FINDING FLINT

Book 2 of the *Unlikely Heroes* series

Written by

Aileen Chorley

Having Fun

"He's going to bottle it."

"Yep. He's totally going to bottle it."

Jenna turned to Graham and Johnson. "He's not going to bottle it."

"How d'you know?" Johnson asked.

Smiling mischievously, Jenna turned around and gave Flint a hard shove.

Flint's shriek died off as he disappeared down the side of the mountain, his flailing body shooting down the blue ice track.

"See you at the bottom," Jenna said, launching herself after him.

Johnson smiled. "The girl's ruthless."

Jenna raised her arms, shouting in exhilaration, freezing air whipping over her face. The ice track entered a cave, thrusting her into a loop-de-loop, light hitting her eyes as it spat her out again. The track became a series of twists and turns, the view stretching for miles... She held her breath as the next drop came up... Curving around an ice bowl at the bottom, she accelerated into more twists, turns, and drops...

Plummeting down the final drop, she let out a cry of excitement.

The group, waiting at the bottom, watched her slide along the run-off.

Brash took her arm and pulled her up. "You liked that?" he asked, smiling.

"It was great!" Unhooking the body-length sledding mat, she glanced at Flint to find him scowling at her. "Did *you* like that, Flint?"

"You pushed me," he said in a hard voice.

"Sorry. But you don't want to be left up there, do you? I was only thinking of you."

Flint's hands balled into fists. Cornelius touched his arm. "It's about motives, remember? Motives, intentions, actions. All needs to be taken into account."

"What you talking about?" Newark asked, eyeing Cornelius, oddly.

"It ties in to Mr. Flint's therapy, Mr. Newark. Therapy can be an ongoing process. Sometimes, a life-long process."

Newark stared at him. "I think I'd rather top myself. Christ, Flint. Just toughen the fuck up."

Cornelius touched Flint's arm again. "And remember what we learned about triggers. Breathe and let go. Breathe and let go..."

Jenna looked around. Over to the right of them, brown hairy elbas pulled aliens on skis. The purple-skinned tourists whizzed over the ice at terrific speed. Over to her left, other tourists prepared to dive beneath the ice.

Johnson came down the drop, yelling, "Fucking ace!"

"Stretch out, you'll go faster!" Jenna called.

Brash's arms snaked around her waist. "There's no holding you back, is there?" he whispered in her ear.

She turned around in his arms. "I could say the same for you." She took in the deep brown eyes, the dark brows, the strong jawline, the soft strands of dark hair grazing his neck. Who knew beneath that caged exterior was a wild card dying to get out? "Shaking off the captain role's done wonders for you," she said, smiling at him. "I like this new Lucas."

He smiled back, leaning down to kiss her.

"Get a fucking room," Newark muttered but the two of them ignored him.

"Remember," Cornelius said, pulling Flint away from the others. "This is therapy in action. Everything you've learned has got to be put into practice, and you can only do this in testing circumstances."

Graham came down, pumping. "That was fan-fucking-tastic!"

Jenna broke the kiss. "Are we going again then?"

Brash turned to Fraza. "Tell the guy we're going again."

Fraza handed a lanky, shockingly white, alien a handful of coins. Second turns weren't included in the excursion price.

"You coming, Flint?" Jenna asked, turning to find his eyes upon her.

"Don't push me again," he said with an undertone of threat.

"Sure."

The crew piled back into the vehicle, sitting on opposite benches. Jenna covertly studied Flint. His loose, ice-blonde hair framed a good-looking, if serious, face, a face that had once been tortured and distant. His body had altered too... firm and lean, not skinny and weedy, as if it had grown up this past year. She sensed he still had anger in him, and she couldn't blame him. Before they'd left on their mission, this crew had treated him abysmally. But there was more to it than that. Flint held some terrible secret inside. Cornelius knew what it was but it wasn't her place to ask. The Erithians and Cornelius had helped him a lot in their absence. He appeared healthier, more together.

His eyes moved to her and her gaze shifted to Cornelius. Cornelius noticed and smiled. She smiled back. This man truly was one of a kind. The only part human, part Kaledian they knew of, his loose white hair covered pointed ears, and his loose-fitting clothes covered a Kaledian pot belly. The man had been having a wonderful time these past weeks, throwing himself into everything with gusto, keeping up with the crew, who were decades younger. Maybe he was making up for lost time. He'd lived with the Erithians all his life but as lovely as those people were, their main hobby was meditation. A pang of sadness hit her chest. They'd probably returned to their own dimension now.

As the craft lifted into the air, her gaze switched to Fraza. A bona fide Kaledian, Fraza stood out with his rotund belly, elfish ears, and orange hair. He appeared calm and contained now. Jenna sort of missed his ear rubbing and strange little rituals. As Fraza had grown in confidence, his torturing mind had lost its grip on him. Performing miraculous feats seemed to have cured his OCD.

Fraza frowned, lips pressed tight. Beside him, Newark scratched his messy brown hair, his elbow perilously close to Fraza's head. As Newark turned to look out of the window, his well-built body shunted Fraza. The frown intensified and Jenna smiled, her eyes lighting with affection as they fixed on Newark. She had once thought Newark the most obnoxious person she'd ever met, but he had grown on her. She wouldn't say he had hidden depths - he wasn't that deep, or clever – but she had come to find him strangely endearing.

Newark laughed. "Look at that," he said, pointing. "That purple guy's lost his skis. Fucker's getting dragged over the ice."

Graham and Johnson moved over to look, joining in with the laughter. "Arse must be numb as shit," Johnson said. She and Graham shared a joyous glance as they returned to their seats.

Unmoved by the event, Skinner leaned back with his eyes closed. Jenna's gaze settled on him. The skinny, brown-haired man sort of hung in the background like... boring wallpaper. It hadn't always been that way. He'd once been a jabbering, cowardly worm. Cornelius had changed that with his *die a thousand deaths* programme. She wondered what it was like to die a thousand deaths. In fact, when she thought about it, she couldn't get her head around it. Skinner opened his eyes and they landed on her. She turned away, quickly, not wanting to re-ignite any interest in her.

Looking out of the window, she breathed in, happy with life. It was weird to think this crew had once wanted her dead... well, all except Cornelius, Fraza, and Flint. Aboard her father's ship, she had been a despised misfit, a girl this crew had wanted to kill for her incompetence. She was over that now. Everything had changed. *She* had changed. The past year had been pretty mind-blowing. She'd learned she had the power, she'd learned to wield that power, and she had taken out SLOB, or the Thunder God, as he called himself. Their mission was complete. Now, they were having fun.

They'd been planet hopping for weeks, picking places like this, finding new things to try. They'd swum on the backs of dukyas – green-skinned whales, they'd skied, jet-skied, paraglided, and had found a weird alien theme park. It had an obscenely fast roller coaster that plummeted below ground, and a *fun house* that wasn't much fun seeing as the whole point was to get through without being eaten alive. Maybe they had translated the sign wrong? The spears hanging inside the doorway should have been a give-away. She, Fraza, and Cornelius had to use the power to defend themselves. The next group of *fun-seekers* would have found a bunch of unconscious creatures, and had probably demanded their money back. Newark complained, of course, saying he'd have liked to try the spears, but Jenna told him they hadn't come to a theme park to bloody kill stuff.

To pay for all these activities, they'd been gambling, though it wasn't gambling when you're using the power and can guarantee the result. Cornelius wasn't too happy about this at first, but Jenna pointed out these places stole from everyone, and she was just taking a little back.

Language hadn't been a problem for them. Both Fraza and Flint were geniuses with language, but Cornelius was the main asset. He could communicate using thought transference which made his lips appear odd when he spoke. Though Jenna was now proficient at reading thoughts, she had only transferred a thought once. Fraza and Cornelius, alone, knew she could read thoughts, and she wanted it to stay that way. If the crew ever found out, it could make life very uncomfortable. Even Lucas didn't know.

"What are you thinking?" Lucas asked, resting his chin on her shoulder.

"I'm thinking of everything we've done."

"I'm thinking of what I'm going to do, to you, tonight."

She turned around and kissed him.

"Get a fucking room," Newark complained.

The craft came down. As they disembarked, Fraza drew Brash aside. "Captain-"

"I'm not the captain anymore, Fraza," Brash said, his eyes travelling over Jenna's slender form. Her long blonde hair had been cut into an edgier style.

"Sorry. Force of habit. We need to make some repairs to the ship. If you're not the captain, who should I inform?"

"Flint's the man."

Fraza scratched his head. "I'm not sure Flint's up to the job, Cap-"

"All he needs to do is delegate. Since Skinner's the technical genius, he could instruct him to sort it out."

"Right." Fraza scratched his head again. "Would it not be better if Skinner took charge then?"

"No. He deals with the technical stuff."

"Right. So... Flint would take overall decisions?"

"Yes."

"What if his decisions are... crap?"

Brash turned to him. "I see your English is evolving, Fraza."

"Yes. The crew seem very pleased about this."

Brash's lips creased. "Look, if Flint's decisions are crap, we'll get rid of him. For now, let's see how he does."

"Shouldn't Jenna be captain?"

"Jenna? Why?"

"She's the one deciding where we're going all the time."

"No. Her time cannot be tied up."

"Why not?"

Brash smiled. "Because she and I are having fun."

"Right. OK, I'll talk to Flint then."

As Brash walked away, Fraza wondered if Flint even wanted to be captain. It had never been formally discussed. It had just been an idea thrown out there. Fraza thought it was a joke. Up to now, the issue had not been pressing, but there might be times when difficult decisions would have to be made.

Fraza joined the line. Flint stood at the back, viewing Jenna with suspicion. One by one, they launched themselves down the track, Fraza's delighted squeal piercing the air.

The crew stood at the bottom, waiting for Flint.

"He's fucking bottled it," Newark complained.

"No, he's coming," Jenna insisted.

"How d'you know?" Johnson asked.

"He's pissed with me. I don't think he's going to back down."

When Flint, at last, appeared, Jenna cheered. They all did. They didn't want to hang around for Flint any longer.

As Flint rose from the ice, his eyes fixed on Jenna.

Jenna smiled at him, pleasantly. "What next?" she asked, looking around.

"Let's go skiing," Fraza said, excitedly.

"Yes," Jenna agreed. "Then we'll do the diving."

Brash took Jenna's hand as they walked over the ice to where guides stood with a group of shaggy elbas, the deer-like creatures as big and hairy as buffalo. The lanky guides handed them skis then attached ropes and harnesses to them. The animals stood perfectly still.

Strapped up, the guides yelled at the creatures to move. The crew raced off in a line, freezing air hitting their faces.

5

"These bastards can shift!" Newark called.

They covered a vast stretch of ground in no time. Jenna smiled over at Lucas. He smiled back at her. *God, that smile was sexy.* Years had fallen from him these past weeks. He was thirty-four, she was twenty-three, but the age gap seemed to have shrunk.

Two dots in the distance became clearer, materialising into a pair of gangly aliens. The aliens shouted commands to the animals and the elbas slowed. Except Flint's elba. It careered off into the distance, taking Flint with it. One of the guides unharnessed Graham, jumped on his elba, and raced after him. The other guide, very apologetic, told Cornelius that particular elba had an escape wish.

The crew had to wait for Flint again.

When he was returned to them, Jenna said, "Bad luck, Flint."

He didn't respond. Nor did he feel like doing the diving.

Donning wetsuits in a heated cabin, the crew dove beneath the ice. Coming up for air, they emerged from a crystal blue pool into a huge, magnificent cavern. Newark shouted, listening to his echo. A group of plum-coloured aliens joined in. Newark stared at them. They sounded like doped-up hyenas. Brash and Jenna glanced at each other, restraining their smiles. As the tour pressed on, they discovered an intricate cave system, extending back into the mountain.

After an hour's exploring, they returned to the cabin with dripping hair. Guides handed them towels. The plum-coloured aliens declined the towels, preferring instead to shake their heads like dogs. The crew gawked at them.

As they walked back to the craft, Newark leaned in to Jenna. "I wonder if we could leash those fuckers."

She laughed.

Boarding the craft, their hosts took them back to the city.

Brash put an arm around Jenna. "Are we having enough adventure?" he whispered in her ear.

"Yes," she whispered back. "But we're nowhere near done yet."

She caught Flint watching them. It was strange to feel a presence behind those eyes, especially when he rarely spoke.

Rubbing her arm, she turned her attention to the landscape. They flew over frozen expanses, a bluey-white wilderness with no signs of life. This planet, Goltan, lay off a trade route, and was a popular port of call for those who enjoyed winter sports, or all-year-round sports as it was constantly winter here. A diversity of species visited the place, including humans. Indeed, after all this time, it had been strange to see other human beings.

6

The city of Iystan eventually appeared, the place a conglomeration of old stone buildings, and newer metal constructions thrown up as the place became busier and wealthier.

The craft came in to land on a concrete concourse. As they disembarked, they looked up, the sky a deepening shade of purple. This was their twilight. In another hour or so it would be dark.

Icy, pedestrianised streets required careful negotiation. Lanky Goltans stood head and shoulders above them. With their shockingly white skin and hair, they appeared like ghosts. A plethora of smells drifted out of eating houses... good, bad, and downright nasty, the place catering for a variety of tastes.

Reaching their hotel, they entered through a tall doorway, the high ceiling and walls coated with insanely thick bushy hair. Dyed elba hair. It kept the heating bills down, together with the ambience. Making a beeline for the dining room, they inspected food laid out on a buffet table. Grabbling plates, they served themselves then sat at a table with ridiculously high, high-back chairs. The human food wasn't great, but at least they weren't wolfing spongy things that wriggled.

"If I see another lanky creep eating that stuff, I'm going to puke," Newark complained.

"Well, stop watching them," Jenna told him.

"I can't help it."

When Cornelius sat down with a bowl of spongy, wriggling things, the crew gawked at him.

Cornelius lifted his eyes to them. "I believe the human expression is, 'when in Rome...'"

They continued to watch as he ate the dish. Newark got up and left the table.

"What are your plans for tonight?" Cornelius asked them.

Johnson dragged her gaze away from him. "We're hitting the pub," she remarked.

"We're not going far," Jenna said. "Are you coming with us, Cornelius?"

"I think I've had enough excitement for one day."

After dinner, they left Cornelius in the lounge, and wandered across the road to the nearest drinking establishment. Elba hair lined the walls, all manner of detritus lodged in it. Brash walked to the bar, ordering drinks by pointing at a picture menu. Newark and Skinner hung around him, checking out the talent. The rest of the crew sat at a long table by the wall.

Johnson stretched her rock-hard arms above her head. "All that fresh air's made me tired."

"Not too tired, I hope," Graham said with a suggestive look.

7

She brushed a hand through her light-brown hair, her striking grey eyes settling on him. "I'm never too tired, you know that."

Graham's heart stuttered, his mouth losing the power of speech. Johnson leaned nearer to him, toying with his dark hair, whispering in his ear.

Flint watched them.

Fraza looked around. "I wonder what Serza and Hendraz are doing now," he remarked, sadly.

Jenna nodded, thinking how strange their friends were galaxies away.

Fraza smiled, fondly. "Do you remember that bet we placed on Venulas?"

"Yeah..." Jenna nodded, reflectively. An impish smile grew on her face. "We could always place another one?"

"There's a balcony up there," Fraza said, pointing.

"So, there is."

The two of them stood. "We'll be back soon," Jenna told the others.

Flint watched them go.

The balcony afforded an excellent view. "Right," Jenna said. "Pick your man."

Fraza looked around. "I'll have him." He pointed to a well-built alien with puke-coloured skin and bulging eyes.

"OK. I'll have the purple guy in front of him."

"You sure?" Fraza asked, surprised. "He looks scrawny."

"Yes, but that species is bendy and stretchy. Could be fun."

"OK, let the games begin."

"Hey, that's my line."

The purple alien's elbow jerked out, hitting the other guy in the ribs. Jenna and Fraza watched, intently. The purple turned and apologised. The larger alien nodded graciously.

Frowning, Jenna refocused. A moment later, her man threw his drink at the big guy's head. That did the trick.

"We're on," she said.

As the fight broke out, the crowd moved back, clearing room for them. The brawling pair lost control of their limbs, the hefty guy orchestrating killer punches, but Jenna was more imaginative. The plum-coloured alien threw himself into a handstand, back-kicking the bulky guy in the face. The crowd cheered their appreciation then winced as the handstand collapsed under a lethal spinal punch. Sliding under the big guy's legs, the skinny alien karate chopped the back of his opponent's knees. As the mammoth dropped, the scrawny alien jumped on his bulky shoulders, doggedly trying

8

to twist his head off. The crowd erupted with wild appreciation, Newark egging the purple guy on.

"Come on, Fraza, you can do better than that," Jenna goaded.

Fraza smiled. The hulking alien abruptly bent forward and charged, slamming his cargo into the hairy wall with such force, the hair did little to dispel the impact. The crowd took a sharp intake of breath as Jenna's man fell to the floor, disorientated. Fraza glanced at her with a satisfied smile but she wasn't done yet. Dazed and senseless, the purple alien jumped to his feet, and spun into a round kick, his addled brain a mere passenger on a ride his body shouldn't have made. The crowd watched in amazement, even more amazed when he dropped mid follow-up punch.

Fraza took full advantage. "Come on," he called out. "I'm pulverising you!" He glanced at Jenna, following the direction of her gaze.

The puke-coloured alien dropped too.

"Would you care to explain yourselves?" Cornelius demanded, his eyes burning into them like lasers.

Jenna worried her lip. She'd never seen him look angry before. She didn't like it.

Down below, the brawling pair remained on the floor, stunned and breathless. Newark tried to incite more action but the dazed aliens sat lost in confusion.

Cornelius's face remained rigid. "I cannot believe two students of mine would engage in such self-serving, gratuitous, and violent actions. Did you instigate this fight?"

They stared at him.

Brash appeared behind Cornelius, looking at them, puzzled. "What are you all doing up here?"

"Well?" Cornelius pressed.

9

Dealing Karma

Cornelius appeared frosty in the morning.

"What's wrong with the old man?" Newark asked as he tucked into his breakfast, cramming as much in as possible. "He's got a face like thunder."

Brash glanced at Jenna and Fraza, both of them quiet and subdued. Although Brash wasn't angry like Cornelius, he was a little surprised... at both of them. Jenna had changed so much in the time he'd known her, had become something of a law onto herself. He couldn't deny finding it attractive but... instigating fights between two innocent aliens? Last night, she had refused to talk about it. Brash suspected she didn't regret what she'd done, only that she had disappointed Cornelius.

Cornelius approached them. "Jenna, Fraza, would you come with me, please?"

His hard voice made the crew looked up. Jenna and Fraza rose to their feet, and followed him out back. Walking over frosty grass, they stared over a frozen pond.

"Now you've had a night to reflect on your actions," Cornelius said, still looking over the pond, "perhaps you'd like to explain them to me."

Fraza looked at the ground. Jenna chewed her lip. "It was just a bit of fun," she mumbled.

Cornelius turned to her. "Ah, fun. So, inflicting bodily injury on two hapless, innocent beings is... fun?"

She said nothing.

"Inflicting injury for your own amusement and gratification is... fun?"

She bit her lip. "OK, when you put it like that."

"How else can I put it? You take out one evil then perpetuate evil yourselves."

"I'd hardly call it evil...?"

"No? So, if someone did that to you, you'd be fine with it?"

She bit her lip harder.

Cornelius raked a hand through his hair. "You both have a great gift, and this is what you choose to do with it?" He shook his head. "You're a kind-hearted, intelligent girl, Jenna. Fraza, you are better than this. Both of you put yourselves at great risk to defend the universe, so I'm struggling to understand your actions last night."

"It was just a bit of-" Jenna stopped herself.

"Fraza?" Cornelius asked, turning to him.

Fraza scratched his ears.

11

"You're bringing back his OCD," Jenna accused.

"Fraza?" Cornelius persisted.

Fraza jerked his head three times then scratched his ears again.

"OK," Cornelius said. "I can see I'm getting nowhere."

He stepped back. Without warning, Fraza punched out, hitting Jenna in the face. She stared at Fraza in shock, her fist slamming into his stomach.

"Cornelius, stop it," Jenna shouted. Fraza performed a low round kick that took Jenna from her feet. "Cornelius!"

The crew, standing near the doors, watched intrigued. "Have Trot and Fraza fallen out?" Graham asked, perplexed.

Johnson shrugged. "My money's on Trot."

"They're not fighting," Brash told them, watching intently. "Cornelius is doing this."

"Cornelius ain't doing shit," Newark said. "He's just standing there, watching."

"I'll put ten on Jenna," Skinner said.

"OK, I'll put ten on Fraza," Graham countered.

Jenna and Fraza battered each other senseless, Jenna so worked up, she couldn't summon the power to stop this. Fraza, punching repeatedly, had no space to focus, either. Jenna tried to make her punches swerve in Cornelius's direction but he had full control, each hit she took brutal, her fists sore from punching Fraza.

"OK, I'm sorry," Jenna yelled. "I get the point!"

"I don't think you do," Cornelius said.

Jenna threw herself into a handstand, and back-kicked Fraza in the face. Fraza punched her in the spine and she collapsed. Almost immediately, she slid along the icy ground, her arms shooting out with lethal force, smashing into the backs of Fraza's knees. As Fraza folded, she jumped up and dove on his back.

"I'm sorry," she yelled again. "I'm really sorry!"

"Fraza?" Cornelius calmly asked.

"I'm sorry," the Kaledian spluttered, his head twisted ruthlessly.

Cornelius relinquished control and they fell to the ground, reclaiming their breath. "Work on your focus," he said, walking off.

The crew stared at Cornelius as he walked past them. They looked at Jenna and Fraza, sitting breathless on the floor. Jenna nursed a bloodied lip. Fraza rubbed his neck.

"Can someone tell me what's going on?" Newark asked.

"They've been well and truly told off," Brash said but Newark frowned. "They've been dealt karma."

"Karma?" Graham asked. "For what?"

Brash walked over to Jenna and reached down to take her hand. She looked up at him, a dazed expression clouding her face. "He's such a bloody good teacher," she whispered.

Newark, still lost, went to finish his breakfast.

About Turn

Jenna and Fraza avoided Cornelius for the rest of the day. The others left to go ice-skating but the pair couldn't summon enthusiasm. Plus, they ached terribly. Brash stayed behind with them. "Feeling guilty?" he asked, vaguely amused.

Jenna scowled. "I'm sick of ice," she complained. "I want sun and beaches and cocktails."

He smiled "We'll have to do some research then. Fraza, did you speak to Flint about the repairs?"

Fraza shook his head. "I'll do it later."

When the others returned, Fraza had a word with Flint. Flint appeared emotionless as he listened.

"So, do you want the job of captain?" Fraza asked.

Flint considered this. "They have to do what I say?"

"That is usually how it works."

A strange light appeared in Flint's eyes. "OK, I accept. You say we need to make repairs?"

"Yes, a red light's been flashing on the control panel. I mentioned it before we left the ship but no-one paid much attention. They were in a rush to get down here."

"OK. Go and instruct Skinner to carry out the repairs. Do we have enough money to pay for them?"

"Yes, though I expect we'll need to visit a casino soon. We'll need more money for the hotel."

"We're not staying here. Once the repairs are done, we're leaving."

"Oh? Where are we going?"

"I'll inform you all later."

"Right." Fraza had a troubled feeling as he walked off to find Skinner.

A sudden cry came from the other side of the lounge. Fraza turned, looking through the high-backed chairs. Johnson and Graham hugged each other.

The crew gathered around them.

"What's going on?" Brash asked.

"I'm getting married," Johnson exclaimed.

"Are you nuts?" Newark said, staring at her and Graham.

Jenna beamed. "That's great."

"Congratulations," Cornelius said. "I'll get us some drinks to celebrate."

The drinks arrived and they sat at a table.

15

"So, when are you getting married?" Brash asked.

Graham hadn't thought that far ahead. He shrugged. "Maybe the next planet." He turned to Newark. "You'll be best man, right?"

Newark sat up, swelling with pride. He sniffed. "Sure."

"You know, marriage is becoming an outdated concept," Skinner put in, thoughtfully. "Studies have shown marriage tends to strangle the life out of relationships."

"What do you know about relationships?" Johnson snapped. "Have you ever had one?"

"Hey, don't shoot the messenger," Skinner said, throwing back his drink.

"Well, it's a brave step," Brash remarked, and Johnson stared at him.

Jenna glanced at him too. "What he means is, it's an exciting step. Not one I would take but for some, it's a whole new adventure."

Brash whipped his head to her. She wouldn't want to marry him? He hadn't given it much consideration, but knowing she didn't *want* to marry him grated.

Flint observed Brash, smiling to himself. He stood. "Well, no-one is getting married for a while. Once the repairs are done, we're heading back to Marios Prime."

"What?" they asked in unison.

"I'm captain now," he stated. "That's where we're heading."

"Captain?" Graham asked, turning to Brash.

"We're not heading back to Marios Prime," Newark piped up.

"Why d'you want to go back there anyway?" Johnson asked, staring at the man, oddly.

"I have a score to settle. I thought I could let it go but apparently not."

"What...?"

"Those Guthrins and that proboscis freak that tied me up. D'you know how long I dangled on that hook?"

"Are you insane...?" Graham asked.

"We're not going back to Marios Prime," Newark said, emphatically.

"You're challenging an order?" Flint asked, stone-faced.

"I'll challenge it with my fists if I have to."

"OK."

"What...?"

"I said, OK."

Newark stared at Flint, his face turning hard. "Got a death wish, Flint?" he spat, getting up.

Newark steamed forward, laying into Flint, but Flint pulled off some crazy moves that had the whole crew staring in shock.

"What the hell's happened to Flint...?" Jenna murmured.

"Oh, I've been training him," Cornelius said. "When he hasn't been in therapy, he's been in my dojo. It was that or meditation, and he wasn't sold on the meditation. In fact, I think the training helped him release some anger. He's been at it for hours every day."

Flint pulverised Newark, and Newark wasn't an easy target. The pure powerhouse of Newark found his weight being used against him, again and again. Flint dodged, and spun, his shots delivered with deadly precision.

"It seems Mr. Newark has forgotten his training," Cornelius remarked. "You used his weight against him too. Remember, Jenna?"

Jenna, too stunned to answer, stared at Flint. He didn't look like Flint. He moved like some lethal, ninja warrior.

"He's fucking amazing..." Johnson muttered, watching rapt.

"Yes," Cornelius agreed. "He seems to have a knack for it. Surprising, really."

The lounge got trashed. Lanky servers stared on, helpless. Brash couldn't tear his eyes away from Flint but, at last, he decided to split it up. As he stood, Flint threw a killer blow that laid Newark out, unconscious.

The crew stared at Newark. Their gazes transferred to Flint.

"We go to Marios Prime," Flint said, looking around the crew before walking off.

"What have you done to him...?" Johnson asked, her eyes following Flint.

"Me? Nothing," Cornelius said. "It's a process. You know, I think the man has remarkable strength of spirit."

"Flint?"

"Yes. With so much repressed rage, he could have obtained a weapon and ended you all. I think he's been remarkably restrained."

"He can fight..." Graham said, at last vocalising what he'd seen.

"We're not going back to Marios Prime," Jenna asserted. "What does he hope to achieve anyway?"

"You made him captain," Cornelius stated.

"And we can take it away again," Brash said.

"Really? Is that how it works? How could anyone be a captain under those circumstances? How would you have fared, Captain Brash?"

"Look, it was a trial period thing."

"And he hasn't even had a trial period, has he? From what I can gather, this crew has been screwing him over for years. You made him captain, and if you have any integrity at all, you'll live by your decision. Or has this past year taught you nothing?"

Jenna straightened, annoyed. "This past year has had us shot through a portal into another galaxy. It's had us assembling an alliance of planets from scratch. And it's had us killing SLOB, all at great personal risk to ourselves."

Cornelius nodded, thoughtfully. "Your point?"

"That is my point."

"Your point does not answer my question. If you are going to engage in gratuitous acts of violence, and treat that man as you always have, I think there are greater lessons for you to learn."

"I never treated Flint like anything," Jenna objected.

"I'm talking to you as a group. The choice is yours, but whatever you decide, I'm heading to Marios Prime with Flint."

"You come down hard on me and Fraza, yet you're backing Flint in his act of revenge?"

"Well, let's compare, shall we, using terms you'll understand. Kick the crap out of innocent aliens for fun, *or* punish a gun-running drug lord who causes misery to many. Yes, I'll agree his motives could be better but they are better than yours. And given the choice, I'll go with Flint, do some good for the planet in the process."

Cornelius left them to think about it.

Brash rubbed his forehead. He didn't want to head back to Marios Prime but Cornelius had a point. They *had* screwed Flint over for years and, in truth, they were doing it again. Flint was only ever intended to be a puppet captain so the rest of them could enjoy themselves.

"Let them go," Johnson said. "Cornelius can handle Daka and those Guthrins."

"What do you say, Jenna?" Brash asked.

She looked at him, torn. She didn't want to go back to Marios Prime but she had already let Cornelius down, and she didn't want to let him down again.

"Skinner?" Brash asked.

Skinner thought about it. "Seeing those Guthrins suffer would be gratifying. They had us trussed in ropes for hours."

"Fraza?"

"Well, I suppose there is a bigger picture here," the Kaledian said. "Daka has been responsible for many deaths. We'd be doing Jakensk a service."

"A place that wanted to imprison you for your late parents' debt?" Jenna pointed out.

"Yes, but Daka is also responsible for slave-driven prostitution rings. Some of the victims are young."

Jenna stared at him for a long moment. She straightened. "Well, what are we waiting for?" She looked at Johnson.

Johnson shrugged. "OK, I'm in."

When Newark woke up, he struggled to process what had happened. Where the fuck had *that* man come from? When the crew told him they were heading back to Marios Prime, he stared at them, confounded. "Are you fucking serious?" Nothing made sense. It was a complete about turn.

Bubbling Beneath The Surface

Newark sniffed. "What's that?" he asked Skinner.

"It's the main drive flux commutator."

Newark stared at him. "The what...? What does it do?"

"It relays current to the drive."

"And... it needs changing?"

"This one's on its last legs." Skinner glanced at him. He wasn't used to Newark asking questions.

Newark sniffed again. "So... how does a spacecraft fly?"

Skinner broke off and looked at Newark. "You don't know anything?"

"I never learned that shit."

Brash walked in. "Listen, you two, seeing as Flint's technically the captain now, Cornelius thought it would be a good idea if we call him captain."

"What?" Newark asked. "I'm not calling that little toad, captain, sir."

"Newark, you don't need to call me sir."

"Yeah, I keep forgetting."

"Come on, we've got to give the man a chance."

"He did kick your butt," Skinner remarked, vaguely amused.

Newark scowled. "He got in a lucky shot, that's all. Listen, I'll call him captain when he proves he's up to the job. Are the others calling him captain?"

"They are going to try," Brash said.

"Just because Flint's come out of whatever stupor he's been in for the last few years, doesn't mean he's capable of shit."

"Well, let's give him a chance, should we?"

*

Flint sat on the flight deck, quiet and thoughtful, a patchwork of lights reflecting in his eyes, a view of space around him.

Jenna walked in and sat next to him. "You OK, Flint... err... Cap?"

He glanced at her. "Yes."

"So, we're going to sort Daka out. How d'you want to play it? Conventional weapons, fist fight, or do you want me to fry him to a crisp?" She'd meant to be light-hearted but he didn't seem amused.

"Must be effortless when you can draw on the power, Jenna," he said with a humourless smile.

Her pleasant expression dropped. "It hasn't exactly been an easy ride. And, in case you've forgotten, I ended up where I did because you lot were trying to kill me."

He frowned. "*I* wouldn't have killed you."

"I know. You said. You knew about it, though, and you didn't warn me."

He looked away, quiet for a moment. "You seem best mates with them all now."

"We've been through a lot. They've changed. I've let it go. Have you?"

He looked at her. "Sure." Gaze lingering on her, he got up and walked away.

Jenna watched him go. She couldn't get a handle on this Flint at all.

Blowing out a breath, she idly looked around the plush deck. The Hellgathens had carpeted it in a deep purple pile, and had installed black leather seating around the perimeter.

Johnson came in and plonked herself down.

"You alright?" Jenna asked.

"Yep. Just wondering if I'm doing the right thing, getting married."

"You and Graham are meant for each other. I suppose it's the natural step."

"Yes, but... sometimes, he does my head in. And he snores."

Jenna suppressed a smile. "That's hardly a deal breaker."

Johnson scratched her temple. "I've been noticing stuff more since he asked me to marry him. Like, when I say his name, you know, to get his attention, I always have to say it twice. It pisses me off."

"Did it piss you off before?"

"Yes, but it's *really* pissing me off now."

"Um... Perhaps all this is a... reaction. I mean, marriage is a big step. Maybe you should have a long engagement. Give yourself time to work things through."

She nodded. "Yeah... That makes sense."

"You calling Flint, captain, now?" Newark interrupted, and they looked up at him.

"Haven't spoken to him since he's become captain," Johnson said, absently. Gradually, she tuned in. "He's not like Flint anymore, is he? It's like, there's life behind those eyes. He was always in some distant sodding universe but he's there now... silent, watchful. It's fucking creepy."

"I don't think he trusts us yet," Jenna said.

"What's not to trust?" Newark asked.

"Maybe we should give him a chance."

Johnson appraised Newark. "Heard you were down in the gym this morning," she said, amused. "Battering the punch bag. Afraid you might get your arse kicked again?"

"He was lucky, that's all."

"Yeah. Sure."

Newark scowled at her. "Think you can do better?"

"Err... yes."

"OK, prove it."

"What?"

"Take him downstairs and kick the crap out of him."

"I don't think Captain Brash would be happy about that."

"He's not the captain anymore, though, is he?"

Johnson stood, looking Newark squarely in the eye. "OK, I'll kick the shit out of him."

The two of them strode out. A second later, Jenna followed. Searching for Flint, the three of them walked through the shiny metal corridors of their top-of-range ship. The craft, the smallest of SLOB's remaining fleet, was more up-to-date than any in this region. It had the Super Mega Hyperdrive, which had allowed the crew to return to this galaxy after killing SLOB. The upper level was the business end, containing the flight-deck, two weapons decks, the engine room, weapons storage... The lower level contained officers' quarters, which the crew had commandeered, a gym, a lounge, and a bar stocked with potent Hellgathen concoctions.

They found Flint talking to Skinner and Graham outside the engine room.

"Flint, I'm going down to do some sparring," Johnson said. "Want to join me?"

Flint viewed her with narrowed gaze, his eyes flitting to the others. Taking a quiet breath, he said. "OK then." Turning, he walked on ahead of them.

Graham and Skinner tagged along, jumping into the lift before it closed. Flint stood at the back, silently, the rest of the crew silent too. Newark and Johnson exchanged a glance.

As they entered the gym, Flint kicked his shoes off, walking straight out onto the mat. Johnson followed suit. He turned, his blue eyes fixing her as she weighed him up.

"Whenever you're ready," he said, calmly.

"Ready," Johnson said, crouching slightly.

Eyes locked together, they rounded on each other. Flint moved, lightning fast, taking her legs from under her, flooring her straight away. She was up in an instant, spinning around, elbowing him in the stomach. As he folded, she back-punched his face then turned to slam her other fist into his jaw. The hand got knocked away, and a hard jab landed in her side. The punch, precisely placed, took her down. Flint finished with a round-kick to her head.

"Come on, Daria!" Graham called but things went downhill from there. Johnson got a few good punches and kicks in, but Flint was tireless, his blows expertly placed - minimum effort for maximum effect. Newark didn't know whether to be pleased she was eating her words, or displeased Flint was winning. Flint shouldn't be winning. In what universe did Flint win? What the fuck had taken possession of that man? Maybe it *wasn't* him. Maybe he *was* possessed. It was the only reasonable explanation.

Johnson hung in but she floundered, Graham wincing as a blow to the head nearly snapped her neck. She was a dead woman walking and crew knew it. She took knock after knock until, at last, she knew it too. Reluctantly, she held up a hand, conceding, something she never did.

Flint looked around. "Anyone else?" he asked. Nobody answered. "Be in the conference room in ten minutes. I'm holding a meeting."

The crew stared after him as he walked out.

"Conference room?" Newark asked, as Graham approached Johnson.

"It's next to the flight deck," Skinner told him. "The room with the long table and black leather chairs."

"Since when do we do meetings in conference rooms?" Newark complained. "The power's going to his fucking head."

"He's just calling a meeting," Jenna said, her gaze transferring to Johnson.

Graham leant down to help Johnson up but she knocked his hand away. He gave her a wide berth as she got to her feet.

Johnson didn't speak as they left the gym. None of them did. Johnson was a formidable opponent but Flint made that look easy.

They entered the conference room to find the others seated around the table. Flint sat at the end. Johnson eyeballed him as she sat down.

"The repairs are done," Flint said. "We're setting a course for Marios Prime."

"Setting a course?" Newark asked, snidely. "With the SMHD, we'll be there in no time."

"It's just an expression," Flint said in a deadpan voice. "Now, I want Daka and his whole operation taken out. Every single one of them."

Newark sniffed to hide errant excitement. Now it was decided they were heading back to Marios Prime, he found himself looking forward to some action. Graham and Johnson couldn't deny feeling the same way. Having fun, loafing about, was good, but kicking butt was good too.

"We'll take them out with conventional weapons," Flint said, looking at Jenna, Fraza, and Cornelius. "Your power is only to be used as a last resort. I take Daka out myself. I want him to look in my eyes as he dies."

The crew stared at him. The man *had* been holding a grudge.

Newark decided *he* was going to take Daka out. Ever since he'd set eyes on the hideous-looking creature, he'd wanted to blast it to kingdom come. Nobody should be that ugly.

"You're just interested in revenge?" Jenna asked, challenging Flint.

Flint's blue eyes fixed on her. "Beings like him think they can walk over whoever they want. I'm not lying down and taking it anymore." The words were spoken calmly and with hard conviction.

She felt oddly inspired. "We should do some gambling and give it to the girls and women caught in his prostitution rings." She glanced at Cornelius. "It will be like stealing from the rich to give to the poor."

"Good idea, Robin Hood," Brash said, smiling at her.

"What? We're good Samaritans now?" Newark asked.

"Of course, we are," Jenna said. "We saved the bloody universe, didn't we?"

Newark paused for thought.

"How are we going to get weapons down there?" Graham asked. "Weapons are taken from you when you disembark."

Flint looked at him. "We'll use theirs. We enter his lock-up when there's no-one around, and wait for him there. Are we clear?"

The crew nodded.

"And remember," he said, "Daka's mine."

As the crew left the room, Jenna approached Cornelius. She was going to ask. "What *did* happen to Flint, Cornelius?"

Cornelius looked at her. "I can't tell you, Jenna. Counsellor confidentiality."

"*You* were his counsellor?"

"One of them. It was a group effort. Pretty exhausting at times, I can tell you."

"Oh... Well... he seems different now."

Cornelius assessed her. "You don't look happy about that."

"It's just... He's not like Flint anymore. He's... hard."

"It's a process," Cornelius told her. "The pendulum swings before it finds its point of integration. Look at Mr. Skinner. He worked through his

25

god-complex then his apathy. If I'm not mistaken, there are even small moments of humour now."

Yeah, moments, Jenna thought. For the most part, she found Skinner boring.

Cornelius smiled. "Remember when you first arrived? Mr. Skinner wouldn't even go to the bathroom by himself. It would have been pitiful if it wasn't so annoying." Cornelius shook his head.

"Has the old Skinner gone for good then?"

"I would say so. It's possible, of course, under certain extreme conditions, old synapses could be triggered, new circuits by-passed. But I don't think it's something we need worry about."

Down the corridor, Johnson let out a yelp. "Don't pinch my arse!" she shouted.

Graham looked at her, confused. "It never bothered you before?"

"Well, it fucking bothers me now!"

Jenna chewed her lip. "I think she's reeling at the prospect of getting married."

"Yes, it's not surprising," Cornelius said, thoughtfully.

Jenna looked at him. "It's not?"

"Johnson had a tough upbringing with a ruthlessly hard mother, a mother who taught her never to rely on anyone, especially men. This marriage proposal might have stoked things up... things that have been bubbling beneath the surface."

"Is there anyone's mind you haven't probed, Cornelius?"

"It was a case of needs must, I'm afraid."

"Ah, yes. Needs must. I remember." Jenna studied him. "And what about you, Cornelius? Are there things bubbling beneath the surface in you?"

"My life has been... uneventful, I'm afraid. You won't find skeletons in my closet."

She assessed him. "Have you ever been with a woman, Cornelius?"

She saw a flicker in his eyes, gone in an instant. He smiled at her. "My path did not lead in that direction. Now, I think we should make ready to depart."

As he walked away, Jenna stared after him. The man had never had sex? That *had* to be rectified.

Making Waves

"This is it?" Cornelius asked, squinting in the bright daylight.

"Yes, this is it," Flint said, staring at the run-down building through his shades. The blinding orange sunlight only affected humans.

"There's no-one inside," Cornelius said, looking around. Down at the bottom was a scruffy back entrance to a bar. The wide alley led out at the other end, the whole area a decrepit backwater.

"We need to get in without breaking the door," Flint said. "Any ideas?"

"I could do it," Jenna offered. "Oh, wait, no. I'd have to use the power."

Flint turned to her. She was being smart, her tongue almost in her cheek. The girl he'd first met wouldn't *know* how to put her tongue in her cheek. "Open the door," he said.

"You sure? We could try other options first?"

He gave her a humourless smile. "Just open the door."

Jenna focused. Using the power and her intent, she turned the locking mechanism.

"Cornelius, Graham, keep watch," Flint said, walking into the building.

The room was in darkness and he located the switch. Crates and boxes materialised before his eyes. "Find the weapons," he instructed.

The crew forced open crates and tore into boxes. They were crammed with bags of drugs.

"He keeps all this shit here?" Newark asked. "Any fucker could take it."

"Nobody would dare cross Daka," Fraza said, looking around. "He has a stranglehold on this city. It is rumoured that even the security forces turn a blind eye, that some are in his employ."

"Look upstairs," Flint told Brash.

Brash got a weird feeling being ordered around by Flint. He forced himself to let it go. He climbed an old staircase to find more crates on the next level. Tearing into one of the crates, he shouted down before riffling through to search out the best arsenal. Newark and Flint came up to help.

Downstairs, Jenna spotted a sink in the corner. Grabbing a couple of bags, she ripped them open, and started flushing the powder down it. "Come on," she said, "let's piss Daka off before we kill him."

Johnson joined in but made a note to keep a bag for herself.

Fraza lifted a couple of bags and came over too. The three of them got coated in white dust. Jenna had another bright idea. She ran upstairs.

"Have you picked our weapons?" she asked and Brash nodded. "Good. Let's piss Daka off even more." Kneeling, she focused, and began twisting metal, destroying weapons. "Fraza, come and help me!" she called out.

"What are you doing?" Flint asked.

"Don't you want him to suffer before he dies. Imagine how he'll feel when he turns up and finds all this."

"When he turns up, we'll kill him."

"Well, we could do that. *Or,* we could leave him to stew for a while then come back and finish the job."

"You're ruthless," Brash said, amused.

"Ruthless? After all the misery he's caused in this city, seems to me he's getting off easy."

"Come back when?" Flint asked.

"Might be fun to leave it a day or two."

"And give him a day or two to prepare for us?"

"That's better, isn't it? You said you wanted every one of them taken out. Well, if he rounds up all his henchmen, we can take them out at once. Make a clean sweep."

"But we lose the element of surprise."

"Oh, they'll be surprised, alright." Chewing her lip, she looked at him, thoughtfully. "I know you said you don't want us to use the power, but we could use it to level the field a little. Daka will be left to you."

Flint was aware the girl was taking over, and he could stop it but she was right. They needed to get as many of Daka's men as possible.

"Fraza," he said as the Kaledian came up. "Clear the room downstairs. Powder the floor. Leave a message in it. Tell Daka he's going to die here in two days-time. Hurry. Do it quickly." He turned to Jenna. "Carry on," he said.

As he watched Jenna pulverise metal, he had the image of a mischievous imp running amok. The corners of his lips creased.

After they'd trashed Daka's lock-up, they headed back to the hotel, their weapons contained in bags, a bag of white powder concealed under Johnson's jacket.

The buildings became classier as they reached the centre. Jakensk, the capital of Marios Prime, or Kaledia, as it was known to the indigenous people, buzzed with life, the cosmopolitan streets crowded. Many species visited the place as it lay on a trade route, but the predominant hair colour was orange. Tall stone buildings edged wide main roads, a labyrinth of seedy alleyways branching out behind them. Hover craft vehicles, called yacts, flew several feet above the ground. When one came dangerously low, Newark let off a barrage of obscenities.

28

"We'll eat then hit the casino," Jenna said, turning to Fraza. "They do have one here, don't they?"

"Yes. There are three. My parents frequented the places. They tried to rectify their financial situation. Unfortunately, it made matters worse."

Flint took Jenna's arm and led her away from the group. "What are you doing?" he asked. Her brow creased. "Are you deliberately trying to undermine me?"

"What? No."

"Then stop making decisions."

"But we need money to pay for the hotel, and we need money to help the prostitutes after we erase Daka."

"I'm aware of that. But I make the decisions, not you. This crew has little or no respect for me as it is. You are not helping matters."

Jenna stared at him. "Sorry. I got carried away. It's just, now we have a purpose, I want to get on with it. If I've got any suggestions, I'll run them by you first in future."

"Make sure you do," he said, walking on ahead.

"What was that?" Brash asked her.

Jenna rolled her eyes. "Flint being a fussy arsehole."

When they arrived at the hotel, Flint didn't eat with the crew. He ate alone in his room, desiring his own company. Graham and Johnson didn't eat with the crew either. They went upstairs to sample Daka's drugs.

The rest of them entered a tasteless, orange-walled dining room, and sat at a high table, high enough to accommodate Kaledian bellies.

Cornelius looked over the table at Jenna. "So, we're giving Daka a couple of days to think about it, are we, Jenna?"

"Thought it might be f-" She coughed, patting her throat. "Thought it might be appropriate."

"I see. I got stung by an atac once. I pulled out the sting. I didn't play around with it for a while first."

"Shouldn't Daka experience some discomfort?"

"Maybe, but who benefits from it? Him or you? He'll be dead in two days so he's hardly going to see the light and mend his ways."

"Maybe not but he'll get a taste of his own medicine." *God, Cornelius was a strait-laced killjoy.*

Newark laughed. "Imagine the ugly bastard's face when he walks into his trashed lock-up. I wish I could get a picture."

"You will," Skinner said. "I placed a camera in the upper right corner, trained on the door. It'll send an image to me." He held up his transceiver.

"When did you do that?"

"Shortly after we arrived. Jenna asked me to rig it up."

Jenna sunk into her chair. Brash turned to look at her.

"So, you had it all planned, Jenna," Cornelius said, his eyes scrutinising her.

"Good one," Newark said. "Why don't I think of shit like that?"

Brash and Cornelius stared at Jenna, Cornelius with a troubled frown, Brash with surprised amusement. *God, she was inventive.* He wanted to scrap going to the casino and take her upstairs.

Jenna focused solely on eating. She didn't look at Cornelius once throughout their meal.

Johnson and Graham eventually came down, and the group headed out, Cornelius saying he'd sit this one out. Flint remained in his room.

*

Housed in a large stone building, the casino comprised one vast, open room. Glaring silver paint bounced off the walls, basic wooden chairs bringing it down to earth. Kaledians hovered around tables, the room buzzing with alien voices.

"I'll take the roulette wheel this time," Jenna said to Fraza.

"I'll take the dice then," Fraza said. Newark and Skinner ambled after him. The others kept with Jenna, Brash lifting a couple of drinks off a tray.

Jenna stood at the table, smiling at fellow gamblers as she placed her bet. She'd learned it was better to be friendly, engage with the clientele, get them on her side. That way, if management got fidgety and suspicious, she'd have support. There had been occasions when she'd been asked to step into a private room. When the clientele had objected, insisting she'd won fair and square, the management backed down.

The wheel spun.

"Shit, that thing's going fast," Johnson said, staring at it.

Graham stared at it too, the pair lost in the spin. Jenna worked her magic, and as the wheel stopped, her number came up. Pressing her hands together, she squealed, feigning excitement.

Brash handed her a drink as she placed another bet. "Remember to lose a few," he whispered in her ear.

Johnson and Graham carried on staring at the wheel, its stillness a palpable thing, as if the stillness could reach out and touch them, maybe give them the answers to existence. The wheel spun and they got transported out of time.

Jenna's number came up, and again she squealed, fellow players and spectators becoming excited for her. Brash hid his amusement. She'd become an expert at working the crowd.

"God, I feel good," Graham said, looking around.

"Everything's amazing…" Johnson murmured, turning to Graham and studying his face. "You're fucking beautiful…"

They wandered around, staring intently at various faces, the faces viewing them, uncomfortably.

"I feel like I'm floating," Johnson said, raising her arms. "Like my body's made of air. Like I'm a breath of fresh air…"

Graham gazed at a bloated Kaledian. "His hair is so orange… It's like blinding sunlight…"

As Graham touched the Kaledian's hair, the guy slapped his hands off.

Newark and Skinner watched Fraza hammer the dice table.

"How does he do it?" Skinner whispered to Newark.

"Wake up, Skinner. He's using the fucking power. Where have you been for the past year?"

"I know that. I mean, how does he actually do it?"

"Why don't you ask him?"

"I have. He says it's all about intent. There's only the power and intent. It makes no sense…"

Newark looked around to see how Trot was getting on.

Jenna took a sip of her drink, preparing to take a fall on the next go. She didn't bet too much. The wheel turned against her, and the crowd let out a sigh of disappointment. Jenna perfected a crest-fallen look, and a female Kaledian patted her arm, encouraging her to try again. She did, coming back to a new run of luck. The management's hired bullies wandered over, watching her closely. She ignored them, taking a fall now and then but steadfastly cleaning the place out.

When a hand came on her shoulder, the crowd turned angry and the hand let go.

"Time to leave," Brash said.

Rounding up Fraza, Newark, and Skinner, they collected their winnings, looking around for Graham and Johnson. They found them gazing, mesmerised, at the silver wall.

"What you looking at?" Newark asked, staring at them, confused.

They couldn't speak.

Brash put a hand on Graham's shoulder and looked into his eyes. "They're tripping. They must have taken some of Daka's drugs."

"How d'you know?"

"Because they're bloody tripping."

31

"Bastards kept that quiet."

"Come on, let's get them out of here."

Newark grabbed hold of Graham. Brash grabbed hold of Johnson.

Outside, they were met by five stocky beings with rubbery faces, and a Kaledian in a funny-looking suit.

"Would you come with us, please?" the Kaledian said, glancing at the large bag of winnings in Fraza's hand. Moving the bag behind him, Fraza translated.

"We won this fair and square," Jenna said, staring the suit hard in the eye.

"Well, there is, as yet, some uncertainty about that."

Jenna's lips tightened. It was alright for them to fleece everyone but nobody is allowed to fleece them? Her look turned mean. "Move," she said, "or these bricks of yours will be scraping you up off the floor."

The Kaledian smiled in amusement. She scowled. Walking up to him, she performed a total body shot. The aliens flew back and hit the deck as if a bomb had dropped. She thought about driving the message home with her fists but decided to leave it there.

"Come on, we're done here," she said, walking off.

Johnson leaned over one of the stunned aliens, gazing into its rubbery, undulating face. Skinner pulled her away.

Brash put his arm around Jenna's shoulders and whispered in her ear. "You're making waves today, aren't you?" he said.

She glanced at him. "Flint's right. You shouldn't put up with any old crap."

Hard Determined Purpose

In the morning, a lot of talk swept around the hotel. Fraza listened in.

"Daka's displeasure is sweeping far and wide," he told the others. "He's out for blood and he's not going to stop until he gets it."

"News travels fast here," Graham remarked.

"Oh, I forgot," Newark said. "Let's look at the pics."

Skinner pulled out his device and they swarmed around him. The picture was priceless. A large proboscis freak staring ahead, wide-eyed. A second shot showed him with his arms in the air.

"Good one," Graham said.

"He looks just as ugly on camera," Newark remarked with disdain.

"What's next?" Johnson asked, looking at Jenna, expectantly.

Jenna glanced at a tight-faced Flint. "Cap?" she asked and all heads turned to him.

"We wait until tomorrow then we take Daka out," Flint stated.

"Yes, but look at the state he's in. Everyone here talking about it? He's hopping mad. Don't we want him to start... worrying, panicking a little? Really pile on the pressure?"

He was curious to know what she'd come up with next. "What did you have in mind?"

"Well," Jenna said as if tossing an idea out there, "maybe we could find out where he lives, trash his house."

Cornelius stared at her. Would she ever stop? Newark was pumping. This had turned into a fun game.

"Cool idea," Johnson said. "Take it onto home turf."

"I'm in," Graham seconded.

"Jenna, this is reckless and unnecessary," Cornelius said. "Let's just finish the job."

"Well, Flint's the captain," Jenna insisted. "It's up to him, not you."

Flint couldn't believe this girl. She had become a manipulative, self-indulgent thrill seeker, who was trying to play him.

"OK," Flint said. "Newark, Johnson, Graham, Skinner, find out where Daka lives and leave a powerful message there. The rest of us will investigate the prostitution rings, find out where they are, and provide the financial assistance they'll need."

"Wait a minute," Jenna piped up. "I need to go with *them*. They might need protection."

"OK. Fraza will go with them."

Jenna's expression turned hard. "*I'm* going with them."

"No, you're coming with me. If you disobey an order, I'll go and finish Daka now."

"He'll kill you."

"Not if I go with him," Cornelius said, looking at her steadily.

The crew knew they witnessed a battle of wills. Cornelius knew, if the crew sided with Jenna, Flint would have a mutiny on his hands. He was intrigued to see how this would play out.

Flint didn't take his eyes off Jenna as he spoke. "We came here with an objective," he said in a hard voice. "To kill Daka. You came here to play games, have a little fun, didn't you? I've gone along with it because I don't mind seeing Daka suffer, and I don't mind seeing him suffer some more. Have fun in the process, if you want to, but you made me captain and you'll follow my fucking orders. Or has every scrap of decency been stripped from you, Jenna Trot?"

Her eyes widened. She was about to respond when he continued. "Why don't you wake up to yourself? Instead of playing your games, come with me today and help the people who need it, people that bastard has been treading on for years. My one objective was to kill Daka but we have the means to do more. We have the means to repair some of the damage he's done. I didn't see it at first but I should have. Some damage goes deep, so deep you can't possibly imagine..." His gaze became intent, he spoke with passion. "You took out SLOB but evil is all around us, festering like pus. *That* is not a game. It's real and you need to come see it. So, follow my fucking orders!"

Cornelius smiled to himself. The pendulum was swinging. Flint was channelling his pain into hard determined purpose. He felt proud of the man.

Jenna stared at Flint, lost for words. She'd never heard him speak like that. She could hear the pain, the anger, the determination, the passion... What *had* happened to Flint?

Still staring at him, she nodded.

Brash sized Flint up. He couldn't reconcile this man with the man he had once known. Where had *this* man been all these years?

"Does that mean we're not trashing Daka's house?" Newark asked, disappointed.

Flint turned to him. "Trash it."

*

34

As Flint could speak Kaledian, and Cornelius could read and transfer thoughts, they had no problem asking various shady-looking characters where they could obtain a woman. One shady-looking character directed them to a build-up area outside the city centre.

The dwellings crowded together, the alleyways narrow and twisted. Dirty Kaledian children viewed them with suspicion as they walked past, sporting shades. Following the directions, they turned a corner to see a longer building with barred windows and two stocky goons loafing outside it. They were the same species they had encountered outside the casino.

"D'you think that's a brothel?" Brash asked.

"Well, we could always ask those gentlemen," Cornelius remarked.

Jenna glanced at him. "If they're gentlemen, I'm a whore."

Cornelius raised his brows to her.

Brash lifted the bag of cash he carried, playful humour lighting his eyes. "Can I afford you?"

She smiled, flirtatiously. "For you, babe, it's free."

Breathing out, Flint walked on and they followed. As they approached the building, the stocky aliens stood straight, blocking the entrance.

"We're looking for prostitutes," Flint said, directly. He brought out a wad of notes to show they could pay. "Is this the place?"

The aliens looked them over, their eyes settling on the bag Brash carried. "What's in the bag," one of them asked.

Flint glanced at the bag of money then looked at Cornelius. "I'll take the one on the left. You take the other."

Flint turned back to the goon, smiled at him, then punched him in the face. As Cornelius laid into the other, Brash and Jenna moved away to give them room.

"This is totally unnecessary," Jenna complained.

"With this much money," Brash said, "we weren't going to get away without a fight. Besides, if we've come to the right place, we'd have to take them down anyway."

"I know that. I mean, fist fighting. Takes forever. Cornelius and I could have this done in seconds."

Brash smiled. "Doesn't seem Flint likes things done the easy way."

"The easy way saves time."

He brushed a hand through her hair. "What's your rush?" he asked, smiling at her, seductively.

Jenna smiled back, responding to his flirtatious manner. "I've got too much restless energy," she replied with a meaningful look.

"Ah, we'll have to do something about that." He leant down to kiss her, the two of them becoming lost in each other.

Jenna broke off, aware it had gone quiet. She looked around to see Cornelius and Flint staring at them, the two stocky aliens laid-out on the ground.

"Oh, that was quicker than I expected," she said. "What are we going to do with them?"

Flint walked around the building, returning a few moments later. "There's a storage bunker round the back. We'll dump them in there."

"OK, shall Cornelius and I transport them?" she asked. "They're quite heavy."

Flint hesitated but agreed.

Brash kept look-out as Cornelius and Jenna levitated the two unconscious goons around the back. Depositing them in the storage bunker, Jenna fused the metal handles together.

Returning to the front, they knocked on the door.

A Kaledian woman opened it. She glanced around briefly, no doubt wondering where the goons were, before motioning for them to come inside.

The four of them stepped in, and Cornelius's eyes bulged as the woman rattled off a list of prices.

"What's she saying?" Brash asked.

Cornelius scratched his head. "She's running through the... err... menu," he replied, uncomfortably. "Now she's saying they cater for various tastes but I think she's already made that clear. Oh, wait a minute, she means they have a variety of species on offer."

The woman called out loudly. Moments later, a group of women emerged. A collection of Kaledians, Guthrins, and Stilgens. Jenna studied them. They did cater for different tastes. The bony, green-skinned Guthrins, with their long green hair and emerald eyes, contrasted sharply with the dark-haired, voluptuous, blue-skinned Stilgens, and the bloated orange-haired Kaledians. Surprisingly, one human stood there.

"Is that human pregnant?" Jenna asked, staring at her.

Cornelius asked the question. As woman the answered, Cornelius's eyes widened.

"Well?" Jenna asked.

"No," Cornelius replied. "But she's not entirely human..."

The Kaledian woman pulled back the human's hair. She had pointy ears.

"Cornelius, she's like you," Jenna said, amazed. "You're not the only one."

"What's she saying now?" Brash asked.

36

"She says this one's very popular," Cornelius replied, "and a little more expensive."

Flint looked around the women... about fifteen of them. "Do you work for Daka," he asked, speaking Kaledian.

The Kaledian woman whipped her head to him.

"They do," Cornelius replied. "But she's not going to tell you. She's too scared. These women are prisoners here. The goons out there are their jailers that also serve to keep out non-paying clients."

"Is this everyone?" Flint asked the woman.

"Yes," she affirmed.

A Stilgen woman stepped forward. "We have younger girls and boys, if you are so inclined."

The Kaledian woman glared at her, hissing out vitriol. The Stilgen hissed words back at her.

"Show us," Flint said, tight-lipped.

The crew followed the Stilgen down a grotty narrow corridor. She opened a door and they stared at a group of children – Kaledian, greens, blues – all looking up with fearful eyes. Cornelius and Brash stared back at them, horrified. Jenna couldn't move. Flint's jaw tightened. He stepped forward to close the door.

The four of them remained silent as they moved back down the passage, Flint hoping to God they did a good job of trashing Daka's house.

On entering the main room, Cornelius lowered into a chair. Flint turned to the women. "We've come here to set you free," he told them. "You have my word Daka will be dead tomorrow." The women stared at him as if he was mad. Flint glanced at Brash. "Have you got the money?"

Brash tipped out the large bag of notes, three hundred thousand quontas in total. With the cost of living reasonably low in Kaledia, it equated to roughly a million pounds.

The women gazed at the money. "Why would you help us?" one of the Guthrins uttered, her eyes finding Flint's.

"Let's just say Daka crossed the wrong human. This money is to be shared between you, to set you up in new lives. Except you," he said, pointing at the Stilgen who had volunteered the children.

"What?" she protested. "Why not me?"

"Why d'you think?"

"You don't know what Daka would do to us. We would be flogged if he knew we were hiding them."

"They're children!" he yelled at her.

The crew looked at him. The woman didn't utter another sound.

Dismissing her, Flint turned to the rest of the women. "You will take care of the children?"

"Yes, we love those children," a Kaledian insisted.

"You need to pack and leave. The men outside are… indisposed for now. Tomorrow, Daka will be dead," he promised them.

The women looked at him, stunned.

"Come on, let's move," he prompted, urgently.

The women crouched down to divide the money, the Stilgen woman looking on, resentfully.

Jenna got up and wandered around the shabby-looking place. Although some attempt had been made at decoration, little money had been poured into it. The faded curtains, and old, worn furniture suggested run-of-the-mill clientele. She wandered into a corridor on the other side of the room to discover more bedrooms down there. The place was dismal, airless, the bars on the windows keeping them away from the world. Flint was right. Evil was everywhere, festering like pus…

She sat on one of the beds, looking around the squalid room, trying to imagine these women's lives. Angry tears leaked onto her cheeks.

Wiping them away, she got up, bumping into the part-human, part-Kaledian woman in the corridor. The woman grabbed her arm. "Thank you," she said.

"You speak English?"

"My father was human."

"I see."

"Are you freeing all the houses in the area?"

"There are more?"

"There are at least five, all prisoners like ourselves."

Jenna stared at her, realising they needed to hit the other casinos.

"I don't know why you're doing this," the woman said, "but you truly are angels."

Jenna smiled at her. "Are there any more like you? Part-human, part-Kaledians?"

"I've never met any. I… I've always been an… outcast."

"Well, you're not entirely alone, you know? My friend out there is like you. The man with the white hair?"

"Really? I thought he was fat."

Jenna smiled. "No. Pointed ears like you."

"Wow…"

"He's lived… alone a long time. Perhaps you'd like to come to the hotel with us then the two of you could… chat. It must be nice for you both, meeting someone like yourself."

The woman smiled a knowing smile. "By lived alone, you mean he's a virgin?"

Jenna bit her lip. "Yes."

"It's OK. I'll come with you. He seems nice. And," she said, looking at the huge wad of money in her hand, "it's the least I can do."

Jenna moved off to re-join the others, wondering about her own integrity. Was that a bad thing to do? She honestly wasn't sure.

Big Mistake

Daka was having a bad day. He'd returned to find his newly-decorated, top of the range mansion trashed – the bastards had smeared what he hoped was mud all over the walls – and he'd just had word one of his sex houses had been emptied.

He looked around. Every inch of his home had been desecrated. A portrait of himself on the wall now had two horns and a pair of breasts. His long dark hair had bows drawn on it. A green, mucus-like substance coated the floor.

"What is this?" he asked, pulling up his foot, the sticky stuff trailing down in strings.

"Looks like pond puke," the Guthrin said, studying it.

"What?"

"That film that collects on the top of ponds. Pond snakes secrete it." The Guthrin's eyes widened as a slippery creature slithered across the room.

"There's a bad smell in here," another Guthrin said, coming in.

Steaming pressure built in Daka's skull. "I'm going to rip their limbs off one by one!"

He strode outside, trampling the scrubby grass. His army of Guthrins had assembled. "Ten of you, come with me. The rest, start cleaning this place up."

Daka made his way to his deserted brothel. A few of his men hung outside, waiting for him.

"Have you found them?" he asked.

"Yes, they're inside. They were locked in a storage bunker around the back."

As Daka walked in, the two Revlans looked up, fearfully. The proboscis freak was scary enough on the best of days. The ominously large body drew closer to them. "Well?" Daka pressed.

"They jumped us, sir. They were fast, like lightning, experts at martial arts."

"They were like trained assassins," the other put in. "Lethal."

"How many?"

"Fifteen, at least. All powerfully built."

A blue Stilgen woman stepped out from the corridor. "There were four of them," she qualified. Daka whipped his head to her. "Human. One girl with blonde hair, two youngish men - one dark-haired, one blonde-haired - and one older man with white hair. They said they'd come here to set us free and gave the others money. A lot of money. One of them said you had crossed the wrong human."

Daka stared at her, trying to make sense of what he heard. His eyes slowly widened. One of his casinos had taken a loss last night. They were human. Had they stolen from him too?"

The steaming pressure exploded. He slammed a fist into the wall making plaster crumble and everyone in the room jump. *Who were they! He rarely dealt with humans!*

He turned to the woman. "You," he said, pointing. "Why did you stay behind?"

"I am loyal to you. I was hoping you would repay my loyalty."

His dark eyes stayed fixed on her. Whatever this was, it wasn't loyalty. He turned his attention to the two Revlans now trembling on the couch. Striding across the room, he grabbed a weapon off a green and shot them both in the head.

The Stilgen woman stared at the slumped bodies, her fearful eyes drawn to Daka.

"I will repay your loyalty," Daka told her. "You will have the pleasure of lying with me tonight. After a night with me, you'll wish you'd run off with the others."

"I-I thought you'd let me work in one of your casinos," she protested, feebly.

"Then you misjudged the situation. Big mistake." He shrugged. "Who knows, maybe you will... if you survive the night."

*

The part Kaledian woman was called Takeza. Jenna watched her and Cornelius chatting in the lounge.

"They're getting on well, aren't they?" she said to Brash.

"Is this a done deal, Jenna?" he asked, raising his brows to her.

"That depends on Cornelius."

Newark came over with the others, grinning at Jenna. "Want to see more pics?"

"Yeah," she said, excitedly. "What've you got?"

Skinner opened his device. Again, the pictures were priceless. Jenna peered closely at one of the images. "Is that...?"

"Dung, yes," Johnson said, smiling. "We collected a bag of it from a nearby field."

42

"Nice touch. So, his house wasn't guarded?"

"Nope," Newark said. "Arrogant fucker thinks he's untouchable."

"Well, hopefully, every one of them will turn up tomorrow. Bye the way, we need to hit another casino tonight."

"Cool."

Flint and Cornelius stayed behind that night as the others headed to the casino. Fraza and Jenna hit the tables, working their magic as their crewmates watched on and drank. They heaped up their winnings but Jenna found it odd no goons had been out to them yet. In fact, it all seemed too easy.

"Come on," she said to Brash, "let's get Fraza and cash in. I've got a bad feeling."

As they walked over to Fraza, a strange hush came over the room. They turned as one to see the imposing form of Daka. An army of henchmen walked in behind him, the patrons backing away.

Daka's dark eyes fixed on them. Newark's stomach turned as his eyes soaked in the aggressively protruding forehead, the shockingly hideous proboscis. The fucker should have been drowned at birth.

Fraza got up and stood beside Jenna. "Flint's not going to be pleased," he said.

Recognition flashed in Daka's eyes. This group of humans had got away from him once before. *They* had been causing all this trouble? He sneered. He would finish the job properly this time.

"Tell them to get out," Jenna said to Fraza.

"Who? Daka?"

"No, everyone else."

"Get out if you want to live," Fraza shouted to the clientele, upon which they stampeded to the doors.

The room cleared to leave the crew facing Daka and an army of at least fifty, made up of thin green Guthrins and stocky Revlans.

Daka's eyes smiled, tauntingly. "For such a small group, you've been causing me a big headache." Fraza translated. "Did you think you would get away with what you've been doing?"

"Did you?" Jenna asked. "Time to face the music, Daka. You're going down."

The proboscis freak laughed. That did it. Jenna was going to end him herself. Newark stared at Daka, transfixed. He didn't think it possible for the guy to look any more hideous but that proboscis shook disgustingly.

"OK, let's get this over with," Daka said to his men. "Keep the blonde girl alive. I'll have a threesome tonight."

Jenna and Fraza focused. Daka's men began firing but the fire hit an invisible barrier and ricocheted back, downing a few Guthrins. A moment of silence followed. Daka's men looked to Daka, who, like them, didn't have a clue what was happening.

"Continue firing!" Daka yelled, and more of his men fell.

Fraza and Jenna dropped the barrier and moved forward, thrusting out their arms, flinging bodies against the walls, deflecting the shots coming their way. Weapons flew out of hands, landing near the crew.

"Blast them!" Jenna shouted, and the crew started firing.

Tables and chairs flew at the enemy, glasses smashed in their faces as the crew fired, repeatedly. Thrown into disarray, Daka and his men went into meltdown. This was supernatural stuff. Bony bodies tried to escape but the doors slammed shut in their faces. The crew systematically annihilated them, the floor becoming littered, until one man alone remained standing. Newark fired at Daka but Jenna deflected the fire. Flinging out an arm, she knocked the gun from Newark's hand. It hit the wall with a crash.

"I'm not finished with him, yet," she shot.

Daka's bloodied face stared at her as she moved closer. "Who are you...?" he whispered.

"Who are you?" she countered. "Do you have a story, Daka?" He stared at her, confused. "You know, some twisted history that's turned you into the mean bastard you are?"

"Would it make a difference?"

"No."

His face turned hard. "Some wield power. Some succumb. It's the way things are."

"I see. You thought no-one could touch you, didn't you? Big mistake." A weapon flew out of Johnson's hand and Jenna snatched it.

"Wait," Daka pleaded. "I'll give you anything. What do you want?"

"I want this." She pointed the weapon at Daka's head and fired.

Daka dropped. A moment of hush descended.

"Flint's not going to be pleased," Fraza said, shaking his head.

Stand-Off

Cornelius and Flint had retired when they got back to the hotel, so the crew left it until morning to tell them.

In the morning, Flint was apoplectic. "Daka's dead!"

"Dead as a doorknob," Newark remarked. "Trot took him out."

"We were ambushed," Jenna insisted.

"Yeah, there was a whole army of them," Johnson told him.

"Wiped out the lot of them," Newark boasted. "Daka was the last man standing."

Flint stared at Newark, his blazing eyes descending on Jenna. "You knew I wanted him! Why didn't you come and get me!"

"What does it matter?" Brash said. "The job's done. We did what we came here to do."

"What does it matter...? She deliberately disobeyed an order, taking matters into her own hands again!"

"Look, if we'd left it any longer, the security forces would have descended on us. Should we have killed them too?"

Flint's look hardened. "The security forces would have thanked you."

"We don't know that for sure."

"This has nothing to do with them and you know it. This is to do with Jenna doing whatever the fuck she pleases!"

"Doing whatever *I* please?" she shot. "You just wanted your pound of flesh. And what does it matter *who* killed him as long as the job's done?"

Newark snorted. "You stopped *me* nailing the bastard."

Flint's eyes whipped to Newark. They returned to Jenna, demanding an explanation.

"Alright," she threw out. "He was laughing at me. I hate that. But the fact remains-"

"The fact remains, you disobeyed my orders!"

Cornelius shook his head. What a shambles. "That's enough," he said firmly. "Listen to yourselves. One of you wants to kill Daka because he laughed at you. One of you wants to kill him because he's ugly." He raised his eyebrows to Newark, who stared at him, confused. "One of you wants to kill him for revenge."

"What do *you* suggest we should have done?" Jenna asked, snidely.

Cornelius looked at her. "You should have got Flint. His motives might not have been any better than yours but he's the captain."

"Well, if his motives are as crap as ours, he shouldn't *be* captain!"

"But he is and you should have got him."

"At risk to ourselves?"

"There was no risk to yourselves. Daka's men lay dead. It would have taken ten minutes to get Flint. It probably took you that long to clean the place out. I presume you collected the cash? You wilfully disobeyed orders."

"Crap orders."

"You disobeyed them for your own personal reasons. So, he laughed at you? Get over it. You are not the girl you were, yet you are allowing the past to drag you down." He turned to Newark. "As for you, Mr. Newark, beauty is merely skin-deep."

"Have you been rooting in my head?" Newark asked, cottoning on.

"I don't have to do much rooting. It's all there on the surface. And, as for Mr. Flint," he said, looking back at Jenna, "this is only half about revenge. The other half is your lack of respect and insubordination. He has every right to reprimand you and, if I were him, I'd throw you in the lock-up."

Jenna glared at Cornelius. "I'd break out."

"Must be good, being a magician, Jenna," Flint said, looking at her, steadily. "Everything easy, no consequences... Must be just like being the Admiral's daughter."

She stared at Flint. Eyes blazing, she launched herself at him, fists flying. Brash caught her and held her back. "Let it go, Jenna," he said.

"Get off me!" she yelled.

"Calm down, Jenna," he said in her ear. "It's not worth it."

She struggled against him, eyes locked on Flint. "What's happened to you?" she fired at him.

"What's happened to you?" Flint fired back.

"Let it go, Jenna," Brash repeated.

"Did you hear what that scumbag said to me!" Her murderous glare fixed on Flint.

"He doesn't know what he's talking about. We have other things to focus on. There are women and children out there that need our help. That should be our priority. Let it go." He glanced at Flint. "You need to let it go too."

Brash steered her away, her angry eyes lasering Flint. At last, she turned, walking off with Brash. Cornelius watched them go.

Glancing at Flint, the crew wandered to the bar, which, happily, never closed in Jakensk.

"That was some heavy shit," Johnson said.

Graham nodded. "That's what you call a stand-off."

Fraza rubbed his ears. "I don't think this is going to be resolved easily."

46

"If you ask me," Skinner remarked, thoughtfully, "there's a lot of sexual tension between those two."

"Which two?" Johnson asked.

"Trot and Flint."

Johnson, Graham, and Newark looked at each other then burst out laughing.

"Maybe they need to get it out of their systems," Skinner thought aloud.

The three of them laughed harder.

"God, Skinner, you're a bloody comedian," Johnson managed.

Newark slapped Skinner on the shoulder. "And you're supposed to be the fucking genius."

"He is," Graham said, "he just doesn't know shit about people."

"Well, here's a head's up," Johnson said, wiping her eyes. "Don't let the cap hear you saying that crap, cos I don't think *he'll* find it funny."

"Which cap?" Skinner asked, studying her, thoughtfully.

"Brash, of course."

Across the room, Cornelius sat down, heavily. The girl had greatness in her. She had already proved that, but she still had a long way to go. At the moment, her greatness was going to waste.

He looked up to see Flint watching him.

Flint sat beside him. "Perhaps I should give this up now," he said, staring at the floor.

"That would be the easy option," Cornelius reflected. "For you... and her." He smiled, sadly. "But I care enough not to make it easy on either of you."

Flint rubbed his forehead. "It... wasn't just about revenge."

"I know what it was, Mr. Flint. It was important he looked into your eyes. And I know why. The point is, Jenna doesn't. Not that it excuses her actions lately."

"So, what now?"

"You tell me. What now, Captain Flint?"

"I don't know. This group has the ability to do a lot of good, right many wrongs. I'm just realising this. But whether they'll want to do that is another matter."

"Then why don't you ask them?"

"Perhaps I'm not the one to..."

"The former captain chose you to be his replacement. They now have to live with that decision. And maybe you *are* the right one."

Cornelius looked up. Flint followed the direction of his gaze. Takeza stood near the bar, her eyes locked on Cornelius.

"Excuse me," Cornelius said, standing.

Flint studied their interaction. The woman kept touching his arm as they talked intently. It was odd to see Cornelius interact this way. They'd obviously slept together last night, obvious she liked him. They spoke for some time then they hugged. The woman walked away, her sullen eyes staring at the floor. Cornelius walked out into the garden.

Flint sat there for a time. He got up and walked out after him.

Cornelius stood on the scruffy lawn, staring ahead into nowhere.

"Why don't you stay?" Flint said.

Cornelius turned, gazing at him for a few moments. "I can't stay. You and the crew need me. And besides, I'm too old for her anyway."

"I don't think the age gap bothered her. And, as for the rest of us..." He shrugged. "We'll manage. If they want to do some good, I'll keep at it. If not, we'll part company. Like you said, it's a process. We'll either get through it or we won't."

Cornelius smiled. "You've come along way, Mr. Flint."

Better Be Convincing

The crew distributed the rest of the money, the women in the sex houses accepting it in wide-eyed wonder. Johnson felt like a liberator, even instigating the trashing of the places, an official act of shutting them down.

As news of Daka's demise spread through the city, this strange group of humans started to gain notoriety. They were eventually tracked down and an enthusiastic crowd gathered outside their hotel. Management had to employ security on the doors. Management had also waived their bill.

Members of staff stared over at them as they ate their evening meal, many coming over to clasp their hands. Though most of the crew couldn't understand what they said, the sentiment was clear.

"We're fucking heroes," Newark said, wishing Kaledians were more attractive. He could have ridden the back of this.

Unlikely heroes, Cornelius considered, but heroes nonetheless.

"Free room and board," Johnson said, smugly.

"It's free anyway," Flint remarked around a mouthful of food. "We don't exactly earn the money we spend."

Johnson shrugged. "Maybe so, but this feels better."

Graham's hand rested on her knee beneath the table. Since she'd agreed to marry him, he was touching her virtually non-stop. She steadfastly resisted the urge to slap his hand away, maybe punch him in the face for good measure.

Jenna experienced similar feelings toward Flint. Brash kept glancing at her, aware of her simmering resentment. Fraza, aware of it too, rubbed his ears, catching himself in the action, and becoming increasingly concerned.

"You're rubbing your ears again," Skinner observed.

"They're itchy," Fraza shot.

After the meal, Flint asked them to follow him into the lounge. He was holding a meeting.

"Another fucking meeting," Newark complained as they got up.

They sat in comfy seats, receiving complimentary drinks. The crew stared at the vivid-looking concoctions then knocked them back.

"We've done what we came here to do," Flint said, ignoring Jenna's glare. "The question now is, where do we go from here? I'm prepared to stay on as captain, depending on which direction you intend to take."

"Which direction?" Brash asked.

"It's obvious to me this crew has the potential to do a lot of good. If that's what you want to do, I'm in. If not, we'll part company."

Result, Newark thought.

"So," Brash asked, "you're proposing we travel the galaxy, being... what? Vigilantes?"

"You took out SLOB," Flint stated. "You're already heroes. The question now is, do you want to carry on where you left off, or are you going to continue your extended holiday?"

"We earned that holiday," Jenna asserted. "Where were you?"

Flint ignored her, which made her anger spike.

"Well?" he asked.

"We could do both," Johnson mused. "You know, have fun and clean up a little as we go." She had to admit, she'd enjoyed these past few days.

"Not a bad idea," Graham agreed. He'd enjoyed himself too.

Newark remained quiet. He didn't mind kicking butt, but he struggled to accept Flint as captain.

Skinner and Fraza, who had no issue with Flint, apart from the discord it caused, were prepared to go along with the group decision. Brash had reservations. He wasn't averse to doing good, but if they followed this course, they needed a strong captain. Flint had no experience, and Brash had no desire to resume the role. Dropping the captain role had done wonders for his relationship with Jenna, but more than that, it was like shedding a heavy skin.

"If we do this," he said to Flint, "using the power cannot be a last resort. We use every weapon at our disposal and do it in the most efficient and effective way."

Flint nodded.

Jenna looked at Cornelius. "Was this your idea?"

"No," he said, simply. "But you have the means to help those who cannot help themselves. Is that a gift you want to waste?" He looked around the crew. "I suggest you all think about it. But if you decide on this course, you need to give Mr. Flint your full co-operation."

"Let me know your decision," Flint said.

The crew got up and migrated to the bar.

"Jenna, could I have a word with you?" Flint asked.

She looked around at him. His tone was conciliatory but she hadn't forgiven him for what he'd said. She reasoned he wanted to apologise. Nodding, she followed him out into the garden. The green twilight glow pervaded the sky. She looked up at it.

Flint turned to her. "I've brought you out here to talk about Cornelius."

"Cornelius?"

"He wants to stay here, with the woman, Takeza."

Jenna stared at him. "He does? Wait. He slept with her last night?"

"I believe he did, and they seem to have a... connection. But he won't stay because he believes, rightly or wrongly, that we need him."

"*You* need him," she said, snidely. "He seems to have your back."

"Maybe you need him too," he countered. "Someone needs to rein you in."

"Really? Is that your considered opinion, *Captain Flint?*" She gave out a laugh. "Captain Flint... D'you know how absurd that sounds? D'you remember how you were, Flint? Remember when we fled Daka last time? You couldn't carry your own weight. Graham had to haul you along. Then, when we travelled through the forest, you wanted to kill yourself. Remember that? Do you really think you are captain material?"

His jaw tightened. "When did you become such a bitch?"

"When did you get ideas above your station?"

Anger flashed in his eyes. "D'you know what I think?" he said in a hard voice. "I think Cornelius is right. You can't shake off the yoke of the past, no matter where you go or what you do. The harder you fight, the stronger its claws dig into you."

"You don't know what you're talking about," she spat.

"I do," he said, looking at her, steadily. "I see through you, Jenna Trot."

"Fuck you!"

He laughed. "Am I ruffling your feathers, Jenna?"

"The only thing you could ruffle is your prissy blonde hair."

The conversation was going in the wrong direction. Flint drew in a steadying breath. "I brought you out here to talk about Cornelius, not to bicker. The man is getting old. This could be his last shot at happiness. We have to let him go, and he'll only do that if he thinks we're going to be alright."

"We're not alright."

"I know." He drew in another breath, resisting the urge to tell her she was a spoiled brat, and more like the Admiral's daughter than she ever had been. "So, are you going to work with me, to ease his mind?"

"Why do you care so much about Cornelius?" she asked, looking at him, strangely.

"You forget, I spent a lot of time with him while you were away. He helped me a lot. I... I've never had that before."

Sense started to prevail. She seriously thought about Cornelius and what was best for him. "What do we do?" she asked.

"We have to make him believe we have resolved our differences, and are moving forward."

"OK, but he sees through everything."

"Then we'd better be convincing."

51

Newark watched them through the window. "What are Flint and Trot talking about?"

"They've been out there a while," Johnson remarked.

Brash and Cornelius glanced through the window. Cornelius noted their body language seemed relaxed. They were talking things through. This was a good sign.

"D'you think that crowd's ever going to disperse?" Graham asked, wandering to the front window. A chorus of cheers erupted when he was spotted.

Newark wandered to the window too, basking in the glory. "It's like being a rock star," he called back, smiling.

"Don't encourage them," Brash told him.

Newark and Graham returned to the table, Newark looking around the bright orange walls. He sniffed. "Kaledians must have sunglasses for eyes." A thought occurred to him. "Maybe these walls aren't as bright to them..." He frowned, considering what he'd said.

Skinner glanced at him. The comment had merit. Maybe bright ideas *did* pop into Newark's empty head in a Zen-like way.

"What's the verdict then?" Brash asked. "Are we going to carry on where we left off or not?"

Johnson sniffed. "I don't mind taking out a few scumbags. I'm in."

Graham nodded. "Might be good to have a purpose again." He'd always dreamt of being an architect but he could put his plans on hold a while longer.

Skinner nodded, thoughtfully. "I'm in."

"Fraza?" Brash asked.

"It has been good to help people," he said. "I'm in, too."

"Newark?"

Newark stared around the lot of them. "You're all happy with Flint being captain?"

"Well... the man's changed," Brash said. "And he seems to have a vested interest in this."

"I know one person who won't stand for it," Newark asserted. "There's no way Trot is going to accept Flint."

Newark looked up to see Trot and Flint walk through the door, talking amiably, even smiling at each other. *What the fuck...?*

The two of them joined the group. "You know, Flint," Jenna said, "I don't even know your forename?"

"Vincent," Flint replied.

"Vincent… Remember the team building exercise we did?" she asked, turning to Brash. "Where we learned each other's names? Flint missed out on it, didn't he?"

"*Okay,*" Brash said, his gaze lingering on her. "I'll start. My forename is Lucas."

Brash looked to Johnson. "Daria," Johnson said.

"Graham," Graham said.

"Excuse me?" Flint asked.

"Graham Graham. That's my name. Blame my dad."

"Right." Flint looked to Skinner.

"Jeremy," Skinner said.

"Fraza is my forename," Fraza said. "Do you want to know my last name?"

Flint shook his head. "That's alright." He turned his attention to Newark.

"John," Newark threw out.

"Now that's done," Jenna said, "have we decided what we're going to do?"

"That depends on you," Brash told her.

"Let's go and be heroes," she proclaimed.

Cornelius studied her. "Have you and Mr. Flint resolved your differences, Jenna?"

"He's apologized for that awful comment," she lied, smiling at Flint. "He realises it was below the belt, and was spoken in complete ignorance. He regrets what he said."

"Yes," Flint agreed, smiling back at her, "and Jenna realises she's been self-indulgent, insubordinate, and pretty juvenile."

Jenna's hands pressed into fists beneath the table. "I got carried away. I should, perhaps, have got Flint, like you said, Cornelius. I've been… disrespectful."

The crew stared at Jenna. Newark thought he was hearing things. Flint and Jenna gave each other a, *what a pair of ninnies we are,* look.

"You must have had quite a talk out there," Cornelius said.

"Yes," Jenna agreed. "It didn't start off too well but I think we're getting there."

Sounds of commotion came from the front of the hotel. The crew looked around to find a small party of Kaledians being ushered inside, one of them looking regal and pompous in a green robe.

"It's the Hefruk," Fraza told them.

"The what?" Johnson asked.

"I think it's like a mayor," Flint remarked.

The Hefruk and his entourage were escorted over to them, the Hefruk beaming broadly. "I believe we are all in your debt," the Kaledian effused and Fraza translated. "I cannot tell you what it means to this city to be free of the scourge of Daka."

The Hefruk sat with them. Glancing around briefly, his voice became quieter. "Now, what is it you want?"

The crew stared at the Kaledian.

The Hefruk continued. "Are you planning to take up where Daka left off, or is this about blackmail?"

"Blackmail?" Flint asked.

"Payment to clear off."

Flint looked at him for a moment. "We don't want anything," he told him. "We were... on a mission of mercy."

The Hefruk and his entourage stared at Flint, suspiciously. "Are you playing some sick game here?"

"No game." Flint realised this wasn't going to wash. "OK, we had a score to settle with Daka. We got what we came for. And we'll be leaving soon."

It took a few moments for that to sink in. The Hefruk's face suddenly transformed into a broad, beaming smile. "Well, in that case, let me welcome you to Jakensk. You are all invited to attend the Hefruk's ball tomorrow night, and will be granted the freedom of the city. The Jakensk games will be starting the day after, and the people of this city would be delighted if you would open them. You have become quite the heroes."

Flint thought for a moment. "OK. We most graciously accept," he said, smiling.

When Fraza translated, Jenna stared at Flint. What was he playing at? They were supposed to be leaving tomorrow.

The entourage eventually departed and Jenna held onto her annoyance until Cornelius retired. When he did, she pulled Flint aside. "What the hell are you doing? We're leaving tomorrow. We're not going to any god damn ball!"

"You don't get to make that decision. You're not captain. I am. And we're going."

"You need to consult your crew," she hissed.

"No. I don't." He drew in a breath, holding onto his patience. "Look, we're going to need a couple of days, at least, to convince Cornelius we're good. He's not buying it yet. He needs more proof. You have to be a lot more convincing."

"I *was* convincing. Do you know how much effort it took to smile that sweetly?"

"It showed. Your body was stiff. Try using your imagination, pretend you are warming to me. Pretend I'm Brash, if it helps, but pull something out of the bag because your second-rate performance isn't going to work."

Her lips twisted, her eyes glaring at him. "By the end of these two days, you'll believe I really do like you, but just remember it's a fucking lie."

"Fine with me."

"Good."

They gave each other hard stares as they parted company, Flint vowing to bring that girl in line.

Keeping Up Appearances

Jenna did such a good job of being nice to Flint, she even danced with him at the ball.

"You can't dance," she remarked, smiling at him, pleasantly.

"Neither can you. You keep standing on my feet."

"That's deliberate."

"Just keep smiling. And watch your thoughts. Cornelius can read minds, remember?"

The Hefruk's staff had purchased evening wear for the crew – there were a number of human shops in Jakensk. Flint wore a dark suit. Jenna wore a short purple dress.

From the side-lines, Brash admired her in the dress. He knew what she and Flint were doing. Jenna had told him about Cornelius wanting to stay. He had to hand it to them. They were doing an excellent job. If she hadn't told him, he might have felt jealous.

Newark, who didn't know about Cornelius, stared at them, agog. What the hell was she doing sucking up to Flint? Fraza moved passed his line of vision and his attention diverted to him. Fraza danced with a female Kaledian, and Newark couldn't decide if it was funny or freakish. Their big bellies made close contact impossible. Newark's brain followed that thought. How the hell did Kaledians do it?

As Graham turned to ask Johnson to dance, she turned to Brash. "Want to dance, Cap?"

Brash looked at her, surprised. "Err... OK. But I'm not the cap, remember?"

"Sorry. Force of habit."

As they walked out over the floor, Brash turned to her. "So, you dance?"

"No, but there's a first time and all that."

"You're not wearing a dress," he observed, his eyes raking over her jeans and t-shirt.

"Nope." She didn't wear dresses nor did she dance. Unless she was desperate.

On the side-lines, Graham looked around the grand, impressive room. Chandeliers sparkled, the wooden floor shone, all completely ruined by the blinding orange walls and chintzy curtains. That seemed a popular colour scheme here – God damn awful.

He turned to Newark. "Not dancing, bud?"

"With what?" Newark asked. "Bloated Kaledians or colour-challenged Stilgens and Guthrins?"

"I'm sure that's racist, you know."

"What's racist is there's no humans here."

"Humans just visit the place. Few settle."

"Oh, my god, look at Skinner." A blue Stilgen was asking him to dance. Now, the old, drunken worm of a man would have snapped her hand off, but this new Skinner was picky. He politely and persistently declined her offer.

Graham laughed. "What d'you think? Think he'll dance with her?"

"Think she'll get her face punched if she carries on."

"It's funny, isn't it?" Graham reflected. "Skinner was always the one getting punched."

"I miss those days..." Newark said, equally reflective.

The Stilgen, at last, got the message and walked away, face intact.

"Trot's still dancing with Flint," Newark observed. "D'you think he's done some freaky mind shit on her?"

"Flint? He wouldn't know how to do freaky mind shit. Mind you... I never thought I'd see him fight like that. It's like he's not Flint anymore, isn't it?"

"The man gives me the creeps."

"Skinner changed and he didn't give you the creeps? Mind you... Skinner never got promoted to captain."

"What does he know about being captain? The worm's been in *therapy* for the past year."

"Daria told me Trot said he's got some deep, dark shit in his past."

"Deep dark shit?" Newark asked, turning to Graham.

Graham shrugged. "That's what she said."

"Well, he'll have some deep, dark shit in his present if he gets on the wrong side of me."

"Everyone getting on?" Cornelius asked, coming up behind them.

"Yep," Graham replied.

"You know," Cornelius said, thoughtfully, "I've lived on this planet all my life but I had never been to Jakensk. I'd heard bits and pieces from Fraza, of course, but it's quite an experience being here."

"So, the Erithians will have gone now, will they?"

"Yes... That beautiful lush valley will eventually return to wasteland..."

A pang of sadness tugged at their hearts.

"Well, all things change," Cornelius said, stoically. "Sometimes, it's just time to move on..." He wandered away in his own thoughts.

Brash and Johnson came over, and Graham asked her to dance.

"There's a reason I don't dance," she said with a sniff. "I'm shit at it."

"You can't be any worse than these Kaledians," Graham said, encouragingly.

"Dancing is for sissies anyway."

He knew that was an end to the matter.

Brash looked around to see Jenna and Flint still dancing. He wondered if they were overdoing it.

"I think we should sit out now," Jenna said. "We don't want to go overboard."

"You're right," Flint agreed.

They wandered over to the others, Jenna talking to Flint pleasantly. Her act was so good, Newark started to feel sick.

As the evening wore on, Jenna grew tired. Being nice to Flint, watching her thoughts constantly, was exhausting. At least, she knew Flint would be having the same problem.

Cornelius approached her with a smile. "Having a good time, Jenna?"

She plastered on a smile and nodded.

"And we have an entire day of games to look forward to tomorrow."

She willed her smile to stay in place.

The next day proved to be just as exhausting. Flint got invited to open the games. Jenna watched as he gave a speech, the pompous arsehole. She whipped her head to Cornelius. He wasn't paying attention. He watched the athletes limbering up on the grass. Kaledians in shorts was *not* a pretty sight. Those fat bloated bellies were quite hairy.

From behind her shades, she looked over the scrubby grassland, wondering how the non-athletic-looking athletes were going to run over that. When the race began, the contestants managed well, Kaledians running far faster than their bodies would suggest. Guthrins and Stilgens raced too and, though they were leaner, a Kaledian won the race. Fraza clapped, ecstatically.

With the exception of that first race, most of the events seemed ludicrous. As competitors lined up for a hand-stand race, the crew wondered how those weedy Kaledian arms would carry those huge bellies. Newark was certain a Guthrin would win, but, again, a Kaledian won. It defied common sense.

The crew stared transfixed as a rolling race began. The contestants simply rolled on their sides to the other end of the field.

"How old are they?" Newark asked. "Five?"

"Look at the Kaledians," Johnson said, trying not to laugh. "It's like, fast, slow, fast, slow…"

A Guthrin won that race.

59

A spinning event had the contestants whirl themselves around then stand still at the sound of a whistle. The last man standing won.

"Is that considered sport?" Graham asked Fraza.

"Oh, yes. They test all kinds of endurance capabilities."

"Right."

Throughout it all, Jenna and Flint exchanged pleasantries. They even laughed together when a punch-up broke out on the field. Cornelius watched them, thoughtfully, and a smile broke on his face. Maybe there was hope for them yet. It was all a lie, of course, he knew, but they were pulling together for the greater good. In this case, his greater good.

A tear collected in the corner of his eye, and he wiped a finger under it. Maybe it was time to let them find their own way, as rocky as that way might be. He thought of Llamia, the leader of the Erithians. She had not wanted him to accompany them on their mission to kill SLOB. She had said, the most helpful things can often be the greatest hindrances. Perhaps it was time to let them go.

Draztis

"You're not coming with us?" Johnson asked Cornelius.

"I'm afraid not," he said. "I've had enough adventure and I'd like to settle now."

"But you don't know anyone here?"

"I have made an acquaintance."

"The woman?" she asked, staring at him.

"You sly old dog," Newark said.

Jenna prodded Newark in the ribs. "We'll miss you, Cornelius," she said, coming forward to hug him. "I'm glad you've found someone," she whispered in his ear.

Flint witnessed the Jenna he used to know, the girl that had been kind to him.

He stepped forward. "Take care, Cornelius, and thank you for all you've done for me."

Brash clasped hands with Cornelius and patted his back. The others said their goodbyes too.

Cornelius watched them walk away with a pang of sadness in his heart. Jenna turned around briefly and he smiled at her. She smiled back, sadly. He had the feeling their paths would cross again.

*

When they boarded the ship, Flint called a meeting.

"We're setting a course for Draztis," he told them, "A planet on the far reaches of the galaxy, and one notorious for its flagrant abuse of citizens' rights."

"How d'you know about this place?" Brash asked. "And, if it's on the far reaches, how is it notorious?"

"I visited the library in Jakensk and studied a travel publication, reading a particular article entitled, *Places not to visit in the Galaxy*." He held up the publication.

Jenna mentally slapped her head. Why hadn't she visited a library and found a *Places to visit* publication? That would have made things so much easier.

"There is a lot of squalor on this planet," Flint said. "Many of the citizens live in a state of subjugation, like the women in the whorehouses here. Only this is slavery on a much larger scale." Flint flicked through the pages. "Misery unimaginable," he quoted. "Slavery sanctioned by the state, wholesale trading of intelligent sentient beings..." He looked up at them. "This place is in desperate need of help."

"You're suggesting we completely re-shape a planet...?" Brash asked.

"Yes, but if we cut off the Head or Heads, we can give the planet back to the people."

"I don't know... It could be a long-term commitment. If we take out the Heads, we create a power vacuum. If we don't see it through, another terror could rise in its wake."

"Then we see it through until a strong and stable government can be formed."

The crew stared at Flint. They hadn't imagined this.

"Slavery is rife in this part of the galaxy," Flint pressed on. "Other planets import slaves from Draztis. It's big business. Children are bred to be exported. We could have a huge effect on the whole region."

"This is bullshit," Newark threw out. "I thought we were clearing up a little, not doing a whole fucking spring clean!"

"It's too ambitious," Jenna said, the pleasant act dropped at the hotel door. "You've only been captain for five minutes, and you're talking about altering whole planets, whole regions of the galaxy?"

"It's a big ask," Johnson said.

Flint sat back and looked at them. "I can't believe what I'm hearing. You travelled regions in a far-away galaxy, you assembled an alliance from scratch, and you took out SLOB, a being who had the potential to effect not one galaxy but many. You have already done so much more. *This* is a big ask?"

He was right, Brash thought. But it was the commitment issue they struggled with; the investment they would have to make afterwards. Once SLOB was killed, their job was done. This was more involved.

"Perhaps I'm thinking too big," Flint said, morosely. "I thought this crew would be more than capable but... maybe I misjudged you..."

"We are capable," Newark piped up. "We're capable of all kinds of shit!"

"Yeah," Graham agreed. "You have no idea what we're capable of."

"And some," Johnson affirmed.

Brash studied Flint. As captain, Brash would never have used manipulation. He wasn't sure he approved of it but maybe Flint needed to use every tactic he had.

"We could do a lot of good there," Fraza said, thoughtfully.

"It's a big commitment," Skinner remarked.

"We didn't sign up for this, Flint," Jenna asserted.

Flint looked at her. "What do you want, Jenna? Do you want to do some good in this universe or not?" He held up a hand. "I know you've done a lot already, but there is so much more to do. These people can't help themselves and we can help them. There are children being bred as slaves, for Christ's sake! What if you were one of them? Wouldn't you want someone in a position to help to actually help? Or would you want them to go on an extended holiday, saying they'd done their bit so the galaxy can go screw itself? What if you were one of those children, facing a life of hopelessness and misery and maybe things a child shouldn't even have to imagine? What if you were one of them, Jenna!"

Jenna stared at him, the passion, the intent, the pain, palpable. What *had* happened to Flint? Again, she felt oddly inspired. At times like this, it was like looking through a window, into him, into herself, a window opening onto the part of her that did want to help, that did care.

"OK," she mumbled.

"What...?" Newark asked.

She glanced at Newark. "You said yourself, we're more than capable." Jenna turned to Flint. "Just because I'm agreeing with you, doesn't mean we're best buddies."

Flint looked around the crew. "Are we agreed then?"

One by one, they nodded, apart from Newark.

"We set a course for Draztis."

*

Draztis was a green planet, two-thirds the size of earth. There were no docking stations, as there were above most planets, where shuttles took visitors down to the capital. They could land themselves but then they could end up anywhere.

Fraza looked at the publication. "Visitors come mostly for commercial reasons," he recited. "Others do arrive but the planet is a god-forsaken hell-hole, the few areas of beauty reserved for the wealthy and elite."

"Can you even breathe on this planet," Newark threw out.

63

"Yes, it has an S1 atmosphere," Flint told him. "OK, we radio down and request permission to land."

"How?" Jenna asked. "Do you speak Draztis?"

Newark shook his head, smugly. The others exchanged glances. Flint was definitely not captain material.

Ignoring them, Flint opened a coms link. "Oppterin par zule. Popa tisis."

They stared at him.

"You speak the language?" Jenna asked.

Flint held up another book: *How to speak Draztis: crash course with pronunciation guide.* "I've been studying it."

Fraza rubbed his ears, excitedly. "May I look at that?"

"Help yourself."

"What did you say?" Jenna asked.

"Permission to land. Respond, please."

Newark's smug look fell away, inadequacy taking its place. Before, they had two geniuses on the ship. Now they had three.

Brash appraised Flint. The man had done some forward planning. At one time, he wouldn't have thought Flint capable of it.

"Joppor goe karo, tisis," came the reply.

"They want us to state our business," Flint said.

"Since we'll want to obtain information," Brash reasoned, "perhaps we should say we are here to purchase slaves."

Flint nodded. He pressed the coms button. "Sop karo," Flint said, taking the book off Fraza and flicking through it, "eel pa soosi ot gonmito folaspio."

Silence at the other end.

"Perhaps you have to go through an agent," Jenna considered.

A reply came. "Oppterin par zule, bati. Jaita komtin, tisis."

"What did she say?"

"Permission to land, granted," Flint replied. "Please follow co-ordinates. She's sending them now."

"We're in," Brash said.

The craft descended through dense cloud, an alien voice directing them to a large black landing platform. It formed part of a line of platforms.

Brash brought the craft down. As they disembarked, they felt light, walking effortless, like they had become five times fitter. They'd visited enough planets to know the small size of this one produced lower gravity. The only thing weighing them down was the pelting rain.

Spotting an entrance to a tunnel, they ran over to it. The long, lit tunnel stretched ahead of them, and a weird-looking being walked toward them in the distance. As it got nearer, Newark winced. The tall creature had six arms, and a long, slightly sunken, narrow face. Large aubergine eyes popped out of its pale grey skin. Newark shivered. It looked like a cross between a zombie, a ghost, and an insect.

"It's got six arms, Cap," Newark said to Brash.

"I'm not the cap." *How long was it going to take?*

The being spoke, its mouth making the most unusual shapes. The crew stared at it, transfixed. When the alien finished, Flint replied to it. "Rap go," he said.

Flint turned to the crew. "He will direct us to a hotel, and will introduce us to an agent in the morning. The agent will discuss options with us."

They followed the weird-looking creature through the tunnel.

"Err... how are we going to pay for a hotel?" Johnson asked.

"It's complimentary. All prospective buyers are given free accommodation. If we don't purchase, we have to pay for the hotel."

"Cheap-skates."

"Is it a man or woman?" Graham asked. The creature's cropped tunic showed off a grey ribbed belly, and it wore leggings under a knee-length shirt. Long grey hair trailed down its back in a braid.

"It's bloody ugly, whatever it is," Johnson remarked.

On entering a terminal, they looked around. Six-armed beings were everywhere. Jenna spotted hairy creatures that looked like bears. Newark thought he saw a couple of humans but when they turned around, his breath caught. They had obscenely large noses and wide, manic lips, as if someone had used a knife on them.

"God, that's just not right," he said.

Jenna followed the direction of his gaze. "I think they're slaves," she remarked. "Look, their hands are bound."

"We've come to rescue *them*?" Newark asked, gazing at their freakish faces.

Flint whipped his head to him. "It doesn't matter what they look like," he snapped. "Suffering is suffering."

As Flint turned around, Newark glared at the back of his head. He turned to Johnson. "I'd be suffering if I looked like them."

They exited the terminal and got pelted with rain again. A closed-topped vehicle waited for them, and they climbed in. Through the sheeting rain and mist, it was hard to see the landscape clearly.

The craft lifted. It took minutes to reach their destination. They climbed out to find they had landed on the roof of a tall building. Rain and mist blocked their view of the surrounding city.

The six-armed being led them to a lift. They descended to the ground floor, the colour scheme of the lobby a shocking contrast to the grey

65

outside. Psychedelic colours and shapes bounced off the walls, making their heads spin.

"Holy fuck," Newark said, looking around.

"Interesting," Skinner remarked. "Says a lot about them."

"Like what?"

"I'm not sure..."

Newark stared at him.

The alien sorted them out with rooms, and showed them to the lounge, the walls painted in those same glaring designs. He told them to enjoy their stay before taking his leave.

Negotiating six armrests, they sat in chairs. Flint got out his *How to speak Draztis* book, and continued to study it.

"Well, they're certainly buttering us up," Johnson said. "Wonder what the grub's like?"

They didn't have to wait long to find out. Waiters loaded the tables quickly, carrying six plates at a time, the crew slower to taste the food. The dish resembled a bowl of grey semolina, with yellow rubbery things floating in it. Johnson stabbed a fork-like instrument into one of the lumps, and tentatively took a bite. "Tastes spicy," she said, beginning to chew with more enthusiasm.

The others tucked in.

"I wonder what this is?" Brash asked, examining the dish.

Jenna smiled. "Better not to ask."

"Well, they're very welcoming," Graham remarked.

Flint scowled at him. "That's because they want to flog us live, intelligent, sentient beings."

Graham sniffed. "I know that."

"God, these walls are giving me a headache," Johnson complained.

"Ask the waiter who does the painting," Newark said to Flint.

Flint looked at Newark. Breathing out heavily, he entered into a short conversation with one of the waiters. The being's face lit up. He looked around the walls with pride as he spoke.

As the waiter walked off, Flint turned to Newark. "A race called the Siltians do the decorating. He said their services are highly prized. They are renowned for their imagination and creative flair."

"They actually like this shit?" Newark asked, looking at the walls.

"Apparently so. The six-armed creatures are called Bortten, by the way."

"Bortten," Brash repeated. "They seem to be the predominant species here."

On finishing the second course, Graham turned to Johnson. "I've got a cure for your headache," he whispered. "Shall we go up to our room and I'll show you?"

Johnson sniffed. "No, I'm good. The bedrooms probably have the same brain-melding designs."

"Then we could turn the lights off," he whispered with a suggestive look.

"I want a drink," she said.

Graham looked at her, disappointed.

"Shall *we* go and check out the bedroom walls," Brash whispered to Jenna.

She turned to him, taking in his strong, lean body, his lazy, confident posture. Loose dark hair framed his handsome face, the deep brown eyes full of promise.

"We could check out the bed too," she whispered back.

They left the table and Graham watched them go.

Flint stood. He'd had enough company for one day. Fraza asked if he could borrow the book. Flint handed it to him. The rest of the crew moved off to look for the bar, but to their complete consternation and disgust, there was no bar.

"Fraza, ask someone where the bar is?" Newark flustered.

Fraza paged through the book. "There is no word for bar or alcohol in here."

"What…?" Johnson asked.

The crew looked at each other, horrified. How long would they *be* on this planet?

Fighting For Command

Three Bortten approached them in the morning. Flint stood to shake one of the eighteen hands but paused, uncertain which hand to shake. As hand shaking was not a custom on Draztis, it was probably for the best.

"You are here to purchase slaves?" one of the sunken faces asked, its aubergine eyes flicking over the rest of the crew.

"Yes, that is correct," Flint replied. Fraza, who had been studying the book all night, followed the conversation well.

The agent sat. "What are your requirements exactly?"

Flint lowered back into his seat. "Well, what... stock do you have?"

"Some species are bred for hard physical work, the price reflecting how much effort we put into feeding and exercising them. Other species are bred for domestic chores... men, women, and children. We have a select group, comprising various species, for sexual gratification. So, what are your requirements?"

"Our requirements are varied." Flint leaned forward. "We are agents like yourselves. Our client is extremely rich. He has recently purchased a number of plantations on Juyra. You know the place?" The agent nodded. "He will require many slaves from all the groups you have listed, and has asked us to examine the stock personally. Would it be possible to have a tour of your facilities?"

The aubergine eyes remained fixed on Flint. "We have many sites scattered throughout the region. You want a tour of all of them...?"

"As I said, our client is extremely wealthy and plans to make a huge investment. He is also choosy. He wants this done right. If we're satisfied, we would like to meet the being in overall control. Like I said, this is to be an enormous investment. Our client plans to expand, so this could be an ongoing arrangement."

The agent glanced at his two cohorts. He turned back to Flint. "I suppose we can arrange this. I need to make some calls. Give me time to sort it out. We will return tomorrow. In the meantime, please make yourselves at home here."

The agent got up, turning back to Flint. "What species are you, by the way?"

"Human."

"Human... Never heard of them." His sunken face stretched briefly then he walked away.

"What did he say?" Brash asked.

"We're getting a tour of their facilities tomorrow. For now, we're staying put."

"Downer," Newark muttered.

They spent the rest of the day wandering around the city. The mist had cleared but the sky remained dull and overcast. They walked past tall, metal and glass structures, the hotel situated in a reasonably modern area. A short walk in each direction and they ended up in shabby territory, the streets drab and dirty, ramshackle grey-brick buildings squashed together. It seemed the central area had been devoted to schmoosing potential clients, the rest of the place neglected.

Residents glanced at them as they walked by. They'd probably never seen humans before, but their lack of interest told Brash they were used to visitors here.

As they strolled further, they passed a few of those bear-like creatures. The bears didn't take much notice of them.

"There's no fucking bars," Newark complained.

"What's that place?" Johnson asked, pointing. A few bears headed into a rough-looking joint through a garish door.

The crew wandered over and ventured in.

The inside was as garish as the outside, the walls the same as in the hotel. Bears sat around on bean bags... smoking bongs...?

"Am I stoned?" Newark asked, staring at them.

"No, but they are," Johnson replied, staring at them too.

"This is the bar then," Newark said, rubbing his hands together. "When in Rome."

"We need money," Graham said.

"Maybe they'll charge it to the hotel," Johnson thought aloud.

"We're not getting stoned," Flint said, definitively. "We're on a mission, remember?"

"Oh, come on, Flint. Live a little."

"It's not happening," he growled.

"Listen, Flint," she said, patiently, "we've followed you across the galaxy. The least you can do is let us have some down time."

"You don't know what's in that stuff. You could end up comatose by tomorrow."

She stared at him as if to say, 'So?'. She turned to Fraza. "Fraza, ask them if they'll charge it to our hotel."

"Fraza, you will not ask them," Flint stated. "If you do, you'll be disobeying a direct order."

Looking between the two of them, Fraza rubbed his ears.

"Stop putting him on the spot," Jenna shot. "Look at him."

70

Flint glanced at the Kaledian. "Why does he keep doing that?"

"His OCD is coming back."

"He has OCD?"

"Had it. Leave Fraza out of this, the lot of you."

"Fraza, go outside," Flint said.

The crew watched their lifeline walk out of the joint.

"Alright," Newark said, annoyed, "I'll ask them with sign language."

"No, you won't," Flint said in a hard voice.

Newark gave Flint a menacing look. "Are you going to stop me?"

Flint let out a breath. "If you want to get high, you'll have to fight me for it. Outside," he said, turning on his heel.

"Will I have to fight you too?" Johnson asked.

"And me?" Graham added.

Flint turned to them. "Very well. The three of you, outside."

"Bring it on," Newark said.

"You can't fight three of them," Jenna insisted. "This is ridiculous. Stop it," she said to Brash.

"OK, that's enough," Brash asserted. "Newark-"

"Stay out of this, Brash," Flint said. "That's an order."

For a brief moment, Brash wanted to punch Flint himself. He forcibly reminded himself Flint was the captain.

This was it, Newark thought as he followed Flint out. The worm was going to be brought down to size.

Outside, Flint stood to face them. Jenna, Brash, Fraza, and Skinner thought Flint was toast. Even if he came out of this relatively intact, he would no longer be in a position to command.

Newark threw the first blow. Flint blocked it, kicking him away as Johnson and Graham steamed in, coming from opposite directions. Flint back-flipped at the last moment, leaving Johnson and Graham crashing into each other. He came back in lighting fast, jabbing Graham in the side then spinning around with a high kick to Johnson's face. Newark swung at Flint's head but Flint ducked, jabbing up into Newark's stomach before dodging Graham's fist, which connected with Newark's jaw.

The rest of the crew marvelled at how fast Flint's reflexes were. A group of aliens had collected, standing with the crew. Bears watched enthralled, a glazy sheen coating their brown eyes. For them, it was quite a show.

Johnson threw a low kick, designed to take Flint from his feet, but the man jumped to avoid it, the spectators gawking at how high he could leap. And that was how he gained the advantage. He moved quickly and nimbly, like an acrobat, steadfastly avoiding their blows, his own blows landing with deadly precision.

Jenna eyes were plastered to him. She'd never seen anyone so lithe and agile. His body twisted, flipped, leaped, his blows expertly delivered each time. A strong punch to the side took Graham down. Newark returned fire with a heavy blow to Flint's gut. Flint doubled over, the crew thinking this might be the turning point, but Flint threw himself into a somersault, avoiding Newark's upper cut.

Graham, Johnson, and Newark couldn't get a handle on him. And they were tiring, getting desperate and angry, their shots sloppy and misjudged. Flint made them look like amateurs, his judgement impeccable. He knew precisely when to move, when to strike, where to place himself. Jenna's eyes remained glued to him, bowled over by his skill. He pitted them against each other. Flint dodged Newark's fist and it landed in Graham's face, taking the man down for good. Flint dodged a second time, and Johnson whacked Newark with full force. As Newark staggered senselessly, Johnson threw a lethal punch but Flint grabbed her arm, pulling off a crazy manoeuvre that flipped her over. They heard the snap of bone as she slammed into the ground. Newark, the last man standing, wasn't in good shape. A swift round-kick to the head snapped his neck and took him out.

Silence descended. The crew gazed at Flint. The aliens gazed at Flint. The bears just gazed.

Jenna made herself move. She surveyed the damage, prioritising Johnson's broken arm. Laying her hands over it, she let the power come up in her, directing it into Johnson, suffusing her arm, mending the broken tissues. When she'd finished with Johnson, she moved on to the others. Newark held his neck. Graham held his face. She worked her magic on them both, then stood to find Flint staring at her.

"You're... healing them?" he asked, incredulous.

"Yes. This power is an all-purpose entity," she said, quoting Cornelius. "You've got some fancy moves, Flint. Were you a gymnast in your former life?"

He looked at her for a moment, stung by the sarcasm. "Yes." He turned and walked off. "No-one goes back in that place," he called over his shoulder.

The crew watched him walk away.

"The man's a bloody freak," Newark snarled.

Johnson wiped her lip with the back of her hand. "He might be able to fight, but all his fancy moves won't stop a laser shot frying his brain."

Fraza wondered why the crew hated Flint so much. Apart from wanting to kill Daka personally, he couldn't fault any of his decisions as captain. And Flint genuinely wanted to do good out there. As he watched the man wander off, he thought he cut a sad and lonely figure. Fraza knew what it was to feel isolated. As a child, he didn't fit in. In fact, being with this crew had given him what he'd never had before. Acceptance. He had the feeling it was something Flint had never had, either.

Dragging themselves to their feet, Newark, Graham, and Johnson dusted themselves down. The crew wandered back to the hotel, passing a new construction, spotting bears decorating the lobby.

"This planet sucks," Johnson threw out, smarting from stinging pride.

"Well," Brash said, "tomorrow we get to see what's really going on here. The faster we get moving, the sooner we can clear off."

"Why don't we clear off now?" Newark spat.

"If we walk away," Jenna said, "what does that say about us?"

"He's started to get to you, hasn't he? He's working his mind-magic on you."

"No, he's not. I think for myself. Just because some of what he says makes sense, doesn't mean he's getting to me. I'm my own person and Flint knows that. I don't follow anyone around."

"Well, technically, he is the captain," Fraza mentioned.

"Captain of what?" Jenna asked. "Are we still in the space corps? We're only doing this because we want to."

"I don't want to," Newark said.

Jenna turned to him. "You enjoyed taking Daka out, didn't you? You'll enjoy this too. You just don't like Flint."

"Taking out Daka was fun because *you* made it fun."

"I did, didn't I?" she said, smug. "Look, don't worry about Flint. I know how to handle him."

Fraza glanced at her and rubbed his ears.

The Right Thing

Jenna stared out at a swathe of wet grassland, the depressingly grey sky a constant shroud of miserableness. They covered miles of it until, eventually, a solitary construction rose up in the distance.

Landing on a concrete concourse, the agent motioned for them to disembark. Ahead, a bridge traversed marshy land, and beyond it stood a high compound with an electric fence running around the top.

Two Bortten stayed with the craft as the agent led them over the bridge.

"We have Velyors here," the agent told Flint. "Bred for their strength. They are put on a certain diet from an early age, and go through a rigorous daily exercise regime. We keep some males back for breeding purposes, of course, to replenish our stock."

As they approached the compound, an outer metal gate swung open. They entered a no-man's land to find a unit of five guards, loafing. The agent had a few words with the guards as the outer gate closed. Three of the guards took up weapons, six each, as another pressed a button to open an inner metal door.

"D'you think they can fire all six at once?" Johnson asked.

"That's dexterity taken to the extreme," Skinner remarked, humorously, but no-one laughed.

"They're like one man fighting units," Graham said.

"So, one of them equates to six men," Newark reasoned.

"Yeah, but look on the bright side," Jenna said, tongue in cheek. "Taking out one is like taking out six."

Newark's brow furrowed. The logic didn't make sense somehow.

As the inner door closed behind them, they faced a metal wall. Turning right, they walked up metal steps. The steps led to a gangway that ran around a training area below. Looking down, they saw broad-chested, pale-green beings. Lots of them. They lifted weights, and worked various pieces of equipment.

"It's an outdoor gym," Jenna remarked.

She studied the creatures' wide, protruding faces and short necks, her gaze settling on their eyes... empty, dispossessed of spirit. She looked around. A couple of armed guards stood on the other side of the gangway.

Walking under a metal archway, they descended more steps, and entered a roofed area, passing row upon row of cells. Jenna peered through a tiny window to see one of those creatures sitting lifeless on its bunk.

"This is like a prison," she said, her gaze lingering on the creature.

75

"We'll take you over to a viewing room," the agent said to Flint. "Let you inspect a sample."

They passed a square courtyard where Velyor children exercised in lines, some of them very young. Guards sat to either side of them, and the instructor held a whip. Flint's gaze fixed on the whip, his eyes lifting to the instructor. The Bortten looked mean. Flint committed him to memory.

Passing more cell blocks, they walked across a second courtyard, and entered a spacious, dimly-lit viewing room. A guard turned on lights to reveal chains hanging from the ceiling. Manacles lay on the floor, and a wooden contraption at the far end resembled a... rack? Jenna frowned. This wasn't a viewing room. It was a torture chamber.

The agent directed them to six-armed seats. The crew sat and waited.

Minutes later, the three guards brought in six inmates. Lined up, the Velyors didn't look at them, just stared over their heads.

As the agent spoke to Flint, Jenna got up and walked along the line. She stared into the creatures' eyes but there was nothing there, no response... until she got to the last one. Something flickered in those green eyes. Something like hatred. She smiled at the Velyor but he glared at her, earning him a clout from one of the Bortten. The green eyes glared at the guard, and Jenna saw what was in his mind. A child whose spirit had been broken again and again. A child wanting to kill all Bortten. A child they had tried to beat into submission. A child grown into a man who could no longer live this way.

"What's his name?" Jenna asked, turning to Flint.

Flint asked one of the guards.

"They don't have names," Flint replied, "just numbers. He is 7498."

The agent recognised that number but couldn't think why.

Jenna looked at the Velyor, opening a channel to him. Though she could read thoughts proficiently, she had only transferred a thought once. *"We are going to free you,"* she impressed on his mind.

She knew language was not a barrier in thought. The thoughts converted into vibrations that matched similar vibrations in the recipient's mind. Still, she wasn't sure he'd got the message.

"Be patient and wait," she persisted.

Still nothing. She wandered back to the seats.

Flint stood and surveyed the line himself. "My client will be delighted with these," he said to the agent.

"You may touch them," the agent said. "They're docile."

Flint's fingers flexed. "I don't need to touch them. I have a keen eye." He visually examined the creatures. "Muscle definition's impressive... Yes, they look like good stock." He turned to the agent. "We'll be placing a large order." The agent's grey skin stretched wide. "I've seen enough," he said, walking back.

"Take the specimens away," the agent instructed.

The guards pushed the Velyors to the door, 7498 being shoved with the butt of a gun. That was a mistake. What happened next was not pretty. 7498 went berserk, reeling around and ripping off one of the guard's arms. The other guards let loose with six guns each, blasting the Velyor to smithereens, before one of them ran out to fetch help.

"Apologies," the agent flustered as the downed guard writhed in pain. He now knew why the number seemed familiar. "That particular Velyor has always been trouble. He should have been put down. I don't know why this hasn't happened!" he yelled at the guard aiming his weapon. He calmed himself quickly. "The others, I can assure you, are docile. But you can see how strong they are. You won't find their equal anywhere."

The crew stared at the severed arm and the bloody Velyor on the floor.

"They seem dangerous," Flint said.

"As I said, he was an anomaly. Why was he brought in here!" he yelled again.

The guard and the agent entered into a heated exchange as the now five-armed Bortten moaned and writhed in pain. Help, at last, arrived and the dismembered guy got carted out.

The agent maintained the Velyors were safe, insisting they continue the tour. Keen to allay their worries, he even approached a couple of Velyors exercising in the outdoor gym. He went one step further, twisting one guy's nipples and getting no response.

"That's fucked up," Newark said.

"Yeah," Johnson agreed, "but he ain't going to do shit with all these guns trained on him."

Flint told the agent he was convinced and asked if they could visit the next facility.

As the crew walked out of the compound, they looked at each other.

"I've never seen a guy get his arm ripped off before," Graham said, soberly.

"They can fire all six at once," Newark said.

"When we come back, that instructor is mine," Flint told them.

*

77

They spent the next few days touring other facilities. One facility housed various species reserved for sexual gratification. Though housed well, in a city called, Iquiem, the crew knew their future was bleak. Other facilities were like shanty towns, surrounded by patrolled electric fences. The one they visited now contained those beings with the big noses and creepy mouths. Water-logged mud formed narrow alleyways, the squalid dwellings affording little protection from the elements, the inhabitants filthy. The ones they'd seen at the terminal had obviously been cleaned up. Clients didn't usually see these facilities but the agent didn't seem embarrassed by the state of the place.

On hearing a commotion, they turned a corner to see a group gathered. Jenna spotted four guards, and a woman screaming hysterically.

"What's going on?" she asked.

Flint asked the question.

"They are having trouble obtaining a child," the agent explained to Flint. "The mother is proving difficult. This sometimes happens."

"They're taking that woman's child away?" Flint asked, concealing his horror.

"Yes."

Swallowing the lump in his throat, he told the others.

The mother desperately clung to her child, screaming at them not to take him. As a guard grabbed the child, a man lunged forward, laying into the Bortten. Jenna stopped breathing as another guard shot him down. Shrieking and wailing broke out. The mother still screamed. It was heart-breaking to watch.

"We need to do something," Jenna urged.

"We can't," Flint told her. "We can't arouse suspicion. We need to get to the Heads."

"But-"

"Jenna, we have to leave it," he said, sadly.

The child got prized from his mother's arms. As the mother ran at the guard, a second Bortten took aim but his fire veered into the sky. The other two guards aimed their weapons. More fire let off into the sky.

"Jenna," Flint growled. Letting out a breath, he turned to the agent. "Tell the guards to stand down," he said. "I've decided to buy the whole compound."

"What...?" the agent asked in disbelief. "You want to buy the lot?"

"My client's requirements are manifold. Tell them to stand down."

"They still need the child, though," the agent insisted. "The child has been paid for."

"Leave the child. I want them all." The agent looked at him, suspiciously. "Is the price of one child worth a billion haglor contract?"

The agent's eyes widened. They lingered on Flint. "Why is the child so important to you?"

"He isn't, but my client will be spending an obscene amount of money. This could be an on-going relationship. He'd like to know he takes priority over other clients. This will be a way to demonstrate that."

The agent studied him.

Flint raised his eyebrows to the agent. "Do you want the contract, or not?"

The agent had a word with his escort who spoke to the guards. The guards stood down, staring at their weapons.

The agent turned back to Flint. "I think my boss will need to meet your client."

Flint nodded. "This can be arranged."

As they walked away, Jenna saw the child reunited with his mother and wanted to kiss Flint.

When the tour ended, the agent took them to a rural waystation. The interior, surprisingly, held no mind-numbing designs, the walls plain and white. Siltians obviously didn't live in these parts. The agent directed them to the lounge as he booked them in. Floor to ceiling windows provided a bright space. The crew looked over water-logged grounds.

As soon as the agent left, Flint called a meeting, explaining the situation.

"So, we need a client?" Johnson asked.

"No. We need to pretend we have a client and get to meet the bosses. By the time they figure out we're bogus, it'll be too late."

"You're... clever, aren't you?" Johnson remarked, looking at Flint, bemused.

Brash was gaining respect for the man. Flint could think on his feet.

"Jenna," Flint said, "could I have a word with you?"

Leading her out of the lounge, he looked around, finding a small empty room. Indicating for her to go in, he followed, closing the door behind him.

"What is this room?" Jenna asked, looking around.

"I don't know. Looks like it hasn't been renovated yet. But I've not brought you here to talk about the room. Today, again, you acted on your own impulses. I gave you no instruction to do what you did."

"What? The weapons? They were going to shoot that woman."

"I know, but you could have put the whole mission in jeopardy. Still might have, if they figure out that had anything to do with us."

"Are you kidding? Should I have let her die? I did the right thing and you know it."

"We're talking about thousands here. Not just one. What is the right thing?"

"So, you were prepared to watch that woman die? How can you be so cold and emotionless?"

Flint glared at her. "D'you think it wouldn't have killed me?"

"I have no idea," she threw out.

"If the mission fails, many will continue to endure a living death, day after day, year after year. Dying is better than that."

"How would you know?"

He didn't answer and she stared at him.

She rubbed her arm. "Well, what are you complaining about?" she tossed out. "It turned out alright."

"We were lucky. But, because of you, the agent is now suspicious. We don't know this is a done deal yet. Never act on your own again."

"I don't take orders from you," she shot. "You were in therapy, remember, whilst the rest of us were out saving the universe."

"Is that what this is about? You lot are a band of brothers, and I don't fit in? Well, you've certainly become like them."

"You don't know them. You think you do but you don't."

"I know you've become a law onto yourself, know you put the whole mission in jeopardy today, know you need to rein yourself in."

"Fuck you!"

"Fuck you? Is that all the Admiral's daughter can say?"

She dove at him, fists flying. He caught her wrists, holding them in a vice-like grip, their eyes blazing into each other. Moments later, their lips crushed together.

Flint?

"Holy fuck..." Jenna mouthed, grabbing fistfuls of her hair. What the hell just happened...? She stared at the soggy ground. *Fuck, fuck, fuck....* Flint? *Oh, this was bad. This was fucking bad.*

"There you are," Brash said, and she turned. "What are you doing out here?"

"Err... Just getting some air."

"Been arguing with Flint again? What did he want?"

"He... err... wanted to tell me off for saving that woman's life."

Brash put an arm around her and she shrivelled inside. "You know, as captain, you have to consider the bigger picture."

"You're saying I should have let her die?"

He breathed out, heavily. "It turned out alright but... it could have gone differently. Sometimes, you have to risk the one to save the many."

"Whose side are you on?"

"Yours. But I'm not going to blindly agree with you." He smiled. "You missed dinner. Let's get you something to eat."

"I'm not hungry."

"Why don't you come to bed then? I can make you feel better."

She smiled, uncomfortably. "I'm going to stay out here for a while. I'll be in soon."

"OK," he said, his gaze lingering on her. "I'll see you soon."

She turned away, staring over the misty landscape. What the hell had just happened? *Flint?*

*

Jenna and Flint didn't look at each other as they ate breakfast.

"So, this is the big day," Brash said. "We get to meet the puppet masters."

"We work fast," Flint told them, "gather information then take them out by any means."

"Gather information on what?" Newark asked.

"On all those involved, every layer."

"Then we liberate the facilities?" Johnson asked.

"Not immediately. The people we free will need homes and money. So, we work with amenable elements of government to sort this out."

"What if there are no amenable elements?" Newark asked.

"Then we sack them and get amenable elements."

"*Then* we liberate the facilities?" Johnson asked.

"Yes."

"And how do we stop them conducting a revolution, murdering the Bortten?" Skinner asked.

"This is going to be a mess," Newark muttered.

"When we liberate each facility, we ask for patience," Flint replied.

"Yeah, that'll do it."

"We explain that elections will be held, a new government formed, and that everyone will have a voice. We make it clear trouble-makers will be dealt with."

"Yep, sure they'll listen to that."

"Once this is accomplished, we hold the elections, and introduce a fair system of democracy."

"That's if we haven't already had the revolution."

Flint turned to Newark. "Perhaps you could be part of the solution here, not the problem."

Newark shrugged. "I'm just being realistic."

"OK, do you have any better suggestions?"

The crew turned to Newark. Newark fell mute then a bright idea popped into his head. "Why not divide up the planet, give each group a land of their own."

Flint's eyes widened. That wasn't a bad idea.

"Could lead to wars," Brash considered. "Might be better to integrate them."

"But the history's not good," Jenna said, thoughtfully.

"Possible wars, or possible revolutions," Newark considered. "Whichever way you look at it, we screw up the planet."

"The planet was already screwed up," Flint said, harshly. "The rich were feeding off the misery of the masses."

"Well," Jenna said, "how about we try integration first. If that doesn't work, we could always split them up."

"Agreed," Flint said, his blue eyes finding hers.

Her heart sped. *Crap.*

"So, we get to be government for a while," Johnson said, importantly. "Wonder what the rich coast's like?"

They flew over a beautiful area... sunshine, clear blue sky, deep green sea... White buildings hugged the coastline. Larger white buildings stood further back, the city dotted with parks and gardens. It looked idyllic. This was where the money was invested.

Jenna drew in a breath. Sun, beaches, and cocktails...

"This is the capital city of Hercillen," the agent told Flint.

They came in to land on a round white concourse, and disembarked to find themselves surrounded by water. A white walkway led over the water to a swish white pad.

"This is where you will be staying," the agent told Flint. "You said your client will be arriving in three days' time?"

Flint nodded.

"We'll have someone collect him and fly him over."

"Will we meet with your boss today?"

"He is hosting a party tonight. You are all invited. Evening attire has been provided for you." He glanced at their unusual clothes. "I will come to collect you later," he said, leading them inside.

The place they entered would have been luxurious, if not for the garish décor.

"Figured out what this mind-melding shit says about them?" Newark asked Skinner.

Skinner looked around, thoughtfully. "No, but it's coming to me."

Newark stared at him.

From the reception hall, a long spacious room branched off to the left. Six-armed furniture dotted the room, together with orange couches that looked like plastic blow-ups. A smaller room lay to the right, and a staircase hid behind the front door. Through an archway ahead, a long kitchen-dinner spanned the length of the building. The kitchen overlooked a lawn and swimming pool. Beyond, Jenna caught a glimpse of a white beach and a green sea.

They stepped out, inspecting the pool, the water coloured yellow.

"I'm not swimming in that," Newark remarked. "Looks like someone's pissed in it."

"It'll be some alien chemical, you know, like chlorine," Jenna said.

"Or some alien piss, you know, like piss."

Jenna smiled at him and ruffled his hair. "You're a big softie, you know that, Newark?"

Flint stared at Jenna, hardly able to take in what she was doing. And the man let her do it? Jenna caught him watching her and he turned away. He rubbed his temple, had been feeling at odds with himself all day. He wanted, desperately, to kiss her again, and he didn't know what to do about it.

"Well, this isn't too shabby," Johnson said, nodding, looking around.

As the agent left, the crew migrated upstairs to check out their rooms. Unfortunately, they were decorated in the same brain-assaulting way. Jenna washed her face, picking one of the three towels hanging on the wall.

"They're inviting us to a party," she said to Brash. "D'you think that's a good thing?"

"I would say so," Brash replied, thoughtfully. "They could potentially make a lot of money from us, so it makes sense to keep us sweet."

"Yeah."

His eyes stayed fixed on her. "Jenna, is there something wrong?"

Putting the towel back, she bit her lip. "Wrong? What d'you mean?"

"You've been quiet today. Are you worried about this?"

She shook her head. "Well, maybe," she lied. She worried about what had happened with Flint. She needed to talk to Flint, knock this thing on the head. *I mean, Flint?* "I'm fine," she said, mixed up.

"Do you want to test out your bed?" he asked, suggestively.

She shook her head, scrambling for an excuse. "You know Flint's going to call a meeting any time soon."

She wandered out onto a balcony, staring over the sea, the dark green an unusual colour. She took a deep breath of the sea breeze. It had an odd flavour, sort of... cinnamon. She turned her head. Flint stood further along, staring at the sea too. His head moved and their eyes locked.

Brash appeared at Jenna's side and the spell broke.

"Can you tell everyone to come down in five minutes," Flint said, heading inside. "I'm holding a meeting."

"You know him so well," Brash whispered in her ear. He stood back and looked at her, regretfully. "I'll go and round them up then."

Jenna watched him go.

"Another fucking meeting," Newark moaned as he and Graham walked down the stairs.

"Suck it up, Newark," Graham said.

The rest of the crew sat in the lounge. Graham and Newark lowered onto one of three orange couches, Newark bouncing up and down a few times. "See-through plastic shit," he remarked.

Flint looked at him, waiting for his full attention. Newark stopped bouncing.

84

"Right," Flint said. "We have three days to gather as much information as possible. We need to identify everyone that is connected to the slave trade. We need to ascertain where the government is located and, if possible, find out how many of them are involved."

"How are we going to find all that out?" Johnson asked. "We don't speak the language."

"Fraza and I will have to get the information. But the rest of you need to keep your eyes open. You can learn a lot by watching interactions, studying body language. We start tonight. We'll need weapons too. Johnson, Newark, Graham, Skinner, that's your department. And remember, nobody takes any action without my command. Is that clear?" He would have looked at Jenna directly but he found himself unable to.

They left the room, Newark crestfallen. "I thought we were going to a party."

"They don't drink," Graham reminded him, "so it won't be much of a party."

"Oh, yeah... Boring fuckers..."

For the rest of the afternoon, they loafed around. Johnson and Jenna braved the pool. They had found swimming costumes in their rooms, but they were far too long, and had three holes down each side, which had cracked them up. In the end, they stripped to their underwear. Newark made lewd comments, which they ignored. Graham and Brash didn't want them parading around in their underwear, but Jenna said most costumes had far less material than this.

Brash sat down, watching Jenna, thoughtfully. She seemed distant, wasn't connecting with him.

Graham sat down, watching Johnson. She had been frosty to him of late, and he wondered if he'd done something. He'd asked the question several times but she'd shook it off.

As Flint watched Jenna, a deep-seated longing arose in him, and he wondered how he could feel this way about someone who infuriated him so much.

Skinner lazily watched Jenna and Johnson, enjoying his appreciation of the female form.

Fraza decided to have a swim. He stripped to his underwear and the crew winced. The Kaledian jumped in the pool, creating a mammoth splash, which made Johnson swallow a mouthful of water.

"How does the piss taste?" Newark called out, laughing.

"Why don't you find out?" Graham said, lurching forward and pushing him in.

The crew laughed as Newark flailed to get out. Hitting the flags, he chased Graham around the pool, then decided it more pressing to shed his piss-drenched clothes.

Jenna glanced over to see Flint smiling. The smile did a lot for him. Their eyes locked, and she averted her gaze.

Still Laughing, Johnson caught Graham's smiling eyes. Her laugh fell away. She couldn't keep up the charade. She had to come clean and tell him the wedding was off. She'd do it after the party. She climbed out, grabbed her clothes, and went to get dressed.

Jenna climbed out, grabbed a towel, and sat beside Brash. She knew she had to talk to Flint. She had to tell him that kiss was a mistake. What the hell was that kiss anyway? *I mean... Flint?*

One Hell Of A Party

"Seriously?" Newark asked, gaping at his reflection. "No way am I wearing this."

Graham couldn't stop laughing at him. "You have to wear it. You might offend them. Besides, your clothes are still wet."

Newark stared at himself again. He wore a golden cropped top, and grey leggings with a short red and gold shirt. "I look like a fucking Egyptian."

"Or a fucking girl," Graham managed.

"I don't know what you're laughing for. You look worse than me."

Graham turned to the mirror, his laughter fading. "Yeah, we look fucking ridiculous."

The crew met up downstairs, all looking ridiculous, apart from Jenna and Johnson, who carried the outfits well. When Fraza came down, the crew gaped at him. Newark burst out laughing. "Oh, my god, Fraza, that's just not right."

The others bit their lips, containing sniggers. Fraza's big belly and orange hair did not go with that outfit *at all*.

"Does it look bad?" the Kaledian asked, looking to Jenna.

She shook her head, vigorously. "No, you look fine. Ignore Newark."

"You look no worse than the rest of us," Flint lied as the agent thankfully arrived.

Jenna poked Newark in the ribs as they walked out. "Stop laughing," she whispered, trying to contain her own laughter

Newark felt so much better. Nobody would be looking at him now.

A short flight took them to the other side of the bay. They landed on another white concourse surrounded by water. Before them stood a luxurious mansion, the grounds of which stretched around them. A short walkway led through the grounds, up to the house. Four Bortten with guns sat on benches, stationed beside the entrance.

"We've found weapons," Johnson said to Newark.

As they approached the house, the agent spoke to the guards, and the crew were allowed in. Entering a spacious, long hallway, they glanced around. The garish walls wrecked the place. A couple of guards with guns sat on chairs, staring at them as they walked by. Passing quiet rooms, the agent led them forward to where the building opened onto a gigantic terrace overlooking the sea. Finely dressed Bortten mingled outside and they did look like Egyptians – only ones dragged back from the dead.

The guests turned to look at them, the aubergine eyes fixing mainly on Fraza, who squirmed under their scrutiny. He rubbed his ears.

"You look fine," Jenna assured him.

Yep, Newark thought, Fraza was a real eye-opener. He looked around. Bright orange sofas surrounded the space. Lanterns sat on a wide wooden railing. Those slaves with the creepy lips stood around with trays of drinks. Together with the Bortten, it gave the place a Halloween vibe.

"Your guests, sir," the agent said, and the crew turned to a man lounging on one of the sofas. The Bortten's aubergine eyes fixed on them as he stood... and did the most unusual thing. He clasped his three pairs of hands together whilst standing on one leg and bending his knee.

Flint glanced at the agent.

"It's a form of greeting," the agent explained, looking at Flint, expectantly.

"Do the same," Flint said.

The crew clasped their hands together, stood on one leg, and bent their knees.

A chorus of laughter erupted. The crew looked around. The boss Bortten smiled broadly, his skin stretching horrifically. "Just my little joke," he said. "Helps break the ice."

Flint translated and the crew stared at the bloke, nonplussed. They forced out a laugh. "The guy's a lunatic," Johnson said.

"Are you the head of operations?" Flint asked him, politely.

"I am. My name is Cliro. And your name is?"

"Flint. My client will be arriving in three days. I hope you can put up with us until then."

"Nonsense. You will be our honoured guests. Now, it's a party." He turned. "Bring our guests drinks!" he called out.

Flint pressed for more information. "Is there anyone else we should meet? Your associates, perhaps?"

"Oh, they're here somewhere..." He looked around. "Hera, Istru, Virta, Pilas, come and meet our guests!"

Four Bortten drew around. They appeared more serious than Cliro, their horrible smiles fake.

Flint's smile hid his distrust of them. "It's an honour to meet you," he said. "We have reviewed your facilities and are impressed. So, the four of you help run the operation?"

They nodded, still eyeballing him.

"No business tonight," Cliro insisted. "The music's starting. It's time to dance!"

Some awful tune blared out and Cliro encouraged everyone to get up. In fact, he did more. He pushed Bortten forward to dance with the crew. As Bortten dancing comprised mainly of hopping and jumping, none of the crew felt enthusiastic. Jenna backed up, crouching down, pretending to fiddle with her shoe. The rest of the crew got knabbed, manhandled by six creepy hands that brought the Halloween vibe to life.

As the mad dash stopped, Jenna breathed out, straightening, her eyes landing on Fraza. He looked over-the-top ridiculous, hopping and jumping with a ghoulish dead-looking Egyptian.

Surviving one ordeal, she was faced with another as Cliro pushed Flint her way. "Dance!" he urged.

Taking hold of each other, they moved together slowly, not even attempting to hop or jump. Jenna glanced at Flint, uncomfortably. "You got spared too," she remarked.

"I copied you."

"Ah. Maybe they take hints." She breathed in, acutely aware of his firm, strong body so close to hers. "He's not what I expected," she said.

"No. The four others don't look friendly. They'll be watching us closely, I imagine."

She looked away, intensely aware of his arms around her. Flint stared at the side of her face. He pulled his gaze away but their bodies drew closer as though charged with a magnetic force. The noise and movement around them existed in a different time frame, each powerfully aware of the other. As their chests touched, Jenna stood back, staring at Flint.

Flint cleared his throat. "I suppose we should get on with the job."

"Yes. We should."

They broke apart to see the rest of the crew trying to extricate themselves from their partners. Graham and Johnson walked over, shell-shocked. Newark followed on their heels. "I need a fucking drink," he said.

A freakish server appeared with a tray. Staring at her mouth, Newark lifted a glass, and took a drink. It tasted like some weird type of tea. Nodding appreciatively, he slugged it back, and within seconds, a buoyant energy filled him.

Jenna scanned the terrace, wondering if there was anyone from government here. She hated the language barrier. It made her feel impotent. Her eyes widened. What was she thinking? She could follow conversations by mind-reading.

She looked around again. Bortten still danced, though most had given up and stood around chatting. Moving to the front of the terrace, pretending to look at the sea, she relaxed and emptied her mind. Soon, she listened to thoughts and conversations. One conversation made her glance around. Two Bortten talked intently.

"So, is the government on board with this?"

"Yes, you'll get your import licence and, as long as the tax returns prove lucrative, and the fees continue to be paid, you'll get to keep it. What did you say the planet was called?"

"Tymos. The creatures should fetch a good price. We're building a new compound already. I think they'll be a high demand for them in the region."

Jenna realised the Bortten on the left was one of the associates. It was so hard to tell them apart. The guy was obviously expanding their empire. She needed to communicate with that governor, somehow. She had to give thought transference a shot.

As the associate moved away, she sat beside the governor, smiling at him, pleasantly. He studied her with inquiring purple eyes.

"You have a beautiful city here," she impressed on him, trying to make her mouth move like a Bortten.

The man stared at her soundless, contorting lips, wondering if the human was deficient in some way. "Are you having... difficulty?" he asked, staring at her, oddly.

Damn, it wasn't working. She had transferred a thought to Newark once. How had she done that? Perhaps nerves or lack of confidence blocked her. She made herself relax, asking herself what was the worst that could happen? He might think her deranged. She could live with that.

The Bortten now viewed her curiously.

"I said, you have a beautiful city here."

"Oh."

Bingo. *"You will have to forgive me. I am struggling with the language."*

"I see," he replied, his narrowed gaze focused on her lips.

"You have some grand buildings. What are they?"

"Libraries, businesses, government."

"Oh? I would like to do some sight-seeing whilst I am here. Perhaps you could point the government building out to me?"

He assessed her for a moment. "I can do that."

He led her to the other side of the terrace, where they had a spectacular view of the city. "You see the building with the glass pyramid at the top?"

"Yes."

"That is the government building. That's where all important decisions are made." He turned to her. "So, I believe you are here to make a lucrative deal with Cliro?"

The man was kept informed. *"Yes, our client arrives soon."*

The Bortten smiled, grotesquely. "Then I'm sure we'll meet again, perhaps even become... better acquainted."

She smiled at him, pleasantly. *In your dreams, creep!*

He stared at her, confused, and she wondered if he'd heard that. *Shit.* He stared at her again so she smiled sweetly, and wandered away. Now she'd switched it on, she had to practice switching it off.

Brash intercepted her. "I've been looking for you."

"Why?"

"Just wondered where you were."

"I'm fine," she said, a little off-hand.

He looked at her for a moment. "Have I done something, Jenna?"

She pulled herself together. What the hell was wrong with her? "Of course, not. I'm just edgy."

"Flint's doing a lot of talking," he said, "but Fraza looks intimidated. I don't think he's getting very much."

"Everyone keeps staring at his belly. It must seem huge to these skinny rakes."

"This tea's not half bad," Newark said, breezing up behind them. "It makes you feel... good."

"Shouldn't you be casing the joint for weapons?" Brash asked.

"Just waiting for an opportunity. Those guards are still in the hall."

Brash looked around to see Johnson, Graham, and Skinner quaffing tea.

He turned back to Jenna. "I've noticed a few intent conversations going on but it's hard to tell who's who."

"I know," Newark said, "they all look the bloody same. You can only recognise them by their costumes."

"We'll have to look closer," Jenna said. "Cliro has got a tiny scar on his chin. We're going to have to pay attention to details."

Cliro came over with two drinks, handing them to Jenna and Brash. He looked around for Flint. "Your friends are not enjoying themselves, Flint! They're offending their hosts!"

Jenna and Brash plastered smiles on their faces, Jenna gently probing Cliro's mind, looking for any malicious intent behind the friendly exterior. She couldn't find any. This man really did love parties.

"Drink!" Cliro insisted, making a drinking gesture with his hand.

They threw the stuff back. He took their empty glasses, depositing them on a tray. Lifting two more, he handed the drinks to them.

Cliro ordered a Bortten to crank the volume up, and suggested to Flint his team showed them how *humans* dance. Flint asked his crew to dance – it wasn't something he could order - and, maybe it was the tea, but four of them did dance. Johnson, though not a dancer, pulled off some bitchin' moves. It felt so liberating to dance tonight. Newark, Graham, and Skinner joined in, their arms and legs going everywhere. The rest of the crew stared at them. When the music stopped, the crowd cheered wildly. Even the four serious-looking associates stretched their faces and clapped their six hands.

"It's weird," Johnson said to Skinner. "I'm not drunk but I feel like I should be."

Skinner nodded. "I want to dance again."

Some of the Bortten tried to mimic the human moves, and after more tea and dancing, Cliro led the whole group around the mansion in the Bortten equivalent of a conga, sticking six arms out here, six there.

"I need more arms," Johnson called out.

"This is insane," Newark cried, happily.

This, of course, would have been a perfect opportunity for them to slip away and search the place for weapons, but weapons were the last thing on their minds.

Fraza, Jenna, and Brash joined the line too. Jenna was vaguely aware of the conversation she'd heard before, but it had sort of slipped into the background. She was lost in the moment, felt like a child again.

Flint remained outside, chatting with the associates, who had now decided the humans weren't all that bad.

They partied into the night and at the end of the evening, they were sent off with enthusiastic hugs, not caring that they had achieved virtually nothing.

Wow, that was one hell of a party!

By Any Means Possible

When they got back to their accommodation, the effects of the tea wore thin.

"What a party," Johnson said.

"They were fun," Newark remarked. "They're not half bad."

"Not half bad?" Flint asked. "They are slave owners and traffickers."

"Yeah, but you know what I mean."

"No, I don't."

Newark shrugged.

"We need to talk," Flint said, walking off into the lounge.

"Does he mean me, or all of us?"

The crew weren't sure.

Flint, who had drunk relatively little tea, sat and waited for them. When they had seated, he spoke. "We didn't acquire any weapons," he said, "but at least you all had a good time."

"I think it was the tea," Jenna mentioned.

"Yes, I imagine it contains some kind of uplifting drug."

"I wonder where you get hold of that stuff," Newark thought aloud.

"Are you mad at us?" Jenna asked, defensively.

"No," Flint replied. "As it happens, it served us well. The Bortten seem to have warmed to us. I got on friendly terms with the associates, and gleaned a lot of useful information."

Jenna wanted to tell him what she had found out but she couldn't. That would blow the lid on her mind-reading ability. So, in effect, what she'd found out was redundant.

"What did you discover?" Brash asked Flint.

"Cliro is in overall control, the four associates beneath him, but there is another layer of ten beneath them, a few of them there tonight. They are the ones that deal directly with the sites. There are also the agents, twenty in all. Then, of course, there are the compound guards, and new slave collectors. The government is working with them. The government here is not elected. The head governor has had the position handed down by hereditary, rather like a monarchy, and he chooses members of the government."

"So, it's basically a dictatorship in the pocket of the slave traders."

"That's right."

"You found out all that...?" Johnson asked, impressed. "How did you manage it?"

The crew looked at Flint, curiously.

Flint hesitated. The four associates were Cliro's sons. Family dynamics were a complex issue. He'd intuited how to respond to each one, whilst delicately teasing the strings of sibling rivalry. It landed boasts, snipes, and results. Most of all, he had managed to gain their trust, though he had to admit, the crew's dancing helped.

The crew's eyes remained fixed on him. Taking a leaf out of Newark's book, he shrugged.

"So, the whole government have to go down," Brash said.

"Yes, but we need to get the fifteen top slave traders together and take them out first. Then we tackle the government."

"How are we going to get the fifteen together?"

"By any means possible. Perhaps we could invite them to a party here."

"We'll need to get some tea," Newark suggested.

"It's not going to be much of a party, Newark, seeing as we're going to slaughter them."

The crew bowed their sombre heads. It was hard killing people they'd partied and danced with.

"So, what's on the cards for tomorrow?" Brash asked.

"We find out where the government is located."

Jenna opened her mouth then closed it again.

As they dispersed, Johnson asked Graham to come outside. She was going to have the talk.

Jenna looked at Flint. She needed to have a talk too but Flint seemed to have a lot on his mind. She decided to leave it. Walking to the door, she glanced back at him. He watched her, a sad expression clouding his face. The sadness transferred to her as she walked out with Brash. She told Lucas she was tired. Leaving him at the bottom of the stairs, she climbed up to her room, and lay awake most of the night.

*

Graham sat at the central counter in the long, sun-drenched kitchen, staring hopelessly at the gaudy surface.

"You OK?" Jenna asked him.

"Daria's finished it. It's over."

She came to sit opposite him. "Why...?"

"Her feelings have changed. Whatever we had has run its course but she hopes we can still be mates."

94

"Oh... I'm sorry..." Jenna rubbed her forehead. "Maybe... Maybe she'll change her mind. Maybe she's not ready to get married yet."

"Or maybe her feelings have just changed." He took a big collecting sniff. "Well, if that's the case, mine will have to change too, I suppose." He got up and walked away.

Jenna chewed her lip. Johnson was making a big mistake.

"Has he gone?" Johnson asked, poking her head around the outer door. She ventured inside, joining Jenna at the counter.

"What are you doing, breaking up with him?" Jenna asked.

"Look, if I don't break up with him, I'll end up murdering him. I can't keep it together anymore. I'm like fuse about to blow. He's irritating the fuck out of me."

"Well, he didn't irritate you before he proposed." Jenna sat, straight. She was going to say it. "Listen, perhaps you need therapy."

Johnson stared at her. "What...? Are you serious...?"

"Yes. I think your mother's had a huge effect on you, and I think she's screwing things up for you now."

Johnson laughed. "God, Trot, I think *you* need therapy. Where d'you learn that psycho-babble?"

"At least think about it. You might find it makes sense. And, if you do need to work things through, perhaps you could talk to Flint. He must be an expert by now."

Johnson stared at her, incredulous. "You want me to talk to Flint about my mother? Are you fucking nuts?"

"I think there are things you need to look at. Anyway, it's up to you, but if you leave it too long, you could lose Graham for good."

"Graham and me are over. End of." She left the counter and walked back outside.

"There you are," Brash said, wandering in.

Jenna turned to him. "Johnson's broken up with Graham."

He frowned. "I thought they were getting married?"

"Apparently not."

Johnson's raised voice travelled through the open door. A moment later, Fraza came in. "She bumped into *me*," he insisted, looking at a loss as he walked across the room and disappeared.

Brash moved to the window, his eyes following Johnson as she strode down the path toward the beach. "So, what happened?"

"I think the marriage proposal has stoked things up. It's... complicated."

"They'll work it out," he said, coming over and wrapping his arms around her shoulders. "Some people are meant for each other. I nearly came into your room last night," he said, nuzzling her neck.

95

"You would have found me asleep."

"I might have woken you up."

"Very considerate."

"I'm sure you'd have thanked me later."

Jenna disentangled herself and moved to the window, spotting Flint walking up from the beach. She turned to Brash. "Do you want something to eat?"

"Yeah, if you're offering," he replied, his gaze lingering on her.

She grabbed a packet of kupto, which, the crew decided, was the equivalent of bread, though it tasted like onions. Perhaps that wasn't a bad thing as there was no butter here. Once you became accustomed to the gritty texture, it wasn't too bad. Opening the three-handled fridge, she pulled out the ufal, which looked and tasted like cheese. Slicing it, she threw it on the bread, and handed a plate to Brash.

Picking up a second plate, she smiled at Flint as he came through the door. The smile took him by surprise. When she handed him the plate, he stared at it, his eyes lifting to her. "Err... thanks."

He took a bite, his eyes remaining on her. "What's wrong with Johnson?" he asked. "She just bit my head off."

"She's broken up with Graham," Jenna told him.

"I thought they were getting married."

"Whatever it is, they'll work it out," Brash said. "Some people belong together." He gazed at Jenna, adoringly.

Jenna smiled, awkwardly. Flint wandered out.

*

They walked through pedestrianised, leafy streets, Bortten staring at them as they passed by. A couple stretched their faces and mimicked fancy dance moves. Newark cottoned on and mimicked back.

"We're celebs," he said, smiling as he watched them go.

"Don't get too attached, Newark," Flint said.

Graham trailed behind the group, his sullen eyes fixed on Johnson.

Jenna turned to him. "Perhaps you should have stayed behind today."

"Why? Why should *I* hide away?"

"No, I didn't..."

Brash touched her arm. "Leave him for now."

Turning away from Graham, Jenna's attention settled on Flint. He walked up ahead with a confident stride. Her eyes travelled the length of him… from his boots, over his lean firm body, to his bare muscular arms. His t-shirt and jeans hugged him in a mesmerising way, his loose, now shoulder-length, blonde hair striking in the daylight. She imagined running her hands through it. Pulling herself up short, she looked away, fixing her attention on Brash. She took in his handsome face, his exquisite form. He noticed and smiled at her. She smiled back.

Passing an enormous square on the left, Jenna stopped. "Look, I bet *that's* the government building," she said, pointing.

Flint turned to her, looking into the square. "Why d'you say that?"

"Because it's got that glass pyramid on the top. That's bound to be it."

"OK, let's check it out."

They moved down the length of the square, looking at the grand white building ahead. It stretched to either side, covering the entire width of the concourse. The white buildings around them, though impressive, couldn't match its grandeur. Bortten stared at them as they walked by, but they were getting used to it now. Newark kept his eyes open for tea shops.

They drew up to the building to find the imposing outer doors wide open, inner glass doors closed. Flint read the words over the entrance.

He turned to Jenna. "You're right."

"D'you think they'll let us in?" Brash asked.

"Only one way to find out."

As they ventured up the steps, two armed guards came out.

"Twelve more weapons," Johnson remarked to Newark.

"What is your business here?" one of the guards asked, peering at the strange creatures, oddly.

"We want to look around," Flint told them. "Would that be possible?"

"Look around?" the guard asked as if the idea was preposterous. "Move," he said harshly, pointing his guns at them.

"I don't think we need treat our visitors like that," a voice said behind, and the crew turned. The Bortten's eyes fixed on Jenna. As he seemed to recognise her, she assumed it was the guy who'd pointed this building out. What a stroke of luck. She smiled, broadly.

"Do you want a tour of the building?" he asked, congenially.

"That would be very good of you," Flint said.

The guard stepped aside, and the crew walked in, staring up at a high-vaulted ceiling. A balcony ran around the space.

"So, did you enjoy the party?" the Bortten asked Jenna.

Jenna had a problem. She couldn't communicate with the guy without giving the game away, but she couldn't not communicate with him, either.

She nodded, imperceptibly, as Flint provided the answer. "We had a great time, thank you."

"Excellent."

The governor proceeded to show them around. They walked up a grand stairway to the balcony. From there, corridors branched off in three directions.

"We have twelve governors," he informed them, "each responsible for a certain department. Down there is finance, justice, home defence..."

As he spoke, Flint translated to the others.

"And which department are you responsible for?" Flint asked.

"I am in overall control," he replied, rather importantly. "My name is Governor Saraquis." He glanced at Jenna. She smiled, uncomfortably.

Flint committed him to memory.

As Saraquis showed them around, he kept turning to Jenna with the odd comment. All she could do was smile.

The tour entered a meeting chamber. The spacious room dwarfed a round table at the centre.

"Camelot," Skinner remarked.

"They're hardly knights of the round table," Johnson said.

"How often do you come together for meetings?" Flint asked the governor.

"I hold a meeting each day. Do it first thing. I like to keep a tight grip on everything," he said, looking at Jenna in a disconcerting way.

Flint nodded, thoughtfully, glancing at Jenna too.

The crew wandered around, examining garish pictures hanging on the walls. The governor lingered near Jenna. "I'm afraid you made rather an impression on me last night," he whispered.

Her eyes widened in a question mark as if to say, Oh?

"Yes, there's something about you I can't quite put my finger on. Damned attractive."

Jenna walked around so her back was to the crew, impressing thoughts on him as she moved her mouth. *I'd hardly think a human was your type?*

His face stretched. "Well, I've always been adventurous. And I'm sure, with your new business arrangements here, we'll become... good friends." The suggestive look made her want to throw up. What she saw in his mind was depraved. "Will you visit often?"

"Yes, I'll be spending a lot of time here." Smiling at him, she wandered off, pretending to examine pictures, her lips screwed up in distaste. She glanced to the side to see Flint looking at her, oddly.

As they continued on, she tried to keep away from the governor but he kept looking at her. She was relieved when the tour finally ended.

"Well, that's the top dog then," Johnson said, outside.

"And he's given us everything we need," Brash added.

"Seemed like a nice guy," Newark remarked.

Flint shook his head. Jenna wanted to tell Newark that nice guy was involved in the import of new slaves... but she couldn't.

"There was no culture department," Skinner remarked.

"So?" Newark asked.

Skinner shrugged. "Says a lot about them."

"Like what?"

"I'm not sure."

Newark stared at him.

"Can we continue to look around?" Fraza asked.

Flint nodded, glancing at Jenna as they wandered out of the square.

They passed white buildings and parks, the buildings becoming less grand as they ventured out of the centre. In these parts, they found Siltians and a bright garish door. The crew didn't even go there. It wasn't worth it.

When they returned to their accommodation, Flint asked Jenna if he could have a word. He took her outside but as the crew came out too, he led her down to the beach.

"What's she done now?" Newark asked, watching them go.

Jenna experienced a riot of feelings as they walked to the shore, most of which she shouldn't have been feeling.

The cinnamon sea breeze brushed over them. They walked out over blinding white sand, Flint quiet and pensive.

He stopped and turned to her, his blonde hair framing a face that got more stunning by the day. She glanced down, kicking at the sand.

"Jenna, what was going on back there?"

She looked up at him.

"The governor seemed to know you. You seemed to be... communicating somehow."

"How could I be communicating? I don't speak the language."

"You stood to face him for a good few moments. He was speaking to you. Are you going to tell me you were just smiling at him? And, if so, why?"

His blue eyes fixed her, intently. It was impossible to think, impossible to breathe. Why the hell was he affecting her so much? It stoked her anger. "I don't know what you're talking about," she threw out.

"Yes, you do. I'm not stupid. Something was going on and we're not leaving until you tell me what."

"Then we're going to get pretty wet when the tide comes in."

"Should I ask the others if they know what's going on?"

"No," she blurted.

99

He raised his eyebrows in a question.

Glaring at him, she let out a breath. "OK. I *was* communicating with him. Happy now? But you can't tell the others. Only Fraza knows."

"Only Fraza knows what?"

"I can read minds and... now I can transfer thoughts."

His eyes widened. "What...?"

"I learned to do it whilst we were away. But the others don't know and you can't tell them."

"Did... Did Cornelius show you how to do this...?"

"He pointed the way."

Flint shook his head. "I'm beginning to wonder if there's anything you *can't* do."

I can't stop thinking about you!

"So... you communicated with the governor at the party?" he asked.

"Yes, I overheard him talking to one of the associates. They're expanding their empire."

"You should have told me."

"I don't want the crew to know I can mind read."

"Why?"

"Because they'll never trust me if they think I can read their thoughts."

He fell silent, staring at her, guardedly.

"I don't read your thoughts," she said, quickly. "Or any of the crew's. I wouldn't do that. I only use it when necessary."

He scratched his neck, glancing at the sea.

"Don't you believe me?" she asked, her voice pleading. "I really don't want to know what you're all thinking."

Chewing his lip, he took in her troubled state. "OK, but you need to be honest with me from now on."

She looked at him, defiantly. This was it. She was going to knock this on the head by any means possible. "You want honesty? OK. I'm attracted to you but that kiss can never happen again. It was a mistake. D'you understand? No way can I ever be with you."

"Why not?"

"Because I'm with Lucas. And because you're... well, you're Flint, aren't you?"

He stared at her, the words a physical blow. His expression hardened and he walked away.

She stared after him, biting her lip. By any means possible didn't feel so good.

Tea

The agent called in to see them the next day, which gave Flint the opportunity he needed. "We would like to host a gathering here for all those we will be going into business with. We enjoyed the party the other night and would like to repay the favour. We thought it might help cement our business relationship if we could meet with all the fifteen."

"It isn't necessary," the agent said.

"We thought it would be a nice gesture."

"It isn't necessary because Cliro has invited you up there today. He thought you could meet everyone over tea. In truth, I think they enjoyed your company. He thinks humans are a… 'most curious and entertaining species'."

"Oh. Right, well, that would be great."

The agent handed him a bag of money. "Cliro wants you to have this. It occurs to him you might not have much currency yet. He thinks this should tide you over for a couple of days. I'll return in an hour to take you up there."

As the agent left, the crew stared at the bag.

"That's really nice of him," Johnson said.

"It's money earned off the back of misery," Flint reminded her.

"We're going to get more tea," Newark said, excitedly.

"We're not drinking tea," Flint stated. "We go in there, all guns blazing. This is it. Time to take them down."

Newark wasn't sure he had the heart for this. They were going to go in and butcher them when they'd been nothing but nice to them. Johnson wasn't stoked about it, either. Graham didn't have the heart for anything. He'd been quiet and sullen since yesterday morning. Jenna stole a glance at Flint, wondering if he'd ever forgive her for what she'd said. He'd not looked at her or communicated with her since yesterday. Brash wondered why Jenna was in a foul mood today. Skinner wondered if they could get one glass of tea before the slaughter began. Fraza hoped they didn't have to put those costumes on again.

*

"This is it," Flint said as they walked up to the house. "You know what to do."

Jenna focused as she approached the guards. The crew hung back and the agent turned to look at them as Jenna performed a total body shot. The agent and the guards catapulted through the air in a soundless explosion. As they crashed into the wall, slammed on the ground, the crew steamed in for the kill.

Loaded with weapons, they entered the house. Cliro and his men waited on the terrace, jugs of tea sitting on a table in front of them. They turned as one, their eyes widening at the glut of weapons trained on them. A few pulled weapons of their own, and got mowed down immediately. The rest stared at the crew in mute horror.

Cliro stood. "What is this...?" he asked, amazed, his six arms outstretched. "Have we not treated you like brothers?"

The genuinely hurt look made Newark glance away.

"Today is your day of reckoning," Flint told him. "Today, you account for the lives you have wrecked."

"What lives...?"

"Seriously? The lives of your slaves."

"Them? They're just slaves. What are they to you?"

"More than you could possibly know," Flint said in a hard voice. "Now, look into my eyes as you die."

That was so totally not necessary, Johnson thought.

"Finish it!" Flint ordered the crew.

The crew hesitated. It was hard to shoot unarmed men, especially men who had treated them so well. Flint and Brash fired, the others watching as the bodies took round after round, falling bloodied and lifeless on the deck.

"This sucks," Newark spat.

"That didn't feel right," Jenna mumbled.

Brash turned to her. "Just remember that child being separated from his mother, or that Velyor being shot down because he couldn't handle the abuse anymore. And the countless others we don't even know about. They needed to be eradicated, Jenna."

"I know..."

"The devil sometimes smiles," Flint said, looking down at the dead Bortten. "But he's still the devil." He looked up. "Get rid of the bodies."

"How?" Johnson asked.

"Use your imagination."

The crew's imagination extended to dragging the bodies into an outhouse and shutting the door on them. It took a long time to move them all, Newark, Johnson, and Skinner helping themselves to tea at intermittent intervals, and when Flint was out of sight. Graham worked mechanically, not communicating with anyone, glaring at Johnson when her back was turned. Jenna could have helped by levitating a few bodies but her mind was elsewhere. As Flint and Brash riffled through Cliro's paperwork, Jenna watched them, realising why they were captains. They kept their eyes on the bigger picture at all times. Maybe Flint really *was* captain material. Who knew? He didn't look at her once, even when she asked if she should mop the deck. She knew she'd hurt him in the worst possible way but she had to. She was with Brash. Whatever this was, it had to stop. The thing was, it wasn't stopping. She had lain awake all night, remembering that kiss, and feeling incredibly guilty for doing so.

When the job was done, they hopped on the craft, and Brash flew them back across town. Landing on the circular white patch, they walked over water, Newark, Skinner, and Johnson, feeling buoyant and uplifted, their previous qualms forgotten. Life felt good. Yeah, they had butchered defenceless Bortten but they were slave traffickers who got what was coming to them. And in the morning, they were going to do it all again.

Indeed, in the morning, they were less reticent. They had gained momentum and wanted the job done. The crew walked up to the government building and, as the guards appeared, Jenna and Fraza wrenched weapons from their spindly arms. Snatching the weapons up, the crew fired. Moving upstairs, they blasted the morning meeting to smithereens. Jenna took Saraquis down herself. What he wanted to do to her was filthy and obscene.

"Well, that's one corrupt regime that's seen better days," Skinner remarked humorously but no-one laughed.

"So, what now?" Jenna asked.

"Now, we advertise for replacements," Flint said. "Let's get the staff to help us."

After locking the outer doors, Flint found the intercom system at the reception desk, and called the staff to the lobby. On arriving, the Bortten flew into panicked hysteria. Newark watched, absorbed, as skinny arms flapped all over the place, the ghoulish bodies desperately trying to find an escape route. All routes were blocked. Flint let them ride it out. When they finally calmed, he told them that a new government would be formed, slavery would be abolished, and he required their help to put everything in place.

"Is this a coup?" one brave soul asked.

Flint considered this. "Yes."

"And what about the army?"

The crew stared at the Bortten, their eyes transferring to Flint.

"The army are behind us," Flint lied, maintaining the appearance of calm. "In fact, get me the commander's number. I need a quick word with him."

"They've got an army?" Johnson asked. Bortten heads whipped to her, the words alien.

"Of course, they've got an army," Newark complained. "Everyone's got an army!"

"Not everyone," Fraza qualified.

"We haven't thought this through," Jenna said. "Overthrowing governments is not our thing."

"Stop panicking," Flint told them. "We'll deal with the army. Skinner, Graham, Johnson, Newark, escort the Bortten back to their offices, and keep an eye on them. Fraza, get me that number."

"We might have another fight on our hands," Brash said, thoughtfully.

It was a delicate conversation with the army commander, although Flint didn't get to say much. The commander flew into a rage, threatening to kebab their bodies on heated skewers. Flint managed to calm him down after mentioning a hefty pay raise.

Flint, Jenna, Brash, and Fraza waited in the lobby. The Bortten commander arrived in person with a weapon-loaded entourage. Jenna's eyes raked over their black skirts, black leggings, and cropped black tunics. A black armband marked the commander out.

The commander looked over the four aliens as he walked in. Whatever they were, they were God-damned ugly. He could have levelled the building, of course, but they hadn't had a pay raise in years and, truth be told, there was a lot of resentment in the ranks.

The crew led them up to the meeting chamber, which had been cleared and cleaned.

"We have one hundred laser-guided weapons trained on this building," the commander lied. They had ten. Budgets had been tight. "So, you'd better explain yourself and quick."

"The old government was corrupt," Flint stated. "We are here to change things."

"Why? Who *are* you?"

"You could call us... guardians."

"Guardians?"

Flint drew in a breath. "We have supernatural powers, so your weapons would be useless." The commander almost laughed. He'd heard it all now. "Jenna, Fraza, please demonstrate."

Jenna and Fraza levitated, hovering in the air. Chairs scraped against the floor as the commander and his men stumbled back, staring at them in mute horror.

"We are here to clean up," Flint told them. "You can either work with us or die."

The commander gawked at the hovering aliens. Was this some kind of trickery...?

"So, what do you say?" Flint asked.

"C... Clean up?" the commander uttered, still staring at Jenna and Fraza.

"We intend to abolish slavery, and introduce a democratic system of government."

The commander's head slowly moved to Flint. "Abolish slavery? Slavery is the backbone of our economy. If the tax intake goes down, how can you give my men a raise?"

"Tea," Flint said, simply.

"Tea?"

"You have a unique blend here. This is something the galaxy has been waiting for. Trust me. I believe you can make far more revenue exporting tea than slaves."

"But... if you free the slaves, you create a boiling pot."

"Not if it's done right. And I'm sure the army can help there. We intend to find gainful employment for the slaves and, as tea production goes up, many could be employed in this area. Things cannot continue as they are, Commander. If you don't work with us... well..." He lowered his head.

"Are you some kind of... gods?"

Flint hesitated. Reluctantly, he nodded.

"But we don't believe in gods..."

The commander grabbed a weapon off one of his men and fired at Flint. Jenna deflected the fire, and the commander stared at Flint in wonder. What Flint didn't know, what nobody knew for years, was that Flint had managed to create religion on Draztis. It was an unfortunate side-effect and one that led to much bloodshed in the future.

"I trust that will not happen again," Flint said. "You don't want to make me angry."

The commander dropped his weapon and held up his hands. "So, tea?" he said with a smile.

Complications

Weeks passed. The army was on board. Everything was being put in place. Jenna and the crew gained a new respect for Flint. The man was restructuring a planet from scratch and they never would have believed him capable of it. The tea growers received a considerable injection of cash. The compounds were finally liberated, the former slaves shipped into suitable accommodation or interim camps. Brash, Jenna, and Johnson went with the army to oversee this. The Velyors exited the compounds in a daze, hardly able to process what was happening. The compound guards were given the option of joining the army or jail, except the instructor with the whip. Flint wanted him jailed indefinitely.

The sex slaves comprised various species but as they were comparatively few in number, they were taken to Hercillen. Flint had given Graham the responsibility for transporting and looking after them. As slaves exited a grey stone building, Newark and Graham stared at a stunning, lilac-skinned race, the women wary of their liberators.

"I don't think they trust us," Graham said. "Fraza, tell them again they're free."

"You are going to live as free citizens," Fraza impressed on them. "You are no longer slaves."

One of the lilac-skinned beauties touched Graham's arm. "Rap go," she said.

"She's saying thank you," Fraza told him.

Graham watched that particular woman as she climbed into the transport.

As the slaves got relocated, Flint began the process of finding representative candidates for democratic elections. Though some demonstrations were held by disgruntled Borttens, the army, who now had a healthy pay rise under their belt, kept the peace.

To fund all this, the slave traffickers' assets and monies had been confiscated. Brash and Flint kept a tight check on the budgets. Financial disaster could bring all this crashing down but for the moment, everything was sweet.

The crew had been kept so busy, personal concerns had slipped to the background. Jenna had plenty of chances to avoid Brash, though it concerned her that she wanted to. Flint still occupied her thoughts but she steadfastly pushed him from her mind, hoping once the feelings for Flint subsided, her relationship with Brash could get back on track. Indeed, she hadn't seen much of Flint and, on the occasions when their paths had crossed, he showed no inclination to talk to her. This grated on her.

Graham talked to Johnson again, even laughing with her at times. Things became as they'd been before they were a couple.

"Graham seems better," Jenna remarked to Johnson as they sat out by the pool.

"Yep."

"Do you regret your decision?"

"No, why should I?"

"Because your eyes are always following him."

"No, they're not. You're seeing things, Trot."

Jenna would have said more, but the woman's fists flexed, and she didn't want to get punched.

Brash, Newark, and Skinner walked out to join them.

"Free samples," Newark said, happily, quaffing a glass of tea. Skinner put a jug and glasses on the table. "There's a whole sack of the stuff in there."

Brash sat beside Jenna. She reached over, poured herself a glass, and took a deep drink. Almost at once, she felt strangely uplifted. This stuff was going to catch on faster than a virus.

"Graham's up to his eyes in it," Newark remarked.

"What d'you mean?" Jenna asked.

"He's trying to rearrange the accommodation for the women. Apparently, you can't put Kelpirs and Landir together. They bicker like mad."

"You didn't hang around to help him out?"

"Hey," Newark said, holding up his hands, "this is his job. Now, if he was helping those Saffria today, I might have stayed behind."

"Saffria?" Johnson asked.

"They're stunning," Newark said with a faraway look. "A sight for sore eyes in these parts, I can tell you."

"We've just liberated them from the sex trade," Johnson snapped. "They don't need you drooling over them."

"I can look," Newark protested.

"Bloody men," Johnson said, shooting up and marching off.

"What's got into her? She could use some fucking tea."

Jenna watched her go.

"So," Brash said, turning to Jenna, "we seem to have some time together."

She nodded, rubbing her arm. "Want to walk along the beach?"

"I had something else in mind," he whispered, suggestively.

"Get a room," Newark remarked.

"I've got one and I intend to use it."

Jenna threw her drink back and refilled her glass. Skinner studied her, thoughtfully.

Fraza came over. "Flint wants us at the government building straight away. We have a problem."

*

The crew assembled in the meeting chamber. Flint waited until they had seated.

"We've got a problem," he told them. "Some of the Velyors have been attacking Bortten."

"They're still in the camps, though, aren't they?" Jenna asked.

"Yes, but Velyors in one camp have attacked Bortten in nearby villages. It seems they've had chance to talk about what has happened to them, and a certain amount of anger has caught fire. If we're not careful, this could spill over into a revolution."

"Told you," Newark said, cleverly.

"The commander wants to steam in there and annihilate them, but I've persuaded him to hang fire for now."

"So, what do you suggest we do?" Brash asked.

Flint looked at Jenna and Fraza. "We need a lesson of biblical proportions."

Jenna smiled. "I have just the thing."

"Can I come?" Newark asked. "This sounds like fun."

*

Jenna scanned the area before they entered the camp. Situated beside a lake, so the residents would have access to water, the prefab huts were an interim measure. Flint hadn't decided what to do with the Velyors yet. They were intimidating to look at, and integrating them needed thoughtful consideration.

"Come on," Jenna said, walking forward.

Fraza, Newark, Brash, and Johnson followed after her. The commander remained out of the picture, though Brash, Newark, and Johnson carried guns.

The camp teamed with Velyors of all sizes. Cute hulky children played in the grassy streets. Velyor eyes followed them as they walked to the centre to where a platform had been erected. Jenna had pre-ordered it. She looked forward to this. It was like putting on a show.

As they stepped onto the stage, Jenna turned to Fraza. "Tell them to gather everyone."

Fraza cleared his throat and shouted out alien words.

Jenna rubbed her hands together. "Let's start with a storm."

She and Fraza focused, emptying themselves. There was only the power and intent.... no from or to... It had taken Jenna a while to grasp this. At first, she had focused on drawing the power up through her, like drawing on a well. Tynia, an old withered being on Cyntros, had taught her to use the immensity of the whole universe. In terms of the power, there was no space and time, no from and to, just the power and intent. This was now effortless to her. Fraza sometimes struggled when his mind got in the way, but he always found it easier with Jenna beside him.

The storm was their intent, and that storm now manifested in reality. The rest of the crew looked up as black clouds rolled in, a fierce wind whipping around them. Rain pounded the earth. Lightning ripped through an angry sky, thunder howling after it.

The crew's stunned gaze transferred to Jenna and Fraza.

The residents couldn't understand where the storm had come from. They stared up, confused, as they ran to the centre. Once they had collected, the storm fell away. The Velyors craned their short necks back to the sky.

Jenna ran her eyes over the assembled throng. "Fraza, translate," she said. Viewing the crowd seriously, she addressed them. "We command the elements, as you have just witnessed." She paused for this to go in, satisfied to see eyes widen and jaws drop. "You Velyors have suffered gravely, and we have travelled from a distant place to free you." An appreciative cheer might have gone up if the crowd weren't staring at her, stunned. "You have the right to live free, and live in peace. We, being omnipresent beings-"

"Jenna, I don't know the word for that," Fraza interrupted.

"Oh. OK, I'll amend." She cleared her throat. "We, being gods, understand how angry you must feel. The injustice you have suffered is unthinkable but please be assured, those responsible for your suffering have been brought to justice."

"Death to all Bortten!" a disparate voice cried out.

Jenna held up a hand. "There will be no more bloodshed, no more violence. If any side instigates violence, they will be met by the wrath of the gods. Please, let me demonstrate."

Jenna closed her eyes. Moments later, a wall of water rose up, curving over the camp and the heads of the Velyors, who cowered in terror.

"Fucking hell," Johnson choked out.

"I've seen her playing with water before," Newark said, proudly. "Pretty cool, huh?"

Brash stared at Jenna. He knew what she was capable of but he hadn't witnessed this before.

The water receded. Jenna looked at the crowd. "Any violence will be met with flood."

Jenna focused again and produced a fireball that hovered above her hands. "And fire." The fireball vanished. "And so much more, you can't possibly imagine. We say to you, live free and live in peace, and on no account, incite the wrath of the gods. This message will only be given to you once."

The crowd stared at her in awe. They dropped to their knees, bowing their heads in reverent submission.

"Job done," Newark said.

Brash's stunned gaze turned to a smile. "You really enjoyed that, didn't you?"

"Yep," she said, beaming.

As they walked away, the Bortten cleared a path for them, their heads still bowed, their whole view of life irrevocably changed.

"D'you know what we should do?" Newark said. "We should travel all the camps. Get the message to the rest of these fuckers. It's fun seeing the looks on their gawky faces."

When they returned to Hercillen, Flint agreed this was a good idea. So, they did more demonstrations and created more gods. What Jenna and Flint didn't know was that in years to come, the Velyors would defend their gods, who, most definitely, were not the same gods as the Bortten gods, despite the fact they most definitely were.

So, peace reigned and the crew were left to get on with the job. Or they would have been, were it not for unforeseen consequences.

Unforeseen Consequences

"What do you mean, the supply of slaves has dried up?" The bulky Reglon stared at his foreman in disbelief. This didn't compute.

"I'm sorry, sir, but our holding stations are not getting the stock. The Draztis government has been overthrown and they are no longer trading in slaves."

"What...? Overthrown by whom?"

"From what we can ascertain, sir, they appear to be a group of... humans? I've never heard of them. An ugly lot, by all accounts. There's talk of... supernatural powers. Some say they're not mortal, they're gods."

"Rubbish!" The rust-coloured Reglon paced around, kneading his knobbly temples. His lavish lifestyle was built on slaves, dependent on them. If they dried up, so did he. "Are the government aware of the problem?"

"I'm not sure, sir."

"Get me a craft ready. I'm heading to Iprian."

*

Jenna couldn't deal with this any longer. She felt like Johnson, felt she was living a lie. She had to tell Lucas. She didn't know if she was making the biggest mistake of her life, but she knew things couldn't carry on as they were. She hadn't been able to stop thinking about Flint, and her relationship with Brash was untenable.

She sat in the garden, stewing. Evening closed in around her. Lucas would be back soon. How would she tell him? She got up and walked down the path to the beach. She needed to clear her head.

The white sand stood in sharp contrast to the growing darkness. A bracing wind swept over her. Even now, she couldn't understand what was happening. She would never have believed she could feel this way about Flint. She kicked the sand, angry at the situation, angry with herself, angry at Flint for ignoring her. It was all one big churning mess.

Lowering to the sand, she stared at the rolling waves. How would she tell Lucas? She thought back to their time with the Erithians, when she had hooked up with him. He'd been the first man she'd slept him, her first boyfriend. They split up briefly on Venulas but had come back together. She thought Lucas was what she wanted. She never imagined this.

"What are you doing out here in the dark?"

She turned to see Flint standing behind her. "You're talking to me now?" she asked, offhand.

"I talk to you when I need to," he said, guarded. "Isn't that what you wanted?"

She turned back around, staring at the waves.

He loitered then lowered to the sand beside her. "Is there something wrong?" he quietly asked.

"Yes," she confessed, miserably. "You're what's wrong. I can't stop thinking about you."

His brow creased, the words not making sense. "But I'm Flint, remember?" he said, bitterly.

"I didn't mean it," she whispered.

"Then why did you say it?"

"I was pushing you away. In the hardest way I could."

He stared at her for long moments, the world shifting on its axis. His hand reached out to touch her cheek. She turned her head, their eyes locking.

His clear blue eyes mesmerised her... so deep, so honest... He leaned closer, their lips connecting softly, gently, inevitably. Every nerve in her body sparked to life, every thought evaporating. His arms came around her, the kiss becoming heated. None of it felt wrong. Her fingers raked through his hair as he pulled her closer. Her barely-functioning mind didn't know what this was but whatever it was, she was done fighting it.

Cold air hit her face as their lips got wrenched apart. A nightmare unfolded before her eyes. Lucas's fist ploughed into Flint's face. Flint recovered quickly but Lucas was a man possessed. She'd never seen him so full of rage.

Dragging herself out of her horrified stupor, she stood, summoning the power, knocking them back, forcing them apart, again and again... Lucas kept going for him, kicking up sand as he steamed in to be thrown back. At last, the futility of his actions registered, and he stood, glaring at Flint. His head slowly turned, his eyes looking at her like she was some vile, unfathomable creature.

"I'm sorry," she whispered, feebly.

Turning his back on her, he walked away

"Jenna," Flint said. She drew her gaze to him. "He'll get over it."

"I should have told him," she muttered. She turned, stumbling off in the other direction.

114

Flint caught her arm. "Jenna, wait."

"Leave me alone." She shrugged his hand off, and he let her go.

Cool air raked through her hair, tugged on her clothing. She barely registered it. Her feet kept walking... until she wandered the streets, the lowest human who had ever lived. The look on Lucas's face haunted her, made her insides shrivel. How could she do that to him...? She wanted to disappear, wanted these god-awful feelings to let up. The solution occurred to her.

She returned to the house to find Newark, Skinner, and Johnson in the kitchen. The three of them watched her as she walked in.

"Flint...?" Newark asked, staring at her, incredulously.

She ignored him as she moved forward.

"Flint...?" Johnson reiterated.

Skinner shook his head. "I knew this would happen."

Staring at Skinner, oddly, Jenna reached beneath the counter, and retrieved the bag of money, before heading out again.

Newark, Johnson, and Skinner followed after her. "Where are you going?" Johnson asked.

"I'm going through a garish door, and hopefully down a rabbit hole. Anyone tries to stop me, I'll lay them out."

Newark stared at her. "Stop you?" He turned to Johnson. "We're coming with you. Flint can't call us out for this after how he's behaved."

"Damn right," Johnson agreed. She glanced at Jenna as they walked into the city. "Flint?" she asked again. "You like Flint?"

"Apparently so," Jenna replied, miserably. "How's Lucas?" She wasn't sure she wanted to know.

"Devastated. He came in, punching the lights out of the furniture, and when we asked him what was wrong, he said, 'she's fucking Flint but don't ask me because I don't know anything anymore!'"

Skinner amended. "His actual words were, 'Ask Jenna or Flint. They're the ones fucking each other! I don't know anything anymore!'"

Jenna chewed her lip. "Have you seen Flint?"

"No. He's not shown his face," Newark said.

"Flint?" Johnson asked again.

Reaching the other side of the city, they entered through the garish door to find bears on bags smoking bongs. Jenna walked to the counter, to where a Siltian prepared the latest order. For the crew's benefit, she pretended to use sign language as she read and transferred thoughts, the bear's eyes absorbed in her hands.

"These drugs might be too strong for your species," he warned. "We Siltians have resilient constitutions but I cannot say how the drug will affect you. Bortten that have used it have gone mad. It's now law they can't take it."

"So, there's no proven side effects on humans?"

"Only because none have ever tried it. Or even visited the planet," he added as an aside.

The pain spoke for her. She handed over the money.

"You'll have to sign a disclaimer," the bear said, handing her a form. "Put your details on there." He passed her a pen.

Jenna turned to the others. "I think we have to sign this, so they won't get prosecuted if we..."

"Get fucked up?" Newark asked, excitedly. "Wow, this must be decent gear."

They were allocated bean bags and an order was prepared for them. Jenna stared at the floor as she waited.

"So, you like Flint?" Johnson asked.

She nodded, morosely.

"Well... I suppose he's not the same Flint anymore."

"Yeah, that would be even more fucked up," Newark said.

"Thing is," Johnson ruminated, "it's going to be awkward, what with Brash..."

"Poor Brash," Newark remarked, sadly. "Losing to Flint..."

The Siltian approached with their bong. "Good luck," he said, shaking his head as he walked off.

"What do I do with this?" Jenna asked.

Johnson took it off her. "Here, let me show you."

The bong got passed around.

Bears stared at the laughing humans. The laughter was insane. The humans kept rolling on the floor at intervals. As the laughter stopped, the humans gazed in awe.

"I can see it now," Skinner said, staring at the dazzling wall. "I can see it all. The colours are speaking to me. They have so much to say..."

"Yeah," Newark agreed, gazing at the wall too, "those colours are off the freaking spectrum..."

"They're moving, undulating," Johnson said, star-struck. "They're definitely saying something..."

"Only... it's a language with no language," Jenna murmured. "I... I can understand it... How can I understand it...?"

The four of them lost the power of language. They got sucked into an alternate dimension where the rules of physics no longer applied. It was the start of a mammoth, mind-bending trip...

Twelve hours later, the four humans got dumped outside their door.

A knock brought Fraza to the front. He stared down, shouting out for the others.

Brash and Graham appeared, staring down in alarm. Brash crouched, checking them over. "They're breathing. No injuries."

Fraza scratched his head. "I think they've been through the door."

Brash looked at him. "Come on, let's get them inside."

They ferried them in and laid them on the sofas, perching Newark in a six-armed chair. Brash slapped their faces but none of them would wake up. "Their breathing's steady. Why won't they wake up?"

Graham left the room and returned, carrying a bucket, chucking water in their faces. It had no effect.

"They're completely zonked," he said. "What if they never wake up?"

"They'll wake up," Brash said, concerned.

Slapping their faces at intervals brought no change. Brash instructed Fraza to go ask the Siltians if this was normal. "See if there's some kind of antidote," he told him.

Fraza returned forty minutes later with Flint.

"What's *he* doing here?" Brash spat.

Fraza frowned. "I thought I should fetch him," he said, looking at Brash, oddly.

"How long have they been like this?" Flint asked, staring at Jenna.

"About an hour," Brash answered, unable to look at the man.

Fraza held out four syringes. "The Siltian said to try this."

"What is it?" Brash asked.

"Some kind of stimulant."

They took a syringe each and stuck them in the comatose arms. Newark and Johnson awoke with a gasp for air. Skinner jerked up, looked around, then wrapped his arms around himself and shrunk into the sofa. Jenna looked around, oddly confused.

"Are you alright?" Flint asked her. She stared at him.

"Jenna?" Brash asked.

As Fraza moved forward to check on her, her eyes widened in shock. "What the hell is that!" she shrieked.

"It's Fraza," Brash told her.

"It's horrible! Get it away from me!"

Fraza backed up. Brash and Flint glanced at each other.

117

"Where I am?" she asked, looking around again. "Where's the ship?"

"What ship?" Brash asked.

"My daddy's ship. Osiris. I want to see my dad! Now!"

Brash looked at her, concerned. "Jenna, you've not been on your father's ship for over a year and a half."

Her confused look hardened. "Captain Brash, if you're playing a sick prank on me, you'll be in a lot of trouble."

Brash turned to the others. "She's lost her memory."

The question was, would she get it back?

The Admiral's Daughter

Flint talked to her but he didn't seem like Flint at all. "Jenna," he said, softly, "it looks like you've lost your memory. You've lost about a year and a half of time." She gazed at him in a trance. The man had never strung so many words together.

Chewing his lip, he pressed on. "During that time, we all got stranded on Kaledia. We were tied up by a dangerous drug lord but escaped into the wasteland. There, we came across a race from another dimension. They told us you had the power, and that you had the potential to save the universe. After months of training, all of you, apart from me, travelled through a portal to another galaxy. There, you killed a being who was using the power for evil. Since your return, we've killed that drug lord on Kaledia, and travelled to this planet, Draztis, to free people from slavery. Does any of this strike a chord with you?"

Her mouth hung wide.

Brash crouched before her. He touched her arm. "You and I were also having a relationship," he gently told her. "Do you remember that?"

Her eyes widened and she backed into the sofa, brushing his hand off. "I d-don't know what's going on here," she stuttered, "but you need to s-stop this now! My dad will be livid when he finds out!"

Newark and Johnson, plugged in at last, came over. Jenna stared at them. They peered at her, concerned, and it didn't compute. Nothing computed. Everyone acted weird. And where the hell was she? The only one that seemed vaguely familiar was Skinner, who curled on another couch, rocking gently.

It hit her. "I'm dreaming... This is a strange, absurd dream, and I'm going to wake up at any moment. You'll be the same obnoxious crew I loathe and hate."

"Good to know," Newark remarked.

"Perhaps she needs to sleep it off," Johnson suggested.

"Maybe..." Brash said, thoughtfully. "Perhaps the effects of the drug are still hanging over her."

"You've drugged me!" Jenna gasped, staring at them in alarm.

"No, you took the drug yourself."

"I would never take drugs," she asserted. She shook her head. "This isn't real... I need to sleep then I'll wake up again."

She lay down and closed her eyes, thinking this nightmare was about to end. The crew looked at each other, hoping this would work.

"Jenna doesn't remember me," Fraza murmured, desolately.

"What's wrong with Skinner?" Graham asked.

Newark shrugged. "Must have had a bad trip."

As Jenna dozed off, Brash turned to Flint. "We need to talk," he said in a hard voice.

Flint nodded and followed him out. Johnson and Newark exchanged a glance.

In the Kitchen, Brash turned to Flint, jaw tight.

"I'm sorry, Brash," Flint said, staring ahead. "What happened last night was... unplanned. There have been feelings growing between us for some time."

"She was with *me*," Brash spat, glaring at him with hatred.

"I didn't set out to win Jenna. It just happened."

"Just happened? Your tongue just happened to slide into her mouth? What else has been sliding into her?"

"Nice way to talk about the woman you love, Brash."

"Cut the crap and tell me!"

"We haven't had sex, if that's what you want to know. It's the truth. If it was otherwise, I'd tell you."

Brash paced around, rubbing his forehead. "You're a fucking dick, you know that! Never in a million years would I have thought..." He plonked himself at the counter, holding his head in his hands, staring at the surface for some time. "If it's you she wants, I'll be leaving soon."

"Leaving? Where?"

"I don't know but I won't be hanging around here."

Flint shrugged. "Perhaps she doesn't know what she wants."

"She's been avoiding me for weeks. I didn't have a clue it had anything to do with *you*."

Newark wandered in. Brash and Flint looked at him, and the man did an about turn.

"Until she comes back to herself," Brash said in a threatening voice, "you keep the hell out of my way."

*

Jenna awoke to the same nightmare. The same unfamiliar place. The same unfamiliar people. She started to become hysterical. "What are you doing to me!" she shrieked, grabbing her hair. "This has got to stop! Daddy will court-martial the lot of you!"

"Jenna, this is no prank," Flint said, crouching before her. "Everything I told you is true."

"How can it possibly be true...? How could I save the fucking universe!" Her hand flew to her mouth and she stared at Flint. "Did I just swear...?"

"You can swear like a trooper," Newark put in with a fond smile, and she gazed at him.

"We just have to hope you get your memory back soon," Flint said to her. "I know this must be unsettling for you but... you are not the Jenna Trot you remember."

She stared at him, lost. Then she broke down and cried.

Flint sat beside her and took her in his arms. The crew glanced at Brash, uncomfortably. Brash's face stiffened but he realised Jenna didn't have feelings for Flint now, didn't have feelings for either of them. If she didn't get her memory back, it was like none of this had happened.

Graham looked at Newark and motioned with his head to the door. Newark followed him out.

"What the fuck's going on?" Graham asked.

"Trot's lost her mind."

"No, why is Flint hugging her, not Brash?"

"Oh. Right. You don't know."

Newark filled him in.

"Flint...?" Graham asked, astonished.

"Yeah, pretty fucked up, right? 'Course she won't know about any of that now."

"Flint...?"

"Yep."

Fraza wandered out. "I never had a friend like Jenna..." he murmured, morosely, as he wandered off.

"Anyone would think she'd died," Newark said, watching him go.

"What if she doesn't get her memory back?" Graham asked.

"Then we'll be stuck with the Admiral's daughter." Newark's face dropped. "And she was *no* fun."

*

Days passed and, as yet, Jenna's memory had not returned. She sat by the pool, arms wrapped around her middle, trying to process this absurd new reality. The last thing she remembered was the day her father suggested she go to Marios Prime with Brash and his crew. She'd wormed her way out of that but did she go there? She'd been upset after her father left because she didn't have anyone else to go with, didn't have any friends. Pain seared her chest anew. Newark had made a remark shortly before that, making her realise everyone on board Osiris thought she was stupid. Nobody truly liked her.

She doubled up in pain. It might have been months ago but to her, it happened yesterday. Tears streamed down her cheeks. She was a despised misfit, reviled, an object of ridicule. Sure, not to her face, maybe, but she could see things she couldn't before... the surreptitious glances and smiles, people veering off in the other direction as she approached. It was all there in vivid detail.

Johnson clocked her crying and did an about turn. She'd let her get it out of her system.

When the tears abated, Jenna looked up, staring at the pool. How could any of what Flint said possibly be true...? But... how could it not be true when they were all so... different? Brash was not the brash man he'd been. These past days, he'd been concerned about her. And he looked different too, his hair longer, a little unkempt... It made him appear younger somehow. Flint was a *completely* different person. He was... there, inhabiting his body, and he appeared confident, self-assured. It beggared belief... Johnson, Newark, and Graham treated her differently... almost like they were... friends. The funny-looking Kaledian constantly came over to her, trying to initiate a conversation, asking if her memory was returning.

Johnson sat beside her. "Hi, Trot. D'you want me to fill in any blanks? You know, help jog your memory?"

Jenna looked at her, oddly. Since when did Johnson help her? "Yes, that might be useful," Jenna said, nodding. "So... we came here to rescue slaves, is that right?"

"We've rescued them. We've set up an interim government, and are in the process of holding elections to introduce democracy. We've been restructuring the planet. The man's a genius."

"Brash is a genius?"

"No, Flint. Oh. Flint's the captain now, by the way."

Jenna stared at her. "Flint...?"

"Well, Brash didn't want the job anymore because you and him were focusing on having fun, so-"

"Wait. I actually *was* having a relationship with Captain Brash?"

Johnson nodded.

Jenna shuddered then shot up, straight. "I'm not a virgin anymore?"

"That ship's well sailed."

Jenna grabbed her head in her hands, totally creeped-out. "I lost my virginity to... Brash?" She tried to imagine having sex with Brash but she couldn't, firstly, because she'd never had sex before, and, secondly, because Brash was Brash.

"I don't think it was a bad thing at the time," Johnson soothed. "You really were into him."

"I don't remember losing my virginity..."

"Yeah, well, you wouldn't be the first one."

"Was I... happy with Brash?"

"Well, err, yeah, for a while. But the night you took those drugs, you kissed Flint, so perhaps you weren't that happy, after all."

Jenna's head moved to Johnson. "I kissed Flint...?"

"Yeah... And Brash sort of caught you."

Jenna stared at the woman, unable to process any of this. "So... I kissed Flint because I was drugged?"

"No. The drugs came later. Apparently, you like Flint now. But, in fairness to you, you would never have kissed the old Flint."

Jenna stared at the floor in a daze. This was like a soap opera. Her life had never had so much drama in it. Did she have some crazy alter-ego she didn't know about? She rubbed her forehead. "Are... you and me... friends now?"

"Sure. You're fun. And you can seriously kick butt."

She looked at her. "I can...?"

"You didn't turn out to be too bad, Trot." She sniffed. "Hurry up and get your memory back, will you? Fraza keeps chewing my ear off. Poor bastard's cut up cos you don't remember him."

"He and I were friends too?"

"Partners in crime, if you ask Cornelius."

"Who is Cornelius?"

"Cornelius is cool. Part-Kaledian, part-human. He trained you. He stayed in Marios Prime because you fixed him up with a former hooker."

"I *did*...?"

"Yeah." She sniffed. "Kind of you, really."

Jenna gawped at Johnson. She was well and truly down the rabbit hole.

*

Newark looked out at them from the kitchen window. There didn't seem to be any change in Trot. He turned when Skinner walked in.

"Alright, Skinner? You look like shit."

"I'm fine," the man snapped.

"Hey, sorry for showing some concern. You heading out with Fraza today?"

"Flint wants us to visit the Velyor camp. Check they're behaving themselves. D'you want to go instead? I'm feeling... off-colour."

"You just said you were fine?"

"Well, I'm not," he snapped. "I'm... under the weather."

"Why d' you have to go and check on them? They got the message, alright. Flint's being a fussy arsehole."

"So, will you take my place?"

"Sorry, I'm helping Graham settle the Saffria in," he said, wiggling his eyebrows. "Helping them furnish their gaffs."

"Thanks for nothing," Skinner spat.

Newark glanced out of the window. "D'you think Trot'll get her memory back soon?"

Skinner glanced out too. "Well, if she doesn't, our powerbase is seriously compromised."

"What d'you mean?"

"If she doesn't remember who she is, how will she remember what she can do?"

"Crap. I never thought of that. We need to get her learning that shit again."

Newark steamed outside to get the ball rolling. "Hey, Trot," he called, "you need to start using your power before it dries up." Coming over to her, he tried to get her to her feet.

"Get off me," she shrieked, batting off his hands.

Newark let go of her. "Raise the water in the pool."

"*What...?*"

"Come on, you need to start pulling your magic shit again."

"Magic doesn't exist," she insisted, looking at him as if he was mad.

"No?" Johnson asked. "Well, how come you could do all kinds of amazing stuff with it. We've seen it, Trot. Come on, why don't you give it a try?"

"Is this a joke?" she asked, suspiciously.

"No, straight up. You were doing this shit all the time."

Gaze lingering on Johnson, Jenna slowly stood. Glancing at Newark, she looked at the pool. "How... do I do it?" she asked, dubiously.

"You're asking us?" Johnson said.

"I could raise water...?"

"Yep."

Jenna took a breath. "Water, I command you to rise," she said.

Nothing happened.

"Try again," Newark said. "Only, you don't usually say stuff."

She repeated the words in her head.

"Use your arms," Johnson suggested.

She used her arms, her thoughts, even said a prayer but nothing would make that water move.

"This is ridiculous," she threw out. "All of this is ridiculous!"

"Well, you've done it before," Johnson told her.

"I've never done anything before," she shot, storming off in a flood of tears.

Newark and Johnson watched her go.

"Thank god we still have Fraza," Johnson said.

*

Flint came out a short time later. "I've come back to check on Jenna. Have you seen her?"

"Yep," Newark said. "She ran off in a hissy fit. Couldn't get the water in the pool to rise."

"Where is she now?"

"I'd say she's crying on her bed."

Flint climbed the stairs and knocked on Jenna's door.

"Go away," she shouted.

He opened the door, taking in her desperate state. Closing the door, gently, he came to sit beside her on the bed. "I know this is all... difficult to believe," he said to her, softly. "It's like, you've had a slate wiped clean and people are telling you things you can't take in, telling you you're something you're not. But that's because of the vantage point you're seeing it from. There is so much more inside you than you know, Jenna. Just because you can't remember, doesn't mean it isn't there. You have greatness in you. I need you to trust me on this."

"Greatness?" she threw out, miserably. "I'm a stupid misfit, and the sad part is, I was too stupid to realise it. I'm a joke. I'm certainly no saviour of the universe..."

"But you did save the universe."

She wiped her eyes and sat up. "If this is true, why can't I remember?" she begged of him.

"The mind-altering drug you took affected your memory."

"Then why didn't it effect the others too?"

Flint couldn't answer that. The others' memories were intact, although Skinner didn't seem himself. He wished Cornelius was here. Perhaps he'd have an answer to this.

She wiped her nose with the back of her hand. "Johnson said I... and you?"

Biting his lip, he nodded.

"It was just a kiss, right?"

"Yes." *It was so much more.*

"And I was with Brash too?"

He nodded, gauging her reaction.

She shook her head. "I lost my virginity and I don't even remember..."

Flint looked down, not sure what to say to that.

"You're not the Flint I remember," she mumbled. "It's weird waking up to find everybody different."

"I can imagine. A lot's happened these past months."

A knock came at the door.

Flint moved across the room and opened it to find Skinner.

"I can't go with Fraza today," the man stated. "I... don't feel too good."

Flint assessed him. "OK, I'll get Johnson to go." His eyes followed Skinner as the man walked off.

Jenna watched Flint close the door and come back over. She couldn't believe he was the one giving orders now.

He sat back on the bed. "Why don't I take the day off," he said, his blue eyes kind. She found herself responding to that look. "Show you around the city. You could do with getting out of here, taking your mind off things."

She wiped her nose again. "OK."

*

Half an hour later, Brash walked in, asking where Jenna was.

"Flint's taken her out for a walk," Johnson said.

Brash hackles rose. The bastard was steaming in *again!*

"Trot's lost her powers," Newark told him.

"Yeah, she ran off in a crying strop," Johnson put in.

"Is she OK?" Brash asked.

"She's better. Flint saw to her."

The bastard, Brash thought.

Newark frowned. "D'you think we're stuck with her for good?"

126

"Who?" Brash asked, confused.

"Who do you think? The Admiral's daughter."

The Weirdest Feeling

Getting over her shock of seeing six-armed Bortten, Jenna looked around the city, taking in the white buildings. She was probably being judgemental, but the beings didn't go with the buildings at all.

Flint led her to the government building, taking her up to the meeting chamber.

"This is where I hold meetings," he told her.

"A round table? It's like Camelot. Your name's not Arthur, is it?"

He smiled. "No, it's Vincent."

Jenna stared at the pictures on the wall. "They've got very bad taste."

He laughed and she turned to him. She'd never seen him laugh before.

"Skinner thinks these designs say something about the Bortten," he said. "But I think you're right. They've just got bad taste."

Jenna stared at Flint's face. The smile transformed it.

Her gaze on him made his heart leap and break at the same time. "Come on, I'll show you around the rest of the place."

He took her through wide, airy corridors, leading her in and out of different offices. Jenna watched the creatures, absorbed. They used all six arms at once. Many of them smiled at Flint, their faces stretching grotesquely.

"They seem to like you," she remarked.

"Well, I find if I treat them with warmth and respect, they treat me similarly."

She turned to look at him. "You've never been treated with warmth and respect, Flint," she said, simply and directly. There was no guile in her statement, just a simple search for answers, and an empathy for how he had been.

He swallowed. "No... I was lost for many years, Jenna. Cornelius and the Erithians helped me a lot. They brought me to myself."

"Well, they've done a good job," she said, smiling at him. "I'm glad, for your sake, we ended up there, wherever there was."

He smiled back, his eyes lingering on her as she moved on.

They left the building and walked through the sunshine to one of the parks.

"This place is really nice," she remarked, looking around. "It's hard to believe they were so corrupt."

"Evil lurks everywhere," Flint said, "even behind the friendliest of facades."

"You must be a good person," she considered, "to want to do all this. And you got the crew to follow you?"

"They followed *you* across the universe. They've already done a lot of good."

"Yeah, I keep forgetting. It's..." She rubbed her forehead. "Was I very different?"

"In some ways, yes. In others, you were the same. I'm sure you'll get your memory back soon." He longed for her to remember what they were becoming to each other. Though he had missed this part of her, he missed the other part too. He wanted all of her.

"Could I see some of the slaves?" she asked.

"Yes. Graham and Newark are helping them settle in."

Flint showed her to the area where the Saffria had settled. Furniture was being delivered to small white apartments. Graham and Newark did most of the fetching and carrying, Newark working bare-chested.

"I've never seen them work so hard," Jenna remarked. "I wonder if they'd help the Bortten with as much enthusiasm?"

Flint turned to her with a fond smile. "You're very perceptive."

The praise made her blush but her attention was taken by Graham, who waved at her. She waved back, awkwardly.

"I still can't get over how different they are with me," she said. "They must have liked her."

"Her?"

"My... alter-ego."

"You're one and the same person, Jenna."

"It doesn't feel like it."

A lilac-skinned beauty came out to talk to Graham. The two seemed on friendly terms. In fact, she would say they were more than friends. Another beauty came out, and Newark stretched. Jenna suspected he was showcasing his muscles.

"It's enough to make your stomach turn," Jenna remarked.

Flint followed her gaze. "You don't like Newark now? You were ruffling his hair a short time ago."

"I was...?"

Jenna turned away, a sudden thought occurring to her. "Did I ever try to contact my dad?"

"No. Perhaps you wanted to... detach from your former life."

"There you are," Brash said and they turned to him. "I've been looking for you, Jenna. Wanted to check you were alright."

She couldn't bring herself to make eye-contact. She'd lost her virginity to this man and it wasn't something she could take back.

"What are you two up to?" Brash asked pleasantly, eyeballing Flint.

"Flint's been showing me around," she said, looking anywhere but at Brash. "Even though I've been here weeks," she added with a frown.

"Right, well, I'll continue the tour then. Flint will be dying to get back to everything, I'm sure."

Jenna stiffened. Flint gave Brash a hard stare. "I think I'm due a day off."

Brash shrugged. "OK, tag along."

Brash was prepared for a fight. He didn't know what charm Flint had used on her these past weeks, but the playing field was level now. He and Jenna could reform their relationship so when her memory did come back, she'd forget all about Flint. The only problem with this plan was Flint. He had to be kept at bay.

For the rest of the afternoon, Brash took the lead, pointing buildings and landmarks out, making references to similar places they'd seen on their travels, places Flint hadn't been. Jenna's brow creased. The remarks meant little to her, either.

A niggling voice told Brash he was being desperate, but a stronger voice told him to drive the slimy toad that was Flint well out of the picture. It didn't occur to him these were traits of the old captain resurfacing, the captain before the team-building captain. *Had* it occurred to him, he might have paused for thought.

Flint got pushed to the background for the next hour. Jenna kept glancing at him, trying to encourage him to join in, but playing games wasn't his style. He trusted Jenna would end up with the right person for her eventually, even if that person wasn't him.

When Flint eventually returned to work, Brash took Jenna back to the house, but already she'd had enough of him. She wasn't at the place he was, even if they *had* had a relationship. She told him she was going to walk along the beach.

"I'll come with you," he said, smiling at her, pleasantly.

"No," she blurted. "Err... I'd like a little time alone."

Nodding reluctantly, he watched her go.

She roamed the beach for hours, like a lost soul. How could any of this be real...?

Returning to the house, she sat by the pool in the darkness. Fraza spotted her and came out with tea.

"You should try this, Jenna," he said.

"What is it?"

"Tea."

"Tea?"

"Special tea."

He poured her a glass and she drank it, experiencing a strange uplifted feeling. "This is good tea," she remarked. She glanced at the Kaledian. "Don't be too upset I don't remember you. I don't remember anyone, really. Or what I do remember of them doesn't exist anymore."

Fraza thought about this, and it made him feel a little better.

"You helped me a lot, Jenna," he said. "I'll always be grateful to you."

"I did?"

"Yes."

"You really like her, don't you?"

Fraza looked at her, thoughtfully "She's you, Jenna. You've... just forgotten a part of you."

"Well, she isn't here now."

"She must be. You can't become what isn't in you."

Jenna thought about this, and it made her feel a little better.

Skinner walked up from the beach. Spotting the tea, he sat with them and helped himself. His tight body hunched in on itself, and, though his mouth wasn't jabbering like it used to, it eased Jenna to see something vaguely familiar. Fraza didn't feel as at ease. He viewed Skinner, oddly. The man looked like he was coming unstuck. Whatever those drugs were, they'd had a profound effect on him. The Kaledian wished they had never gone to that place.

After draining two glasses, Skinner lifted from his chair, and walked back to the beach.

"What on earth possessed you to take those drugs?" Fraza scolded Jenna.

"I can't remember."

"No... Of course, not."

"Johnson said I kissed Flint that night and Brash caught us."

Fraza stared at her, dumbfounded. "You kissed Flint...?"

"Don't ask me," Jenna threw out, shrugging helplessly.

Fraza had been shocked when he found out she was having a relationship with Brash, but Flint...?

"You have to help me, Fraza," she said, more urgently. "I think Captain Brash is trying to... win me over. You've got to help me avoid him."

"That's going to be hard, seeing as we all live here."

"I know but I'm not in the place he is. I woke up thinking I was a virgin. I hadn't even had a boyfriend. All of a sudden, I'm involved with two men, and I've fixed an old man up with a hooker. I think my brain is going to explode."

"I understand," Fraza said, touching her arm, trying to calm her. "Perhaps you should get more involved with Flint."

"More involved with *Flint?*"

"No, I don't mean that. I mean, you could help him, keep yourself occupied, keep out of the house."

"Doesn't Captain Brash help Flint?"

"He's not the captain anymore, Jenna."

"Yeah. I forget."

"He's up there sometimes. Although, mostly, Flint sends us out on various jobs. Even if you do come into contact with Brash there, you'd be at work, so it might be easier."

Jenna nodded, thoughtfully. "Thank you, Fraza. You're so nice. I can see why we were friends."

Fraza beamed.

Johnson walked out and sat with them. "You should have seen how reverent the Velyors were today," she remarked. "That show you put on certainly did the trick." Jenna frowned. "Sorry. Forgot you can't remember. So, what have *you* been up to today?"

"Flint showed me around Hercillen," Jenna replied. "We saw Newark and Graham helping the slaves settle in. Newark was showing off."

"Figures."

"And I think Graham has got a soft spot for one of the Saffria."

Johnson stared at her and Jenna rubbed her arm. After a few moments, Johnson got up and walked off.

"Did I say something?" Jenna asked.

Fraza's face looked heavy. "She and Graham were having a relationship but she broke it off."

"She and Graham?"

"Yes."

"God, more revelations... So, if she broke it off, what's the problem?"

"That's a good question."

Jenna glanced after Johnson, catching sight of Brash in the doorway. Fraza noticed him too. "I've got this," he said, standing.

Fraza intercepted Brash, telling him they needed time alone as he was going to instruct Jenna in using the power again.

Relieved to dodge Brash, Jenna's misery grew when she failed to raise the water.

"You have to believe you've got it," Fraza said.

"This is ridiculous! Magic doesn't even exist!"

"It's not magic, Jenna. It's the power. Watch, I'll do it."

Her eyes widened when a wall of water rose from the pool. Stumbling back, her gaze shifted to Fraza.

Fraza let the water fall back. "Why don't you try again, Jenna," he said.

She stared at him. This must be a dream. A never-ending dream...

"You can do it," he gently prompted.

Drawing her gaze to the water, she tried again. And again. To no avail.

"I can't do this," she threw out, miserably.

"You can. You've done it before."

"I've never done anything before," she shot, storming off.

Newark wandered out, glancing at Jenna as she rushed past. "Is she having another hissy fit?" he asked Fraza.

Brash caught Jenna's arm in the kitchen. "Jenna, what's wrong?"

"Leave me alone," she snapped, wrenching her arm free.

She charged upstairs, threw herself on the bed, and cried. She was trapped in some strange, surreal, no-man's-land, where magic existed, where she was surrounded by people she didn't know, who knew a Jenna Trot that wasn't her. She couldn't even pine for her old life because she didn't want to be *that* girl anymore. She felt completely adrift. It was the weirdest feeling.

A Mystery

"So, what *do* these walls say about them?" Newark asked Skinner.

"They've got bad taste," Skinner replied, pouring himself a glass of tea.

"That's it? That's what I've been waiting for? I thought you were going to come up with some clever, insightful shit."

Skinner took a deep slug of tea. He looked at Newark. "They have no culture secretary, little, if any, entertainment here. They don't even have religion. Their imagination is unevolved. These walls, as horrendous as they are, speak to an undeveloped urge for expression. Since the Siltians are the only ones that express creativity, and the Bortten have no basis of comparison, they think this is good. In short, they have no taste which, in this case, equates to bad taste."

Newark stared at him.

Johnson came into the kitchen. "Anyone seen Graham?" she asked.

"Think he's gone out," Newark said.

"I'm bored of this planet," she grumbled. "I think we should fuck off now."

"We can't leave till the elections are over. It could still all turn to shit."

Johnson sat at the counter. "Hand me some tea, Skinner."

Trot ventured in, looking around, warily. "Is Captain Brash around?"

"Think he's gone for a walk," Newark said, his gaze lingering on her, his mind going off in the wrong direction.

Jenna grabbed a slice of kupto then scuttled back out.

"D'you think she likes Brash again?" Newark asked.

Nobody answered, Skinner and Johnson lost in their own worlds.

Fraza bumped into Jenna in the hallway. "I've spoken to Flint," he said. "You can come over there today, if you want."

"Great. I'll be quick. Brash could come back at any moment."

"Perhaps you should just talk to him."

"I'm not very good at that."

*

Johnson wandered over to the area the Saffria had settled. The small white apartments looked like holiday rentals. She stood behind a tree, watching activity across the street. Carts arrived, loaded with furniture.

135

How much bloody furniture did they need? She stiffened on seeing Graham come out of an apartment with a lilac beauty. The pair of them talked and smiled at each other. Johnson's fists clenched, itching to ram into that lilac face. When Graham leant down and kissed the woman, restraint flew out of the window. Within seconds, the woman was in her grasp, taking a hard blow to the face.

Graham dragged her off. "What the fuck are you doing, you mad bitch!"

"What am *I* doing? What are *you* doing!"

"You dumped me! Remember?"

"Well, maybe I made a mistake!"

Graham stared at her. "What? Suddenly, you've made a mistake? Now I'm with someone else?"

"You're *with* her...?"

"Yes, I'm with her. You and me are over, remember? The relationship had run its course."

"I didn't... I..."

"Listen, you need to leave. Touch her again, and I'll knock you out."

She stared at him. He'd never spoken to her like that before. She watched in a daze as he walked over to the Saffria, checked her face, then led her away from the street.

Johnson hung there, still staring. She'd never seen Graham with anyone else. It felt like a bad dream.

Wandering away, desolately, she turned a corner, lowering herself onto a low wall. A couple of Bortten looked at her but she ignored them. She stared at the ground, struggling to deny this was all her fault. She'd pushed him away when she obviously still loved him. But why...? Why had he been getting on her nerves so much? Scrambling for answers, she wondered if Trot had something with that theory of hers. And what did Trot know of her mother? Johnson rarely thought of her mother. The woman scared the shit out of her. Her mother had been in the corps too, but Johnson never measured up, no matter how hard she tried. The woman abhorred weakness, frightened the crap out of most men. And she didn't do namby-pamby relationships. Relationships were a crutch for the weak. Johnson's father had been a one-night stand. But what did any of this have to do with her and Graham...?

*

136

Brash had turned up at the government building, and was currently showing Jenna the budgets, explaining it all to her.

"So, you see, once the tea production increases, it should offset the loss of revenue from slavery."

"Right," Jenna said, rubbing her forehead, wishing he would go away. If she hadn't lost her virginity to him, she might have found this new Brash charming. As it was, she could barely stand to be around him.

"You know, no-one expects you to be working here. Flint's got it all covered. You should be focusing on yourself."

"I'd like to keep busy. It takes my mind off things."

He assessed her. He didn't like her being here at all. "It's strange to think you don't remember what we had," he said, sadly, and for a moment she felt sorry for him. "We were good together."

She nodded, uncomfortably.

"I'd... err... try to avoid Flint, if I was you. He's changed. I expect you can see that but he's become a little... manipulative."

"Manipulative?"

"Yes. I don't think his intentions toward you are honourable. Before you lost your memory, he tried to split us up."

"He did?"

"Yes. All I'm saying is, be careful, Jenna."

He smiled at her, pleasantly, and told her he'd see her back at the house.

Jenna stared after him, wishing she could remember things. She was working blind here, not knowing who to trust. Flint seemed genuine to her. She didn't get any creepy feelings from him, but what did she know? She didn't know any of them, didn't even know herself.

Johnson ambled in. "Alright, Trot?"

"Yes. Nice to see you," Jenna said, pleasantly, deciding to reformulate her relationship with the woman.

Johnson looked at her, oddly. "Just seen Graham. He called me a mad bitch."

"He *did...?*"

"He's with another woman and I punched her in the face." Jenna stared at her. "Bastard didn't take long."

"Err..."

Johnson sniffed. "You were right. I do still like him and I've screwed it up."

"Oh."

She sniffed again. "You said it's down to my mother and... I dunno," she said, shrugging, "maybe you had something there."

"I did?"

"Perhaps Flint could... you know... help shed light on stuff, like you said."

"He could?"

"All that therapy crap worked for him, didn't it?"

"I suppose it did."

She sniffed again. "Maybe I'll... err... you know?"

"Talk to him?"

"Yeah, I think you're right. I might talk to him."

"OK."

She sniffed again. "Right, I'll see you later then. And... err... thanks."

"That's... OK."

Jenna stared after her, wondering what the hell she knew about Johnson's mother. Jenna Trot was a complete mystery.

*

When Jenna and Flint returned to the house, they found most of the crew in the kitchen. The pair stopped in the archway, staring at Johnson, who was... preparing a meal?

Stirring a pot, Johnson left it cooking, walking past them to lay the table on the other side of the room. Throwing spoons down, she walked back, looking to the door. As yet, Graham had not got back.

"God, you must be bored," Newark said. He turned to Flint, a thought occurring to him. "We should get ourselves some servants."

"We've come *here* to serve," Flint said, and Newark frowned.

Fraza whispered to Skinner. "I don't think Flint and Brash should be sitting around the same table."

Skinner ignored him and moved to the counter to get a drink of tea. Brash came into the kitchen, his dark eyes fixing on Jenna, before flitting suspiciously to Flint. A meaty aroma grabbed his attention, and his gaze shifted to Johnson.

"Is it ready?" Newark asked.

"Yep." Looking at the door again, Johnson grabbed the pot.

Brash jumped in beside Jenna as they sat around the table. "Are you OK?" he asked, meaningfully, glancing at Flint.

She looked at him, puzzled, but nodded, inching her chair away.

Johnson dumped a huge pot down, hot splashes landing on the tabletop.

"So, what's this then?" Newark asked. "Stew?"

"I shoved a ton of stuff in a pot," Johnson said, absently. "Cooking's not my thing."

Flint placed bowls on the table.

Newark grabbed the ladle and filled his bowl, tucking in straight away. "Doesn't taste too bad," he remarked.

Brash took the ladle and handed a bowl to Jenna. "So, how was your day, Jenna?" he asked, pleasantly. "Not sick of paperwork, yet?"

"Err... no."

"Well, I hope you're being appreciated. I know I'm not captain anymore, but it's important to praise the crew." He glanced at Flint.

"Perhaps you're right," Flint said. "Jenna's been very industrious today." He turned to her and smiled. "I'd never have managed all that filing on my own."

"You've been giving her filing? She saved the bloody universe and you've got her filing?"

"I don't mind," Jenna mentioned.

"Well, I mind. Flint obviously doesn't see your worth."

"I see just fine," Flint said, giving Brash a hard stare.

Brash returned the stare. "I see just fine too."

"And what do you see?" If Brash was determined to hang himself, he might as well get on with it.

"I see what a snake you are."

Fraza rubbed his ears. Johnson stared at the door. Skinner wasn't eating. He drank tea at the counter. Newark stuffed his face, eyes flitting between Brash and Flint.

"A snake, Brash?" Flint asked.

"Yes, worming your way into Jenna's affections and no doubt into her knickers!"

Jenna spat out her food. "Stop taking like that," she shot, incensed. "My knickers are my own business!"

Newark stifled a laugh.

Brash looked at her. "I'm trying to help you," he insisted.

"Or trying to help yourself," Flint remarked, looking at him, steadily.

Brash stood, threateningly. Flint stood, too. The others stood and backed away, Newark grabbing his bowl quickly. Brash flung the table away as he steamed in, landing a hard, right hook in Flint's face. Flint recovered quickly and came back with a jab to Brash's side. The kitchen started to get trashed as they slammed against the counters, knocking pots and plates to the floor. Jenna watched, horrified, staring at Flint, confounded. The man could fight.

Johnson wandered outside. Skinner grabbed the jug and followed after her.

"Isn't anyone going to stop this?" Jenna shouted against a backdrop of destruction.

"How?" Newark asked. "The bastard can take three of us at once?"

"Who? Brash?"

"No, Flint."

Flint? Her head moved to watch him. Already, he was getting the better of Brash. He looked lethal, his body nimble, his punches deadly.

Fraza stopped rubbing his ears and, focused, using the power to split them up.

"Fraza, stop it!" Brash yelled. "That's an order!"

As Brash was no longer captain, Fraza ignored him.

"Fraza, you'd better break this up," Flint warned, "or I'm going to kill him."

"You can try," Brash spat. "You always were a worm and you still are. We should have left you dangling on that hook!"

Fire burned in Flint's eyes. "Fraza, don't break it up. That's an order!"

Fraza, out of his depth, looked to Jenna, but the girl stared on, horrified. Newark took his bowl, and moved out into the hallway.

"Newark?" Jenna pleaded.

"Believe me, there's nothing I can do."

She couldn't watch anymore. Skirting the wall, she ran out into the garden. "They're going to kill each other," she flustered but Skinner and Johnson, lost in their own worlds, ignored her. "This is all because of me, isn't it...?" She held her head in her hands. Two men fighting over her? It was unreal.

Gross, barbaric sounds came from the kitchen. Jenna had never seen men fight before. She prayed for it to stop. The sounds abruptly cut off, and her eyes moved to the window. It was eerily silent.

She ran back to the door, staring at Brash laid out on the floor. Flint stood over him, a cold look on his face. The look made her shiver.

He turned to Fraza. "Can you do the healing that Jenna could do?"

Jenna stared at Flint, bewildered. The Kaledian nodded. She watched Fraza crouch down, and place his hands over Brash. Minutes later, Brash pulled around. Flint walked out.

"What did you do...?" Jenna asked, edging toward Fraza.

"I used the power to heal him."

"And... *I* could do that?"

"Yes."

The rabbit hole widened.

140

Brash sat up, groggily.

Jenna drew her eyes to him. "Are you alright?" she asked.

Brash stared at the floor, acutely embarrassed. No-one had beaten him in a fight before, especially not Flint. And for Jenna to witness it...?

"Perhaps you should go and lie down for a while," she suggested, more softly.

Embarrassment dropped away as opportunity presented itself. "Ouch," he said, holding his side.

"Are you in pain?"

"A little," he said, stoically. "I think I *will* lie down. Would you come up with me? Keep me company?"

"Err..."

"Just for a while," he said, his face wincing.

"Err... OK."

She helped Brash to his feet, and Fraza watched them go, concerned. He hadn't thought Brash capable of manipulation but maybe love or jealously did strange things to the human mind. He would have tagged along but something else concerned him. Healing Brash had taken time. The power hadn't come through as freely. Limiting thoughts had got in the way, taunting him, mercilessly. *There's only you now. Jenna can't help you anymore.* Something insidious was creeping back in. He needed Jenna, wished she would come back to herself.

Jenna helped Brash onto his bed then stood back quickly. "I'll... err... sit in this chair."

"Do you remember that room we shared in Marios Prime?" Brash asked, fondly. He shook his head. "No, of course, you don't. That's where it began for me. I started to see you in a different light. There was more to you than people realised."

Jenna's interest piqued. "There was more?"

"Yes. You were quite perceptive... about my crew anyway."

She rubbed her forehead. "Everyone thinks... I mean, everyone thought I was stupid. I'm just starting to realise this..."

"Cornelius said you blocked it out."

She looked at him. "He did? Why did I do that?"

"He said your subconscious was trying to help you but was actually making things worse."

"So," Jenna said, scratching her head, "this old man I don't remember has been rooting around in my *brain?*"

"He rooted in everyone's brain," Brash said with a purposefully charming smile.

She looked at him, seriously, desperately wanting answers. "D'you think I'm stupid? I mean, do you think I was born that way?"

"I don't think you're stupid at all, just... misunderstood."

"But I was shunted from sector to sector. They all tried to get rid of me because I was rubbish."

Brash remembered *that* Jenna Trot but he didn't want to dwell on her; one, because he didn't have the answers, and two, because he didn't want to bring the mood down.

"I think you're amazing," he said, smiling that smile again.

Jenna was in no mood for agendas. "Well, I think you look fine now," she said, getting up and walking to the door.

He tried to protest but she resolutely walked through it. As she closed the door on him, she felt she was more of a mystery than she had been before.

Therapy

Flint called a meeting the following evening.

"The elections are going to be held next week," he said. "Everything is in place. Once the government is established, we can let go of the reins."

"Can we leave then?" Johnson asked with a spark of hope.

"Depending on how things go. We have to watch the government bed in. Hopefully, it will all go well."

"You've done an amazing job," Jenna said, at which point Brash got up and left the room. She glanced at the door. "Perhaps you should try to talk to him," she suggested.

"I don't think he'd listen to me." Flint looked around. "Where's Graham, by the way?"

"Screwing his whore," Johnson spat, at which point she got up and left the room.

Newark sat, straight. "What whore?"

"He's seeing one of the Saffria," Jenna told him. "Johnson's upset about it."

"The crafty devil," Newark thought aloud. "He kept that quiet."

Jenna turned to Flint. "I think she wants to talk to you about it."

Flint's eyes widened. "Talk to *me*?"

"Yes. It's got something to do with her mother but I'm not sure what. Apparently, my former self suggested she talk to you because you know about therapy." Jenna shrugged. "Don't ask me." She bit her lip. "Do you think *I* could have a word with you?"

Assessing her, he nodded. "Let's go into the other room."

As they walked out, Newark turned to Skinner and Fraza. "Wonder what she wants to *talk* about?"

Fraza looked at him, puzzled. "What do you mean?"

"Maybe they're doing more than *talking*." He looked at Skinner for his take but Skinner curled on the couch and closed his eyes. Fraza thought someone should talk to Skinner.

Flint turned the light on in the other room, and gestured for Jenna to sit on one of the chairs.

"What do you want to talk about, Jenna?" he asked, sitting opposite her. He shifted a little, wondering if this had anything to do with him or Brash.

"What it is... Well... I don't know who I've been this past year and a half but the past I do remember is becoming a mystery too."

"How do you mean?"

"Do you remember me from the ship, Flint? I mean, before I joined the crew?"

"Yes."

"Was I really as stupid as everyone thought? Apparently, Cornelius said I blocked it all out, so I didn't know what people thought of me, but I do now and it's... horrible... But why was I so bad at everything? Do you think a person is born stupid?"

"You're not stupid, Jenna."

"Well, I must be if that's what people think of me."

"They don't know you at all. This crew knows more about you than those people ever will. You need to leave those people behind."

"But it tortures me. As far as I'm concerned, I've come straight off Osiris." She wrapped her arms around her middle. "I'm drowning in these feelings. I just need answers."

He leant forward and touched her arm. "I can give you a theory but the answers are in you, not me."

She looked at him with pleading eyes. "What's your theory?"

"Well..." he said, sitting back slightly. "You have had high expectations placed on you from an early age, expectations that perhaps, you didn't think you could meet. Lacking in confidence and terrified of failure, you became a self-fulfilled prophecy. You see, when you approach something from a position of confidence, your whole being is aligned to success. When you approach it from a position of fear, you screw up. When you screw up once, your confidence is knocked further, taking you on a downward spiral, and establishing a pattern. Now, your amazing subconscious, aware of the pain you are in, starts blocking things out, and this probably started a long time ago. So, I'd say your problem was not stupidity, but lack of confidence. You were not born stupid, Jenna. In fact, compared to most people, you are highly intelligent. What those people saw was a projection of your fear. You were misjudged, as much by yourself as anyone else."

Jenna stared at him, transfixed. That made her feel so much better.

"The thing is, Jenna, no amount of theories, as correct as they might be, can change anything. The realisation has to come from deep within you. You have to see the truth yourself, and when you do, nobody else's opinion of you will matter."

She stared at the floor, absorbing what he'd said. Gradually, she looked up at him. "There's so much more to *you* than anyone's ever seen..."

He smiled at her, sadly. "Most people take things at face value."

Her big blue eyes remained on him, and he wanted to tell her how much more there was, how much he felt for her, how much he wanted to take her in his arms and kiss her again. But he couldn't. All he could do was wait and hope.

"I think Johnson should talk to you," she said. "Could I get her?"

"Err... OK."

She got up and walked to the door, but doubled back, threw her arms around him, and kissed his cheek. "Thank you, Flint," she said, squeezing his shoulders.

As she left, he touched his cheek, his gaze fixed on the door.

Johnson spent over two hours in there with Flint, and she came out, shell-shocked, lingering in the hall.

Jenna emerged from the kitchen. "How did it go?"

"He's good..." Johnson said. "He's bloody good... I can see things I couldn't before. It's like my eyes have been opened. He suggested I come back for hypnotherapy."

"He can do that?"

"I'm beginning to think that man can do anything. I never thought, in a million years, I'd be talking to Flint about my mother."

"D'you think it can help you with Graham?"

"Well, it might if he wasn't with someone else."

"Oh, yeah. Well, perhaps this thing is a... fling."

Johnson nodded.

Graham came through the front door.

"Hi, Graham," Jenna said, her eyes flicking to Johnson.

Graham didn't look at Johnson. He still hadn't forgiven her for punching his girlfriend. "Hey," he replied. "I need a word with Flint."

"He's in there," Jenna said, pointing.

Graham moved past them, and entered the room. He came out with Flint five minutes later. Flint called another meeting, and the crew assembled in the living room.

Flint told the crew Graham would be staying with his new girlfriend from now on. The crew stared at Graham, surprised. Johnson stared at him, horrified.

"Since when do you have a girlfriend?" Brash asked.

"I've been having a relationship with one of the Saffria," Graham told him.

"He's been doing more than helping her move in," Newark jibed. "You sly old goat. You kept that to yourself. How do you even communicate with her?"

"Sign-language, mostly. But we've been picking up each other's language."

"You're alright with him moving out?" Brash asked Flint.

"I can't see any problem with it at the moment, as long as he keeps in constant contact with us."

"Is it serious?" Brash asked Graham.

"We have become close," Graham replied, his eyes flicking to Johnson. Brash's eyes flicked to her too.

"You sky old goat," Newark said again, wondering if *he* could get a Saffria girlfriend.

"Report in to me regularly," Flint told Graham.

Graham nodded. Glancing at the crew, he left.

"Bastard can't wait to get back to her," Newark remarked.

Johnson put her head in her hands and cried. The crew stared at her, unnerved. They'd never seen her cry before. It was totally surreal. Even Skinner took time out of whatever stupor he was in to stare at her.

Jenna tentatively placed a hand on her arm. "It'll be alright," she said, gently.

"How can it be alright?" Johnson sobbed.

Johnson wouldn't stop crying, and Brash rubbed his forehead. "You ended it with him, remember?" he said, softly.

"She's not just crying because of Graham," Flint told him. "There are issues with her mother too."

"How d'you know that?"

"Because she told me."

Brash's gaze narrowed. "Have you been messing with her head, Flint?"

"No. She came to me."

Brash glanced at Jenna with a *see what I mean?* look. He crouched before Johnson. "What's Flint been saying to you?"

"Just because she's crying," Jenna asserted, "doesn't mean it's a bad thing. Maybe she needs to cry."

"He'll have been messing with her head," Brash insisted.

"He's not been messing with anyone. He's trying to help."

Brash let out a frustrated breath. "The old you was always far too trusting."

"She was, wasn't she?" Flint mused, giving Brash a meaningful look.

"What does that mean?"

"You do not want to go there, Brash, believe me."

Brash's eyes widened. He backed off. If this Jenna ever learned they had tried to kill her, any hope he had of getting her back would be dashed.

"Go and sleep it off, Johnson," Brash said.

Johnson pulled herself up and walked out, her shoulders heaving with silent sobs.

Newark watched her go. "That was... weird," he said, disconcerted.

146

Jenna, Newark, and Flint wandered out. Jenna and Flint had had enough of Brash. Newark needed some tea. Brash looked around the rest of the crew. Fraza rubbed his ears. Skinner's arms wrapped around his middle, as if holding himself together. Brash's thoughts had been so consumed with Jenna and Flint lately, he'd barely paid Skinner any attention.

"What's the matter with you, Skinner?" he asked.

Skinner looked up. "Feel a bit under the weather."

"D'you need some kind of doctor?"

"I need tea," the man said, dragging himself to his feet, and walking out as if he had hypothermia.

"He has been like that since he took those drugs," Fraza said.

"But that was days ago."

"He's been drinking tea incessantly since then."

Brash frowned. "Perhaps we need to keep him off the stuff."

"I think it's what's keeping him together."

"When he goes to bed tonight, hide the tea. We need to know what's going on with him and if the tea's masking it..."

"Do you think that's a good idea?"

"We need to know what we're dealing with here."

"Perhaps we should ask Flint."

"Flint's done enough damage tonight," Brash shot, annoyed. The crew looked to Flint for direction now?

Newark walked back in with a glass of tea. "That was weird," he said, feeling thrown. "You'd think Trot would be the one crying, wouldn't you?"

"What d'you mean?" Brash asked.

Fraza shook his head at Newark but Newark carried on, oblivious. "Well, he's had them both in that room tonight. Trot was in there first."

"What...?"

"Yeah. She came out with a smile on her face."

"So, Skinner?" Fraza asked, attempting a change of subject.

"What was Jenna doing with Flint?" Brash demanded.

"Just talking," Fraza said, stepping from side to side as he rubbed his ears. "She wanted a quick word with him."

"It wasn't that quick," Newark remarked.

Fraza glared at Newark. "So, Skinner?" he persisted.

"Get rid of all the tea," Brash snapped.

"Get rid of the tea?" Newark asked, horrified.

"Hide it somewhere Skinner won't find it."

"Oh. Good idea," Newark agreed. "The bastard's emptying us out."

Brash stormed off, slamming the door behind him.

147

"Who stood on his tail?" Newark asked and Fraza stared at him.

Newark turned and dumped himself on a sofa. "I tell you, seeing Johnson like that has totally freaked me out. Poor cow..."

As freaked out as Newark was tonight, he was to be even more freaked out tomorrow.

Falling Apart

"What's wrong with him?" Newark asked, gawking at Skinner as he tore the place apart.

Fraza's ears took a battering. "He's looking for tea."

"Where is it!" Skinner roared, slamming a cupboard door, trying to pull the whole thing off the wall.

Newark looked around, frantically. "Where's everyone else?"

"Johnson's walking on the beach," Fraza replied. "Jenna's at the government building, and Brash will be up there now, too."

Newark wished he had stayed out. Skinner was a man possessed but not by anything good. "Calm down, bud," he said in a placating voice.

Skinner's manic eyes fixed on him. "Where's the fucking tea!"

"I don't know, bud. I don't know."

Skinner strode off to tear up another room.

"Where's the fucking tea?" Newark whispered to Fraza.

"Brash took it with him. Said we'd cave."

"Damn right, we'd cave. The bloke's demented."

Newark breathed a sigh of relief when Johnson came through the back door. She wandered through the room, head down.

"Skinner's cracking up," Newark told her against a backdrop of destruction. "What do we do?"

"How long's he been like that?" she asked.

"About ten minutes," Fraza said. "He came down, looking for the tea. When he couldn't find it, he went wild."

"I'll deal with this," Johnson said.

She pulled open a cupboard door, retrieved the largest pan she could find, walked into the side room, and whacked Skinner over the head with it. Skinner dropped like a dead weight. Newark and Fraza stared at her from the doorway.

Fraza moved forward to check Skinner over. "You could have killed him," he said, looking up at her.

"He was going to give himself a seizure," she said. "Tie him up before he comes around." Turning her back on them, she wandered into the living room, and dumped herself on a sofa.

Fraza retrieved some thick string from the kitchen. He and Newark tied Skinner's arms behind his back and bound his legs.

"I could do with some fucking tea myself," Newark said, rubbing his brow. "What do we do when he comes around?"

149

"I don't know. I think we should get the others."

"Good call. Let *them* deal with this shit. Err... I'll go and get them," he said, quickly.

As Newark left, Fraza moved to the living room, stepping backwards and forwards on the threshold. He entered to find Johnson in her own world.

The woman shot to her feet. "She was a complete fucking bitch!"

"Who?" Fraza asked, rubbing his sore ears.

"My mother! God, when I think of all that shit!"

Johnson screamed in anger. Fraza retreated as she began tearing up the room. Hopelessly out of his depth, he attempted to get out of the house, his progress halted as he stepped in and out of the doorways. Escaping at last, he left the noise and madness behind him, moving down the path to the beach. Sitting on the white sand, he brought his arms around his knees and made himself into a tight ball. He couldn't cope. He needed Jenna back. The strong, resilient Jenna, the one that made *him* feel strong.

*

Flint, Brash, Jenna, and Newark arrived back at the house, looking around in shock. Debris littered the place, far more than when Newark had left. He scratched his head. A tied-up Skinner writhed on the floor in pain. In the other room, Johnson sat on the sofa, her knees up to her chin, sobbing uncontrollably.

"This is fucked up," Newark said, holding his head.

"Where's Fraza?" Brash asked.

"Looks like he's bailed."

Brash went to talk to Johnson as Flint approached Skinner. Newark followed Flint. Jenna watched on from the hallway, not knowing what to do.

"Skinner?" Flint asked. "What's wrong?"

"We're all going to die," he moaned inaudibly.

"Nobody's going to die, Skinner. Why do you think that?"

"We're going to die," he moaned again, trying desperately to curl into the foetal position.

Brash came to join Flint, looking down at Skinner. He crouched. "What's going on, Skinner?"

Skinner didn't answer. He shook violently. It reminded him of the Skinner he used to know. Realisation hit. "The programming's broken down." He turned to Flint. "That drug must have screwed his brain up. The *die a thousand deaths* programme has been wiped."

"Oh, crap," Newark said. "We're not getting the old Skinner back, are we?"

"Cornelius mentioned that," Flint said, thoughtfully. "It looks like his old response mechanisms have kicked back in with a vengeance."

"Well, how do we get rid of them?" Newark asked.

Flint looked at Skinner, perturbed. "I've no idea..."

Fraza returned, relieved to see the others at last. Brash glanced at him. The little Kaledian looked shell-shocked.

"Newark, untie him," Flint said.

"D'you think we should?" Newark asked.

"I think he's spent. Untie him."

Newark untied Skinner, bracing himself for impact. Skinner crawled into a corner and curled into a ball.

"The old Skinner was never *this* bad," Newark remarked.

"Maybe it's just hitting him," Flint said. "Everything he's done these past months."

"We'll need to keep a constant watch on him," Brash told them.

Flint stood and looked around the crew. They weren't in good shape. Skinner was a quivering mess. Fraza didn't look too good, either. Through the other door, Johnson appeared a wreck on the sofa, and Jenna, standing around like a lost soul, didn't even know who she was.

Things didn't improve as the hours passed. Skinner did not budge from his corner. Newark got a strange feeling of déjà vu as he spoon-fed the man. He'd done this once before for Brash, had promised he would never do it again, but it was this or keeping an overnight watch on him. Brash was taking the nightshift. Newark rubbed his forehead, feeling unsettled. Trot was different, Johnson was different, Skinner was different.... Even Fraza looked weird. The crew was falling apart. He consoled himself. At least, he wasn't a fucked-up mess.

Johnson and Fraza had worn themselves out, and though it was only the middle of the afternoon, they slept upstairs. Jenna kept an eye on them.

In the living room, Brash sat down, wearily. "Well, Captain Flint, do you have a plan for all this?"

"We get the elections over then we head to Marios Prime and find Cornelius. See if he can help."

"Let's hope we can find him." Brash leaned back and closed his eyes.

"How's Skinner?"

"Newark's feeding him. Not sure how much of the stuff's going in. Skinner looks shattered. Hopefully, he'll pass out then we can take him upstairs."

"That's the problem with quick fixes," Flint reflected, shaking his head. "They're like buildings with no foundations."

"Perhaps he needs a few months of therapy," Brash remarked, snidely.

Flint ignored the comment.

"You've been trying that therapy on Jenna too?" Brash kept his tone even.

"She came to me."

Brash smiled, sourly. "Quite a magnetic person now, aren't you?"

Again, Flint didn't respond. He was in no mood for a slanging match.

"Well," Brash said, "your crew's a mess. It's a good job we're nearly done here."

Flint got an alert on his communicator. Brash heard him speaking Bortten.

When Flint stood, abruptly, Brash's eyes shot open. Flint held the back of his neck, his staring eyes fixed on the floor. As he ended the communication, he looked at Brash. "We've got a big problem."

Facing Invasion

"There's a *what…?*" Brash asked.

"There's a fleet of ships approaching the planet." Flint raked a hand through his hair, his mind racing.

"Who the hell are they?"

"I don't know but I doubt they're friendly. Stands to reason they'll be heading for Hercillen. I've called in the army. We need to defend the capital, defend the government building." He strode to the door. "Jenna!" he called out.

Flint fetched a weapon from a cupboard under the stairs, and when Jenna came down, he handed it to her. "We need to see if you can still fire one of these."

He led her outside and instructed her to shoot at a chair. She handled the weapon awkwardly but when she aimed and fired, her shot was perfect. "I can use this thing…?" She stared at the weapon, mystified. Pointing the gun again, she shot up the remaining chairs. "Wow… I'm really good at this…"

Flint turned to Brash. "Take Skinner to Graham. I'll wake Johnson and Fraza. The rest of us will go to the government building. You make your way over once you've dropped Skinner off."

"Maybe we should abandon this," Brash said, shaking his head. "With Jenna out of commission, we're seriously compromised."

"We still have Fraza and an army of Bortten."

"But we don't know what firepower this approaching fleet has got. We could be sitting ducks here."

"I can't abandon the place now, Brash," Flint snapped. Drawing in a calming breath, he let it go. "If you want to leave, that's up to you but I stay. The rest of the crew can decide for themselves too."

Jenna found her voice. "Approaching fleet…?"

Flint glanced a her. "Maybe you should leave too, Jenna."

She stared at him. *Approaching fleet?*

The jaded crew assembled in the living room. When Flint told them the news, they stared at him, alarmed, apart from Skinner, who was still in his corner and being kept out of the picture.

"I'm staying, whatever," Flint told them. "But the rest of you can leave if you want to."

Johnson, who didn't care if she lived or died, and who had a lot of latent anger to discharge, told Flint she was staying. Fraza felt he had to stay as he was the one with the power. Newark wasn't going to look like a pussy.

"I'm in," he said.

Jenna's heart pounded in terror. She didn't think she could do this.

"Jenna, you should come with me," Brash said. "You're not the person you were. You're not up to this."

"Brash is right," Flint agreed.

A surge of indignance shot up in her. She was being compared to her *other* self and coming off badly. "No, I... I'll stay," she said.

"That isn't a good idea, Jenna," Flint told her.

"I can help," she insisted. "I can fire a gun."

"We have many guns," Brash said. "We don't need you."

"Yeah," Newark said, slightly miffed, "what we need is the other Jenna Trot."

Her lips twitched. *The other, more wonderful version.* Despite the terror, she wouldn't be bettered by her *better* self. "I stay," she said with conviction.

Brash frowned, exasperated.

"Stay close to me then," Flint said.

"Or me," Brash countered.

"We'll take up position near the government building," Flint told them, standing. "Get your weapons."

Brash went to fetch Skinner, his body racked with tension. This was a big job for a fully functioning crew, and this crew wasn't fully functioning.

*

Jenna's former bravery wilted as they approached the square. A fleet of craft roared over her head, ready to defend the city. She looked up, watching them circle. The sun, setting over the sea, gave the blue sky an orange hue. The beauty and terror didn't go together. Was any of this necessary?

As they turned into the square, Fraza felt himself buckle under the pressure. Troops had assembled outside the government building, more of them arriving.

Striding through the enormous plaza, Flint led them forward. Jenna had always loved open spaces. Now they made her feel like a target. The orange

154

hue of the dying sun reflected in the windows of the government building. Guns were being set up before it.

As they neared, Flint searched for the black armband. Spotting it, he approached the commander. "Your men are ready?"

Aubergine eyes fixed on him. "As ready as we'll ever be."

"Do you have any idea who is attacking us?"

The Bortten threw all six arms in the air. "You've cut off the supply of slaves. No doubt made a few disgruntled enemies."

Flint's eyes bore into him, speaking in a hard voice. "I asked you who was attacking us, not why."

"I couldn't say for sure. We've never been attacked like this before. Everything was sweet. Still, I'm sure this will be straightforward, what with you being gods and all."

Swallowing, Flint nodded. "Have you started evacuating the city?" It was a redundant question. Panicked Bortten poured into the square from a side street.

"Yes, the order to evacuate has been issued." The commander turned to one of his men. "Get them out of this area!"

Flint turned to Fraza. "Do you know how you're going to play this, Fraza?"

Fraza looked at Jenna but Jenna wasn't there anymore. This girl stood rigid, her eyes flitting all over the place. He rubbed his ears, stepping from side to side.

"What's he doing?" the commander asked.

"It's a god thing," Flint replied, perturbed. If the army found out they weren't gods, they might lynch them themselves.

*

Brash tugged Skinner along the street. It had taken enormous effort to get him out of the house, and now, the sight of Bortten sent him into meltdown.

"Get a grip, Skinner," Brash said, exasperated.

"They're hideous!" Skinner screamed.

"You've seen them before."

"These ones are like ghouls!"

"They're the same bloody ones!"

Reaching Graham's apartment, Brash banged on the door. The door opened.

"Graham, you need to take Skinner." Brash tried to push the man forward but Skinner clung to him like a barnacle.

Graham stared at Skinner in shock. "What the hell's wròng with him?"

"He's messed up. That drug has brought the old Skinner back."

"What...?"

"Listen, I haven't got much time. We're facing invasion."

"What...?"

Skinner fell to his knees, wailing, becoming demented.

Shit. Brash hadn't meant to reveal that.

"Invasion?" Graham asked.

"There's a fleet heading this way. You have to take Skinner and go."

"No, I'm coming with you."

"You need to take Skinner. The man's psychotic. They're issuing an order to evacuate. Go. Now."

"But-"

"Those are orders, Graham."

Brash couldn't prize Skinner off him, so he punched him hard in the face. As Skinner dropped, Graham caught Brash's arm. "I can't just sit this out."

"We have the army. One more gun won't do much good. I'm going to try to get Jenna to leave too. As things are, she a spare part. Take Skinner and get out of here."

Brash left Graham staring after him.

*

"Any sign of them yet?" Brash asked, striding up to Flint.

"According to our radar, they're minutes away."

"Jenna," Brash said, turning to her, "you should go now. Graham's taking Skinner out of the city. If you hurry, you'll catch up with them."

She looked around, nervously, the offer tempting.

"We don't need you here," he said. "You may as well go."

The words cut into her. "No," she asserted. "I stay."

He blew out an angry breath, "You're still as bloody obstinate."

Raking a hand through his hair, he looked around. Flint had situated them away from the government building, further down the square, Bortten troops stationed at other points. The size of the square gave an expansive view of the sky. They would see them coming. His eyes moved to the anti-aircraft guns, standing ready before the government building.

Brash wondered how effective they were. Maybe they should have increased the defence budget. He looked at their own weapons. Flint had requisitioned the best arsenal for the crew. These weapons had long and short-range settings, nowhere near as effective as the big guns, but they could do *some* damage.

He turned to Fraza. "You ready, Fraza?"

Fraza nodded, not ready at all. He tried to calm himself. This all rode on him. He missed Jenna so much it hurt.

Above, fighters moved into attack formation, roaring away from them. Johnson paid them no mind. She pictured Graham leaving the city with his new girlfriend, starting a new life without her. Her lips tightened and her face turned hard. She hoisted her weapon, ready to rumble.

"Here they come," Newark said, peering at dots in the distance.

Fraza drew in a deep breath, and focused, recalling words Jenna had spoken to him. *A blank mind is a canvas for creation. No space, no time. No from or to. Just the power and intent. No you, Fraza.*

Emptying his mind, he removed himself. There was just the power and intent. He intended shields around the Bortten craft.

Dog fights began in the distance. The shields held, the enemy craft taking hits.

"They're not getting through," Newark said, smugly.

Johnson watched, vaguely disappointed. She needed to kill something.

Flint studied Fraza. The Kaledian's eyes were closed, his body still. No ear-rubbing at all. His gaze moved back to the sky, hope building.

Unfortunately, Fraza couldn't keep it together. His mind interfered. *How long can I hold this for? I'm on my own now.* He tried to push the thoughts away, tried to return to emptiness.

The first Bortten craft nose-dived to earth. Then another.

"We're taking hits," Brash said.

Fraza heard, and his confidence nosedived too. Soon, the enemy got through. The army and the crew prepared.

Enemy craft descended, letting off rounds, chewing up stone flags. Johnson and Newark went berserk, firing like crazy. Brash and Flint were with them, but Jenna stood, frozen, a thought looping in her head. *I'm going to die as I've lived, a complete and utter failure...* Something in the depths of her raged against it. She lifted her weapon and fired, shooting the thought down.

Fraza managed to knock a craft out of the air. It plummeted toward the sea, but it had taken a lot of effort, and he knew he wasn't making a dent.

"Get back!" Flint shouted, shoving them into a doorway as a craft swooped low, reining fire. Bortten bodies flew as it carpet-bombed the square.

The commander watched in horror, wondering why their gods weren't protecting them. He got the niggling feeling they weren't gods, after all.

"I can't do this," Fraza moaned, helplessly. "I need Jenna."

"I'm here," Jenna said.

"You're not Jenna," he shot.

The words, like bullets, wounded her. Hurt turned to anger. "Well, you're stuck with me, so stop moaning and get on with it! Can't you do anything without her? What is she, your bloody mother!"

"Well said," Newark called out. "Now grow a dick, Fraza!"

Fraza was past growing a dick. He'd put too many barriers in his way. The enemy fleet eviscerated the city. The Bortten army fired like crazy but enemy firepower proved way superior. The square got shredded. Building fronts exploded. Soldiers ran for cover as casualties mounted.

"We need to go," Brash yelled, ducking to avoid shrapnel. "It's over, Flint! We need to get the hell out of here!"

Silence fell as the carnage abruptly stopped. A loud voice blasted over a speaker. "Give up the usurpers and no-one will be harmed." The message came in Bortten. "We have no wish to take over the planet, merely overthrow the government that has overthrown your government."

The commander, seeing his heavy losses, and angry these so-called gods had failed them, walked out with his six hands held high. Above him, an enemy craft came down.

"Run," Flint shouted.

Skirting the buildings, they charged down the square, but Bortten soldiers blocked their path, pointing weapons at them. Staring at the guns, they turned to see knobbly-headed troops emerge from the craft. The Bortten commander spoke to a guy at the front, before pointing their way.

Their only hope was Fraza, but Fraza rubbed his ears, chanting Kaledian words, over and over. The guy had lost it.

"Should we take a few with us," Johnson spat.

"Put down your weapons," Flint ordered.

"They'll kill us."

"This way we stand a chance."

Reluctantly, they put their weapons down.

The knobbly-headed leader approached with the commander, eyeing the group of them up. "So, these are the fearful gods," he said, vaguely amused.

Newark stared at the guy. Had he been in a fire? The reddened skin looked burnt.

"Tell me, how did you manage this coup?" the alien asked, intrigued.

Though the alien spoke Bortten, Flint offered no reply. All their hard work had been for nothing, and whatever they faced now couldn't be good.

"Should I order my men to fire?" the commander spat with disdain.

"No, they owe me," the alien said. "They should fetch an excellent price."

The commander nodded to his men, and the Bortten soldiers stepped forward, knocking the crew out with the butts of their weapons.

Strange Things

The crew woke up with banging heads, trying to make sense of where they were. Metal walls surrounded them.

"Is everyone alright?" Brash asked.

They nodded, morosely. Flint didn't nod. He wasn't alright. He was devastated. Draztis would return to being a slave traders paradise, and what this crew now faced didn't bear thinking about. He had failed them, failed everyone. He should have prepared for this eventuality, but he hadn't.

Brash raked a hand through his hair. "Well, Flint, this is a right mess you've got us into."

"He gave us the option to leave," Jenna pointed out.

"Why are you always defending him?" Brash asked, exasperated.

"I'm just pointing out the truth."

"I'm sorry," Flint mumbled. "I failed."

"Damn right, you failed," Brash spat.

"Of course, he failed," Jenna retorted, angrily. "Probably because he was doing it all himself. Perhaps he should have foreseen this but shouldn't you have foreseen this too? You've been captain a long time. He hasn't."

"But *he's* captain," Brash shot.

"But *you* could have shared your experience with him. You didn't see this either, and you should have."

"I take responsibility," Flint said.

"Yes, you would, but I'm not letting him put all this on you."

Flint's eyes moved her. No matter how much she changed, her irrepressible spirit remained in place.

She smiled at him.

The smile stoked Brash's anger. "You don't know what you're talking about. You don't even remember who you are!"

Jenna glared at him. "I can see what's right in front of me. Can see you're the same obnoxious captain you've always been."

Brash stared at her, winded. Is *that* what she saw...?

Noises in the corridor shifted their focus. Brash looked at Fraza. The Kaledian was in his own compulsive-driven world, nodding his head and muttering. Even Newark and Johnson didn't look up for a fight.

Doors opened. Knobbly-headed guards strode in, motioning with their weapons.

161

Escorted through metal corridors, they emerged from a spacecraft under a pale green sky. They were on an airbase. Butts of weapons shoved them forward to a line of smaller craft. Already, Jenna and Johnson were being separated off.

"We stay together," Brash shouted, earning him a crack over the head.

"We'll find you," Flint called, earning him a crack too.

"Why are we being split up?" Newark whispered.

Flint didn't want to voice the answer to that. He stared at Jenna, who stared back at him.

Bundled into separate craft, they flew off in different directions.

*

"I think these are holding stations," Flint said, looking around the wooden walls. The tiny windows provided meagre light. "They'll be deciding what to do with us."

"Do with us?" Newark asked.

Flint stared at him. "You do realise we're slaves now, don't you?"

"Slaves? I ain't no goddam slave! I thought this was a prison. How are we going to break out of here?"

"The guard is too strong. It's not the best option to try to escape now. And Fraza's still out of commission." He glanced at the Kaledian.

Brash looked at him too. Fraza's hands fidgeted wildly, scratching his ears at intervals, his eyes staring at the floor.

"Fraza," Newark said, crouching before him. "Pull your shit together. We need your freaky magic to get us out of here."

"I failed," Fraza groaned. "I let Jenna down."

"Stop wallowing in misery and pull off some shit!"

"Leave him, Newark," Brash said, becoming more concerned about Fraza. "He can't focus."

*

Jenna and Johnson were housed in more luxurious accommodation, the building like a spa. They'd been pampered, had their hair done, and been given a facial. Their nails had been trimmed, and they now wore long white, sleeveless gowns. Painted murals lined the spacious room they

162

shared with five others. Quilts covered the beds. Elegantly furniture dotted the place. A couple of roman couches perched in the centre.

"Why do you think they're treating us so well?" Jenna asked.

"Seriously?" Johnson asked, staring at her. "You haven't figured it out yet?"

"Figured what out?"

"We're going to be pimped off."

"Pimped off?"

"We're whores now, Trot."

"What...?" Jenna stared at her, horrified. "I... I can't be a whore... I'm a virgin! I don't want to be a whore!"

"Well, you're not a virgin, remember? And d'you think I want slimy alien hands all over me? Not to mention whatever else..."

"Oh my god..." Jenna said, holding her head. "This is like a bad dream..." She looked at Johnson. "What are we going to do?"

"Well, the old Jenna Trot would have got us out of this but we're stuck with you."

Jenna glared at her. "The old Jenna had magical powers, didn't she? Must be easy when you can do anything!"

"She was fun too."

"I'm fun!"

Johnson rolled her eyes. She sniffed. "She was cool. I miss her."

"She's me!"

Johnson looked at her. "No, she's not."

Fuming, Jenna stared at the quilted bedcover. It was like she had a twin sister that was better at everything than her. She was jealous. *How could she feel jealous of herself?* Easy. This other Jenna had remarkable powers. No wonder she was cool. Who wouldn't be cool with remarkable powers? Everything must be effortless when you can do anything. She almost detested this other her. *How could she detest herself...?* Well, the other Jenna Trot had it easy, she decided. This one was going to have to get by with more than remarkable powers... if she didn't want slimy alien hands roaming all over her.

She didn't speak to Johnson for the rest of the day and, in the morning, they were taken to market. Low platforms surrounded a busy square. Sandy stone, roman-like buildings looked down on them. The pale green sky didn't stop it being sunny. Those ugly, knobbly-headed creatures milled around the platforms. They wore long loose gowns - the men's gowns having full shoulders, the women's with shoulder straps. All revealed too much skin. The reddish-brown hue and uneven texture reminded Jenna of burned bacon. Her stomach turned over.

Various species in pretty dresses stood on the platforms. Jenna didn't think the dress did anything for the creature on the opposite platform. It had a trunk and the dress made it look ridiculous. Still, it attracted a lot of attention from prospective buyers. Her thoughts cut off as hands touched her legs. She slapped them away.

The knobby-headed alien laughed. "She's going to be fun," he remarked to the agent, turning his attention to Johnson. Johnson glared at him, threateningly. "I think she's going to be fun too. I'll take them both."

"They're a rare species, so very expensive."

"I don't care. I want them both. You know I'm good for it."

The deal was done. Johnson and Jenna were sold.

"No way am I sleeping with that thing," Johnson whispered to Jenna as they were taken down off the platform. "Let's see if we can make a break for it."

Unfortunately, their buyer came with three weapon-toting creatures as ugly as him. Jenna and Johnson got bundled into a vehicle and air-lifted away.

Jenna's heart hammered. She sneaked a peek at one of the creatures. Its slit eyes travelled over Johnson, the knobbles on its head highlighted by its lack of hair. She took in the burnt-looking flesh, wondering if the whole body looked like that. She shuddered, turning to look out of the window.

The vehicle flew over a sprawling city. Beyond the centre, a collection of poky dwellings tumbled over each other. Further out, leafy areas contained grand, regal villas. In the distance, she saw a craft descending, coming in to land in the city. But they ascended, until she stared at a grand stone villa, sitting atop a steep, high hill.

Landing in grounds behind it, the aliens motioned for them to disembark. As they stepped out of the craft, they saw two guards sitting on benches outside the villa entrance.

"He must be someone important," Johnson remarked to Jenna, realising it wasn't going to be an easy escape.

Their buyer walked on ahead of them. One of the guards motioned for them to enter the villa.

The air was cooler inside, the wide main corridor painted with impressive frescos and lined with ugly statues. Their guard prodded them to keep moving forward. Light and heat hit them as they walked out over a spacious courtyard. Water tumbled from a fountain in the centre. A knobbly-headed servant watered colourful arrangements of potted flowers. He turned, looking them over as they passed by.

The wide corridor continued beyond the courtyard but they didn't reach the end. Prodded to move left onto a narrower corridor, they turned right into a scruffy, undecorated passageway. Reaching the end, they got deposited in a basic room. As the door closed behind them, they looked around. The room had two beds and bars on the window. Johnson tried the door. It was locked.

"This is our prison," she said, rubbing her forehead. She looked at Jenna. "Try and break the bars."

"Are you serious...?"

"Just give it a go."

Jenna looked at the bars but no matter what she tried, they wouldn't budge.

Johnson shook her head and dumped herself on the bed.

"Stop looking so disappointed in me," Jenna shot. "You can't break the bars, either."

Johnson said nothing.

"What's going to happen now?" Jenna asked, drawing her arms around her.

Johnson didn't answer.

Jenna sat on the other bed, staring at the bars.

A few minutes later, a knobbly-headed female appeared, gesturing for Jenna to join her. Jenna looked at Johnson.

"You can fight, Trot," Johnson said. "Bear that in mind."

"I can?"

"Cornelius taught you. You were good at it too."

The woman made frantic movements with her arms. Jenna shook her head, so the woman stepped back, and two armed guards appeared, motioning with their weapons. Reluctantly, Jenna stood. Following the woman to a nearby room, she stared at a steaming bath tub. The woman pointed for her to get in. Jenna knew what this was about and her mind scrambled for a way out of it. The woman pestered her to get in and eventually she did, her mind working overtime.

When she climbed out, a fresh white dress got thrown at her. Her body shook as she fumbled to put it on.

The armed guards waited outside the door. The woman led her through the villa, over shiny mosaic floors, the two guards following behind them. Jenna wrapped her arms around her middle. The thought of that creature touching her made her want to throw up.

Entering a large, expensively-decorated bedchamber, she was taken out onto a wide terrace where the vile-looking creature waited. The spectacular view of the city behind him barely registered.

He turned, his slit eyes lighting up.

165

"Look, I'm not doing this," she insisted, and he gazed at her, confused. "Does no-one speak English here?" She looked around to find the guards and woman gone.

"I haven't got a clue what you're saying but you look so devilishly appealing." He came forward and stroked the side of her face. She knocked his hand away.

He laughed. "I've sampled many creatures but I've never tried a human before." His anticipation mounted. Placing his hands on her shoulders, he tried to lower the straps of her gown.

She twisted out of his grasp. "I'm not doing this!" she shrieked.

Her wildness only served to excite him. Grabbing her wrist, he pulled her toward the bed. She dug her nails into his disgusting flesh, drawing a brownish-coloured blood. The alien looked at the damage she'd done, and a deadly passion arose in him. Slapping her face hard, he grabbed her with both hands, and tossed her on the bed, his slit eyes wide with excitement.

She seethed with desperate fury. Fury like she'd never known before. With every fibre of her being, she wanted to hurt him. A chair flew across the room, the alien dodging it, before it smashed against the wall. He stared at the chair. Jenna stared at it too.

Backing away, the alien shouted, and the guards ran in, the three of them entering into a confused discussion. Heart thumping wildly, Jenna shot up, searching for a way out. She ran to the edge of the terrace, staring at the steep drop. She made a dash for the door but one of the guards caught her and flung her back on the bed.

The three aliens talked some more. One of the guards lifted the chair, taking it with him as both guards left.

Her tormentor turned to her, ready to pick up where he'd left off. His vile, lustful eyes fixed her as he stalked forward. Helpless rage exploded in her chest. She wanted to kill him, wanted him to suffer horribly. She had never wanted anything so badly. An object flew through the air, lodging in the alien's privates. He doubled-up, screaming in agony. Jenna stared at him. What that a letter opener? The guard came running back in. The alien clutched his groin, howling in agony, his white gown stained a sickly brown. As the guards attended to him, Jenna looked around, fearfully. Was this place haunted? A more comforting thought arose. Was the ghost trying to protect her?

The guards shouted for back-up, and more came running in, some hands grabbing her, others lifting the writhing, bleeding man.

As the injured alien got carted off, Jenna was taken down town to be locked up with a disparate and scary bunch of cell-mates, whose eyes never left her. She huddled in a corner, watching them fearfully, hoping the

166

puddles on the floor were water. Fortunately, the torture didn't last too long. Two Reglons picked her up, and returned her to the house, depositing her in her jail room.

Johnson sat up, looking at her, concerned. "Did he...?"

"No. But don't ask me what happened because I've no idea..."

Jenna explained the strange series of events.

"That wasn't a ghost, Trot. That was you."

"What...?"

"Yeah. It used to come out unconsciously before you learned to control it."

Jenna stared at her.

"Well," Johnson said, leaning back, pleased, "you've put him out of commission for a while. Good one. It'll give us time to figure out an escape plan."

"That was me...?" Jenna asked.

*

The injured Reglon, a high-ranking city governor, would be laid up in bed for several days, and out of commission for weeks. He'd secured his slave's release by reporting the incident a freakish accident. Secretly, he started to believe in ghosts. These were strange things. He hadn't mentioned this to anyone but he didn't sleep soundly at night.

His fearful thoughts preyed on him. He needed to communicate with that slave.

Jenna got called up again but this time she didn't get a bath, and she knew the alien's parts would not be in working order for some time.

As she entered his chamber, another alien stood in the room, fiddling with a slim device that made high-pitched sounds. He looked up briefly, pointing for her to sit on the bedside chair. Glancing at the bed-ridden alien, she did. The other guy kept talking into the device, and all manner of weird noises came out of it. They sounded like different languages until, at last, she heard words that made her eyes widen. English?

"Tell me when you understand me," the alien said.

"I understand you," Jenna replied.

"At last." He passed the device to the governor.

"What is that?" Jenna asked.

"A translator," the governor replied. "You may go now," he said to the other man. As the door closed, he turned to Jenna. "I need to communicate with you. The day of the... accident... did you see anything peculiar?"

Jenna considered how best to play this. She could use this to her advantage.

"Actually..." she said, thoughtfully, a plan formulating, "I thought I saw a strange shadow in the corner of the room." The slit eyes widened. "Yes. A dark, sinister-looking shadow. I thought I'd imagined it."

The governor rubbed his knobby brow, looking extremely worried.

Jenna pressed on. "People have said I am psychic. I pick up on these things." She leaned forward, whispering conspiratorially. "I have the feeling this place harbours dark secrets."

"Dark secrets? What kind of dark secrets?"

"I don't know. I get this ominous feeling. My father was psychic too. He used to help people get rid of... unpleasant things."

"You think there might be more than one ghost here?"

Jenna nodded. "I think the place is teeming with them."

He stared at her, horrified. "Can you help us get rid of them?"

She looked him straight in the eye. "Yes. In exchange for my freedom and that of my friend."

"Your freedom? Do you know how much I paid for you?"

She shrugged. "Well, it's up to you."

The governor's expression hardened. "You're mine. Body, mind, and soul. You'll get rid of the damn things, and your reward will be that I carry on feeding you! Do you understand me!"

She left the room, defeated.

Johnson listened to Jenna's report. "Well, maybe you have to up the ante."

"What d'you mean?"

Johnson sat up. "Make the place so haunted, he'll be begging to give you our freedom."

"But I can't control the power, can I?"

"No, but you can get angry. Imagine stuff that makes you angry. Make strange bumps in the night." Johnson smiled. "We could have fun with this. And, if he folds and grants you our freedom, we won't be hunted. It'll be a clean break."

"But don't I have to be in the area where stuff happens? We don't get let out of this room much."

Johnson frowned. "I don't know... Perhaps you could imagine yourself in another part of the house, picturing that creep doing sick shit to you.

Picture the guards doing sick shit to you too." Jenna stared at her and Johnson shrugged. "You've got nothing to lose by giving it a try."

Jenna lay back, wondering if this could work. She'd wait until nightfall.

As stars appeared in the window, she closed her eyes. In her mind's eye, she took herself back to that creature's bedchamber, bringing it into vivid focus, imagining she was there, imagining that creep doing nasty things to her. She worked herself into a murderous frenzy. Taking her attention to a different part of the villa, she imagined the guards doing the same. Hate-filled fury consumed her.

At last, she had to stop. She was giving herself a seizure. Sounds of shouting drifted down the corridor

She and Johnson sat up.

The door burst open and a wide-eyed guard barged in.

Ghost-Busting

"Culli," the man urged, motioning for Jenna to follow.

"You're on," Johnson said, smiling to herself.

Jenna stood and followed him along passageways to find the household in disarray. Servants cowered in the dark courtyard. Guards loitered there too, holding their useless weapons. Other knobbly-headed beings stood around in a wide-eyed daze. The governor hobbled toward her with his translator. "We need your help," he said, staring at her, intently.

"Do we get our freedom?"

"You're my slaves! You do what I say!"

Jenna summoned some exasperated fury, and pots smashed against columns. The household screamed, banding closer together.

"I do it if we get our freedom," she bravely maintained, staring him hard in the eye. Inwardly, she braced herself to be struck.

The governor glared at her but he paused for thought, turning briefly to the shell-shocked faces around him. He let out a defeated sigh. "OK, but you stay until all the strange things have gone. When we are free of this for weeks, then you can leave."

"I need a legally binding document," she asserted.

"Fine," he threw out.

"Attend to that first thing."

"OK. Just sort this out."

She wandered through corridors, pretending to scope the place out, the governor following warily.

"What's your name," she decided to ask.

"My name...?"

"My name is Jenna. And yours?"

"Flaydir," he replied, looking at her, oddly.

She didn't think there was anything odd about wanting to be treated with respect. If she wasn't getting it, she was going to ask for it.

Affecting a serious expression, she moved in and out of rooms, placing her hands in front of her, speaking strange words she made up. Inwardly, she smiled, smugly. She'd managed to secure their freedom. How amazing was that?

"What are you doing?" Flaydir asked.

"I'm seeking out energies," she replied. "Seeing where they are."

"How are you going to get rid of them?"

"Let me worry about that."

Over the next few days, she wandered around the villa as if haunting the place herself. In the meantime, a legally binding document was drawn up. The disturbances settled down, and the occupants slept easier in their beds. Flaydir talked to her at intervals, coming to view her as more than just a slave.

"Do all humans have this gift?" he asked.

"No. It's a rare gift."

"I see..."

"So, what do you do?" she asked, glancing at him.

"I am a city governor."

"What's this city called? In fact, what planet am I on?"

"The planet is Juyra. This city is Pyshirian. It's the second largest city on the planet," he boasted.

"It's not the capital?"

"No. Iprian is slightly bigger but not by much."

"And what do you govern?"

"I run the finance department."

"Budgets and stuff?"

"Yes, you hogas tart-"

Jenna turned to him. He adjusted his box, picking up where he left off. "You know about budgets?"

"A little. I... worked in government too."

"You did?" he asked, studying her curiously.

"Yes." She exaggerated, she knew, but it felt good to be well-thought of, even if it was by a slave owning rapist. She rubbed her brow. Was she that desperate for respect? She didn't like *that* at all. What did Flint say? Getting to a point where others' opinions didn't matter. She was so far from that point.

As the quiet nights continued, Flaydir became more talkative. Even Johnson was allowed out of the room, until she would often be seen loafing around the place.

"Whatever you're doing seems to be working," Flaydir said to Jenna, pleased. "Why don't you take a break. Come and have lunch with me."

He led her to a lavishly decorated sitting room, and out onto a terrace. She gazed over the city, and the sun-bathed land beyond it, all set beneath a pale green sky. Here under other circumstances, the stunning view would have captivated her.

A table had been laid and they sat down. Flaydir smiled at her, pleasantly. She tensed. He walked erect again, and she wondered if he was in good-working order. As lunch progressed, she got the feeling that was not what he had in mind.

"You're not your average slave," he remarked.

"I'm not a slave at all. I was kidnapped."

"I see. Very unfortunate," he said with a quick smile.

"Very."

"So, you worked in government?"

"Well, I only worked there for a short time." *Please don't ask any involved questions.*

"And you know about budgets?"

"A little."

"I've been looking through some paperwork as I've been laid up, and I'm having a problem balancing the books." He reached behind him and grabbed a file. "Perhaps you could help me."

Crap. Now he would find out what a complete imbecile she was. She'd only done filing. "I'm sure you don't need my help," she said, feebly.

"Nobody in my department can find the problem. You see, the totals on the paperwork don't match the revenue, but I can't see where the shortfall is."

"Well, I'd love to help but I won't be able to understand the language."

"I've managed to get all the revenue forms transcribed into your English. You're such a genius when it comes to ghosts, I thought you might be a genius at this too."

"I'm not sure the logic works out."

Maintaining the smile, his slit eyes remained on her. "Well, it took our translators an age to transcribe it all, so I'd appreciate it if you could take a look."

"OK," she said in a high-pitched voice, knowing they'd wasted a colossal amount of time.

She took the file and retired to her room, knowing Flaydir was going to be disappointed in the morning, and she would look like a fool.

As she stared at the papers, her mind went blank, the figures becoming blurry nothings.

"What you doing?" Johnson asked, ambling into the room.

"I've no idea..." She looked up at her. "He's asked me to look over this paperwork but I haven't got a clue."

"I thought you were the ghost-buster, not the accountant?"

"So, did I. I've no idea what I'm doing."

"What you panicking for? Look at the stuff. If you fix it, great. If not, who gives a fuck? We've got our freedom anyway."

Jenna stared at Johnson. Looking back at the papers, she realised she wasn't as concerned with the governor's opinion as she was with her own. Her self-esteem couldn't take another battering. She also realised nobody had been able to solve this problem, so, even if she failed, she wouldn't have done worse than anyone else.

Examining the paperwork, she stayed up long after Johnson had fallen asleep. At last, she noticed something.

In the morning, she explained her findings to Flaydir. "The figures do balance," she said. "The figures at the front on many of these returns seem higher because..." She turned the page over. "If you notice this section overleaf, a certain proportion of the revenue has been deducted. I think they've called it a building allowance? But the letters are tiny and it's sort of buried in the notes. Anyway, this is the discrepancy. If you take that into account, the figures match. This has happened on a lot of them."

The governor stared at the paperwork. "You're right. That's the discrepancy."

"So, the totals generated by the system are correct." Jenna looked at the governor. He stared ahead, distantly. "So, why have they put it on the back then?"

"Building allowances were scrapped last year..."

"Wouldn't this have been questioned when the payment was processed? Who processes payment?"

"My department..." Flaydir rubbed his forehead. "I attend meetings mostly. The operational work I leave to my team... who are a bunch of corrupt, extorting, bastards! They've been taking payments to let others fiddle the system!"

Over the days to come, the governor was kept busy, sacking his department and filing prosecution orders. Jenna felt pretty pleased with herself. In such a short space of time, she had secured their freedom and uprooted a corrupt finance department. It was one in the eye for the other Jenna Trot.

*

Flint, Brash, Newark, and Fraza laboured in the fields under a pale green sky. Flint thought about Jenna and the awful things she must have endured by now. The thought of it crushed him. Brash had similar thoughts, knowing the old Jenna wouldn't be able to handle it. He swallowed hard, knowing what a mess she'd be. As yet, they'd had no opportunity to escape. There were too many weapons trained on them and Fraza... God knows where Fraza was. He barely spoke, if not to chant strange repetitive words that sounded like gibberish. His face was black and blue from being hit so much. The guards didn't understand or care that he broke off to do strange rituals because he had too.

"We're going to have to chance it," Newark said.

"We chance it, we die," Brash told him.

"I'd rather die than do this shit any longer."

The crew looked up. An elaborate open-topped carriage rode by, carrying couple of Reglons, and a more beautiful being."

"I wonder who *she* is?" Newark asked, gazing in wonder.

A fluid sleek mane of long black hair fell down her slender back. Her skin glowed with a silvery sheen.

"Could be a slave," Brash mused, staring at her, entranced. He wasn't usually this affected by beauty but the woman bewitched him.

"I doubt they'd treat a slave so well," Flint said. "And look at her bearing and posture. That's no slave."

The guards yelled at them, whacking them over their heads. The carriage stopped and the beauty shouted over at the guards. She stepped out and walked toward them, her walk devastatingly alluring.

She approached Brash and touched his face, examining it. The touch sent tingles through his body. His eyes were glued to her. So were Newark's. The only repulsive thing about her was her six fingers, but in a world of knobbly-headed Reglons, Newark could overlook six fingers.

"Are you OK?" she asked Brash, her lips not matching the sounds.

"You can transfer thoughts, read minds?" Brash asked.

"I am a Sentier." Her head tilted as she studied his handsome face. "You are human, are you not?"

"Yes," he replied, gazing at her pearlescent grey eyes.

"You need attending to," she said, leading him away.

Flint and Newark watched him go.

"Your face looks more of a mess than his," Newark remarked, sourly. "Mine's aching like mad."

Newark got hit again and his face ached even more.

As the carriage drove away, Brash stared at the Sentier, feeling like he was falling in love.

Love Spent

The Sentier led him into the plantation house, a sprawling stone villa. Brash couldn't keep his eyes off her. Her dark mane shone. Her slim, perfectly-proportioned body moved with grace and elegance. He didn't notice the mosaic-stone floor, or the impressive murals on the walls. He barely noticed the servants bowing to her, graciously.

She led him into a luxuriously furnished room. Sitting him on a quilted bed, she attended to his face... using her hands alone. He stared at her, too absorbed to ask questions, lost in those pearls of grey light.

After she'd seen to his face, she gently pushed him back, her lips connecting with his. He couldn't think, the feel of her lips, paradise. Was he dreaming...? His arms came around her. He rolled her over as the kiss became heated. Blood pumped through his veins. His heart pounded, senses bursting to life. She pulled at his shirt and he knelt up to tear it off, before unfastening her thin chiffon dress. Clothes discarded, their skin pressed together, his body melting into hers. He kissed every inch of her, imbibing her jasmine scent, the soft sounds she made, sheer poetry. His hands touched and explored, her body yielding beneath him.

She rolled on top of him, taking control, her lips and fingers working magic. His chest rose and fell. His eyes squeezed shut, pleasure wrecking him. *Christ, this woman was good.* It was too much. He could wait no longer. He brought her onto her back, his heated gaze raking over her as he entered Eden... and was transported out of time...

As they fell back, spent, Brash stared at the ceiling.

"I love sleeping with humans," she breathed out, satisfied.

"You've met other humans...?" he managed.

"Humans are rare in this region but I have travelled extensively."

He turned to her. "Who are you...? What's your name?" He bit his lip. "Perhaps I should have asked you that first."

She smiled, serenely. "My name is Allessa. I am a Sentier."

"A Sentier?"

"We are like... empaths, psychics. We are highly valued and honoured on certain planets." She smiled again, breathtakingly. "We never have to worry about food and board. We are allowed to stay where we like. At the moment, I am staying here because the family are having trouble with their youngest son. I am helping him."

"You're sort of a therapist?" he asked, still taking in the incredible vision before him.

"Our therapy works at a deeper level. At the energetic level." Brash looked at her, lost, but it didn't matter. Nothing mattered, lying here beside her. "And," she said, smiling, "we have lots of energy ourselves."

She rose over him, and the heavenly experience began all over. This woman knew what she was doing. Her fingers seemed to have fingers... unimaginable bliss.

He entered into a night of unquenchable passion.

*

In the morning, Brash was taken back to the fields, stiff and aching. The wonderful memories took the discomfort away. Newark kept looking over at him, and when they got back to their grotty barracks, he gave Brash the third degree.

Brash didn't need the third degree. The words spilled out of him. "She's amazing... We made love all night..."

"You lucky bastard," Newark said. "All night?"

Brash nodded, reflectively.

"Aren't you worried Jenna will find out?" Flint asked, studying him, thoughtfully.

Brash's eyes widened. He'd forgotten about Jenna. "I'm not with Jenna at the moment, am I?" he spat, conflicted. Brash glared at Flint, realising the man knew too many of his secrets.

"How long is she staying?" Newark asked. "D'you think she'd like a variety whilst she's here? You could put in a good word for me."

Brash didn't like the thought of that at all, but Newark lived in hope.

Newark's hopes were dashed the next day when Brash was summoned to see Allessa again. And it was another mind-blowing experience. One he was becoming fiercely addicted to.

Weeks flew by like this; all thoughts of escape pushed from his mind. His only thought was when she would summon him next. Their love-making was insatiable, but they talked in the breaks. Brash discovered the Sentier came from a planet called Lixia. They were born with their gifts and, in order to develop them further, they had a very disciplined training. Allessa, as intrigued by Brash, found his account of the past year gripping. He told her about Jenna, though he neglected to mention what they'd been to each other.

"You did all that and now you are a slave?"

"We were kidnapped."

"Oh... I wish I could help you. We have a lot of influence but... It is assumed we will not interfere with matters of commerce. If I free one slave, I could free many and then..."

The fact he was a slave didn't matter at that moment. Nothing mattered.

It mattered very much to Flint. Flint's thoughts were consumed with Jenna and the suffering she must be going through. He needed to think harder of a plan to break out. There must be some weakness he could exploit. At last, he decided it was Brash. Brash had mentioned Allessa's healing abilities. He would use this.

As they laboured in the fields the following day, Flint drew his scythe across his leg. "Ah!" he cried out in genuine pain.

"What've you done, you stupid fuck?" Newark asked.

"I've nearly chopped my leg off! Get help!"

Flint hoped to god they didn't send him back to the barracks in agony. The guards appeared, standing over him, poking his leg and extracting more cries. Brash turned to the guards. "Allessa," he impressed on them, saying her name over and over.

Cottoning on, they fetched the Sentier. Allessa instructed the guards to bring Flint to the villa. Brash's prayers got answered when he was brought along too.

Cooler inside, Flint detected the sweet smell of incense. He noted every passageway as he got carted through the elaborately decorated building. Servants ran after them, wiping blood off the tiles. They directed Allessa to an unoccupied guest room, and the guards placed Flint on a quilted bed.

"I will see to him," Allessa said, dismissing the guards and the servants.

Brash gazed at her as she placed her hands over Flint's leg and worked her magic. He moved to the window, staring over yellow fields, praying she would take him to her bed. He indulged in a fantasy, where he was the landowner here, and she was his wife.

Flint's face screwed up in pain. He kept his mind blank. She couldn't know what he planned. As the pain faded, his face relaxed.

She smiled at him, serenely. "The leg is healed," she told him.

"Thank you," Flint mumbled, his eyes purposefully heavy. "D'you think they'd let me rest here for a while?"

She assessed him. "I will see to it."

She left the room to sort it out. Returning, checking on Flint briefly, she took Brash's hand, and led him to her room.

After hours of love-making, Brash and Allessa pulled themselves apart, and went to check on Flint. They opened the guest room door to find the room glaringly empty.

"Escaped?" Newark asked, dumbfounded.

"It was all a ploy," Brash said.

"And the bastard left us *behind...?* Some captain!"

"He must have spied an opportunity and taken it."

"You've had tons of opportunities! You didn't leave us behind!"

Brash scratched his ear.

"That bastard," Newark said, shaking his head. "I bet she got into trouble too."

"No. The Sentier are treated like gods here."

"Yeah, I remember what that was like..." Newark rubbed his brow. "So, how are *we* going to get out then?"

Brash frowned. "Well, we can't copy Flint. They'll be wise to that now. Leave it with me. I'll think of something."

Newark waited for Brash's plan but days turned to weeks and the plan did not come forth.

Until Brash made a colossal mistake. He told Allessa he loved her. The grey eyes fixed him, staring at him for a long while. "I... do not do love, Lucas. I do sex."

"But don't you have feelings for me?"

"I have favoured you more than any mate. That is all I can say."

Though disappointed, Brash decided that was a good start. She had feelings for him. She just didn't want to admit it. His optimism, however, dwindled as days passed and she didn't summon him again. When he saw her riding away, he ran after the carriage. "Allessa!" he called.

A weapon swung at his chest like iron bar. He dropped. Through the winding pain, he raised his head, staring after the carriage.

Back in the barracks, he nursed a broken heart and bruised ribs. He looked at Newark. "Let's get out of this shit-hole."

A Fortunate Coincidence

The day of their release finally arrived. Before they left, Jenna asked the governor how they might find their friends.

"They could be anywhere on the planet," he said. "I could make enquiries but it will take time."

"Well, I would be grateful if you could. The other option is to set off and go looking for them."

"You can't go wandering around the planet. Many regions aren't safe. Inhabited by wild people. At one time, we tried to capture them, turn them into slaves." Jenna frowned at him. "The thing is, they're fierce. They fight to the death and have no fear of death. Ones we did manage to capture, killed themselves. It was a useless endeavour. And, if you survive the wild men, you have to watch out for poisonous plants. Some of the plant-life here is nasty."

Jenna's eyes lingered on him. "Well, if you could help find them, we would be grateful. I'll make sure you get our new address."

The governor gave them a translator and cash to find lodgings in the city. Jenna and Johnson were very appreciative until they found the cash would only buy one week's rent in a poky and virtually uninhabitable hole. The place sat squashed between two other uninhabitable holes and was a far cry from the villas of the rich.

"Stingy arse," Johnson complained. "He must be bloody loaded."

"I'll go and give him our address. Let's hope he gets information soon."

"Well, if we're staying here for a while, we need to earn money."

"How are we going to do that?"

Johnson shrugged. Then an idea occurred to her. "Perhaps we could go into business doing what you do best."

"What's that?"

"Ghost-busting." Johnson grinned. "Could be lucrative. We'll get started tonight."

As night descended, so did chaos. They picked an affluent part of the city, wandering past grand villas. Using her imagination, Jenna whipped up some fury but they didn't hear any bumps or sounds of commotion.

"Why's it not working?" Johnson asked.

"I can't take myself into a house I haven't been in. I can't imagine what I've never seen."

"Right, so we need to break in then. Leave it to me."

"Err... Do you think we should be doing that?"

Johnson turned to her. "You're OK extorting money under false pretences, but we shouldn't break in? Get real, Trot."

"I hadn't thought of it like that... I suppose this *is* about survival... OK then."

They picked three houses, scoped them out, and caused mayhem. A chorus of screams broke out, lights went on, and the two of them ran off down the street.

Jenna's heart pounded with naughty excitement. When, at last, they stopped, out of breath, she turned to Johnson. "See, I can be fun?"

Johnson glanced at her. "Yeah, in a kiddy kind of way."

Jenna scowled. "I'm not a kid."

"You *are* naïve."

"I'm not naïve!"

"You've got a lot of growing up to do, Trot."

"I am grown up," she insisted, hands on hips.

Johnson looked at her. "I state my case."

Jenna stared at her, exasperated.

When they got back to their hovel, Johnson emptied her pockets.

"What have you got there?" Jenna asked.

"Food. We've got to eat."

"You *stole* it?"

"It's about survival, remember?"

"I don't like stealing."

"So, starve then." Johnson glanced at her. "You keep your principles if you want to, I'd rather eat."

"Would... the other Jenna have stolen?"

"If she had to. But if she was still around, we wouldn't have ended up on this planet in the first place."

"Stop saying stuff like that! She's not here, I am. So, cut out all that crap!"

"Nice one, Trot. You're swearing again."

"So, I'm *swearing*. Good for me. I think *you* need to grow up."

"And we're back to moaning brat."

Jenna couldn't win. She sat on her bed and ignored Johnson.

Tearing off a bite of bread, Johnson dumped herself on a dusty chair. "Bet Graham's not eating second-hand bread," she complained, miserably. "He's probably eating some delicacy his new woman's whipped up for him. Bastard..." She tore off another chunk. "Didn't take him long to find *her*..." Johnson stared at the floor, forgetting about the bread.

Despite everything, Jenna felt sorry for the woman. She wasn't sure what to say. "Chin up, Johnson."

182

Johnson turned to her. "Chin up? That sounds like something your dad would say. For god's sake, when are you going to get your memory back?"

"I was only trying to help," Jenna shot. "Perhaps if you were a little nicer, Graham might be with you now."

The forlorn look on Johnson's face brought a stab of guilt, but perhaps the woman should know what effect unkind words had.

Jenna lay back and stared up into the darkness, a firm resolve forming inside her. She was going to learn to control this power. She already was controlling it, in an indirect way. True, she had to whip herself into a frenzy, and it *was* exhausting, and she never knew what the exact effects would be, *but* she was using it with intention. She had all the proof she needed now she had it. Fraza told her she had to believe she had it. Well, she did. Surely, it was a step away now.

She turned her head to Johnson. Focusing on the chunk of bread in her hand, she imagined this power surging up in her, lashing out, knocking the bread away. The bread flew out of Johnson's hand. The woman turned to her. Jenna stared back.

She jumped to her feet. "I did it! I actually did it!"

Johnson smiled. "At long fucking last." She sniffed. "Well done, Trot."

*

In the morning, a fierce banging came at the door.

"Looks like we're in business," Johnson said, springing up and grabbing the translator.

The governor and a hoard of frightened citizens stood out on the street, looking far too well-dressed for the area.

"We need your help," the governor said with urgency.

Johnson perfected a serious frown as last night's events were relayed to them. Jenna said they'd come over straight away.

And so, their work began.

As Jenna performed her rituals, the governor asked an uncomfortable question. "It seems odd all these incidents have happened since your arrival?"

She glanced at him, thinking fast. "It has nothing to do with me," she said, trying to remain calm. "You'll often find with things like this they reach a critical mass. You know, the energies increase and feed off each other until a time arrives when all hell breaks loose."

Flaydir considered this, nodding thoughtfully.

183

"In fact, if I hadn't arrived when I did..." She shook her head. "Well, I wouldn't like to think where you'd all end up."

"So, your arrival was a fortunate coincidence?"

"I would say so."

He nodded, thoughtful again. "Then we're grateful you're here."

Jenna felt pleased with herself. She could think on her feet. Who knew?

Each day, she performed her rituals, Johnson assisting, keeping up her serious façade. The nights brought more disturbing reports, and, consequently, more money. Soon, business boomed until Jenna and Johnson moved out of their squalid little dwelling. They now resided in the upmarket part of the city. Indeed, they had become well-known in Reglon society, being invited to parties, and dining at the best tables. Unfortunately for Johnson, Reglons didn't drink. Still, it was better than being a slave, and the grub was decent and plentiful. As for Jenna, she had never known such notoriety. Well, maybe she had, but not for being good at anything. Sure, she was using remarkable powers, but she had been inventive too.

Although Reglons were the predominant species, other beings attended these events... attractive beings, not in any way repulsive. At one party, they were introduced to a stunning, silvery-skinned woman.

"It is nice to meet you," the woman said, and Jenna stared at her lips. They didn't match the sounds.

"You're speaking English?" Jenna asked, amazed.

"She's using thought transference," Johnson remarked, eyeballing the woman.

"I am a Sentier," the woman said. "We have psychic abilities."

"You do...?" Jenna asked. "Wait, are you reading my mind?"

She tilted her head. "I have to, to understand you. I only read when you speak. Otherwise, it would be the height of bad manners."

"Bad manners? It would be like... rape."

"I'm with you on that," Johnson agreed, still eyeballing the woman.

The woman smiled, serenely. "We Sentier know how to behave. I believe you have become the celebrities. I would very much like to come out on one of your... ghost-hunting excursions."

Jenna stared at the woman, now seeing her as a threat. If she was psychic, she might discern there were no ghosts.

"Well," Jenna said, keeping a careful check on her thoughts, "I'd love you to come but-"

"Wonderful," the Sentier said. "I will join you tomorrow then."

"No, I... I really need to work alone."

"You will not even know I am there." The woman gave her a breath-taking smile. "It is so unusual to see humans on this planet. And to see six...?"

"Six?"

"I met four other humans a brief time ago, working on a plantation. One of them was extremely..." She broke off, touching her chest. "Of course, we seldom form relationships but I always find sex with humans exquisite."

Jenna stared at her. She couldn't believe she'd said that. The humans *had* to be them. "Did you catch any of their names?"

"The one I formed an attachment with was called, Lucas."

Jenna's eyes shot open. A stab of jealously hit her heart and it didn't make sense. Yes, she'd had sex with him but she couldn't remember. "Lucas Brash...?" Jenna asked.

"Yes. Do you know him?" Allessa's eyes searched hers.

"We were separated. We need to find them."

"They are on a plantation, south of Iprian. But they are slaves."

"They are not slaves. They were kidnapped, like us. Could you excuse us, please?" Jenna led Johnson away. "She's seen them," she whispered.

"I've got ears, Trot." She sighed. "I suppose we'll have to sell up and go get them then." She'd enjoyed the good life here. Yet, she knew herself enough to know she'd eventually get bored. "Maybe we can buy their freedom."

"Yes. How long does it take to sell a house here?"

"A few weeks, I believe," the Sentier said, coming up behind them. "You mean to free your friends?"

"We do," Jenna replied, thinking the woman was a rude, eavesdropping slut.

Allessa's eyes probed hers. "Forgive me for asking but... were you having a relationship with Lucas?" Allessa experienced an unusual, and unsettling, pang of jealously.

"No," Jenna said, off-hand. "Apparently, I had a relationship with him but I don't remember."

Allessa studied her, curiously. "You do not remember?"

"It's a long story."

Johnson lifted her chin to the woman. "So, how far south of Iprian?" she asked.

Allessa's eyes lingered on Jenna. She turned to Johnson, giving her the exact location. "So, meeting me seems to have been a fortunate coincidence, does it not?"

"Yes," Jenna said, wondering how many times Brash had had sex with her. "Well, we should be going now." Jenna gave Johnson a meaningful look.

"Yep, I'm bushed," Johnson said, yawning.

"I will see you tomorrow," Allessa said, watching them go.

*

As Jenna de-ghosted a villa the next day, she looked up, horrified, to see the Sentier walk into the central courtyard.

Allessa smiled, serenely. "You will not know I am here," she assured them.

Jenna moved her hands around, uncomfortably. For the first time, she felt like a fraud, and compensated by producing evidence. A pot smashed against a pillar and the Sentier's eyes widened.

"Extraordinary," Allessa said, tilting her head to Jenna.

"Yes, there seems to be a couple of entities in this place."

"Really?"

"I need to concentrate to try to dispel the energies."

"And... where are you sending them?"

"They need to move on. Sometimes, they need a little shove."

"I see..."

Jenna glanced at Johnson. She looked down and thrust out her arms a few times in a made-up ritual, whilst shouting, "Be gone!"

Johnson rolled her eyes. Even she could do better than that.

Finally, Jenna looked up. "All done," she said.

"They have moved on now?" Allessa asked.

"Yes."

"Um..." The woman smiled a knowing smile. "Well, you certainly put on an entertaining show."

"Excuse me?"

"You and I both know there were no entities in this place."

"Then how do you explain the smashed pot?"

"Lucas mentioned your powers."

"He did...?" She almost felt betrayed.

"I understand. You found a way to survive here. But it has to stop now. We Sentier attend to things like this, and we do not exploit people for it. Yes, we get lodging and food but it is given to us freely."

186

Jenna stared at her, feeling like a complete low-life. Then she started to feel cross. "Well, if you get free lodging and food, you're not struggling to survive then, are you? Bet *you've* never been bound into slavery, subjected to... degradation, having to use any means possible to get by. How *can* you understand when everything's given to you on a plate!" Jenna shook her head. "I can't understand what Brash saw in you!"

"Are you jealous of me?" Allessa asked, tilting her head.

"No, I'm not jealous of you. I merely detest you. You're more of a freeloader than I am. Here's a thought. Instead of sitting there in judgement, why don't you do some good, like trying to free the slaves on this planet."

"We never interfere with matters of commerce."

"This isn't about commerce. This is about suffering, about being deprived of your liberty and dignity."

"It would be impossible to free all the slaves."

"Have you ever tried? No. Well, one man has. If you'd slept with him, I might have felt jeal-" Jenna stopped herself. What the heck was she saying?

"Who is this man?" Allessa asked, intrigued.

Jenna shook her head. "Never mind..." What was wrong with her? Feeling stabs of jealously over Brash, blurting that out about Flint? It was like stuff she didn't know about was bubbling up.

"You seem conflicted," Allessa said, tilting her head again.

"No shit," Johnson remarked.

"I'm not conflicted," Jenna shot. "I'm with no-one. I'm not jealous of anyone. End of." She drew in a breath, turning to Johnson. "We'll sell the house and get the crew. In the meantime, we've got more than enough to live on."

"I am not judging you," Allessa said, gently. "I have been brought up a certain way. It really is an honour to meet the humans who saved the universe. If I could free the slaves, I would. As I said, certain things have been drilled into me."

Jenna looked at her, oddly. "Well, maybe it's about time you started to question those things."

Allessa stared at her, her eyes widening. "Oh, no. Olixder is here."

"Olixder?"

"He is the head of our order. He will sniff out this deception straight away."

"Great," Johnson threw out. "Looks like we'll have to piss off now then. When's the next shuttle?"

"No, you do not understand. He is outside."

"Outside?"

187

"Yes."

"So, what's the worst that could happen?"

"He could have you executed."

"Shit."

Passive Observer

Flaydir arrived with an older, male Sentier. The tall, slim being glided out into the courtyard, his draping garment caressing the stone flags. His grey eyes, like a tethered storm, fixed on Jenna and Johnson.

"This is the human who has been saving our city," Flaydir said, indicating Jenna.

Olixder's eyes honed in on her. Jenna tried not to think, started humming a tune in her head.

The Sentier assessed her. "I hear you are doing an excellent job here. I have never come across so many incidents of hauntings in one place. Flaydir told me of your theory." He tilted his head. "Critical mass...?"

The grey eyes unsettled Jenna. They had a mocking quality. She reacted to it strongly.

"It's just a theory," she said with a purposeful shrug, holding steadfastly onto the tune.

"I see..." Olixder looked at her, oddly, his grey eyes probing. "What is that incessant noise in your head?"

"My business, seeing as it's my head!"

Johnson's gaze whipped to her. What the fuck was she doing? Jenna, regretting her outburst, realised it wasn't the smartest move.

Olixder's eyes widened fractionally. Nobody had ever spoken to him that way before. "I have to read your mind to understand you," he said, studying her, curiously. "I know how to conduct myself."

Flaydir shifted on his feet. He didn't know what they said but he hoped the human wasn't offending the Head Sentier.

Olixder wondered if this species was temperamental. Dragging his gaze away from the human, he looked at Allessa. "I believe you have been watching them. Was this place haunted?"

Allessa found herself in an impossible position. It had been drilled into her not to lie but she couldn't let these humans suffer.

"I believe so, sir. I witnessed a pot smash to the ground. There was no reasonable explanation for it."

Olixder's eyes lingered on her before moving back to Jenna. "The work you are currently doing should be undertaken by Sentier. Allessa and I will take over from here." Johnson breathed out. "But I would like to see you work."

Johnson breathed in again. Jenna fumbled for a way out of this. "To be honest, I would feel embarrassed," she said, awkwardly. "I'm sure you are far more proficient at this than I am. I just happened to be in the right place at the right time. I might look... amateurish next to you."

He gazed at her, curious again. "You have low self-esteem?"

"You could say that."

"It is unusual for someone who does not believe in themselves to have the fortitude of spirit to undertake this work."

She shrugged. "I suppose I'm a contradiction. And... some spirits can be trapped, can't they?" she said, humorously. "Only come out at certain times and places?"

Olixder stared at her. She wasn't sure he got the humour.

"Well, I am sorry to cause you discomfort," he said, watching her steadily, "but, as I said, I would very much like to watch you work."

It wasn't a suggestion; it was an order. The man either didn't trust her or was curious. Either way, they were done for.

Olixder did not trust her. He had come across many charlatans in his time. Some of the gimmicks were inventive but he always got to the bottom of their deception.

"Lead the way," he said, extending an arm.

The grey eyes followed them as they walked out.

Moving on to the next haunted residence, Johnson whispered in Jenna's ear. "You'd better pull something out of the bag, Trot, because I don't want *my* spirit separated from my body."

Jenna's frantic mind worked overtime.

The residents at the next place, overjoyed to see them, ushered them inside. They'd set up beds near the entrance, and they scarpered fast now, hoping whatever this group did would work.

Jenna walked down a wide passage, and out into a grand courtyard, the centre dominated by a statue of a naked male Reglon. She had minutes to produce a ghost. She didn't think smashing pots would do the trick. Olixder needed to sense the entities.

Exiting the courtyard, she walked in and out of grand-looking rooms, smashing the odd vase to buy time. Olixder stood there, impassively, unmoved by the event.

Jenna bit her lip, thinking hard. How could she produce a ghost? What *were* ghosts? What did their energy feel like? She'd heard somewhere malevolent spirits were dark and dense. Were they? Well, that's all she had. Somehow, she had to use this power to compress energy. Up to now, she had only smashed pottery. How the heck was she going to compress energy...?

Olixder glanced at her as he wandered around. "I do not feel anything," he remarked.

Time was running out. Pulling herself together, she focused, bringing the power up in her. She started to imagine this power reach out as giant hands, hands squeezing the energy in front of her, kneading it into a thick dense ball. She couldn't allow herself to doubt or question, couldn't allow herself to fall to pieces. She kept her focus in place.

Olixder, drawn to that spot, reached out with his hands. Johnson stared at those hands. Weird, long, tentacle-like protrusions extended from his fingertips, stalking through the air like ghostly worms. Jenna noticed them and lost her focus.

"I have dispersed the energy," she said, quickly.

Olixder stood there for a good long while. Jenna and Johnson stared at him, their lives hanging in the balance.

"That was amazing..." the Sentier said, drawing his gaze to Jenna, staring at her in awe. "No-one has ever removed a ghost so quickly."

Yes! Jenna mentally punched the air. She'd done it. She bet the other Jenna Trot had never done *that!*

Allessa looked at her, confounded. Johnson experienced dazed relief.

*

Jenna and Johnson walked down the street, away from their ghost-busting life. Staring at the stone pavement, Jenna reflected on what she had done. Johnson, still dazed, was sure Trot would have screwed that up.

"Jenna," Allessa called, coming up behind them. They waited for her. "How did you do that...?"

"I... compressed energy."

"Only Sentier can compress energy, and only the most skilled of us. That was... amazing..."

Yeah, Jenna thought, it *was* pretty amazing.

"Are you leaving now?" the Sentier asked.

"Yes. Olixder won't find any more ghosts and he'll start to wonder why." She turned to Johnson. "We should leave first thing. Take what cash we can."

Johnson nodded. "We won't have enough to buy their freedom, though. We'll have to break them out somehow."

A wave of inexplicable sadness washed over Allessa. "I hope you free them," she said. Smiling at them briefly, she turned and walked away.

Jenna watched her go. "I think she's in love with Brash."

"How d'you make that out?"

"Just a feeling. Would the other Jenna have ripped her eyes out?"

Johnson shrugged. "Maybe. Least, before she had that thing with Flint."

"Maybe it's best I don't remember... It all sounds like a mess..."

"Well, it sounds as if Brash is over the other Jenna now."

A sad feeling took hold of Jenna as she turned and walked on.

"I can't believe you actually did that," Johnson said, still stunned.

"You don't need to sound *so* surprised."

"I suppose the old Jenna's still in you," Johnson remarked, thoughtfully.

Jenna glared at her. "Maybe she is, but *I'm* the one that did that! Has the other Jenna ever done anything like that?"

Johnson shrugged. "Don't think so."

"So, she's not better at everything then!"

Johnson looked at her, oddly. "You talk like you're jealous of her."

"Is it surprising when you're constantly comparing me to her?"

Johnson shook her head. "This conversation is seriously fucked up."

"Oh no, you don't get to do that. You're partly responsible for the fucked-up-ness of the conversation by always making out she's better than me! You can't turn it all around now!"

"OK, keep your knickers on."

"Leave my knickers out of it! No wonder Graham moved on. Sounds to me, he couldn't bloody win, no matter what he did!"

"You don't know shit," Johnson growled.

"I know what an unreasonable woman you are! Did he never measure up, either?"

"You'd better shut the fuck up, Trot."

"Make me."

"Oh, I fucking will."

Johnson steamed in, throwing a mean punch that took Jenna from her feet. The one thing that got Jenna up again was pure unadulterated rage... a lifetime of it, like a lid had blown off and her life sprayed out. She saw it all. The disdainful looks on the ship, the hushed remarks, the judgements, the ridicule... Every repressed image exploded in a horrific firework display. She wanted to kick it all to pieces. Her fists flew. Her legs performed insane manoeuvres that would have made her stop to think if she hadn't been so driven. Johnson fought back with as much rage, her punches and kicks as precise, as deadly.

They were lethal fighting machines, hitting the deck, getting up relentlessly, neither of them backing down. Blood spilled onto their clothes, and the pace slowed, but they weren't giving up, each powered by a mountain of hurt and anger, Johnson toward her mother, Jenna toward everyone, but mostly toward herself. She threw a high kick that hit Johnson in the head. The woman dropped. Jenna was about to follow it with a knock-out punch when a voice screamed, "Stop!"

Jenna turned to see Allessa running toward them. "Stop this!" the Sentier shouted, appalled.

Jenna looked down at Johnson and unfurled her fist. She dropped to the ground, exhausted.

"What are you doing?" Allessa asked, looking between the two of them, assessing their injuries.

"We had a disagreement," Johnson mumbled. Wiping the back of her hand over her mouth, she looked at Trot. "Told you, you could fight."

Jenna said nothing.

"Why were you fighting?" Allessa asked. She turned to Jenna, waiting for an answer.

"Because I'm angry," Jenna whispered.

"You are angry at Johnson?"

"Not really."

"Then who are you angry at?"

Jenna's eyes lifted to her. "I'm angry at me."

The Sentier stared at her. The human's eyes looked tortured.

Crouching, Allessa touched her arm, tuning in to her. "Ah... I see it... You have been a passive observer in your life." She smiled at Jenna, sadly. "It all registers. Silently, quietly. Deep down, we know."

She let go of Jenna's arm, and sat beside her. "We know," she repeated, quietly. "I came back to ask if I could come with you tomorrow."

"Because of Lucas?" Jenna asked, looking away from her.

"No. Because everything you said about me was true."

A Sticky Situation

The sticky red stem choked Newark, the plant trying to drag him below ground. "Get this fucking thing off me!" he spluttered.

"Fraza, do something," Brash yelled.

Fraza did do something. He walked in circles, rubbing his ears, vigorously.

"Fuck's sake." Brash ran to their bag of provisions and retrieved a scythe. He came back, swinging at the thing, ripping into sticky flesh. The plant writhed manically, thrashing Newark all over the place, its grip on him tightening. Brash sliced and slashed, the flesh repairing as quickly as it got torn.

Stepping back, he looked around, frantically. Turning to the plant, his eyes fixed on the boggy ground at the centre of those snaking red tentacles. Moving back, he charged, jumping through the wriggling stems, splashing into bog, his scythe coming down, again and again and again...

The stems stopped flailing. Newark dropped, gasping for air.

"You OK, Newark?" Brash asked, crouching beside him.

"No thanks to him," Newark spat, hoarsely. He glanced at Fraza. "Thanks a fucking bunch."

Fraza had stopped circling. Brash strode over to him and shook him by the shoulders. "Pull yourself together, Fraza. You're useless to us like this."

"He's dead weight," Newark spat, bitterly.

Brash agreed. All that power going to waste. The Kaledian could have been a real asset. Instead, he was going through some insane meltdown. Brash had no idea how to get through to him.

Giving up on Fraza, he looked around. "Well, now we know how dangerous this place is, we need to stay on full alert. You ready to move, Newark?"

Newark dragged himself to his feet.

"I'll take lead," Brash said. "Keep your eyes peeled."

They set off, scythes at the ready, avoiding patches of boggy ground. Warm air clung to their skin. Ahead, a vast swathe of forest stretched to either side.

"It's too big to skirt around," Brash said. "We might be safer in the trees, anyway," he considered.

The light got gloomier as they entered the forest. Keeping their wits about them, they stepped over twisted, snaking roots. Humid air hung around them. They wiped sweat from their foreheads. As they wove deeper in, the ground got soggier, not drier, until they skirted a patch of bog.

"The trees are whispering," Newark said, looking around, unnerved.

"It's just the wind," Brash told him.

"What wind?"

"There's a slight breeze in the canopy."

"I think they're planning an ambush."

Brash turned to look at him. "Are you going crazy now, too?"

"I know it sounds crazy but... this place doesn't feel right."

"There are no planets in the universe where trees plan ambushes. Got that?"

"How d'you know?"

"It's common sense. Now, come on."

Brash turned back, his eyes widening in shock. A hole swathe of branches blocked their path. He reeled around. Downward-pointed branches hemmed them into a circular prison. "There fucking ambushing us!" he yelled, going berserk with his scythe, trying to break his way through.

"What do they want?" Newark yelled, thrashing out wildly. "They can't eat us, can they?"

Brash looked around. "No, but that thing can!"

Newark turned to see a huge plant rise out of the bog. An enormous venus-fly trap bore down on them.

"Climb the trees," Brash shouted. "Come on, Fraza! Move!"

Pushing Fraza up, Brash climbed after him, the branches trying to swat them off. Brash swung out, slicing into bark.

"Make him go faster!" Newark yelled from behind.

The plant swooped but they were out of reach. Making the uppermost branches, they looked down. The horror of nature remained there, waiting.

Newark tentatively touched a branch. "These ones don't move," he said, relieved.

Brash drew a hand over his mouth. "Maybe we're not the usual type of prey." Taking a composing breath, he looked around the dense canopy. The trees packed close together, the knotted, sturdy branches strong enough to provide foot bridges. "We'll have to stay high, move from tree to tree."

"These trees are fucking alive," Newark said, freaked out.

"All trees are alive, Newark," Brash told him.

"Yeah, but I mean, alive alive."

"It's just a response mechanism. Come on. Be careful. Watch your footings."

Newark looked down to see the plant sink back into boggy ground. "That was fucked up," he said, shell-shocked.

Gripping boughs above, Brash tested branches as he guided Fraza along. Fraza let go to rub his ears. "Fraza, don't do that! Newark, grab hold of his belt."

"No way," Newark protested. "If the fucker falls, I do too."

Brash focused on picking their way through the trees. Newark discerned the trees were arranged in circles, no doubt with a murderous freak of nature in the middle.

"How big d'you think this forest is?" Newark asked.

Brash didn't answer. He'd been wondering that himself.

Some branches buckled under their weight. Others snapped and they had to re-route. It was slow going. As the light began to dim, Brash became concerned.

"It's going to be dark in a couple of hours, Cap," Newark said.

"I know."

"If we get stuck in this forest overnight-"

"I know."

"If any of us dozes off-"

"I know, Newark! Quit pointing out the obvious."

Fraza slipped. Brash grabbed his arm, clinging on, desperately, his shoulder tearing. "Newark, help me!"

Newark moved in and grabbed Fraza's collar, the two of them straining as they hoisted him up. Newark shoved Fraza against the trunk. "Don't fucking move," he shot, turning to Brash. "Bastard didn't help me out."

"Let it go, Newark." Rubbing his shoulder, Brash assessed Fraza. "Fraza, I need you to concentrate. We need to get through this forest, so we can see Jenna again."

"Jenna...?" the Kaledian murmured, his eyes moving to Brash.

"Your Jenna. The Jenna who was your friend."

"Jenna...?"

"Yes. She's herself again and waiting for you. Think how proud she'll be if you get through this forest." It was cruel, he knew, but he had to be cruel to be kind.

"Jenna...?"

"Yes. Your partner in crime. She's waiting on the other side of this forest."

A spark of life returned to Fraza' s eyes. As they pressed on, the going got easier, Jenna like a holy grail to the Kaledian, bringing his spirit back to life.

The mention of Jenna brought a painful ache to Brash's heart. What would she think of him if she knew? God knows what she'd been going through, whilst he had been...

He swallowed hard. Birdsong echoed around him. He hadn't noticed it before now. It brought a deceptively normal quality to the forest. But it was a lie.

They pressed on, quietly, light leaching from the world.

"Cap-"

"I know, Newark," Brash snapped. "It's getting dark."

"No, I think the trees are thinning out."

Brash looked up. Ahead, patches of sky brought hope.

"We're nearly there," Brash said, bolstering Fraza.

As the forest thinned, they lost their foot bridges. Brash turned to Fraza. "We need to go down and make a mad dash for it," he said. "Remember, Jenna's waiting."

As they climbed down, the lower branches took a swipe at them. Reaching the bottom, they dragged Fraza, running to break free of the forest. A plant rose up in front of them, and they swerved to avoid it, chopping through branches, hacking and slicing. Pulling Fraza through, they jumped over roots, making it out at last.

Walking over open land, Newark glanced back at the forest. "That was fucked up. What d'you suppose was in it for the trees?"

Brash glanced back too. "Nutrient rich soil?"

"Well, I'm not setting foot in another forest here. Bet Flint's toast by now."

"Forget about Flint. He abandoned us. Goes to show he was never captain material."

Fraza gazed around. "Jenna...?" he asked.

"There's no Jenna," Newark said. "He lied. And even if there was, I doubt the cool Jenna's coming back."

"Newark," Brash shot. "What did you tell him that for?"

Newark looked at Brash in earnest. "Bastard didn't even pick up a scythe."

"Not coming back...?" Fraza whispered.

"Ignore Newark, Fraza." Scowling at Newark, Brash scanned the distance. Wild grassland stretched ahead of them. Night closed over it. He tested the dry, solid ground. "We need to get some sleep."

"I vote we move away from the forest," Newark said.

They walked on, Fraza trailing behind in a spiritless daze. Picking a patch of ground, they camped down. Fraza curled into a ball. "She's never coming back..." he murmured, distantly. His eyes closed and he was gone.

198

Brash rubbed his forehead. "Well, we've no idea where we are, no idea what planet we're on, and with Fraza out of commission, we're not going to be able to communicate with anyone."

Newark viewed the Kaledian with disdain.

Brash clocked the look. "Drop it, Newark. The guy's out of it."

Newark sniffed. "So, what now?"

"We need to find a main road, head for a city." He glanced at Newark. "Get to sleep, Newark. I'll take first watch."

Newark lay down, the stress of the last few hours coming over him. He closed his eyes and within minutes, he snored

Squawking birds didn't wake him. Brash looked up, following the silhouetted shapes as they soared through the sky. They reminded him of the aruks in Erithia. His heart squeezed. He and Jenna had been happy there. That seemed like such a long time ago...

*

Newark kicked Fraza awake in the morning.

"Newark, I told you to let it go," Brash said, frowning.

"What? I was just waking him up."

"With a little too much force."

Fraza came to life... well, as much life as they'd seen in him lately. Maybe even less. He didn't do any of his ear-rubbing or fidgeting.

Brash looked around. A strange mist caressed the ground. The mist lingered as they pressed on, the grass becoming longer, the ground swampy. Newark thought he saw a long thin shape slither passed him.

"Scythes at the ready," Brash said, scanning the ground.

Eyes down, they failed to notice what surrounded them. Fraza saw, yet it held no meaning, brought no response from him. When the others looked up, they froze.

The creatures stood on two legs - big, muscular bodies, covered in hair. With their knobby heads, they could have been a Neanderthal version of the Reglons. And they carried spears.

"No sudden moves," Brash said.

Newark glanced at him. "No sudden moves? I say we bolt for it, otherwise we'll end up in a cooking pot."

"We're not going to end up in a cooking pot. For all we know, they might welcome strangers." Brash wasn't buying that himself but if they bolted, they'd be speared in the back.

199

One of the ape-like figures came forward slightly, motioning for them to drop their scythes.

Brash stared at the spears surrounding them. "Drop your scythe," he said, letting go of his.

Reluctantly, Newark followed suit. The Neanderthal gestured for them to move, so they moved. Fraza didn't move. One of the creatures shoved him.

"We're fucking dinner," Newark insisted, looking around at the apes.

"We're not dinner," Brash told him.

The creatures led them to a settlement. Outward pointing spears formed a wall around it. Hand-held spears encouraged them to move inside. As they entered, the whole settlement gathered around them, cheering and shouting.

"I tell you, we're dinner," Newark maintained.

"We don't know that," Brash said. "We could be-" His eyes fixed on a large pot hanging in the centre of the settlement, the pot big enough for human-size prey. "Shit." He turned to Fraza. "Wake up, Fraza! We're going to die if you don't wake up!"

The words didn't register but Fraza registered with the villagers. They pointed at his orange hair and big belly.

"If he doesn't snap out of it soon," Newark spat, frantically, "I'll toss him in that bloody pot myself!"

Pushed to a round wooden hut, they got thrown inside.

Newark rattled Fraza's shoulders. "Pull off some shit, you insane freak!"

"That's not going to work," Brash said, raking a hand through his hair. He peered through a hole in the door. There were a ton of them out there, guarding them like prized possessions.

"What's the plan then, Cap?"

Brash turned to Newark. "We need a bloody miracle."

Hearing Voices

Their first stop was a small town called, Camyra. Allessa led them to a hotel. The pale stone, three-storey villa had balconies jutting over the square.

As they entered a spacious, mosaic-tiled lobby, a couple of Reglons approached, fawning and fussing over the Sentier.

"I reckon we're going to get free room and board," Johnson said.

The Reglons ushered them forward, leading them to a dining area. Tables edged a bright, flowered-studded courtyard. Tiny Reglons ran between the pots, chasing each other.

Directed to a table, the three of them sat, Jenna breathing in flowers, imbibing the holiday feel.

"So, did we get this free?" Johnson asked.

Allessa nodded, her eyes moving to the happy children.

Food arrived quickly, Jenna marvelling at the awe and respect the Reglon servers showed Allessa. In contrast, those slit eyes viewed her and Johnson oddly. Johnson thought she'd rather be viewed oddly than have a stupid fucking knobbly head.

"So, we couldn't catch a direct flight to Iprian?" Johnson asked, inspecting the food. Reglon food was decent. Meat and vegetables. Not liquidly stuff with weird shit floating in it.

"Direct flights leave only once a week," Allessa replied. "Other flights stop en-route. We will be getting on another shuttle tomorrow."

"Did we get that free too?" Jenna asked.

"Yes," Allessa replied, looking down at her plate.

"It's great being a Sentier on this planet," Johnson said.

After they'd eaten, they were shown up to their rooms, congregating in Allessa's room, which was far more spacious. Johnson's eyes brushed over expensive, Romanesque furniture as she wandered out onto a narrow balcony. Platforms had been set up in the square below, and slaves were being traded. "There's a couple of hulks down there."

Jenna came over and looked out to see two Velyors. "Do all the slaves here come from Draztis?" she asked, turning to Allessa.

"I believe so."

Jenna shook her head. "I can't believe the Sentier allow this. It's not very... spiritual."

"No..." Allessa agreed quietly, staring at the tiled floor. She looked up at Jenna. "I would like to meet this man you spoke of, the one that was freeing the slaves."

Jenna didn't like the thought of that. She didn't want the woman getting her tentacles into Flint too. "I suppose we'll be leaving as soon as we find them," she said, trying to hide her irrational jealously.

Allessa tilted her head. "Have you had a relationship with him too?"

"I can't remember," Jenna replied, off-hand. "I can't remember anything."

Allessa studied her, thoughtfully. "Perhaps there is a reason you lost your memory."

"There is. The other me took a mind-bending drug."

"*I* didn't lose my memory," Johnson put in. She shrugged. "Mind you, I wasn't playing off two men."

"I wasn't playing off two men!"

"How d'you know if you can't remember?"

"Because... because I wouldn't do that!"

"Ah, *you* wouldn't do that but what about the other you? Do you know, you and Fraza used to start fights in bars and place bets on them?"

"What...?"

"Yeah, you used the power, took control of their bodies. Cornelius was hopping mad at you."

"I would never do that!"

"No, well, *you* wouldn't but the other Jenna would. I miss her..."

Jenna stared at her, horrified.

"Maybe it was you," Allessa suddenly said. The two of them turned to her. "Maybe this part of you made you forget."

"What...?" Jenna asked, screwing up her face.

"Perhaps this part of you did not approve of the other part." Allessa tilted her head, her grey eyes probing. "Perhaps you reasserted yourself, made yourself forget her... especially if the love triangle proved too difficult."

"This is getting fucked-up," Johnson said, turning her attention back to the square.

Allessa's grey eyes remained fixed on Jenna. "Maybe that is the reason." She tilted her head. "Change that happens quickly leaves little room for assimilation. Perhaps you moved too far, too fast. Perhaps you left important parts of yourself behind. Maybe there was something you had not quite comes to terms with."

"Or maybe," Johnson offered, staring at an unusual being with a shell-like head, "that brain-melding drug just wiped out the cool parts."

"*I'm* cool!" Jenna insisted.

"Whatever the reason," Allessa said, gently, "you have now lost a part of yourself... a part that must always have been in you, whether you have known about it or not. If you do not remember that part, Jenna, you will never be all of yourself."

Jenna lay in bed that night, considering Allessa's words. Had she re-asserted herself? That made her feel smug. That meant she was stronger, didn't it? Maybe the other Jenna was no match for *her*. Maybe it was the other Jenna who should feel jealous.

She dozed, feeling satisfied, listening to the drapes ruffling in a breeze... It sounded so far away... Almost in a distant galaxy...

She dreamt of blonde-haired beings with the oddest anatomy. She dreamt of a blonde-haired man, a bitter, twisted youth. A psychopath. Why was she hugging him? She dreamt of crystal towers and angelic faces, of flying on the backs of enormous birds, of an old man with white hair.

"*Jenna, where are you? Can you hear me?*"

He looked worried, sounded concerned.

"*Jenna, where are you?*"

The words became irrelevant as she got swept up in a dance with a dashing Captain Brash. *God, he was attractive.* The scene switched. She lay on grass, Brash leaning over her, making love to her... It was... amazing...

She awoke with a start, her breathing fast, her mind racing.

Climbing out of bed, she poured a glass of water and drank thirstily. Filling the stone basin, she splashed water onto her face. Looking up, she stared at her flushed reflection in the mirror. The memory of the dream hung over her in vivid detail. She could smell the grass, feel the air on her skin, smell the coconut scent of his hair... It wasn't a dream. It was a memory... Images and faces flashed before her. Weird-looking ogres with yellow skin. Beings with pink skin and violet hair.

Her eyes widened in the mirror. The other Jenna Trot was trying to reinstate herself. A strange feeling took hold of her body, a strength, a confidence rising up, reflected in the eyes staring back at her. But she wasn't going to be muscled out. She fought against it, pushing the memories away, shrugging off the increasingly confident posture. The eyes in the mirror looked determined. She didn't know if they were her eyes, or if they belonged to the other Jenna Trot.

The battle lasted through the night, and in the morning, she crawled out of bed, exhausted.

Wrapping her arms around her middle, she moved down the stone steps, walking over the tiled floor to the dining area. Allessa smiled as she approached. Jenna nodded, trying to hold onto her control.

The Sentier assessed her. "Are you alright, Jenna? You seem... tense."

"I'm fine," she said, sitting at the table. "Had some bad dreams. Didn't sleep well."

Johnson lifted her head. "Yeah, you look like shit."

"I'm fine."

"Where's the next stop then?" Johnson asked the Sentier.

"Ishia," Allessa replied. "It is by a lake. Quite beautiful..."

Johnson sniffed. "Maybe we could go swimming."

"I would not recommend it. The fish there are... vicious."

Johnson stared at her. "We swam on the backs of whales once," she recalled, remembering how cool it was.

"Yeah, they were lovely creatures," Jenna said, retrieving a gloopy roll, her hand stopping mid-air, her eyes fixing Johnson.

Johnson whipped her head to her. "You *remember* that?"

She shook her head quickly. "No. I'm thinking of something else. Can you pass me the... whatever that stuff is?"

Johnson eyed her, oddly. Jenna busied herself with breakfast.

Alessa looked at Jenna. "Have you thought about what we spoke of yesterday?"

"I think it was just the drugs," she replied, dismissively.

"You know, I was thinking about that," Johnson said. "I don't think the other Jenna would go down without a fight. She was ballsy. No way would this Jenna have wiped her out."

Jenna shot to her feet, grabbing Johnson by the collar. "Say shit like that again and I'll knock you out! You hear me!"

Staring at Johnson, horrified, she let go of the woman, and backed away. Turning, she ran off, desperate to resume control.

Johnson and Allessa stared after her.

As they hopped from town to town, Jenna struggled to hold onto herself. She became quiet and withdrawn, taking little interest in the places they visited. The nights brought more memories, but she steadfastly pushed them away as she tried to cling to herself. Dark circles appeared under her eyes. Johnson asked her if she'd been taking drugs. Allessa wished Jenna would talk.

The Sentier watched her now as they ate their evening meal.

"So, what's *this* town called?" Johnson asked.

"Latrina," Allessa replied.

Johnson spat out her food, and Allessa studied her, curiously. Johnson looked between the two of them. "Come on. That's not funny?"

"If you say so," Jenna mumbled.

"Jesus, Trot, lighten up." Grabbing her glass, she sat back. "You used to be much more fun."

Jenna glared at her.

Allessa thought Jenna looked pale. "We should take a walk after the meal," she suggested. "Get some air."

They left the hotel, strolling through quaint, pale-stone streets. Johnson spotted a couple of Reglons staggering out of a doorway. She halted. "We've found a bar?" She turned to Allessa. "I thought Reglons didn't drink?"

"Places like this are frowned upon by the state," Allessa replied. "They are very much an... underground phenomenon."

"Bloody kill joys."

"Well... Reglons do not handle alcohol well."

A grin spread on Johnson's face. "What are we waiting for?"

As they walked in, slit eyes stared at them. Sentier never entered these places, and what the hell were those creatures with her? Johnson scanned the joint. The tiny hovel didn't look like a bar, more like someone's living room. Still, it was gold. She was about to ask the Sentier to order for them, when drinks were brought their way. Fawning, the man directed them to a table.

Johnson smiled. "It's good to have a Sentier on tap."

She took a deep swig, pleasantly surprised. The brown liquid had a kick.

Allessa didn't touch her drink. Jenna took a sip. Normally, she didn't drink but she'd try anything to relieve her tension. The problem was, she couldn't stop drinking. She threw the stuff down her, matching Johnson glass for glass. Except, it wasn't her doing it.

"I didn't know you liked a drink, Trot?" Johnson asked, eyeing her, thoughtfully. "Well, not the *you* you." *That sounded plain weird.*

"I've always liked a drink," she lied.

Johnson's eyes lingered on her. "We've not had a drink in ages," she complained, looking around the bar. "They didn't have alcohol on Draztis. Flint should have changed that." *Why didn't they press for that? Oh, yeah, they had tea.*

Jenna's hand reached for the glass again. She grabbed hold of her wrist and a battle of wills ensued. The hand broke free and grabbed the glass. She desperately tried to stop it reaching her mouth.

Johnson took in glazed eyes and swaying bodies. When a knobbly-headed drunk fell off his seat, she laughed. Allessa tilted her head to her.

"Oh, come on?" Johnson asked. "That's not funny?" She turned to Trot.

Jenna let go of her wrist and beer splashed in her face.

"What the fuck you doing?" Johnson asked, staring at her. "You just threw that at yourself."

"I think I'm getting drunk."

"Already? God, the other you would have drunk you under the table." *Again, just plain weird.*

Allessa's curiosity transferred to Jenna. Jenna, aware of their suspicious looks, let the hand do what it wanted. She ended up, plastered. Johnson had to carry her back but not before having one hell of a night, watching a group of pissed-up Reglons that couldn't handle their drink. They couldn't fucking sing, either.

*

In the morning, Jenna awoke, ashamed and demoralised. She curled into a tight ball. The other Jenna was getting stronger. If she didn't stop this, she would disappear. But it was *exhausting*.

"Jenna," Allessa said, coming into her room. The Sentier sat on the edge of the bed. "Tell me what is troubling you?"

Jenna hadn't wanted to say it out loud. That made it real somehow, and she knew Johnson would be rooting for the other Jenna, which she could do without. But she had to talk to someone. "She's coming back," she whispered.

"Who?"

"The other Jenna. I can feel her. I'm remembering things. She'll take over and I'll disappear."

Allessa touched her arm. "Jenna, she is you. Maybe she is your friend."

"I don't know that."

"Listen to me. She let go for a reason. She must have wanted you back."

"What reason?"

Allessa tilted her head. "Maybe she went too far. She had been passive for so long, after all... I cannot say for sure but you are here, so you are here for a reason. Perhaps now is the time to be all of you. You cannot carry on being at war with yourself."

"She'll take over," Jenna pleaded with her. "Just like my dad."

"Your dad?"

"He was always... directing, controlling, sorting things out."

"I see... Well, she is not your dad. She is you. These things that are happening are coming from yourself. Perhaps you need to trust that you know what you are doing."

"She doesn't feel like me."

"That is because you are not allowing yourself to remember. These feelings and this situation will not resolve until you do." Allessa looked at her, sadly. "Are you too unwell to travel today?"

She nodded.

"Very well. Sleep."

When the door closed, Jenna summoned a new wave of determination. She was going to fight with everything she had left, which wasn't much as the hangover was killing her. She closed her eyes, riding it through.

Allessa joined Johnson at the table. "We will not be travelling today."

"I knew she wouldn't be able to handle her beer," Johnson complained.

Allessa tilted her head. "Why are you so hard on her?"

"I'm not hard on her."

"You are, almost like you... resent her."

Johnson sniffed. "Maybe I do a little." Johnson looked at her. "She took the place of my friend. I never had female friends. Jenna was the first one."

"She *is* Jenna."

"She's not the same. I want Trot back. This one's... prudish. She hasn't been through what we've been through."

"I see... Then it seems this Jenna never stood a chance with you, did she?" Johnson chewed her lip, staring at the table. "Perhaps, if you had not met the first Jenna, you might have grown to like this one."

Johnson sat there, soaking that in.

*

"Jenna, where are you? It's Cornelius."

Jenna sat up and looked around, the room quiet and empty. Realising she'd been dreaming, she lay back down.

"Jenna, please. Let me know you're alright."

She sat back up, looking around, trying to shake the alcohol from her brain. The shaking made her head ache terribly. She had to lie back down.

"Very clever..."

She shot up. She wasn't imagining it. She was hearing voices.

Jumping off the bed, she charged for the door, rushing down the stairs, and hurtling into the dining room. "I'm hearing voices," she blurted, hysterically. A few Reglons turned their heads.

Allessa took in her panicked state. "Calm down, Jenna."

"Calm down?" Johnson asked. "She sounds psychotic." ·

"What did you hear?" the Sentier asked.

"One voice said he was Cornelius. But then there was a second... more sinister voice."

Allessa studied her, thoughtfully. "Jenna, can you read minds?"

"What? No. Of course, I can't read minds."

"Could she read minds?" the Sentier asked, turning to Johnson.

Johnson shook her head. "If she could do shit like that, she would have told me."

"Are you certain?"

Johnson viewed Jenna with suspicion. "Have you been holding out on me, Trot?"

Jenna stared at her. "How do *I* bloody know!"

"Jenna, keep calm," Allessa said. "It is possible that you can link minds and there are two beings trying to communicate with you. If that is the case, you need to find out what they want."

"What...? This is insane..."

"Get into that relaxed state again. Do not panic or you will break the link. Should I come with you?"

Jenna stared at Allessa. "You really think I can mind-read...?"

"Considering what else you can do, it is a strong possibility."

Johnson frowned. "You've been able to mind-read all this time and you didn't tell me? God, when I think of all the shit you might have heard."

"Not me," Jenna said, exasperated. "Your so-called friend!"

"God, if she ever comes back, I'll be having words with her."

"This is freaking me out," Jenna said, holding her head. "I can mind-read...?"

"Jenna," Allessa said, gently, "you need to find out what they want. You are perfectly safe. Do you want me to come with you?"

"Course, she does," Johnson mumbled, annoyed. "Go and hold her hand."

Glaring at Johnson, Jenna straightened. "I don't need anyone to hold my hand."

Turning her back on Johnson, she headed to her room, wondering how many more things the other Jenna could do she didn't know about. Mind-reading...? This was unreal. Well, if the other Jenna Trot could do it, she would damn well do it too.

Lying on her bed, she took a few minutes, trying to dispel the nerves. Nothing happened and eventually, her eyes drooped.

"Jenna, where are you? We're looking for you."

Her eyes shot open and the link broke.

Drawing in a breath, she calmed herself, closing her eyes once more. "C... Cornelius? Is that you?"

"Thank god. Tell us where you are, Jenna."

His voice soothed her. She trusted it. *"We're on a planet called, Juyra. We're heading for the capital, Iprian. I'm with Johnson. We are going to rescue the others."*

"Wait for us in Iprian. Tell me where we can meet you."

"Look for the main square. All the towns and cities have them here. We'll wait for you there."

"OK. So good to hear you, Jenna. Are you alright?"

"Fine... except, I lost my memory. I'm... not the Jenna you remember."

Cornelius paused. *"I remember you just fine. Wait for us in Iprian. I'll be there soon."*

She felt his presence leave, and lay there thinking about what she'd done. She'd talked to a man she didn't know across miles of space. Could the rabbit hole grow any wider?

"Very clever, Jenna Trot."

Wait? What? This didn't feel like Cornelius. *"W-Who are you?"*

"The question is, who are you? There were no ghosts, Jenna, so that must mean, somehow, you manipulated energy. And you also committed a crime. An arrest order has been issued-"

Jenna sat bolt upright. Olixder was coming after them?

No Way Out

"It was definitely him," Jenna insisted.

Allessa's wide eyes did nothing to dispel Jenna's fears. "Olixder will find us," the Sentier said. "He has huge influence here. Every resource will be made available to him, and it will be virtually impossible to leave the planet."

"I say we avoid Iprian then," Johnson said. "Head straight to the plantation."

"We cannot do that. We would not survive. The land is treacherous and populated by fierce wild men. We need to take transport from Iprian."

"Is there no transport from here?"

"No. All roads lead to the capital."

"So, there's no way out? That's fucking stupid!" Johnson rubbed her forehead. "Wait a minute. Why are we panicking? Trot's got some of her powers back now."

"I can smash a few vases," Jenna said, helplessly. "I doubt I'd be able to take on an army if he has back-up."

"Olixder, himself, is formidable," Allessa said. She glanced at them. "The Sentier have powers too."

"You do?"

"You do?" Johnson asked. "Well, you're our secret weapon then."

"Even if I was prepared to go up against the Head Sentier, Olixder is stronger than I am. And he might bring other Sentier with him."

Jenna and Johnson stared at her.

"So, we're well and truly fucked," Johnson said.

"What can the Sentier do?" Jenna asked.

"We work with energy. We can move energy and manipulate it, like you can. And, we have been doing it for a very long time."

Jenna rubbed her brow. "What will happen to us? He wouldn't actually execute us, would he?"

Allessa grey eyes looked troubled. "With any other Head, you would probably get away with a warning but... Olixder does things differently. He is very... strict."

"And that translates *as*?" Johnson asked.

Allessa looked at her, concerned. "He might take your heads."

Jenna's hand came to her throat.

"Just because we pulled the wool over his eyes?" Johnson asked. "That hardly warrants a death sentence."

"Like I said, he does things differently." Allessa looked away from them.

"He's not spiritual, at all, is he?" Jenna threw out. "Maybe the Sentier have lost their way."

Allessa lowered her head.

"Wait," Jenna said. "I spoke to Cornelius too." She turned to Johnson. "He said he would meet us in Iprian. Would Cornelius be a match for Olixder?"

Johnson stared at Jenna. "Cornelius is coming here?" She smiled, somewhat relieved. Then she frowned. "Cornelius can kick butt but I don't know how strong he is compared to this Olixder." She sat down, defeated. "The only one who could really fix this was Jenna. The girl had turned into a fucking miracle-worker."

Jenna waited for the scathing look that told her she was an imposter in her own body. It didn't come. Johnson looked worried. Jenna had never seen her look that way. And she had every reason to. A group of powerful Sentier, backed up by an army of Reglons, might be more than Cornelius could handle. They might all lose their heads, and Brash, Flint, Newark, and Fraza, would rot on that plantation for the rest of their days. The outlook was bleak. Desperately bleak. But the answer stared her cruelly in the face.

Self-Sacrifice

"I'm going to lie down," Jenna told them, expecting a sarcastic retort from Johnson. Nothing came. She walked away but paused and turned. "I'm sorry you lost your friend," she said to Johnson. She smiled at the woman, sadly. "We had *some* fun, though, didn't we?"

Johnson watched her go with a puzzled frown.

Jenna realised this was inevitable. It was going to happen sooner or later but at least, this way, she was giving her consent.

When she entered her room, she took a long look in the mirror. She was about to die so another her could live. It seemed surreal and absurd. Her heart sped. She wanted to cling to herself, as a needy child clings to a teddy, but she knew she couldn't.

Taking a deep breath, she summoned the conviction she needed then walked over to lie on the bed. Closing her eyes, she took a moment then she opened herself to the inevitable.

The room was quiet and still. The stillness seemed to hold her, waiting, as she waited...

Slowly, an odd sensation invaded the calm. An energy rising from the depths, flimsy at first, suffusing her like a ghostly possession. She had the feeling she was about to launch onto a roller-coaster ride...

A mish-mash of images flickered through her mind, a dizzying kaleidoscope...

Then the past two years replayed at lightning speed...

She saw the fateful trip to Marios Prime. The escape through the wasteland. Meeting the Erithians and Cornelius. Learning to use the power. And every single event that happened after. Lucas got resurrected as each detail of their relationship played out before her. She experienced it all, felt it all... the uncertainty, the highs, the lows, the overwhelming fear, the joy, the pain... Throughout it all, she felt herself toughen, harden, change... It was like she had died and her life flashed before her.

None of it felt alien. It was all her life. She'd woken from a dream of forgetfulness to an oh yeah *feeling. The missing pieces fit perfectly, slotted into place with ease. And she wasn't disappearing. She was still there, watching it all, reliving it... only, from a different vantage point. From this crystal-clear place, she was both Jenna Trots and neither at the same time.*

Llamia flashed into her head. "Stop looking in the mirrors. Look inside yourself."

Flint had been right. The people on Osiris just reflected her own lack of faith. She could have been anyone. It really wasn't personal. Allessa had been right too. She had *been a passive observer. A part of her had always known what went on around her, had watched silently in the background. That part was watching now.*

She was no longer angry with the mirror, no longer angry with herself. Everything had been inevitable, the character born of circumstance, denial born of pain. Yet, she couldn't be who she was now without being who she was then. The pendulum swings until it finds the centre, and the centre was where she was meant to be.

Two halves merged together. Her scattered energies reassembled. It was the most profound, almost mystical, experience.

When she opened her eyes, she was herself, all of herself.

A knock at the door turned her head. "Trot, it's me," Johnson said, opening the door. Looking awkward as she walked over, Johnson sat on the bedside chair. "Listen, I've been thinking, and I reckon, maybe, I've been a little hard on you." She scratched her neck. "Maybe you're not the Jenna I remember. That doesn't mean you're *all* bad."

Jenna watched her and the woman offered more. "You know... you're sort of alright. And... err... we did have fun in Pyshirian. That was cool." She scratched her neck again. "I reckon you're sort of a friend."

Jenna sat up and gave her a broad grin. "You never called me friend before? You going soft in your old age, Johnson?"

"What...?"

"Come on. Tonight, I'm going to drink *you* under the table. Loser has to pay a forfeit."

Johnson stared at her. "Trot...? Is that you...?"

"Always has been."

A Bloody Miracle

"We've been in here for days," Newark threw out, brushing a hand through his hair.

"Maybe we're being saved for a special occasion," Brash thought aloud.

"What? Like Christmas? We get to be the fucking turkey?" Newark shot to his feet. "Try him again."

Fraza's gibbering and ear-rubbing was a thing of the past, the guy barely there at all.

"It's no good," Brash said. He looked up at Newark. "Listen, when they come for us, we fight. We'll die, of course, but we're not going down without a fight."

Noise and merriment started up outside. A strange tribal chanting began.

"Shit," Brash said. "This might be that special occasion."

"Fuck."

The villagers whipped themselves into a frenzy. The chanting carried on and on...

"What the hell are they doing?" Newark asked, peering through the hole in the door. He caught snippets of frenetic movement.

"Sounds like some kind of ritual."

"Bastards!"

Darkness closed around them, the wait excruciating.

"Fucking cannibals!" Newark spat, banging his fists into the wall. He glared at Fraza, eyeing the tripped-out, pot-bellied bastard with disdain.

The door opened and he spun around. The first Neanderthal to appear got dragged inside to a fury of fists. Brash and Newark did damage to two more before they were speared in the legs and punched in the face. Fraza got punched in the face for good measure. Bloodied and bruised, the three got dragged to the centre of the village, to where a fire blazed beneath a huge steaming pot.

"They're not going to throw us in alive, are they?" Newark asked, quaking.

Dumped on the ground, Neanderthals with spears started dancing around them, the looks on their faces, crazed, demented.

"Think of something," Newark pleaded with Brash. Death he could accept but being boiled alive made him want his mummy. Course, his mummy wasn't the cuddling type and, with nine siblings, cuddles were rare, but that was irrelevant at the moment. Any bloody mother would do!

Brash racked his brains but could come up with only one solution.

"Newark," he said, decisively. "We need to grab a couple of spears. I'll kill Fraza then we stick each other in unison."

"That's the plan...?"

"You'd rather be boiled alive?"

Newark stared at Brash. "That's a good plan."

They gave themselves a moment to process what they were about to do.

"It's been a pleasure serving with you, Newark," Brash said, seriously.

"You too, Cap."

"You ready?"

"Yes. Let's ruin their fucking party!"

"On three. Three..."

Newark didn't stop to wonder what had happened to one and two. Charged with adrenaline, they jumped up in unison, wrenching spears from gyrating Neanderthals. Brash turned to Fraza and took aim. At that precise moment, all hell broke loose. Villagers' huts went up in flames. Rounds of weapons sounded. Neanderthals dropped all over the place.

Stunned for a moment, Brash grabbed Fraza, shielding him as he and Newark backed up, keeping their spears poised. The Neanderthals, presently focused on staying alive, didn't notice them. Through the flames and darkness, Brash caught a brief glimpse of an elusive figure. Whoever or whatever it was, it moved with stealth. How many of them were there? Who were they?

"We need to move," Brash urged.

Hobbling on injured legs, they dragged Fraza between blazing huts. A couple of Neanderthals came at them but got shot in the back.

Staring at the lifeless bodies, they staggered past them until, at last, they made it through the gates.

"Keep moving," Brash said.

Holding onto Fraza, they picked their way through the darkness, the village burning brightly behind them, flames roaring in their ears.

"What just happened...?" Newark asked, glancing around.

"I've no idea," Brash said. "A bloody miracle. That's what happened."

As they put more distance between them and the village, their adrenaline calmed down and the pain kicked in. "My leg's bloody killing me," Newark complained.

"I know but we need to keep moving."

They struggled through the pain and kept on through the night, Fraza silent, Newark constantly complaining.

As the light of a new day rose into the world, they dropped down, exhausted. Fraza flaked out.

"*He* didn't get speared in the leg," Newark said, glaring at him.

"Get some sleep, Newark," Brash said. "I'll take first watch."

Movement behind made them reel around. Their eyes fixed on a bizarre sight. Holding a gun in one hand, and bag of arsenal in the other, Flint wore a ripped, dirty t-shirt, and a bandana over his forehead. He looked like a special forces' operative.

"Flint...?" Brash murmured.

"You all OK?" Flint asked, looking them over.

"Was that *you*...?"

Flint threw his bag on the ground and sat with them. "I saw you being captured."

"You saw?" Newark asked, staring at Flint, confused. "But you left weeks ago?"

"I ran into some trouble," he said, wiping his dirty brow.

They waited for him to elaborate but he didn't.

"So, you waited days to rescue us?" Newark asked, still confused.

"I had to find weapons. You were closely guarded. It would have been a suicide mission to go in there, unarmed."

Brash and Newark stared at Flint, marvelling at this one-man army.

Newark shook his head. "I can't get a handle on you, Flint. One minute, you run out on us, the next you're risking your life to save us."

"I didn't run out. I needed to get to Jenna and Johnson. Brash had no intention of escaping, so I took the best shot."

"He had every intention of escaping."

Flint's eyes fixed on Newark. "No, he didn't. He was too wrapped up in the Sentier."

Newark turned to Brash, waiting for him to refute it. Brash lowered his head. It was the truth but he couldn't bring himself to admit it out loud. He'd been selfish. Blinkers fell from his eyes. He realised he had lost himself on Draztis. The egotistical old captain had pushed to the surface, the man he'd become slipping away from him like a delicate dream. He wanted that man back, whatever the cost.

He looked up at Flint. "Thank you, Flint. You saved our necks."

Newark sniffed. "Yeah, thanks." Being saved from a boiling pot had done wonders for his opinion of the man.

Flint looked at Fraza. "Still no change?"

"He's worse," Brash said. "He's completely shut down."

"We need to gather the crew, get off this planet, and find Cornelius."

"Any idea which way?"

Flint looked at the sky. "I've seen craft heading in that direction." He pointed to his left, to a large swathe of forest. "We either go through the forest or skirt around it, which could add days to our journey."

"I say we skirt around it," Newark suggested.

Flint brought a spray gun out of his bag. "Or, we could go through it."

"What's that?" Brash asked.

"An effective poison. Reglons use it. It's potent stuff."

"Where did you get it?"

"It's a long story."

Again, they waited but nothing was forthcoming.

"Can you walk?" Flint asked, looking at their injured legs.

"Not too well," Brash said.

Flint reached into the bag and pulled out cloth, which he ripped into strips and threw at them. "Make bandages," he said. He brought out a bag of leaves and passed it over to them. "Take some. It's a natural painkiller. The Reglons use it."

Brash and Newark looked at the bag, their eyes drawn back to Flint. The man was a complete mystery. They took the leaves and bandaged their legs.

"Come on then," Flint said, standing. "We'll use as much of the day as we can."

They woke Fraza, who stared out, vacantly. Flint took hold of him, and they headed to the forest. Brash and Newark kept glancing at Flint, Newark viewing him as badass. Fint was cool. Brash wanted to be like him.

"Have you got a sense of humour, Flint?" Newark asked.

Flint glanced at him. "Yes, though it's probably not the same as yours."

"What d'you call a hungry Neanderthal?"

Flint raised his eyebrows.

"A crazed, demented bastard."

Flint's lips curled. "A crazed, demented, dead bastard."

Newark and Brash both smiled.

A Few Home Truths

Johnson stared at Jenna as if she was the reincarnation of some revered deity. She couldn't believe she had her mate back. Her attention shifted as they walked into the central square of Iprian. Grand classical buildings surrounded the space, all built in that pale stone. The huge noisy square heaved with Reglons carrying placards.

"What's going on?" Jenna asked.

"It is protest day," Allessa replied. "Once a month, the citizens are allowed to protest."

Jenna glanced at her. "Allowed to?"

"What are they protesting about?" Johnson asked.

"There are different protests going on. That group," Allessa said, pointing, "want slave prices driven down. The placard reads, 'cheaper slaves for all!'"

Jenna looked at Johnson. "The poor downtrodden masses." Johnson smiled. "What about them?" Jenna asked, pointing to a smaller, yet no less vocal group.

Allessa followed the direction of her gaze. "They are protesting against protests." Jenna raised her eyebrows. Allessa leaned in close. "It is rumoured that group is a covert government department."

Jenna studied the group. They appeared furtive, their eyes flitting around as they chanted. "What are they shouting?"

"Protests lead to anarchy'."

"Not very catchy."

"They are saying, 'protests lead to a- nar-chy'."

"Still lacks imagination. They must be a government department. What about them?" The group she looked at now had a stall with pamphlets set upon it, the Reglons behind silent, almost demure.

"They want compulsory religious instruction in schools."

"So, Reglons have religion?"

"Some are religious but they are in the minority."

"And what do they believe?"

"They believe the universe started with a big explosion and is still expanding. They believe that every aspect of the universe is an expanding aspect of the divine. Indeed, that the divine lives in all things with a progressive tendency to create."

Jenna and Johnson stared at her.

"The big bang is science, isn't it?" Johnson asked, scratching her head.

"That is what I believe, yes."

"So," Jenna asked, thoughtfully, "if religious Reglons believe in the big bang, what do non-religious Reglons believe?"

"Many believe in a judgemental creator, but since no-one ever laid down any rules, it is impossible to know how to please him. So, they just get on with their lives and hope for the best. If they do not think about it too much, it does not affect them."

"So, in effect, they are religious but they're in denial?"

Allessa considered this. "I suppose that is true."

"It all sounds back-to-front," Johnson remarked. "Don't they have any scientists here? How the hell do they built spacecraft?"

"Yes, there are scientists. Indeed, a large proportion of scientists are religious."

"And they buy into the *divine in all things* part?"

"Science has never been able to explain consciousness. It is the missing part of the equation. I think the scientists here are progressive, accepting that there is, indeed, a *ghost in the machine.*"

"Or a machine in the ghost..." Jenna pondered, thoughtfully.

Johnson looked at her. "What?"

"Just thinking about something Cornelius once said... I think I might take a pamphlet."

As she walked over to the stall, she noticed a lone protestor standing silently with his placard. "What's he protesting about?"

Allessa read the sign. "He wants to abolish slavery."

"He *does...?*"

Approaching him, Jenna used thought transference to communicate. "You look like you're being muscled out," she said with a smile, indicating the hordes of vocal demonstrators.

The Reglon stared at her lips. They made the oddest shapes. "What are you?" he asked, gazing at her, curiously.

"I'm human."

"Are you against slavery?" he asked. "Or have you come to taunt me?"

She chewed her lip, studying him, thoughtfully. "Are you all there is?"

"Is that a taunt?"

"No, just a question."

"There are others but they are too frightened to make their opinions known. Being against slavery is not a popular stance on this planet."

"I can imagine." Jenna noticed the protest against protests protestors glancing over. "This protest day is just a sham," she said to the Reglon. "A way to let the masses get it out of their system. You must realise that, surely?"

"I do, but it's important to stand up for what you believe."

"I suppose you're right." She looked around at the large group shouting loudly to drive slave prices down. "They're far too noisy," she remarked to Johnson.

Johnson nodded, her lips curving.

Using the power and her intent, Jenna summoned a localised blast of wind that hit the protestors squarely in the face. The shouting stopped, momentarily, but started up again. She hit them over and over until they looked around, dazed, their former fervour quelled.

"What did you do...?" Allessa asked, gazing at her, curiously.

"Blew their own hot air back at them." She turned to the stunned Reglon. "They seem to have lost focus."

"No, I think they're starting up again," Johnson said.

Jenna turned back around with a frown. "Persistent buggers."

She focused again. Their placards flew out of their hands and they ran around the square chasing after them.

Johnson laughed. "They'll get them back, you know?"

"No, they won't. Watch."

The placards rose on a sharp updraft, landing on the top of the buildings.

"Nice one, Trot."

Jenna turned to the staring Reglon. "I think what you're doing is admirable," she said. "I'd hang around with you but I'm looking for someone." She smiled at him then moved away, keeping her eyes open for Cornelius.

"Why did you do that?" Allessa asked, tilting her head.

Jenna looked at her. "I'm making my own protest."

"But... is that not unfair? They have the right to protest, even if we do not agree with them."

Jenna considered this. "Well, what about all the opponents of that view who are silenced because they are afraid to speak out? Or the slaves, who don't even get a voice? If everyone can't have a voice, no-one should."

Allessa stared at her.

"Yeah," Johnson said, haughtily. "Who stands up for the silent majority?"

"Not the bloody Sentier," Jenna remarked under her breath.

Allessa's silvery lips tightened. "At least, we do not act rashly," she accused.

"You don't act at all."

"Look," Johnson said, "she could have brought down fire and brimstone. She's been remarkably restrained. A few months ago, there might have been injuries."

Jenna chewed her lip. Yeah, there might have been injuries.

The Sentier fell silent as they moved through the crowds. They saw no sign of Cornelius, and when Johnson spotted a few soldiers, they made a swift exit.

"What's our next move then?" Johnson asked.

"We find somewhere to stay," Jenna replied. "Come back tomorrow."

"That's risky. Perhaps we should head to the plantation now."

"I want to give Cornelius a little longer. Can you get rooms for us, Allessa?"

Allessa secured a top hotel and, again, they were treated like VIPs. As they sat in the mosaic-floored lounge, soft drinks were brought for them. Jenna and Johnson stared at the walls. Frescos of nude Reglons showed intimate detail, making them realise what they'd been spared. Guests stared at them but they barely registered now.

"I need a piss," Johnson said, getting up.

Allessa pointed the way.

"Are you alright, Allessa?" Jenna asked, studying her, curiously.

The Sentier looked at her. "Since I have met you, I do not know what to think of anything anymore. I thought I knew the right way but now…"

"You think it's right people are bound into slavery?"

"It is not the Sentier way to interfere in civilisations' progress. We work on an energetic level to heal, to help, but we do not steer. Each race must find their own way, evolve at their own rate."

"If you ask me, that's a cop-out. Maybe sometimes progress gets stuck and can only evolve by being challenged."

Allessa stared at the floor. "I do not know who I am anymore…" She rubbed her forehead. "Whoever I am, I am an outcast now."

"Olixder doesn't know you're with us."

"He is not stupid. He knows I covered for you, though he will not understand why."

"Do you think he's here yet?"

"I do not know…"

"Well, there's been an arrest order issued," Jenna said, thoughtfully. "I expect the authorities have been more concerned with the protests today. Tomorrow could be different."

Allessa nodded. She stood. "I am going to lie down," she said, quietly.

Jenna watched her go, feeling sorry for the woman.

Johnson returned and took a swig of her drink. "We should see the others soon," she remarked.

"Yeah."

Johnson sniffed. "Is it still Flint you want? Or is it Brash?"

"A lot of time's past. Maybe they won't want me."

Johnson considered this. "I suppose Allessa's in the frame now too."

"Yeah..." Now she remembered her history with Lucas, him sleeping with the Sentier started to hit home.

"What was it like, getting your memory back?"

"Like waking up."

Johnson scratched her neck. "I might have been... a little hard on the other you."

"I remember."

"You do?"

"Of course. I was there."

"Didn't seem like you were. And, I tell you, the other you didn't like this you, *at all*. Jealous as hell, she was."

Jenna smiled and leaned over the table. "She's listening."

Johnson's eyes widened. "She is?"

Jenna laughed. "She's me. We are one person. I... just forgot things for a while."

"Well, don't forget again. It was weird getting the Admiral's daughter back. A total head fuck."

Lifting her glass, Jenna sat back, her smile fading. "I think Flint was right. I did need to rein myself in."

"Flint plays by the book. I wouldn't put too much stock in what he says."

"The thing is, when everything's easy, you can do anything. No consequences. It's hard not to get... carried away."

"Yeah, but you get to kick ass."

Jenna smiled. "As long as it's the right ass."

"You're not going to get fucking boring on me, are you, Trot?"

Jenna looked at her. "Now, come on, you know fun's my middle name."

Johnson smiled. Her smile dropped. "You can read thoughts?"

"Ah."

*

Jenna lay on her bed, staring up at the ceiling. She would see the others again soon. Now she had her memory back, it would be an uncomfortable meeting. Fortunately, Flint and Lucas would have had plenty of time to deal with it all... although, it seemed Lucas already had. Did he have feelings for the Sentier? As far as Jenna was concerned, that night on the beach with Flint had only just happened. She'd had no time to process it, had no idea how it would have played out. One minute, she had broken Lucas's heart; the next he'd slept with someone else. She found it hard to get her bearings.

Tossing her thoughts aside, she dozed.

"Ah, there you are."

Olixder. Jenna drew in a breath. *"I thought you knew how to conduct yourself, Olixder? Barging into someone's head is the height of bad manners, wouldn't you say?"*

"As is conning a whole city."

"Not a whole city. Just the wealthier parts."

"Your levity belies your situation, Jenna."

"Well, if you haven't got a sense of humour, what have you got?"

He paused. *"You seem... different."*

"Is there a reason for you contacting me like this? Want to rub salt into the wounds?"

"I would like you to tell me how you did it. I have uncovered many deceptions in my time, but I have never met anyone, other than a Sentier, who could manipulate energy. So?"

"Ah... Perhaps you should have asked that question before you told me about the arrest order. Not the smartest move. Guess you wanted to score your goal. Tell me, Olixder, is your ego so fragile?"

"You are insulting me? Is that a smart move? You could be making things far worse for yourself."

"Really? Can you chop a person's head off twice?"

He paused. *"I sense you are trying to get a reaction from me, Jenna. It will not work. I have many years on you."*

"A reaction from the wise old Head Sentier? I bet equanimity is your middle name."

"Do not play games with me. That is a dangerous game."

"Dangerous? You've already decided my life is forfeit. That game is played. But here's another one. We have to figure out why a mighty Head Sentier is so desperate to punish a girl, simply because she pulled the wool over his eyes."

"You conned the people of Pyshirian. You committed a crime."

"Oh, please. You don't give a damn about the people of Pyshirian. The people there merely serve to trump you up, and offer you a free meal ticket. At least, be honest with yourself, if not with me."

He paused again, stunned to be spoken to like this. *"You have no idea what the Sentier are."*

"Then enlighten me."

"We are overseers, we provide assistance. We work with energies..."

"You provide assistance to some but abandon others."

"Abandon who?"

"The slaves."

"We do not challenge cultural norms."

"So, I've heard. But maybe you should. If you don't challenge slavery, you condone it. You not only condone it, you perpetuate it, for if the wise old Head Sentier offers no protest, it must be sanctioned."

"You do not understand the way things are."

"I think I do... I think if you challenge the norm, you run the risk of losing your position here, losing your privileges and status. The ego wants gratification. It might be wrapped in a veil of wise authority, which I'm sure you buy into, but it's all bullshit, Olixder."

"How dare you speak to me like this!"

Jenna smiled. *"Ah, is the ego coming out to play now? Did the nasty woman prod it too hard?"*

"Do you think your goading will make me reverse my decision?"

"Your decision is irrelevant to me. I'm asking you to wake up to yourself."

"Wake up to myself...? You are addressing the Head Sentier!"

"I'm addressing some kind of imposter."

"You will regret speaking to me like this," he hissed.

"You're losing your cool, Olixder. Years on me? A few insults and the whole edifice comes tumbling down. Did you know you were so fragile? You know, when I first saw you, I wasn't sure what to make of you, but I have to say... you're something of a disappointment."

"What...!"

"Don't get me wrong, I'm sure there's a better Head Sentier in there, somewhere. But the thing is, the role you are playing is bogus, and you need to face up to it."

"You dare to prescribe to me!"

"And there's the god complex coming out. I've met that before. Classic sign of a fragile ego is a god complex."

"I can hardly believe what I am hearing...!"

"Yeah, it's difficult to face home truths, isn't it? I suggest you take that righteous anger and have a good hard look at what lies beneath it. You could be so much more, Olixder. I think, underneath all the crap, you're probably not that bad. So, here's a thought. Instead of freeloading off the

Reglons, why don't you use your influence to start the process of abolishing slavery. No-one should have their liberty and dignity taken away. That's plain evil. Are you evil or good, Olixder? Think about that."

"You think I will change course on your say so! On the whim of an ignorant little girl!"

"And now the put-downs. I have no idea but it's worth a shot. I'm looking at the bigger picture here. I think you should too. Sleep on it."

She opened her eyes and broke the link.

Miles away, Olixder sat, reeling.

Olixder

Olixder lay awake all night. This girl had got to him. Nobody got to him. His feathers seldom got ruffled. He couldn't believe he had managed to prove her right. He *had* lost his control. And so easily. But why? The answer stared him in the face. Nobody had challenged him like this before. No-one had dared. A small voice told him he had failed a test, a voice that started to question whether he was as wise and controlled as he thought.

She was controlled. Not scared at all. Why wasn't she scared? She should be scared. Does she not know what will be brought to bear on her! She should have been pleading for mercy, begging for forgiveness!

He shot up and paced around, hurling an ornament at the wall. He froze, staring at the broken shards in horror. Some part, deep inside, suspected the words she spoke might be true, yet another part raged against it.

The battle lasted through the night, Olixder swinging from indignant anger to bewildered questioning. By daybreak, one side had risen to dominance. It was the side that set off to meet Jenna Trot.

Coming Prepared

Compared to yesterday, the square was virtually empty. Allessa, Jenna, and Johnson stood under a columned portico, keeping to the shadows. Johnson watched Reglons walk by, wondering if the men wore anything under those gowns. The thought of loose Reglon junk turned her stomach.

"It is dangerous to still be here," Allessa said. "They will be looking for us. Every Reglon we have passed has stared at you. Humans do *not* blend in here."

"We need to meet Cornelius," Jenna said, looking around. "Without him, we're not going to get off this planet."

"Why d'you think Cornelius was looking for us?" Johnson asked. "D'you think his woman dumped him?"

"I hope not."

"She was too hot for him anyway, despite her big ears and fat belly."

"Maybe she's travelling with him. Maybe they got sick of Jakensk."

"Yeah... Or maybe she just dumped him."

Jenna frowned. "How does he know we're in this region?"

"Flint would have told him. They were in each other's pockets, weren't they?"

"You know, I've really missed him."

"Who? Flint?"

"Cornelius."

"You haven't remembered him for the past few weeks."

"*Yeah,* but I missed him before that."

"You sure? You did a lot of squabbling."

Jenna bit her lip. "He took a lot of crap from me. I need to say sorry."

"If I were y-" Johnson broke off and stared into the distance. "Oh... my... god..."

Jenna followed the direction of her gaze, her eyes fixing on what seemed like a mirage. Four bedraggled figures walked across the square, all of them familiar.

"It is Lucas..." Allessa murmured, star-struck.

Jenna glanced at the woman, having the sudden impulse to deck her. Ignoring it, she turned back, staring out at them.

Johnson walked forward. The two of them followed.

The figures drew nearer, stopping, staring back at them in awe. Brash stood frozen, his gaze moving between Jenna and Allessa. Jenna's gaze moved between Brash and Flint. It settled on Flint, who looked like some wild rebel combatant. The look was good.

Flint soaked Jenna in. She appeared like a vision in the white dress, an apparition that might disappear at any moment. He stepped forward. "Are you alright?" He wanted to touch her, test she was real, but he held himself in check.

"I'm fine," she replied, her gaze lingering on him.

Brash didn't step forward. Not only was this extremely awkward, it was utterly confusing.

"Lucas, you are hurt," Allessa said, moving over to him. She crouched, laying her hands over his leg. Brash stared down at her. Hadn't the woman dumped him...? His eyes flitted to Jenna. Jenna's eyes locked with his.

Newark's shock turned to a broad grin. "You're alive, you jammy bitches," he said, hobbling over to Johnson, throwing an arm around her.

Johnson smiled and punched his arm. "So are you, you jammy bastard."

"Good to see you, Trot," he said, acknowledging her with a nod of his chin. "Never thought *you'd* make it."

Jenna smiled at him, stealing at glance at Brash. As Allessa rose to her feet, Brash backed away slightly. He surmised now the Sentier and Jenna had been talking.

Jenna's attention shifted to Fraza. The Kaledian stared at the ground. "Is Fraza alright?" she asked.

"He hasn't been himself since we got here," Flint told her.

"Yeah, he's completely out of it," Newark remarked, sourly.

Jenna walked up to Fraza. He didn't register her. "What's wrong with him?"

"He's flipped out."

"Fraza, it's me," she said, touching his arm. His eyes remained on the ground.

Brash cleared his throat. "We haven't been able to get through to him."

Jenna shook Fraza's shoulders. "Fraza, it's me. Jenna. The Jenna you lost. I'm back."

Brash, Flint, and Newark looked at Johnson.

"Yep. She's back," Johnson said.

"She's back?" Newark asked, staring at Trot in wide-eyed wonder. A smile possessed his face and he hobbled over to her, lifting her into a bear hug. "Welcome fucking back, Trot!"

Jenna laughed. "Good to see you too, Newark."

As the man put her down, she turned to Allessa. "I think Newark could use your gifts too," she said, looking at her, steadily.

230

"Of course," the Sentier said, coming over and crouching before him. Newark looked down at her, wondering what *she* was doing here. His gaze moved to Brash, before switching to Jenna.

Jenna chewed her lip. "I'm worried about Fraza."

"I wouldn't worry too much," Newark said. "The bastard let me get eaten by a plant."

Jenna's brow creased. Sounds of commotion turned their heads. Reglon pedestrians rushed out of the square.

"Oh, no," Allessa said, straightening, staring down the square in horror.

At the bottom, a small army of Reglons stood behind a line of silvery Sentier. The crew turned to find more soldiers blocking their escape.

"All this for a handful of fugitives?" Brash asked, stunned.

"It's me and Trot they're after," Johnson said.

"What?"

"It's a long story."

Flint unpacked arsenal, handing out the weapons.

"Jenna, we have to plead for mercy," Allessa urged.

Jenna glanced at her. "You have to pick a side, Allessa. If you want to go, go now. And quick."

Allessa stared at the line of Sentier, caught in a horrible dilemma. Go against her own people, or do what she felt to be right. "I stay," she said.

"Right. All of you, keep back."

"What are you doing?" Brash asked, concerned.

"I'm just going to talk," Jenna said, walking forward.

Flint caught her arm. "Jenna, what's this about?"

"No time to explain."

"Don't do this," he implored, his blue eyes begging her.

She smiled at him, gently. "It's OK. I've got this."

Releasing herself from his grasp, she walked forward. Allessa hesitated, then reluctantly followed after her.

Further down, Olixder walked forward too, his long garment trailing on stone. *"We meet again,"* he said, his sights fixed on Jenna.

"How are you feeling this morning, Olixder?"

"Very well. I did not sleep soundly last night but I am much improved. I want to thank you for making me take a good hard look at myself. It is important to question one's motives."

"And you have done that?"

"I have."

"And what did you find?"

"I find you to be a threat to public order. A criminal that is about to be held to account."

231

Jenna stopped several feet away from him, looking at him for a long moment. "You really do disappointment me, Olixder."

Olixder's face tightened. His eyes moved to Allessa. "You betray your Order, Allessa?"

"I have no wish to do that but I think... I think there is a better way."

"I see she has got inside your head. She is good at that. Come and stand in my ranks and all will be forgiven."

"I am afraid I cannot do that."

From behind, the crew watched this odd exchange, baffled as to what was going on. Flint's weapon pointed at the Sentier, his heart hammering in his chest. He couldn't bear to lose her when he had just found her.

Olixder's grey eyes lingered on Allessa, turning hard as they fixed on Jenna. "I will not kill you now. There is to be a public execution."

Jenna shook her head. "You're such a hypocrite, aren't you? You say you do not get involved, yet, here you are, taking the law into your own hands."

"That is because you pose a dangerous threat to these people. Only the Sentier can be trusted to work with energy."

"Ah, I see. It's all about you then. I think *you* have a dangerous gift and it's called, manipulation. I prefer to talk straight. So, here it is. There will be no execution. As from this moment, you are no longer Head Sentier. Allessa will take your place."

"What...?" Allessa asked.

Olixder's eyes widened, incredulously. "Bold words but I doubt you can back them up." The grey eyes turned hard.

A pressure tightened around Jenna's throat. Focusing, she blasted the energy back at him and Olixder stumbled slightly.

Looking at her, surprised, he raised his hand. The line of Sentier stepped forward. Within moments, Jenna felt that pressure again, stronger this time, tightening ruthlessly.

Resisting the pressure, she focused her power and intent, breaking the chains of energy wrapping around her throat.

Olixder raised his arm again and the army fired. Jenna created a shield around her and Allessa, the fire deflecting, some hitting Olixder's shield.

"She really is back..." Newark murmured. "I *missed* her..."

"Is that all you've got, Olixder?" Jenna asked, viewing him with disdain.

An enormous weight crushed down on her. Focusing again, she blasted the compressed energy to smithereens, creating a shower of light above her head.

"Still not enough, Olixder," she said.

The Sentier concentrated their efforts repeatedly, but her shield could not be penetrated and, at last, they were forced to give up. Dropping her shield, she focused on the Sentier, intending invisible walls around them, walls that squeezed, crushing them. Their arms pressed to their sides. They struggled to breathe. Olixder stared at her, his grey eyes bulging.

She released them.

"You underestimated me," she said.

"How did you do that...?" Olixder choked out, struggling to reclaim his breath. "No-one can manipulate energy like that."

"I'm not manipulating energy." He stared at her, bewildered. "Now, this is what will happen. You will walk away with your men. There is no need for anyone to die. You will relinquish your position and hand it over to Allessa."

Still staring at her, Olixder turned, making a gesture to those behind. Jenna waited. Nothing happened and no-one left.

"Walk away," Jenna said, giving him a hard stare. "You have no idea what I'm capable of."

"I think I am beginning to understand, but I always come prepared."

She viewed him, oddly. Noise erupted in the air above. She looked up. Craft hovered right over them, a yellow mist raining down. She looked at Olixder, who wore a mask, those behind him masked-up too.

Struggling to breathe, she, Allessa, and the crew behind, fell to the ground.

Olixder stood over Jenna. "There will be a public execution," he said.

The words rang in her head as the world disappeared.

Family Day Out

The populace headed for an arena. Cornelius watched them, some holding hands with their children. There had been no trace of Jenna in the square, but Cornelius was intrigued to know what was going on here. He asked one of the knobbly-headed beings.

"There are to be executions," the Reglon replied, gazing at Cornelius's stomach. "We haven't had an execution for many years. It is very exciting."

Cornelius stared at the man, a bad feeling settling in his gut. He tried, again, to contact Jenna, but still nothing.

"What's going on?" Graham asked.

"Executions. Come on." Cornelius followed the crowds.

"Shouldn't we be looking for the crew?" Graham asked.

"I just want to take a look."

"Didn't know you had a gore streak, Cornelius?"

Cornelius didn't respond.

The open-air arena heaved with spectators, a palpable feeling of excitement and anticipation in the air. Down below, an executioner's block sat in the centre of the floor. Around it, stood a number of wooden carriages with metal bars on the windows. It was the oddest and most barbaric sight. Cornelius observed a line of silvery-grey beings sitting on a platform near the block. They looked serious, emotionless. A handful of soldiers lined the perimeter.

"Do we really want to watch this?" Graham asked.

Cornelius didn't answer.

A food seller walked between the rows. Graham gestured that he had no money but the guy handed him a small package anyway.

"God, they *are* in the holiday spirit, aren't they?" Graham remarked. He sniffed the food then tucked in.

Cornelius glanced at him. "You're going to eat before you watch an execution?"

"Hey, you're the one that wants to watch. Besides, I've not eaten all morning."

Down below, the Sentier may have appeared emotionless but they felt hugely conflicted. They obeyed and followed their Head, unquestioningly, but certain questions swirled in their minds. Was the punishment not extreme? Did it really demand the death penalty? And why was this execution being conducted so publicly? That was not the Sentier way. It was almost as if their Head wanted to humiliate his victims. Over to their

235

right, the governors and their families sat in fancy boxes, tucking into treats and snacks. The family day-out atmosphere unsettled many of the Sentier. This should be a necessary evil for the greater good, not a sport to be enjoyed. Why would their Head allow this?

Olixder stood and walked off the platform. The crowd fell silent as he addressed them. "Citizens of Iprian," he called out, loudly, "it is a long time since executions have been held here. And it is not a decision taken lightly. But the law must be respected, as must the Sentier. The beings facing justice today are not from this planet-"

"Death to the aliens!" a fervent voice shouted.

"They are a divisive and disruptive force that pose a threat to you. That threat will be removed here today."

"Kill the aliens!"

Graham sunk down in his chair.

"What is their crime?" someone shouted. The Sentier, alone, heard this voice.

Olixder whipped his head, searching the crowd. "They have used fear and deception to exhort money from hard-working Reglons. They have challenged the authority of the Sentier. These beings wield dangerous powers and, if left to their own devices, would pose a serious threat, not only here but on other planets too."

"Have they killed anyone?"

Olixder continued to search, and Graham wondered what he was looking for. He glanced at Cornelius. "Are you communicating with him? he whispered.

"I want to know why they deserve to die," Cornelius whispered back.

"Seriously? Let him get on with his speech and let's get the fuck out of here."

Olixder sights honed in on them. "As yet, they have not killed anyone but it is a matter of time."

The crowd voiced their agreement.

"Today, we put an end to this threat," Olixder vowed, his sights lingering on the white-haired being. "Today, we stamp it out."

The crowd cheered in accord.

Olixder walked back to the platform, taking a front-row seat. Some of the Sentier didn't have the stomach for this.

The crowd became animated as the first victim got dragged out of a wagon. Cornelius's eyes bulged. Graham spat out his food, staring down in horror.

Cheering and jeering got louder. Jenna pulled her listless eyes open, her addled brain struggling to make sense of where she was. She lay on a wooden floor in a confined space, a barred window a couple of feet above her. As she moved a heavy arm, a chain rattled. The chains attached to manacles on her wrists and ankles. She tried to stand but her body wasn't working.

Memories filtered through, the situation becoming clear. Her tingling arms regained feeling. By force of will, she reached and grabbed the bars, hauling herself up, her limp legs daggling beneath her. She gazed out at a huge arena and a baying crowd, her eyes widening in shock on seeing Johnson dragged, kicking and punching, to an executioner's block.

Desperately, she tried to shake off the listlessness, tried to focus, her mind as sluggish as her body. Mounting panic worked against her. She screamed inside. Her friend was about to die and there was nothing she could do.

In another wagon, Flint rattled the bars. Chained like an animal, he couldn't break free. He watched, helpless, as Johnson was forced to her knees, three guards holding her in position. Rattling the bars harder, he started praying to gods he didn't even believe in.

What happened next could turn an atheist into a believer. The guards hurtled back. Other guards ran forward and flew back too, some landing unconscious. Shots exchanged. Pandemonium filled the arena. Flint caught a glimpse of Johnson being thrown a gun by... Graham...? Then he saw their saviour.

"It's Cornelius," Flint said, staring out in wonder.

"Cornelius? Is Johnson alright?" Brash yanked on his chains.

"Yes. She's here."

"What?"

The door of the wagon burst open and Johnson appeared, throwing them a key. As Brash and Flint freed themselves, Johnson charged to next wagon, firing as she went. Grabbing the key from a hook outside, she glanced behind her. Graham, stationed behind a wagon, fired at the remaining guards, giving her cover. Cornelius held his own against the group of Sentier.

She opened the door to find Allessa lying out of it. Cursing, she fired more rounds as she ran on.

Flint and Brash ran out, lifting dead guy's weapons, and firing like crazy.

Opening the next door, Johnson found Newark awake. Throwing him the key, she moved on, finding Jenna at last.

"I can't do anything!" Jenna yelled in helpless frustration.

Johnson came in to free her, spotting a needle on the floor. "They've injected you. Can't you move?"

"I'm getting some feeling back but I can't stand. And my mind's fuzzy. I can't focus it."

"Come on, Trot, pull your shit together."

"I'm fucking trying!"

Jenna attempted to stand but fell to her knees. Johnson carted her out.

As the remaining guards went down, Brash, Graham, and Flint turned their focus to the Sentier, but their fire kept being deflected. Cornelius knew this was a losing battle. They used energy manipulation, coming at him from all angles. What he was doing wasn't going to work. He needed to change tack. Focusing on one Sentier, he managed to get in close, going hand to hand with him. The other Sentier held back, unwilling to hurt one of their own. Even Olixder restrained himself. He didn't want to be the first Head to kill a Sentier. Allessa didn't count. She was a traitor.

Discharging round after ineffective round, Flint searched for Jenna. Johnson carried her out, setting her on her staggering feet. Jenna's face contorted in horror. Flint whipped his head back to see Cornelius land semi-conscious on the floor.

"End him!" Olixder yelled.

"No!" Jenna cried.

Dropping their useless weapons, the crew charged the Sentier, getting knocked back, again and again. Sentier dragged Cornelius to the executioner's block. Jenna battled to free herself. Sense returned to her body. Her mind started to clear, but not quickly enough.

Time slowed as the executioner's axe fell.

Sick cheers rang in Jenna's ears as she dropped to her knees.

The crew stared at the lifeless form of their much-loved mentor.

Changing Heads

A primal scream tore through the arena, as if someone's soul had been ripped from their body.

Jenna slowly pulled herself up. The walls of the arena crumbled as she punched out her arms, blasting stone, wanting to tear the whole place down. Shrieking Reglons ran. Bodies flew through the air, as if the wrath of the gods had descended. A stone block broke free, hanging in the air as Jenna searched for Olixder.

"Where is he!" she screamed, her wild eyes scanning the place. She couldn't see him through the commotion.

A hand touched her arm. "Blind rage, Jenna? After all this time?"

The block dropped, squashing a couple of Reglons. She turned to stare at an apparition. "C... Cornelius...?"

The rest of the crew gazed at him too, their eyes transferring to the headless corpse on the ground. Sentier followed their gazes, staring in horror at their fallen comrade.

"How...?" Jenna uttered.

"Projecting thoughts is one thing. Projecting two images simultaneously is quite another. But," Cornelius said with a shrug. "I actually did it."

"What...?" Newark asked, gawking at him.

"The Sentier I knocked out appeared to be me, and I appeared to be him."

"What...?"

"It's a mind trick, Mr. Newark." Cornelius scratched his neck. "Never been able to pull that off before. Damn glad I did."

"No shit...?"

"Shit, Mr. Newark. Pretty cool shit, too."

Jenna threw her arms around Cornelius, squeezing him tight. "I thought you were dead."

"Err, these fuckers are trying to get away," Johnson said, and Jenna turned to see the Sentier running off.

She frowned. A deep rumble started, and an avalanche of stone blocked the exits. The Sentier looked around, fearfully, some attempting to climb the destroyed seating. She dragged them down, slamming them on the floor near the others.

Scowling, she walked over to them. "Where is he?" she barked.

"Think the fucker's bailed," Newark said, looking around. "He sure as shit scarpered fast."

Jenna took a deep, calming breath, surveying the group of Sentier. A few nursed injuries. A couple had been knocked out. She sneered at them. "Not so high and mighty now, are you? Things are going to change," she told them. "Allessa is your new Head. You do whatever the fuck she says. Got that?"

The Sentier stared at her, helplessly.

"Where *is* Allessa?" Brash asked.

Johnson pointed. "She's flaked out in that wagon."

Jenna's eyes followed Brash as he walked off to fetch her.

One of the Sentier spoke and she reeled around. "Shut your goddam mouth," she shouted at him. "You speak when I tell you."

Johnson sidled up to her. "Can I punch one of them?"

Jenna looked at Cornelius. "Can she?"

"Help yourself," Cornelius said, extending a gracious arm.

As Johnson took the shot, Jenna raised her eyebrows to Cornelius. "I thought you didn't approve of that sort of thing?"

"What sort of thing? Bearing the consequences of your decisions?"

Brash entered the wagon to find Allessa sitting up, groggy.

"Is everyone alright?" she asked, concerned.

"They are now," he said, stiffly, bitterness taking root. "Come on, Jenna's made you Head Sentier."

"What...?"

He helped her up.

As Brash and Allessa approached, Jenna turned to the group of Sentier. "This is your new Head," she said, indicating Allessa. "Anyone questions this, they'll have me to answer to."

One of the Sentier held his hand up. She nodded for him to speak.

"The Head has to be inaugurated by the old Head," he told her.

"Well, in that case, she will be acting Head until we find the old Head, and get him to swear her in."

"What... What if he will not do that?"

Jenna pursed her lips. "What happens if the old Head suddenly dies?"

"Then a new Head is voted in."

"What happens if the old Head absconds and doesn't come back?"

"Then a new Head is voted in."

"Right, well, if he comes back, he'll either agree to inaugurate her, or he'll die. Either way, it comes down to a vote, so let's cut the crap. Raise your hands if you want Allessa to be Head." She glowered at them, threateningly.

"But... there are many Sentier in the region, hundreds on Lixia. They all have to vote."

"All of them...?"

The Sentier nodded.

"Jenna," Allessa said, "you haven't even asked me if I want to be Head."

"Well, do you?"

"Not really."

"But you're the only one who can change things."

Allessa bowed her head. "I know..."

"This is not going to be a quick process," Cornelius said. "We have to work this through."

Jenna slowly nodded. He was right. She looked at Flint. "We need to finish what we started on Draztis, and we need to work with the Sentier."

"You want to carry on?" Flint asked her.

"Those slaves can't help themselves."

Flint stared at her, a smile breaking on his face. The smile absorbed her.

Johnson glanced at Graham, her heart lifting. He had fetched Cornelius and come back to save her. He *did* still care. The day had turned from one hell of a nightmare into a pretty good fucking day.

Lixia

The crew escorted the Sentier to their ship. Flint determined they would hold a general Sentier meeting before Olixder could hold one. They would travel to Lixia straight away. It would take Olixder weeks to get there on a bog-standard craft. They had the SMHD.

Their craft was parked outside Iprian on an area of flat grassland. As they walked toward it, Newark kept his eyes peeled, wondering if any Neanderthals lived in these parts. Flint glanced at Jenna, knowing she had her memory back. Brash glanced at Jenna, wondering what she thought of him.

The gangway lowered as they approached. Walking up into the boarding area, Johnson pulled Graham aside. "You rescued me," she said, staring at him like a love-struck teenager.

He looked at her, uncomfortably. "I came to rescue you all."

"Well, I know but-" Her heart stopped when she spotted *her*. The Saffria came forward and took Graham's arm, looking at Johnson, warily.

"I'm still with Yasnay," Graham said, awkwardly, leading his girlfriend away.

Johnson stared after him.

Takeza appeared, embracing Cornelius. Brash hung, awkwardly. He was on a spaceship with two ex's and he wasn't sure how either of them felt about him. His own feelings were equally confused.

Flint turned to the group of Sentier. "There's a lounge on this level. Sit down and use your mind-reading abilities to get assembling." He looked at the crew. "I'm holding a meeting straight away."

Jenna gave the silvery beings a hard look. "If you so much as think of bailing on us, I'll hunt you down."

The Sentier's eyes widened.

As they left the boarding area, and walked down the passage, Newark sidled up to Jenna. "You're scary."

She smiled at him. "Good."

Graham and Yasnay chatted as they walked ahead. Johnson eyes ran over the lilac-skinned woman, over the prissy cream dress, and glossy purple hair. Jenna's eyes tracked Fraza. He reminded her of a cow, mindlessly following the herd.

The group entered the lift, Flint taking fleeting glances at Jenna. Brash kept his head down. Allessa watched him, thoughtfully. Newark clocked

Graham and his bird holding hands. Cornelius and *his* bird held hands too. He frowned, staring at the floor. Why did he never get a bird?

Emerging onto the upper deck, they entered the conference room, and sat around the long table.

"Right," Flint said. "I need to know where everyone is. Jenna and I are committed to carrying on with our mission. What about the rest of you?"

"Wait a minute," Jenna said. "Where's Skinner?"

"Mr. Skinner is in his quarters," Takeza told her.

"Is he alright?"

"Well... no," Cornelius said, rubbing a hand over his mouth. "I'm afraid I've got my work cut out there. We would have been here sooner but we had a problem with a drive-plate, and Mr. Skinner was not on top form."

"That's putting it mildly," Graham remarked, sourly.

Jenna looked at Graham. "So, you got to our ship then went back for Cornelius?"

Graham nodded.

And took that bloody bitch with you, Johnson thought, bitterly.

"So, where are you all with this then?" Flint asked. His eyes brushed over the crew, omitting Fraza as Fraza wasn't anywhere.

"I could do with some payback," Newark said, eternally grateful to Flint for rescuing him from a horrific death.

"Me too," Johnson seconded, glancing at the Saffria.

"How about you, Brash?" Flint asked.

Brash nodded. He owed Flint. "I'm in."

"OK. Our first port of call is Lixia. If we gain the support of the Sentier, and install Allessa as Head, this could prove of great benefit in the region. After that, we return to Draztis, and finish what we started."

"I bet it's a mess," Newark said.

"Yes... And we no longer have the support of the army."

"Then we get it back," Jenna asserted.

"How?" Newark asked.

Jenna's lip curved. "I have a few tricks up my sleeve."

Brash smiled, fondly. Allessa noticed and experienced a surge of jealously.

"So, the drive's fully operational now?" Jenna asked.

"Yes," Cornelius said.

"Good. We should be on Lixia in no time."

*

244

The crew gathered on the flight-deck, looking out as they descended. Lixia possessed a strange beauty. Craggy grey mountains towered up to a lilac sky. Johnson hated that sky. Lakes and rivers, too, had a lilac gleam as if the place taunted her.

"There is Estria," Allessa said, pointing. Brash corrected course.

The capital city sat in a bowl of mountains, the towering rocks dwarfing its grey stone buildings.

Bringing them in, Brash set down on a huge, circular patch of stone outside the city.

Collecting the Sentier, they disembarked. Fraza and Skinner stayed behind in their rooms. Takeza agreed to remain with them.

The crew looked around, breathing in uplifting air. Before them, the city perched on a low mound of rock.

"Well, communicating should be easy," Cornelius remarked, surveying the city. He smiled at Jenna. "The Sentier can do the work for us."

"What do you mean?" Brash asked, frowning.

"He means," Johnson said, "that like Cornelius, Jenna can read minds and transfer thoughts."

"What...?"

Brash, Newark, and Graham stared at Jenna.

Jenna cringed. "It's true," she quietly confessed.

"Since when...?" Brash asked, stunned.

She scrunched her face. "Since we left Cyntros."

"Cyntros? Why didn't you tell me...?"

"Err..." She chewed her lip. "I thought it would make things... awkward."

Brash fell silent, processing this.

Jenna, keen to brush over the topic, turned to Flint. "Do you think Allessa should speak?"

"I think *we* should speak," Flint said.

"OK, but *I* don't want to speak."

He raised his eyebrows to her. "Any reason?"

She bit her lip. "I tend to be... rash." Since they'd left Juyra, she'd been beating herself up. She'd thought herself invincible but she wasn't. She'd put the crew and herself in danger because of her arrogance.

"Should I speak, Mr Flint?" Cornelius suggested.

Flint turned to him, thinking Cornelius would be an excellent choice. He nodded.

Brash's eyes widened. *That was how she knew about the shape-shifting prostitute on Cyntros!*

245

Cornelius tilted his head, studying Brash. Clearing his throat, he turned to the loitering Sentier. "Please, lead the way," he said, extending a gracious arm.

The Sentier led the crew away from the landing area, the silvery-skinned beings subdued. *They* had been thinking on the short journey too. They did not approve of that public execution, and a few of them wondered if Olixder had lost his mind.

Newark walked beside Jenna, viewing her, critically. "You've not been reading my thoughts, have you?"

"I wouldn't do that." She glanced at him. "Honestly. No way do I want to know what goes through your mind."

He nodded then shook his head. "You're one freaky little mother, aren't you?"

She thought about that. "Yeah. Guess I am."

Walking up worn, uneven steps, they entered under a wide stone arch. The Sentier took them through a maze of narrow walkways, the whole city pedestrianised. The place had an old feel as if the stone had stood for hundreds of years. Passers-by tilted their heads, their grey eyes fixing them. A few heads bowed, graciously.

Turning onto a wider walkway, they approached another impressive arch. The grey building behind it resembled a castle, with turrets rearing up. It stretched from left to right, built from great chunks of stone.

"That is the Parnithian," Allessa informed them.

"Government?" Jenna asked.

Allessa tilted her head, assessing. "A cross between government and a university."

The crew looked at her, puzzled.

"We take a holistic approach here," she explained.

Whatever that means, Newark thought. Personally, he wouldn't let students near politics. He frowned. What did students know about life? A stint in the school of hard knocks would bring *them* down to earth. He stared ahead at the ancient building, imagining ghosts and cobwebs.

Walking under the arch, they entered a cobbled forecourt. Most of the Sentier walked off, leaving one remaining.

"Where are they going?" Jenna asked, suspiciously.

The male Sentier turned to her. "It will take weeks for all the Sentier to arrive back."

"Weeks...? We haven't got weeks."

"Shit," Newark said, looking around. "This place looks dull as sin. And I bet they don't have tea."

"We can't stay weeks," Jenna insisted.

Cornelius touched her shoulder. "There is nothing we can do about that."

"We have accommodation prepared for you," the Sentier told her.

"Really?" Jenna asked. "After everything that happened?"

"We Sentier do not hold grudges."

"You sure about that?" Jenna asked, thinking of Olixder. The man looked down. Jenna rubbed her forehead. "Well, it's up to Flint. He's the captain."

Flint and Cornelius registered the comment.

"OK, we stay," Flint said. He looked at the Sentier. "We accept your kind hospitality."

Nodding graciously, the Sentier led them across the forecourt, and down a long, gloomy tunnel that stretched to a circle of light in the distance.

"D'you reckon we've died and don't know it?" Newark joked to Johnson.

Johnson gave no response.

Allessa walked beside Brash. "This city is my home," she said. "Perhaps I could show you around it."

Jenna turned to look at them. Brash's eyes flitted to her. Flint watched Jenna, thoughtfully.

They emerged into a courtyard, surrounded by doors.

"This is where the novices are housed," Allessa told them, looking around in reminiscence. "The dormitories must not be full at the moment."

Taken through one of the doors, their eyes examined a sparse, bleak room. Apart from the beds and washing facilities, the place was barren.

Jenna chewed her lip. No wonder they went planet hopping.

"You sure they don't hold grudges?" Newark said. "Don't they have hotels here?"

"I am afraid we do not," Allessa replied, sitting on one of the beds.

Jenna looked at her, oddly. "Aren't you going to your own home, Allessa?"

"I would like to stay with you," she said, glancing at Brash. Brash's eyes flitted to Jenna.

Johnson looked around. No way was she sleeping in a dormitory with Graham and his new bird.

In fact, none of the crew were happy about the sleeping arrangements.

"Sod this," Newark said. "I'm sleeping on the craft."

"Good idea," Cornelius agreed.

*

The days clocked by. Even the ship felt cramped. Johnson kept bumping into Graham, who was constantly attached to his woman. The sight of them made her feel sick. They appeared awkward on seeing her but she didn't give a toss how awkward the fuckers felt.

Brash felt awkward all the time. Being in the same place as Jenna and Allessa proved stressful. How much did Jenna know?

Newark wandered around, aimlessly. He didn't have many people to talk to. Graham was all loved-up. Skinner and Fraza were out of it. Brash kept disappearing. Johnson kept biting his head off. And Cornelius was always with his woman. He couldn't believe the old goat had so much stamina. Jenna told him Cornelius would be making up for lost time, but still...?

Allessa knew Lucas was avoiding her. She'd hurt him but she had left because her feelings were becoming too strong. Those feelings had not subsided since they'd been apart. If anything, they had grown. She wasn't sure how things were between Lucas and Jenna, but she couldn't hold back any longer. She needed to talk to him.

She found him in the bar with Newark, Flint, and Jenna.

"And he just walked around in circles," Newark complained. "Choking to bloody death I was."

Jenna bit her lip, hiding a smile. Newark provided a wonderful buffer. If he hadn't been there, she would have felt extremely uncomfortable. She, Lucas, and Flint had not discussed what had happened on the beach. In truth, she didn't want to because she was more conflicted than ever. She would look at Flint and feel an overwhelming attraction. Then she'd look at Brash and her heart would melt. Lucas didn't try to win her over anymore. If anything, he seemed uneasy around her. Did he want the Sentier now?

"Excuse me," Allessa interrupted and they looked up. "Would you like me to show you around the city now, Lucas?" she asked.

Brash's eyes flicked to Jenna. Jenna studied him, curiously.

"I owe you an explanation," Allessa added.

His eyes flitted to Jenna again. He looked at Allessa, about to decline, but those enchanting grey eyes bewitched him. Nodding, he rose from his seat.

Jenna's chest tightened. She and Newark watched them walk out together. Flint watched Jenna. "Would you like to take a walk with me, Jenna?" he asked.

She turned to him. His blonde hair had grown. He appeared rougher, wilder. She forgot about Brash.

248

"We'll be back soon," she said to Newark.

Newark slugged back his drink, knowing he'd been sacked off.

Jenna and Flint headed away from the city, walking beside a lilac river, the huge mountains towering around them. Jenna drew in a breath of uplifting air, a tiny breeze caressing her face. The place was perfect. She hoped he didn't ask about that kiss.

A purple-feathered bird came to land in their path.

Jenna smiled. "Johnson wouldn't be pleased." Flint turned to her. "Everything's purple or lilac here. It reminds her of Graham's girlfriend."

"Ah..." He smiled. "It's like the universe is conspiring against her."

"Something like that, only those weren't her exact words."

Smile fading, he rubbed his forehead. "Jenna, I need to ask..." *Crap, he was going to ask her.* "Did anything... happen to you when you were a slave?"

Her brow creased. "Oh," she said, cottoning on. "No, nothing," she said, shaking her head. "It nearly did, but it didn't." He breathed out, and she saw how worried he'd been. "In fact, I spent most of my time ghost-busting."

He raised his eyebrows to her, and she told him about the series of events leading up to their near-execution. He listened, absorbed. When she finished, he looked at her, awkwardly. "So... you remember everything now?"

"Yes." *He was going to ask her. How did she feel about him? Why was it so confusing?*

"Right." He looked around at the mountains. "So, do you want me to carry on where Newark left off?"

"Excuse me?"

"With the story."

"Oh. Yes. Yes, course." *He wasn't asking...? Had his feelings changed?*

She kept her eyes on him as he spoke. He seemed younger than the Flint she used to know, yet more mature too.

"Wild men?" she asked. "They were going to eat them?"

"Yes. Newark's been very nice to me since."

"Ah, that's how to get on his good side. Save him from a boiling pot." She smiled and he smiled back at her, their eyes locking together. His eyes were the clearest blue, like pools of beautiful crystal. "Why don't you ask me?" she whispered.

"Because it's clear you don't know what you want."

Her eyes watered. "I'm sorry..."

He gave her a gentle smile. "Don't be."

Over in the city, Brash had a similar conversation. "You left because you had feelings for me...?"

Allessa nodded. "I... do not do relationships, Lucas. It... took me by surprise."

"I see..." He stared at the ground. "I thought you'd been... using me."

"At first, maybe but... I am sorry... Do you still have feelings for me, Lucas?"

He looked into her beautiful eyes. "Yes..."

"But you have feelings for Jenna, too, and you are not sure what you want."

He lowered onto a stone bench, looking over pristine flowerbeds. "It was always Jenna before. When you came along, it threw me." He bit his lip. "She hurt me. She kissed Flint."

Allessa sat beside him. "I know. I know what happened."

He nodded. "I assume she knows about us?"

"Yes." She smiled at him, sadly. "I will back away and let you decide what you want. Perhaps you should talk to Jenna."

He nodded.

Brash did talk to Jenna and she apologized for hurting him. "It... sort of crept up on me. I was baffled myself."

"Weren't we happy?" he asked.

"I... thought so."

"Is it Flint you want?"

"I don't know... Is it Allessa *you* want?"

Neither of them could answer each other's questions.

In another part of the ship, Cornelius stood in Skinner's room, wondering what to do about the man. Newark stood there too. He was bored.

"Perhaps we should give him some more of those drugs," Newark suggested. "Maybe they'll sort him out again."

"Or maybe they'll make him worse."

"Can he get any worse?" Skinner lay on his bunk, curled into the foetal position.

"There's always worse, Mr. Newark." Cornelius scratched his chin. "I'll try a series of hypnotherapy. See if I can kick-start the right networks again. I just need to tap in to the other Mr. Skinner."

"He's still there?"

"Oh, yes. He's lurking about in there somewhere."

"What about Fraza?"

"Fraza gained a lot of confidence in a short time. Stands to reason it would fall apart so quickly. We need to retrieve him too. I'll start on Mr. Skinner. Now, could you leave us, please?"

Newark looked glum. He had bugger-all else to do. Cornelius appraised him. "OK, you can watch but I shouldn't imagine much will happen for a while. It's going to be a slow process."

Newark watched for five minutes then got bored. He went to the bar to get a drink. Takeza sat in there. Cornelius's bird liked a drink?

He poured himself a blue drink and sat with her. "These are Hellgathen drinks," he told her. "You should try this blue one. It blows your head off."

The woman smiled.

After another drink, he asked her what it was like being a prostitute. Cornelius had told Takeza all about this crew, and she felt she knew Mr. Newark already. Consequently, she was not offended. They chatted easily, and Newark thought she wasn't half bad.

Over the weeks, they shared many drinks, Cornelius kept busy with Skinner and Fraza. If Takeza didn't have a pot belly and pointy ears, it might have felt inappropriate, but Newark knew Cornelius had nothing to worry about. She definitely wasn't his type. The more she mentioned her former life, the more Newark realised how shit it had been. He was glad they had freed them. She even thanked him and it made him feel proud.

Johnson materialised one afternoon. She came into the bar, looking miserable. Pouring a drink, she threw it back. "I wish he'd fuck off with his whore," she threw out.

"Who? Graham?" Newark asked.

"He should go and find himself a cosy house somewhere, and settle the fuck down. They're making me sick to my stomach."

Newark could relate. It turned his stomach too. Graham had no time for him, either. He didn't know what to say to Johnson. Something came out of nowhere. "Perhaps he's punishing you."

Johnson stared at him. She shook her head. What did Newark know?

Johnson continued to be miserable. Jenna and Brash continued to be conflicted. Flint and Allessa continued to wait. And Newark continued to be bored.

Jenna wanted to ask Cornelius about his mind-trick but each time she remembered, she found him tied up with Skinner or Fraza.

The days dragged. They spent a lot of time wandering around the city or the surrounding area. Though the Sentier were gracious, they were not very chatty. Newark thought they were arrogant, stuck-up bastards.

Newark became so bored, when he stumbled across gardens in the city, he almost wet himself. The novelty wore off quick, though. Jenna tried to help him, suggesting they take an expedition up a mountain. She persuaded Johnson to come too.

The three of them set off, negotiating craggy ledges until they collapsed a third of the way up. Taking in the view, they watched a craft come in to land.

"They're starting to arrive back," Jenna remarked.

"No shit," Newark said

Sentier numbers grew by the day, the circular landing patch getting crowded. Other circular patches around the city filled up too.

"How much longer?" Newark complained to Takeza as they sat in the bar. "How many fucking Sentier can there be?"

Takeza looked up. Newark turned to see Skinner walk in, his back erect. Skinner glanced at them. "I want a woman. Are there any whores in this city?"

Newark would have shaken his head, vigorously, if he wasn't staring at Skinner in shock.

Cornelius walked in behind him. "I'm bloody good, if I do say so myself."

Challenging Wisdom

Weeks of pain and struggle brought Johnson to a sobering conclusion. She had to find a way past Graham and move on. She wanted to get this meeting over with, get off this planet, and throw herself into action. Indeed, all the crew wanted to get moving now.

Except Fraza. He hadn't moved out of his room for weeks.

Cornelius approached Jenna in the lounge. "Jenna, I wonder if you could come with me. Fraza's becoming more receptive, and I think we need your input now."

"My input?"

"Yes. You were like a mentor to him, in more ways than one. You were also a crutch. We'll deal with that later but, for now, we need to reintroduce you."

"Oh. OK."

Jenna entered Fraza's room to find him sitting on his bed, sort of present, yet... despondent.

"She's here," Cornelius said, and Fraza's head lifted, the Kaledian's brown eyes fixing her. Recognition shone in those eyes but it was weak.

Jenna crouched before him. "Fraza, it's me. I'm back."

"Jenna...?" he asked, looking at her, dazed.

"Yes. Your Jenna. I'm sorry I left you. I couldn't help it but I'm back now."

"You're back...?"

"Yes."

"You left me..."

"I know. I'm sorry. Remember the fun we used to have?" Cornelius frowned. "I've missed you these past months. You've left me too, you know?"

"I'm sorry," he mumbled, his eyes taking her in.

"Are you going to wake up now? Come back to me?"

He nodded, mutely.

"You can do it, Fraza," she said. "I know you can."

A day or two later, Fraza scratched his ears. Cornelius saw this as a positive sign. Newark didn't but Cornelius told him Fraza was coming back from the brink.

Fraza shadowed Jenna, her presence a rope reeling him up from the murky depths. She talked about the things they'd done together, and Fraza hung on every word.

At last, Jenna found time to ask Cornelius about his mind-trick. "So, how did you do it?"

"Well, transferring thoughts is one thing. Transferring images quite another. It takes a lot practice to make them solid and real, more practice to do it whilst fighting." He boasted a little, so he qualified. "I've been at it, on and off, for years."

"It would have to be a very strong transmission?"

"Yes. It's about practice, commanding your mind, and using the power. I could give you a few sessions, if you like, but it takes years to master."

Her first session was interrupted when Allessa informed them all the Sentier had arrived back.

*

They sat in the belly of an enormous mountain. Newark looked around the huge chamber carved out of rock. He surmised it was the only place big enough to house all these Sentier. That, or they were weird fuckers.

"This is an odd place to hold a meeting," Graham remarked, and his girlfriend nodded as she looked around. She caught Johnson's eye and turned her head away, quickly.

A Sentier graciously extended his arm, and Cornelius stepped onto a stone block in the centre. The citizens remained quiet as they waited for him to speak.

Cornelius coughed to clear his throat. "It is nice to meet you all," he said, congenially. "You have a lovely city here. Beautiful, in fact. It reminds me of somewhere I left behind. That was a beautiful place too." He smiled in sad reflection. "They were not my people, you understand, but they came to be. In fact, they were from another dimension."

The Sentier stared at him, and he paused for this to go in.

Newark stared at him too. "Is he giving them a history of his life?"

Jenna shrugged.

"Many would describe them as a wise race," Cornelius remarked, "but how can you tell if someone is wise, unless you are wise yourself? How can you tell if *you* are wise?" He shook his head, engaging them in the puzzle. "It's quite a conundrum, isn't it?"

The Sentier viewed him, curiously. It was indeed a conundrum.

"How *can* you tell?" a young voice asked.

Cornelius looked toward the voice, appearing surprised by the question. "Well," he said, thoughtfully, "if you are asking me, I would say you have to take it down to basics. What *are* the basics of wisdom?"

Jenna looked around. The Sentier appeared thoughtful. They weren't questioning why he had come here; they questioned wisdom. Interesting detour, she thought.

"Knowing when to act, when not to act," a female voice suggested.

Cornelius nodded in consideration. "And what do you base your actions or non-actions on?"

"On whether your actions do good or harm."

He nodded again. "But an action that does harm might turn out to the good in the future, and vice-versa."

"You cannot *possibly* know all the connotations," a man said with conviction.

"That's right."

"Just do nothing then?" a curious voice asked.

"But doing nothing could have harmful effects."

"What's he doing?" Newark whispered.

"I'm not sure what he's doing," Jenna said. "Just leave him to it. I'm sure he's going somewhere."

"Then how can we know the wisest course?" a woman asked, tilting her head, intrigued.

"We can't," Cornelius replied. "That is the point. However, I believe that deep inside, sometimes way down deep, we all have an internal radar. It connects to our feelings, and to access it, we have to get out of our own way. Edifices are built on this part, huge stiff structures, years of conditioning, years of what others have told us, years of ignorance upon ignorance. In fact, even to call yourself wise is another deluded edifice. Are you wise or are you open to wisdom?"

The Sentier stared at him, wondering where this man had come from.

Cornelius drew in a breath. "I have come here today with my friends to appeal your internal radar. Not to the edifices on which the ego rests, but to your own true internal compass. Slavery is rife in the region. Beings are subjugated, having their dignity stripped from them. If no action is taken, this will not change. The Sentier have huge influence here. If we work together, we could wipe slavery out. Your leader turned a blind eye. Will you?"

"It is not the Sentier way to interfere," a male voice said.

"So, I believe. But who says that? You? Or someone else? Perhaps at times, it is right not to interfere. Yet, sometimes it is wrong. If you accept

255

what is handed down to you, you will never test it against your own internal radar, and your own wisdom will escape you."

The assembly fell silent, soaking in his words.

"Why's he going to all this trouble?" Newark asked. "Just get up there, Trot, and scare the shit out of them."

Jenna smiled. "We need their full commitment."

"I would like to suggest," Cornelius continued, "Allessa, here, take over the leadership role. I believe your current Head has been putting personal considerations before the greater good. I believe the public execution he ordered was to satisfy a need for power and revenge. Is that the Sentier way?"

All had now heard of the failed execution. Sentier never held public executions. Executions were extremely rare, a necessary evil performed by the authorities on the particular planet. In fact, before Olixder, they couldn't remember executions being ordered by the Sentier. *Was* Olixder losing his way? Or did he see a bigger picture they could not?

Olixder's voice boomed out around the cave. "You are listening to this manipulation?" he accused. "This group is very good at that." He walked to the front, viewing Cornelius with disdain. Cornelius smiled at him, pleasantly. Olixder turned to the assembly. "Do not be duped. Do not be deceived. These imposters are manipulating you. They are threatening our values, all that we hold dear. They need to be eradicated, not humoured!"

The Sentier looked between the Head and Cornelius.

"Lock them up," Olixder bellowed. "But watch out for that one," he said, pointing at Jenna. Jenna shook her head at him and this enraged him. "Can't you see what is going on here!" he shouted at them as if they were stupid. "This-" Olixder paused to sum Cornelius up, "whatever he is, is a charlatan!"

Eyes continued to move between Olixder and Cornelius. The being with white hair had a calm temperament and a basic honesty. Olixder, on the other hand, came off... scary. Internal radars went off all over the place.

"Can you not see!" Olixder shouted.

"Yes," a woman said, stepping forward, bravely. "I can see." Olixder's face relaxed. "I see that you are giving in to anger, you are holding a grudge, and you are treating your people with disdain."

"What! I'll have your head for this!"

"I say we vote," a man asserted. "All in favour of Allessa?"

Every hand raised.

Wow... Jenna thought. Olixder had scored an own goal.

The former Head Sentier strode off, knocking bodies out of his way. Jenna watched him go. He needed taking out, but that wouldn't go down well with the Sentier.

"Well done, Cornelius," Jenna said as they walked out. "Looks like he's been sacked."

"I don't think that was all my doing. The man has anger issues."

She smiled at him. "You plugged into the zeitgeist, didn't you?"

"The people here believe themselves to be wise. I got their attention."

"What you said was true, though, wasn't it? It is a conundrum."

"Right," Flint said, coming up behind them, "Allessa is Head now. We'll talk to her about how we're going to move forward. After that, we'll head back to Draztis.

"You haven't called a meeting, Flint?" Jenna asked, smiling with a hint of humour.

"Very observant. I wonder what means," he said, frowning, smiling back at her.

Her eyes followed him as he moved past. Cornelius watched her, his gaze moving to Brash. The man talked to Allessa. Um... He'd been so tied up with Skinner and Fraza, things had slipped his notice.

*

Allessa, still not thrilled to be Head, told Flint that from now on, the Sentier would make their views on slavery known. They couldn't oppose it with force. None of the Sentier would agree to that, but they wouldn't keep their silence any longer.

As they prepared to leave, Allessa remained on the craft.

"Aren't you disembarking, Allessa?" Jenna asked.

"No, I am coming to Draztis with you."

"But...?"

"The Sentier now know how to conduct themselves. It is not imperative I remain here. Heads often travel around the region."

Especially when they're chasing a bloke, Jenna thought, sourly. She shrugged it off. She didn't even know how she felt about Lucas.

So, with Allessa aboard, they set off for the mess of a planet that was Draztis.

"Are you back?" one of them asked.

"I'm back," Flint said. "Take the rest of the day off." The day off was given in case the commander decided to nuke the place.

The staff didn't disappear straight away. They hung around to talk to Flint, seemingly pleased to have him back. The crew stood, watching.

After the building had cleared, Flint contacted the commander.

"Where are you?" the commander growled. "How did you escape?"

"You betrayed your gods," Flint said. "Are you going to beg for forgiveness?"

"You're no god! You're nothing but an imposter!"

"Then meet me and find out."

"Where," the commander spat.

*

Sun bathed the shallow valley outside the city. The commander scanned the low-lying hills. No sign of the imposters yet, but if they pulled any stunts, he had a few tricks of his own.

"Keep alert," he ordered, turning to his men.

A sudden wind got up. The commander looked at the sky. Black clouds hovered overhead and he stared at them, confused. Rain lashed the ground. Lightning struck. Where the hell had this storm come from...? As quickly as it had come, it disappeared. His men started shouting. The commander turned to see a wall of water rise from the river. *What the...?*

More men shouted. Balls of lightening whizzed through the air, soldiers ducking, running in all directions. The fireballs disappeared, and the soldiers looked around, fearfully.

"How are you doing this?" Cornelius asked, staring at Jenna.

"I'm not drawing from a well, Cornelius," Jenna replied, staring down at the results of her work. "I'm drawing on the whole. An old woman on a planet called, Cyntros, taught me to change my perspective when working with the power."

"Right," Flint said, standing. "Time to have a chat."

As the crew walked down the hillside, the commander and his men drew their weapons, firing frantically. The fire bounced off an invisible shield, the imposters walking inexorably forward. The commander called in back-up, looking to the sky as aircraft streaked in, chewing up the ground in a merciless battery assault. Through the smoke and debris, the commander watched intently. The figures emerged, still moving forward. Raking a

261

skeletal hand through his hair, he looked to the skies again. The aircraft zoomed in for the next fly-by but got shunted by vicious blasts of wind. Engines roared as they struggled for control, their crews finally forced to retreat.

Realising these aliens really *were* gods, the commander dropped to his knees. The army followed suit.

Flint stood over the commander.

"Forgive me," the Bortten pleaded, his six arms outstretched.

"Where is your second-in-command?"

The commander pointed, nervously.

Flint addressed the other man. "You are in charge now." He turned back to the cowering former commander. "You are going to prison. Arrest him."

The second wasted no time.

The army was back in line.

*

As they entered the city, Flint turned to Jenna. "You were amazing."

She stared at him, shocked, her shock transforming into a smile. "I thought you didn't like things done the easy way."

Smiling back, he leaned in to her. "To quote Cornelius, 'needs must'."

Brash watched their exchange with a churning feeling in his gut.

Cornelius felt troubled. He drew Jenna aside. "Jenna, what you did was very impressive but... you have to be careful."

"Yeah, I know, they could bring nerve agents or something, but this army can't afford chemical weapons. I've seen the budgets."

"No, I don't mean that. There could be side-effects from such a public demonstration of your power."

"Side-effects?"

"Religion."

"Religion?"

"When people see things like this, they want to do something with it, build an edifice around it. This could have long-term effects we cannot yet foresee."

"No, they'll forget about it when we've gone."

"I'm not sure..."

"So, they get religion? What's the worst that could happen?"

"Bloodshed, war, intolerance, persecution..."

"Oh. OK, I'll... not do things so publicly in future."

"Thank you, Jenna."

"For what?"

"For being reasonable."

She scratched her neck. "Yeah, I... should apologise for being a pain in the arse. I think I did get a little out of hand."

He smiled at her, gently. "It's a process."

*

Their work began in earnest. The slave traffickers were arrested, pleading they'd had the jobs foisted on them. The excuses didn't wash. They'd been creaming it in. The process of freeing the slaves began again, as did the process of re-introducing democracy.

Being the interim government, the crew took possession of their former pad, and rehoused the Bortten family, giving them a large injection of cash for their trouble.

Over the following weeks, they were kept busy. Graham moved back in with his woman, and Johnson breathed a sigh of relief.

Allessa didn't see much of Lucas. Often at the government building, sometimes elsewhere, when he did come back, he was tired. She sensed he was avoiding her. She had promised to back-off, so she didn't question him, but it troubled her.

She spent much of her time wandering the area. As she set off now for an evening stroll, she stopped in the kitchen doorway. Lucas sat out by the pool with Jenna. The Sentier watched them laughing.

"Yes, I remember," Jenna said. "When you look back at it all, it was kind of... fun."

"Yeah."

"But scary too." She turned to find his deep brown eyes upon her.

"You changed me," he said.

She smiled. "I think Cornelius might have done that with his mind-altering drug."

"No, I was changing before that."

She swallowed the lump in her throat. "You were the first man I've ever felt anything for. Before you, there was nothing..."

Their eyes locked for several moments but the spell broke when Newark and Skinner came out with tea. "We've got the good stuff back," Newark said happily, putting a jug on the table.

"Should you be drinking that, Skinner?" Brash asked.

263

"I'm fine," Skinner said with a shrug.

Skinner seemed to have his brave self back, but Jenna knew how easy it was lost.

"Can you believe they threw a ton of this stuff away?" Newark said, disgusted. "What's wrong with these people?"

"Well, the plantations are in full throttle again now," Brash said. "Flint's re-establishing trade-links."

Jenna noted there was no malice or bitterness in his voice.

"We've also got scouters patrolling the planet," he mentioned, "so we'll have advance warning of any attack."

Jenna chewed her lip. "Juyra and the other planets aren't going to be happy when their supply of slaves dries up," she said, concerned.

Brash nodded. "Flint has increased the defence budget. He's also been working to strengthen their fleet. They've been drawing up plans and tactics. The man's efficient, I'll say that for him."

Brash and Newark looked almost reverent. Jenna stared at them.

"We won't be able to leave until the threat's past, though," Skinner remarked.

"Yeah," Jenna agreed, "and it could take years before the Sentier's influence is felt, if it ever is..."

Newark's face would have dropped if he hadn't been drinking tea.

"Juyra's the main importer, isn't it?" Jenna said, thoughtfully.

"Yes," Brash replied.

"Perhaps we could help change their attitudes."

"How?"

"Fear."

"Fear?"

"The non-religious Reglons believe in a judgemental creator."

"That fucked up," Newark said.

"So... we plug into their fears, and let things spread on their own."

"How would we do that?" Brash asked.

"The creator could visit senior officials in the night, challenge their conscience, and hopefully their policies." She was aware of the conversation she'd had with Cornelius but this could be done covertly. Just a few senior officials.

"Jenna, you were nearly executed on Juyra," Brash said, frowning.

"That was Olixder."

"The populace will revolt if they abolish slavery," Skinner remarked.

Jenna chewed her lip. "Yeah... I suppose we'd have to visit them too."

"You can't visit the whole planet," Newark said. "That would take centuries."

"No, just a few citizens in various cities. You know how news spreads. We could plug into the zeitgeist."

"The what?"

Jenna looked at Newark but didn't bother. She reasoned she wouldn't be creating a religion as most of them already believed in a creator god, whether they'd packaged it as religion or not. Still, she decided to run it by Cornelius.

"So, it's like what you did on Lixia," she said to Cornelius. "You know, you plugged in to what was there. Well, the Juyrans already believe in a creator god, so I wouldn't be *changing* their beliefs. And, if I don't do this, Cornelius, Draztis will never be safe."

Cornelius thought about it. "OK, but no public displays." He looked at her, seriously. "And be careful, Jenna."

Having got it by Cornelius, she spoke to Flint. Flint rubbed a hand over his mouth as he considered her idea. "You're expanding the ghost-busting theme, I see," he remarked, a hint of humour in his eyes.

"Well, I'm not happy about going back there, but if we don't act, this could be a long process. I mean, we can't leave until the threat of invasion is past, can we?"

"I know. That has been troubling me." He looked at her. "OK. But take some of the crew with you."

"Who should I take?"

He hesitated. "You choose."

She tapped her chin, thoughtfully. He watched, captivated, every fibre in his body craving her. Would she pick Brash?

"I'll take Johnson and Newark," she said. She'd have to have a long chat with Fraza.

"OK. Just promise me one thing, Jenna."

"What's that?"

"You'll take care and come back safe."

Looking into his blue eyes, she touched his arm. "I'm coming back."

Shock And Awe

Newark had tons of fun, standing outside villas, hearing pots smash, furniture fly, voices cry out. He pictured the looks on their gawky faces. "I wish we could go in there."

"We made a living out of this for ages," Johnson remarked.

"Lucky bastards. We slaved away on a plantation."

They stood in the wealthier part of the city, where most of the slaves were located. Since Jenna had her full powers back, she didn't need to see inside first. Consequently, no break-ins were required.

The noise inside calmed, and she transferred thoughts. *"Set my children free, or you will feel my wrath!"*

"What c-children...? I d-don't have children."

"The slaves. As your creator, you are all my children. None shall be slaves! Those buying slaves will be punished!"

She knew she'd hit the mark, when the voice in her head pleaded for absolution.

She looked up. "Our work here is done."

They moved around the area, creating more mayhem.

"So, how do you get them to hear what you're thinking?" Newark asked.

"I get into a certain state and tune in to whoever's in there. It's like... radio waves but it's mind waves."

"That's crazy shit, Trot. Have you ever considered you might actually be a god?"

Jenna laughed and looked at him. "I love you, Newark."

Over the weeks that followed, the three of them travelled from city to city, heading gradually for Iprian, and their final goal, the government.

*

Jenna's absence left an impression on Brash, Flint, and Fraza.

"How d'you think she's getting on?" Brash asked Flint.

Flint smiled. "Knowing Jenna, she's having a ball."

Brash's smile echoed his. "Yeah." He rubbed his forehead. "It's funny, isn't it, how you can completely misjudge a person. When I first met Jenna Trot, I had written her off."

"You were different then."

Brash looked at him and smiled. "So, were you."

Allessa moved through the kitchen to the garden, smiling at them both as she passed. Brash's eyes followed her. Flint watched him, thoughtfully.

Allessa came across Fraza, sitting by the pool. The little Kaledian still looked fragile.

He glanced at her. "She's left again..." he said, rubbing his chest.

Allessa sat beside him. "Sometimes, you have to let people go, Fraza. People should not be a crutch."

He didn't reply.

She reached out and touched his arm, feeling his life in her hand. "Ah... She was the first person to truly see you..." She tilted her head, looking at him, sadly "Perhaps now, you need to see yourself."

Brash watched them from the window. He didn't notice Flint leave nor Skinner arrive. Skinner stood beside him, looking out too. "It's the tentacles, isn't it?" the man said.

Brash turned to him. "What...?"

"You've barely spoken to her since she pulled them out."

"Don't be ridiculous! I'm not *that* shallow." Brash looked at Skinner, suspiciously. "What's Newark told you?"

"Newark tells everybody everything."

"So, you know she and I...?"

Skinner nodded.

"Great."

"Hey, it's your business."

"Apparently not." Brash forced an abrupt change of subject. "Where's Cornelius?"

"In his room with his woman."

"Again?"

Graham walked in with his girlfriend. He nodded a hello then raided the food cupboards. "Are they not back yet?" he casually asked.

"No," Brash replied.

"They've been gone weeks."

"Could be gone many more."

Graham pulled his head out of a cupboard. "D'you think they're safe over there? We still don't know where Olixder is."

"Wherever he is, his power base is lost now, isn't it?"

Graham shut the cupboard door, without retrieving any food. "Has Cornelius contacted Trot? Checked they're alright?"

"Yes. They're fine."

Graham nodded. "Good. Right, well, I'll see you later."

Skinner watched him go.

After weeks of targeted action, Jenna, Newark, and Johnson arrived in Iprian. Bumping into a Sentier, they secured a plush place, the hotel offered free for the duration of their stay. The Sentier told Jenna their position on slavery had been explained to the government.

"How did they take it?" she asked.

"They smiled and nodded respectfully. We will keep reminding them of our position."

"Good."

He gazed at her, curiously. "You and your group of friends challenged us, and I feel we should thank you."

She smiled at him. "Well, we all lose our way. I think I need a map." He stared at her, nonplussed, and she remembered Sentier didn't do humour. "So, do you happen to know when the next protest day is?"

"In five days-time, I believe," he replied, tilting his head. "Why?"

"No reason."

The Sentier bowed slightly and left. Jenna turned to the others. "Right, we've got five days to scare the crap out of the government."

"Cool," Newark said.

They located the government building, which overlooked the square, and found out who the main players were. One by one, they followed them home, terrifying the hell out of them.

They filled in the time scaring ordinary citizens too. On protest day, the square was packed, the vast majority protesting against slavery.

"This is a good show for five days work," Newark said, pleased.

"They're from all over the place," Johnson told him, "not just here."

The vocal protestors hefted plaques, shouting with conviction. Jenna hoped this wouldn't get out of hand. Walking through the crowd, she stumbled upon that original sole protestor. He looked around, mystified.

"See you've gathered support," she said to him.

"This has nothing to do with me," he replied, shell-shocked.

"Nonsense," she said, kindly. "It only takes a spark to light a fire."

He stared after her as she wandered away.

Jenna's eyes fixed on the high balcony of the government building. "They're not coming out," she said.

"Maybe they need more persuading," Johnson reasoned.

269

"Um… If they don't come out, we'll carry on working until the next protest day."

Nobody came out, so they put in another month's work.

During the days, they loafed around, or did the touristy thing, scoping out underground bars. As darkness fell, Jenna performed nightly visitations, hoping for next-day results. As yet, nothing. The governors would have nervous breakdowns before they abolished slavery.

As the month progressed, Newark and Johnson became bored. The novelty had worn off, and the fearful cries, rather than amusing, now started to annoy Newark. "Fucking pussies."

On the next protest day, the square heaved, demonstrators spilling out onto neighbouring streets. A counter-demonstration had been organised, which was every bit as vocal. The friction culminated in sporadic fights until the violence threatened to get out of control.

A couple of governors came onto the balcony, calling out for calm.

"We've started a fucking war," Newark said.

"Crap." Jenna looked around at the angry faces.

"We need to move," Johnson told them.

They squeezed through the mob, getting pushed and shoved.

"This way," Johnson said, forcing through to the nearest doorway.

Barging into a spacious, empty hall, they ran up stone steps, heading to the front of the building. Reglons crammed the balconies, staring down in wide-eyed wonder.

Jenna turned, retracing her steps. "Let's take a back window, get up to the roof."

Climbing through the window, Jenna used the power to levitate herself. Newark and Johnson gaped at her as she hovered, mid-air. They'd seen her levitate before but it was still a head fuck.

"Come on," she said, quickly. "D'you want me to lift you?"

Dragging her gaze away, Johnson craned her neck. "No, I can manage it."

She and Newark scaled the wall as Jenna came in to land on the flat roof. She moved to the front to see fights becoming one mass brawl. The melting pot boiled over, and it didn't look pretty. Members of the government crowded the balconies, shouting out for calm. One of them got pelted with fruit.

Newark and Johnson joined her.

"This isn't good," Jenna said, worrying her lip.

"Let 'em kill each other," Johnson said, looking down. "That'll be one way to sort them out."

"*I* need to sort this out."

"What are you going to do then?"

"Shock and awe?" Newark suggested.

Jenna was reluctant to do that but what choice did she have? They had stirred up so much feeling, it could lead to civil war. Civil war or irrevocably change their view on life? It was a desperate choice.

Aware that Newark and Johnson probably weren't the best ones to ask, she put the choices to them anyway.

"Leave them to it," Johnson remarked, looking down with disdain.

"Open the fuckers' eyes," Newark said, excitedly.

That didn't provide much clarity. Newark suggestion had the added benefit of abolishing slavery, so she decided to go with it.

The shock and awe began - the regular routine of storm and fireballs. The crowd stopped fighting. The crowd cowered, mutely, except those pulling at their hair and screaming. Jenna transferred thoughts to one of the governors. Oddly, the man felt compelled to speak.

"Abolish slavery!" his voice boomed out. "Abolish slavery or the wrath of God will descend on this planet!"

There was definitely shock and there was definitely awe.

"Job done," Newark said. "Can we piss off now?"

Jenna bit her lip hard as they turned to leave. Cornelius was going to kill her. Maybe she wouldn't tell him.

Soon after, slavery was abolished on Juyra but a new religious movement was spawned. In time to come, this new religious movement would persecute the minority religion, leading to bloodshed and tears. As most scientists came from the dwindling religion, it also halted scientific development. The governor, who Jenna had spoken through, led that new religious movement and was treated like a god himself. Generations down the line, his successors came to see the Sentier as evil and banished them from Juyra. If Jenna had been around to see it all play out, she would have considered Cornelius's talk on wisdom, for in sticking up for good, she had created a new evil.

Yes, if Jenna could have seen all this, she would have been horrified.

If Johnson could have seen all this, she would have said, "Leave them to it."

If Newark could have seen all this, he would have said, "Stupid fuckers."

Final Decisions

Jenna squirmed as Newark relayed every detail of their adventure. She'd asked Newark and Johnson not to provide details, but Newark couldn't help himself. Newark regarded Jenna with pride. Cornelius looked at her, alarmed.

"It was spiralling out of control," Jenna insisted. "It could have led to civil war. It seemed like the best option at the time."

"Jenna, you've altered the view of a whole planet," Cornelius said.

"They believed in a creator god anyway?"

"In a repressed way. Now, religion will get a stranglehold on that planet."

"That can't be worse than slavery," she protested. "Can any consequences be worse than slavery?"

"I don't know..." Cornelius said, concerned. He rubbed his brow.

She chewed her lip. "Are you angry with me, Cornelius?"

Cornelius looked up. He shook his head. "You acted for the greater good. That is much better than being wilful and self-indulgent."

Jenna looked at Flint. He gave her a gentle smile, knowing, like her, trying to fix things wasn't easy.

*

The new government bedded in well. Flint let go of the reins. Tea production was good, the former slaves were now wage-slaves, and democracy ruled. Juyra was no longer a threat, and no other planet would challenge Draztis without them.

As their duties wound down, the crew had more time to themselves, more time with each other. Brash couldn't avoid Allessa any longer. He chatted to her and was friendly, but Allessa felt things were different. He didn't speak to her in quite the same way. She clung to the shred of hope they would find each other again. And that concerned her. Sentier didn't cling.

Flint and Jenna talked together too and, though she couldn't deny the attraction she felt, she found herself having nostalgic thoughts about Lucas. She and Lucas hung around each other a lot. They would laugh about things, dissect their journey together. It was a way of coming together. Flint saw them getting closer. His heart broke but he wouldn't interfere if that was what she wanted.

Fraza, happy to have Jenna back, became his old, if compulsive-driven, self. The confident Kaledian he'd been was lost in the ether, but at least he'd tuned back in.

Graham knew the crew would be leaving soon. He didn't know what he'd do when that time came. Slowly, he arrived at the painful decision to remain behind with Yasnay.

And the day came when Flint held his final meeting.

"Well, I think our work here is done," he said, smiling as he looked around the group. "Thank you for following me out here, and for all the hard work and commitment you've shown. You really are a pretty amazing crew."

The crew had reciprocal feelings. Flint was a pretty amazing captain. Who'd have guessed it?

Jenna viewed Flint, curiously. This man had been lost for many years, but finally, he was the man he was born to be. Flint had found himself.

"What's next then, Cap?" Newark asked.

"Well?" Flint said. "What's next for you?"

"I would like to head back to Marios Prime," Cornelius told them, looking at Takeza.

"What about everyone else?"

"Sounds good," Brash said.

Allessa gazed at him. He had decided but he hadn't even told her. Swallowing the hard lump in her throat, she stared at the floor.

"Err... I'll be staying here," Graham said, uncomfortably. Johnson looked at him, her heart shattering. "I... err... think that's what I want."

"You can't stay here," Newark objected.

"I'm sorry, bud. I've made my decision."

Newark and Johnson stared at the floor.

"Right, well," Flint said. "That's sorted then. We'll leave in a couple of days."

As they dispersed, Flint took Jenna's arm, holding her back, waiting for the others to leave. "I think you've made your decision, haven't you, Jenna?"

"I have?"

He looked at her with a sad smile. "Haven't you?"

She breathed out, heavily. "I think I have," she said, guiltily. "I'm sorry, Flint."

"Don't be."

"I..."

He put a finger to her mouth. "Nothing needs to be said."

Allessa pulled Brash aside in the hallway. "You have decided who you want but you do not have the courage to tell me, do you?"

Brash looked down. "I'm sorry..."

"Don't be," she said, walking off.

Johnson followed Graham out of the house. "Graham," she said and he turned. "I just want to say... I'm sorry I hurt you."

"It's OK," he said with a shrug.

"No, it's not. I still loved you when I broke it off. It was never that." Graham looked at her, confused, and Johnson rubbed her forehead. "Don't ask me to explain... Anyway, it doesn't matter now. I'll be leaving soon, and I want you to know, I'm sorry."

He viewed her, suspiciously. "Are you trying to get me back?"

She shook her head. "No. I accept you're with... Yasnay now. I know it's over between us. I just wanted to say sorry."

"OK," he said, studying her. "Apology accepted." He smiled at her, the first smile in aeons.

She smiled back. "I'm saying goodbye now. Easier that way. Take care," she said, stepping forward, punching his arm lightly.

"You too."

She walked away but turned around briefly. "Oh, and if you have any lilac kids, don't fucking bring them to visit me."

"You hate kids?" he asked.

"I hate lilac." She shrugged. "Had to get that in." She smiled then walked out of his life.

Graham stood there, staring at the empty spot. He wandered away, processing the fact he would never see her, or any of them, again. It was the hardest decision he'd ever had to make, and one he hadn't taken lightly. But he was with Yasnay now, and they were building a life together.

*

The house was quiet. Jenna lay on her bed, staring up into the darkness. She had made her decision. Flint had been a... fling. She and Lucas had history. They'd been through a lot together. A part of her wondered if she was clinging to the past but why would she...? She had left her father behind, hadn't she? She hadn't clung to him. It was real with Lucas. She'd forgotten that for a while.

The balcony doors stood open, the sound of the sea lulling her to sleep...

She stood in a cave, surrounded by gods and demons. Jagged rock pricked her arm, and she stared at the cave wall as it receded away from her. Rubbing her arm, she gazed round, unable to figure out the good guys from the bad guys. They were all so deceptive. A beautiful being moved toward her, his heavenly smile turning sour. The cave became oppressive. She couldn't breathe. A heavy weight crushed her chest.

Her eyes shot open. A body lay on top of her. Hands pressed over her nose and mouth. As her eyes adjusted, she registered a hate-filled face. She desperately tried to buck him off but her limbs had no strength. She tried to focus her sluggish mind.

Wrenching her head to the side, she broke his grip, screaming at the top of her lungs. Barely a sound came out, cut off in its prime. Screaming inside, her heart pounded wildly as she battled to free her useless body.

"Not so clever now, are you?" Olixder goaded, a mad gleam in his eyes.

Panic overwhelmed her. She was going to die and there wasn't a thing she could do about it.

"The execution is going ahead," he said with a cold smile, "with or without an audience."

The room started to spin. She had no air left in her lungs. She was blacking out.

The pressure released. She gasped for air, her addled brain scrambling for focus.

Fraza stood over the Sentier, a hard look on his face. Olixder couldn't breathe, couldn't move his arms, couldn't wield his power. Trapped in a choking box, he experienced the panic he'd inflicted. His bulging eyes stared at Fraza but he found no mercy there. They were the last thing he saw as he fell back, dead.

"Jenna, are you alright?" Fraza asked, rushing over to her.

"Welcome back, Fraza," she managed before passing out.

A Rude Awakening

The crew hung in the kitchen, eating breakfast.

"Newark, Johnson," Flint said, "when you're finished, take the trash out, would you?"

"I always get the shit jobs," Newark complained. "Where d'you want us to put it?"

"Bury him at the bottom of the garden. Brash, Skinner, dig a grave."

Newark felt slightly better.

Flint moved over to Jenna. "Are you sure you're alright?"

"Yes, I'm fine."

"You had us worried there."

"I didn't know you knew CPR, Flint?"

He smiled, glancing around to find the crew staring at him. "Turns out I didn't need it. You were drugged. Anyway, I'm going to the government building to wrap up. Keep an eye on this lot while I'm gone." He smiled at her then walked off.

Jenna watched him go.

Johnson tapped her fingers on the counter, the day stretching ahead of her. She wanted to be out of here now. She shot up. "Get me a shovel."

Upstairs, Allessa kept to her room, wanting the day over too, needing to see as little of Lucas as possible. The pain in her chest was excruciating. This was why she didn't do relationships, and one thing she was certain of, she would never open herself to this again.

Brash found a convenient moment to take Jenna aside. "Am I reading the signs right, Jenna? It is me you want?" Jenna stared at him and nodded. "Then why don't we stay here for a while? Have some time to ourselves?"

"How would we get back to Marios Prime?"

"We'll take a Bortten craft. I'll sort it out with Flint. They owe us that much."

"It'll take months to get back on one of them."

"So? We could tour around a little on the way. We've never really had time to ourselves, have we? The crew's always been there."

Jenna chewed her lip. Maybe Lucas was right. Maybe that was why she had kissed Flint. They'd never been alone and fully explored their relationship.

"OK," she said.

They broke apart as Skinner moved passed. The man's gaze lingered on them.

*

Allessa remained in her room that night. Brash called the crew to the living room to tell them he and Jenna were staying on for a while.

"Staying?" Newark asked. "Why the fuck do you want to stay?"

"Jenna and I are reforming our relationship, and we need some time to ourselves."

"What...? I thought you were crazy about the Sentier?" He turned to Jenna. "I thought you were crazy about Flint?"

"Catch up, Newark," Johnson said.

Newark looked at Johnson. "Well, you should have seen him on that plantation. Completely fucking love-struck. We stayed weeks longer than we needed to."

The crew looked down, uncomfortably.

"Newark, shut up," Brash growled, his eyes flitting to Jenna. Jenna didn't know where to look. "Don't listen to Newark," he told her.

Cornelius viewed Brash with interest. "Are you going to return to Marios Prime eventually?" he asked.

"Yes."

"Then I must give you my address."

"How are you going to get there?" Newark asked. "Walk?" *Weeks they had been on that fucking plantation!*

"Flint has sorted a craft out."

"I've sorted out two craft," Flint said.

"Two?" Jenna asked.

"I'm not going to Marios Prime, either. I'm going to take some time out. I'll drop Allessa off at Lixia. After that..." He shrugged

Jenna stared at him. "You *are* going back to Marios Prime, though, aren't you?"

"I'm not entirely sure..."

"But you're the Cap?" Newark said.

"I'm not sure about that, either."

"What about your mission to do good?" Jenna asked.

"I can help in many ways, big or small."

"Like what?"

"I'd like to help... damaged children."

278

"You want to be a fucking therapist...?" Newark asked.

"You mean we might not see you again?" Jenna said, her throat constricting.

"I'm sure I'll head back to Marios Prime eventually." Flint looked away.

Jenna stared at him, not knowing if she believed that.

Skinner studied Flint. "Can you fly a Bortten craft?"

"Yes," Flint replied. "I've flown one a few times."

Skinner continued to study him."

"Can't you kick butt *and* do therapy?" Newark persisted. "Cos, let's face it, you already have."

Flint smiled at Newark, fondly. "I'm going to miss you too."

The crew looked down. None of them wanted to let him go. After all his bitching, Newark now wanted to follow Flint. Flint was badass and loafing around too long wasn't Newark's thing. Johnson and Skinner felt the same way.

"When are we leaving?" Johnson quietly asked.

"First thing. Perhaps you should go and see Graham now. I've already said goodbye."

Still quiet, the crew rose to their feet. Fraza wandered out of the room, heart-broken. He wouldn't see Jenna for months. Jenna glanced back at Flint. He smiled at her. She smiled back, sadly.

Newark walked to the front door. "I'm going to say goodbye to my mate," he muttered, dejectedly.

Skinner, Jenna, and Brash followed him. Johnson stared at the door.

Flint remained in the living room, knowing a chapter had ended. Jenna was happy. He had to feel happy about that. And he would. When his heart had mended.

*

In the morning, Jenna awoke early, anxious and sad to be separated from the crew.

When they assembled in the hall, ready to leave, she hugged them tightly. "Take care of yourselves," she said, her eyes lingering on Flint.

Flint's blue eyes held hers. "You take care too."

Allessa and Brash gave each other a hug. The Sentier did not hold grudges. Brash felt a tug of sadness and guilt. If it hadn't been for Jenna, maybe he would have overlooked the tentacles. At the moment, they didn't seem important.

"I'll see you in Marios Prime," Fraza said to Jenna. "I'll be waiting."

"I'll be there," she told him.

When the crew left the house, she stared at the door, wiping tears away.

"We'll see them again," Brash said, gently. "Come on. Let's take a walk along the beach. It'll be like a honeymoon."

She smiled at him, and they left the house through the back door.

"They'll be in Marios Prime in no time on our craft," Jenna remarked.

"Yes."

"It'll take Flint weeks to reach Lixia in that Bortten craft."

"Yes."

"I wonder what he'll do after that."

"With Flint, it's anyone's guess. He's... a remarkable man."

"Yeah..."

As they wandered along the shoreline, Jenna picked up stones and bits of shell. "I never had a holiday when I was young," she remarked. "My dad was always too busy."

"Well, you deserve one now."

"You were right," she said, "we've never had time to ourselves. The crew was always there in the background."

"Well, it'll be just you and me now."

He held out a hand to her, and they walked, arm in arm, breathing in the morning breeze, silently enjoying each other. They stopped, watching as their craft flew by, heading out into space. A second craft flew by moments later. They stared after it then turned to face each other, looking into each other's eyes. Brash brushed hair from Jenna's face. He leaned down to kiss her, their lips connecting for the first time in months... but... it didn't feel right. In fact, Jenna didn't feel anything. Neither did Brash.

Pulling apart, they stared at each other, Jenna realising with horrible clarity what the nostalgic feelings had been. Deep down, she knew their relationship was at an end, and even if she hadn't admitted it, some part of her had been saying goodbye. Brash realised he *was* a shallow bastard, but he had just got a whole lot deeper.

They turned in unison, staring at the empty sky.

Graham ran up behind them. "Have they gone? Am I too late? I've made a terrible mistake!"

***

Printed in Great Britain
by Amazon

49424143R00160